# EGO & SOUL

# EGO & SOUL

## THE MODERN WEST
## IN SEARCH OF MEANING

## JOHN CARROLL

COUNTERPOINT
BERKELEY

This edition published by arrangement with Scribe Publications, Australia.

Library of Congress Cataloging-In-Publication Data

Carroll, John, 1944-
Ego & soul : the modern West in search of meaning / John Carroll.
p. cm.
Includes bibliographical references and index.
ISBN-13: 978-1-58243-553-4
ISBN-10: 1-58243-553-7
1. Civilization, Western. 2. Civilization, Modern—1950-
3. Social history—1970- 4. Western countries—Social conditions. 5. Meaning (Philosophy) 6. Social values. 7. Quality of life. 8. Conduct of life.
I. Title. II. Title: Ego and soul.

CB245.C347 2010
909'.09821—dc22

2009040511

Printed in the United States of America

COUNTERPOINT
2117 Fourth Street
Suite D
Berkeley, CA 94710

www.counterpointpress.com

Distributed by Publishers Group West

10 9 8 7 6 5 4 3 2 1

# Contents

# PREFACE

Humans are meaning-seeking, meaning-finding, and meaning-creating creatures. *Ego and Soul* assumes that a life which loses its meaning is not worth living. It assumes that individuals need ties, and points of reference, beyond themselves; and that their lives are dependant on commanding stories to give them plausible shape. The book's conclusions are, on balance, optimistic. I argue that people today, in the modern West, continue to find traces of coherence in their everyday experience, despite being cast into a world in which uncertainty has become the norm—particularly, uncertainty about the big questions.

*Ego and Soul* first appeared in 1998. This edition is heavily revised and updated. One of the five theses that undergird the argument of the book has been recast, and a former chapter on Princess Diana has been scrapped, on the grounds that her mythic presence has dramatically waned. There are also three new chapters (including one on the 'Do-It-Yourself Home') and a new Part IV on 'The Future'), and new segments have been introduced that deal with the Olympic Games, Las Vegas, and new modes of democratic practice. There have also been some structural adjustments, and segments of the argument have been recast. I'm grateful to Henry Rosenbloom and the staff at Scribe for their invaluable contribution to this process.

# FIVE THESES

Who lives well? What characterises the good life? More specifically, what may we, in the modern West, claim about ourselves? And does how we live, and what we do, make any ultimate sense?

Debate about the quality of modern life has surged for over a century, without resolution. It is fed by unease about the times: fears about the loss of our bearings and of the attachments that once somehow secured our ancestors, and also a general discontent about who we are. Alternatively, many believe that this is a very good time in which to be alive.

Questions about the value of the lives we lead have become difficult to answer because the traditional signposts are gone. Old certainties have eroded. They include belief in a God who rules benevolently; optimism that material progress will make people happier; and humanist confidence about a virtue in individuals inclining them to build better societies.

Many who reflect on these issues today are not sure that there is any higher order shaping the human condition. They are uncertain about any absolute framework within which it is possible to make judgements. And, indeed, anyone who thinks seriously and honestly

1

is compelled to move tentatively. They must balance 'doubting wisely', as John Donne put it, with a respect for the integrity with which individuals try to live their lives.

Friedrich Nietzsche wrote that a people is only worth as much as it is able to 'press upon its experiences the stamp of the eternal'.[1] I argue in this book that, by this criterion, modernity has its value. Through describing many of the central activities of modern life — what ordinary people do — I shall propose that there is a method to be found here. That method gropes instinctively, if at times erratically and blindly, to make sense of things. There is both success and failure. Signs abound of a driving dynamic that is opposite to the negative one often attributed to modernity.

Widespread pessimism is common amongst social commentators, from sociologists and philosophers to artists and journalists. They read modern life as driven by a base reality of selfish pleasures, covered over by a veil of illusions. The pleasures are extravagantly serviced by a consumer society — consumerism itself being mindless materialism floated on a profane concoction of greed, aimless leisure, and an insatiable craving for entertainment. Commentators inclined to the political left tend to blame the capitalist economy, and lament a general decline of social conscience.

Conservative commentators stress a fraying of moral standards, deriving from a weakened family unit. Childhood is being destabilised. The security of the regular presence of two loving parents has become less common. Familiarity with the most extreme degradations of adult behaviour is readily available to children, through the visual media. The prevalence of drug and alcohol abuse, like higher rates of depression and youth suicide, tell of a sense of a failure of hope about the future.

It is true that the traditional answers to the three age-old, fundamental questions that face all humans are gone: 'Where do I come from?', 'What should I do with my life?', and 'What happens to me at death?' New answers have not appeared.

It may be that we find ourselves placed in history between epochs, stranded in a sort of cultural no-man's-land. What is to come is struggling to be born. Or, more likely, living with uncertainty has become our permanent condition. For us, sure answers belong once upon a time, to a lost past. At best, what we know flickers obscurely, like fairy-lights glimpsed haphazardly through a dense mist. Anything deep is an enigma.

This is a fertile and exciting place to be. But it is prone to cultural pathology. For instance, today, strongly asserted religious or political beliefs, where they exist at all, are to be found among minorities, and at the extremes. Two nodes of dogmatism have risen in reaction to the fluidity at the centre. There is, at one pole, religious fundamentalism, which regresses into a medieval assertion of creed and practice. At the other pole, there is militant secular atheism, deeply hostile to religion, with its own fundamentalist beliefs in science and codes of human rights.

The vast majority in the West belong to neither extreme. They are left, whenever they raise their heads from their daily doings, to spend their psychic energy struggling to find some overarching sense of meaning. And they worry about the futility that otherwise threatens to swamp them. This book is concerned with their story.

Every historical epoch obeys a sort of inner logic. Since Georg Hegel, German thought has postulated a *zeitgeist*, a spirit of the time. Max Weber, in the work which endures as sociology's masterpiece, *The Protestant Ethic and the Spirit of Capitalism,* argued that the modern world had been generated out of a new cultural blueprint. Weber went on to chart a disenchantment with life, and the spread of a profane bureaucratic rationality, of 'specialists without spirit, sensualists without heart', that would inevitably follow from the waning of faith in the formative culture.[2]

I shall suggest in what is to follow that Weber was too pessimistic.

He misread a decline in church-going Christianity, and the retreat of sacred communities to the margins, as the whole story. While his work discovered and traced the inner logic, it lost track of some of its main workings. It missed the creative adaptability of the modern West, its capacity to reorient its everyday ways to seismic shifts in social, economic, and cultural conditions.

Modernisation has driven the most radical transformation in the history of our species, especially at the material level—it has conquered most of the hardships that afflicted our ancestors, including disease, famine, poverty, and brute labour. It has ameliorated the struggle for existence to a degree hitherto unimaginable. That it has not managed to neutralise the Old Testament wisdom that we do not live by bread alone—and it has baked a lot of bread—is obvious.

What is perhaps less obvious is the extent to which modern activity disguises a search for meaning. The everyday pursuits themselves reveal a quest for answers to the three great metaphysical questions. And answers *are* to be identified there.

My argument proceeds by means of five theses, which serve as directing threads running through the whole story—a bit like the string that led Theseus through the labyrinth.

## Thesis One

*Unconsciously, all humans know the true and the good, and are inwardly compelled to find what they know, through their lives and what they see. They sense that there is some higher order framing their existence. The West continues to grope for the frayed metaphysical tissues.*

## Thesis Two

*Culture is those myths, stories, images, rhythms, and conversations that voice the eternal and difficult truths on which deep knowing, and therefore wellbeing, is dependent.*

## Thesis Three

*Cultures are singular. Fundamental moral laws and human rights are universal. The crisis of meaning in the modern West is an issue of culture, not of morals.*

To clarify Thesis Three, it is necessary to distinguish three different types, or levels, of truth.

The base level is that of facts, such as: *Yesterday, I had lunch at one o'clock.* This is true, but of trivial significance. The life of the individual is largely composed of everyday routines and habits that can be described in such a manner. But a life-story that is little more than a compendium of such ephemeral facts is hardly worth living.

There is a middle order of truth — the ethical order. It is composed of the moral laws that constrain behaviour: the commandments, or 'thou shalt nots'. Many of these are petty, such as the rules of politeness, and these petty rules vary from one society to another.

The backbone of the ethical order is a body of cardinal laws. They are universal; that is, they are found in every human society. They include 'thou shalt not kill'; 'thou shalt not strike or damage another human without due cause'; 'thou shalt protect the innocent'; 'thou shalt not betray trust'; and 'thou shalt not lie about important things'. These laws constrain all humans, except those whom we classify as 'psychopaths' — people who transgress major interdicts without conscience.

Furthermore, all societies esteem courage, and scorn cowardice. A film clip of an adult jumping into a raging torrent to save a drowning child will be understood in all cultures — with admiration expressed for the courage of the adult.

There are also important laws governing other roles and conduct. There is the 'good mother', the 'good father', the 'responsible leader', and moral support for 'doing a job justice'.

What varies from one society, or culture, to another is the specified circumstances under which it is permitted to break one of the cardinal laws. Some societies, for instance, have permitted infanticide—under the rationalisation that the baby is not yet human, so the normal prohibition on murder does not apply.

In the West, the recognition that all humans are equal in terms of the cardinal moral laws, and some of their derivatives, has come to be called 'universal human rights'. These apply irrespective of tribe, ethnicity, age, sex, status, wealth, or power.

This is an exceptional historical development. Humans have generally been tribal. The tribal view constrains me to treat members of my own tribe, nation, or culture justly, but those outside may be dealt with by looser standards. Outsiders—distinguished disparagingly as barbarians, gentiles, heathens, infidels, or savages—are legitimate prey to my self-interest.

It is only since the mid-twentieth century that a belief in universal human rights has become predominant in the West. This is one of Western civilisation's great achievements. It has its sources in the teachings of Jesus and in classical Greek philosophy, consolidated in the European Enlightenment and, since then, developed into a staple of the liberal-democratic political form.

The third and highest order of truth is Culture. The central task of every culture is to provide convincing answers to the three big questions about the human condition. This is the order of capital 'T', or metaphysical, truths.

The answers are provided through stories—what the Australian Aborigines call Dreaming stories. These are archetypal narratives from a long time ago that provide structures of meaning, and ideal character types, through which each individual may make sense of his or her life. Each generation needs to retell these timeless stories in ways that speak to it.

Popular culture—from tabloid journalism to Hollywood, from

television soap-opera to sporting legends—taps into these stories. In them, the classical themes of the hero, romance, duty, fate, evil, tragedy, and redemption are endlessly reworked.

Here, every culture is different. It is a central and incontrovertible difference. The archetypes of Western culture are particular and unique—coming from Homer and Greek tragedy, and from the four accounts of the Life of Jesus. They are very different, for example, from Aboriginal Dreaming stories. They are different from the foundation body of Hindu stories told in the *Mahabharata*; although, in this case, there are strong parallels.

Likewise, the sacred sites of culture vary—from Mecca to the River Ganges, from Rome to Mount Fuji. What they represent is not negotiable.

The great weakness in the West over the last century has been in the domain of Culture. The mainstream of literature, art, music, and philosophy has largely abandoned its mission to retell the timeless stories in new ways, and to interpret them. It has betrayed its responsibility to help people make sense of their lives and times. In its relativisms, surrealisms, deconstructionisms, and postmodernisms it has denied that there are fundamental truths. It has sometimes even denied that there are universal moral laws.

It is in the interest of everybody that all cultures are strong and independent. As Aboriginal wisdom puts it, if you lose your Dreaming you die. Insecurity about belief tends to breed a range of pathologies, including fanaticism.

Western civilisation today stands on three legs. There is Helleno-Christian culture—the Western Dreaming. There is the political form of liberal democracy, wedded to a belief in universal human rights. And there is technological, industrial society—the ever-evolving capitalist economic system.

The defence of universal human rights depends on the recognition that they are independent of culture in the big sense. The cardinal moral laws are constitutive of the human condition. They form a central component of being human, irrespective of tribe or culture. A democracy must, of its nature, apply its laws to everyone, irrespective of cultural orientation. Likewise, it is fundamental to liberal democracy, and to the separation of church and state, that all citizens be free to set up churches as they wish, and to worship how they choose. Modern democracy guarantees enough social stability to allow a high degree of freedom of Culture.

The three legs of the tripod are inherently different from each other in their fundamental natures and in their inner logics. Yet their historical evolution has involved complex interactions. Notably, the separation of church and state, indispensable to the rise of both modern democracy and capitalism, has its roots in the teachings of Jesus—a cultural factor. Even the monolithic Roman Catholic Church has largely respected this separation. Also, as Max Weber argued, the Protestant ethic—a cultural factor—was an essential precondition to the emergence of the capitalist economy.

It is the business of each culture, at home in its own backyard, to cultivate its singular understandings of mortal life. It is the business of all humans, wherever they dwell, to defend cardinal moral laws and universal human rights.

## Thesis Four
*A triple neo-Calvinist logic drives through modernity: individual conscience, worldly vocation, and* anima mundi.

Modernity is culturally Protestant, and remains so long after the God of Luther and Calvin has faded into obscurity. The Reformation undermined church hierarchy and the authority of the clergy with one simple doctrine: individuals should be guided in life, both morally and spiritually, by their own conscience. God spoke directly, through what Milton described as his representative in man:

*conscience.* The highest authority on what to do and how to live was thereby democratised, down to each individual human being, irrespective of his or her age, sex, race, or social station. Not only bishops and ministers thereby lost their privileges; so did secular authorities — kings, prime ministers, civic leaders, and magistrates. Finally, in the last quarter of the twentieth century, the same logic struck families, eroding the capacity of parents to discipline their teenage children.

Social commentators often claim that the defining cultural quality of modernity is liberal humanism, with its central belief in the freedom of the individual. Indeed, the mainstream of modern thought, at all levels, has worked on the assumption that freedom is progress. Individuals will be happier and better, their lives more fulfilled, the more they are released from constraints: the constraints of parents, of employers, of social hierarchies, inequalities and expectations, of political orders, even of personal psychological repressions. *Repression is bad.* The language of modernity has centred on the word 'freedom'. Yet the deeper truth is that such liberal optimism has only been able to spread so fluently because of a prevailing assumption that there remains one controlling authority — the conscience of the individual. Not everything is permitted.

Max Weber pointed out the degree to which capitalism depended on an inversion of the traditional, negative attitude to work. The view of the leisured aristocracy had been that no one in their right mind would choose to work, unless they had to: the common people laboured in order to eat. Calvinism brought about the revolution by stressing that the principal illustration of the state of the individual soul was the way that humans conducted their central life activity — their *vocation.* Ideally, they did so with dedication, discipline, rigour, and skill. Work became the new form of prayer: the individual alone, head bowed, in silent concentration, hour after hour, day after day. The seventeenth-century Dutch painters

Vermeer and de Hooch evoked the mood of pious devotion. This ideal of work, including the notion of vocation, has continued; whatever the reality of modern occupations, there is usually a feeling of discontent, a sense of failure, even a guilt over failure, when the reality does not live up to the ideal.

The Reformation tendency was to take religion out of the churches, and into everyday life. Indeed, implicit, if unintended, in the Calvinist logic was what came to virtual completion in the twentieth century: the disappearance of the churches. Calvin even wrote that the church which mattered was the invisible one, with its membership known only to God.

Vocation was one aspect of the secularisation of worship. The other was what the ancients had termed *anima mundi*—finding a soul in the things of the world, a spirit that may breathe through ordinary, everyday things, including matter. Vermeer painted the way a water jug, a loaf of bread, or a richly woven rug becomes illuminated with a divine glow when handled with reverence. Individual humans have the power of sacred presence, strong enough to endow the world in their vicinity with grace.

The primary domain of *anima mundi* would become Nature. From the late eighteenth century, Westerners would increasingly go out of doors, and away from town and city, in search of the sacred—in the beyond. They were in retreat from civilisation, striving to immerse themselves in landscape, seascape, or wilderness, and there commune with the spirits of the Earth and the heavens. Calvinism had unwittingly encouraged a new paganism.

The Calvinist logic driving through modernity shows little sign of faltering. Not only have the churches been emptied, but most other forms of community are losing vitality, as sociologists have lamented for more than a century. It seems that modern society likes its collective experience in small doses: its yearning for cosy, intimate, secure communal life is not to be much acted upon, but rather soothed by fantasy idealisations in television soap-opera. At the same time, a range of secular activities — from sport, through intimate relations, to encounters with nature — is gaining a status somewhere intermediate between the profane and the sacred.

## Thesis Five

*Western progress has been through ego, sometimes at the expense of soul. While the East has tended to emphasise soul at the expense of ego, the West was founded on a balance of the two, as formulated in Greek tragedy, and revitalised in Protestantism.*

*Ego* is full of character. It is the self in its defined and unique presence. It knows what it likes and what it needs. But it also has to be brought up. The child self, alternating between an omnipotent me and a timid nonentity afraid of the dark, has to be metamorphosed into the adult. The latter is, ideally, whole and integrated, deepened by experience, knowing itself, its talents and flaws, at ease in itself, satisfied by who it is, finding the path of what it has to do in life. This fulfilled ego is virtuous, too full of itself to tolerate its own cowardly or unjust impulses. It is also compassionate, not caught up in its own anxieties, freer to feel with others.

The ego, for good and for ill, rules the person. La Rochefoucauld called it self-esteem (*amour-propre*), and attributed to its vanity most of human motivation outside what is necessary for material survival, especially in personal affairs. He described it as the greatest of all flatterers, and 'more clever than the cleverest man of the world'.[3] The ego is vital to individual wellbeing. The clichés of modern counselling are that you need to believe in yourself, feel good about yourself, not put yourself down. They still underestimate the nature, power, and range of the ego. The ego, moreover, has the power to mobilise hatred, spite, intrigue, charm — indeed, the entire repertoire of human emotions — as its weapons of attack and defence.

Freud pictured it differently: in his system, the ego is contrasted with the id and the superego, and is diminished to a puny entity without its own drives, known mainly by its capacity to reason. It is as if Freud, in denying the existence of the soul, felt the need to eviscerate the ego.

Everybody strives to do, and to be seen to do, whatever expands the size and narcissistic pleasure of the ego. Everybody is vulnerable — it is merely a question of manner and subtlety — to flattery, to the massaging of the ego, which gleams like a new car when it is polished by the praise of someone whose judgement is valued or, in bad times, by anybody at all. At the same time, as Aristotle pointed out, anger is usually the result of a feeling of belittlement, of being made to feel smaller than one believes oneself to be, of being put down.[4] In English usage, the ultimate 'put down' is death, which is what is done to end the misery of very sick pets.

The impulse to know important people, to be in the live presence of stars when they perform, to identify with success — whether in the form of one's football team, political party, or nation — are all ways of increasing one's own size. Likewise, gossip about others — especially in criticising them, and exposing their supposed foolishness ('Can you believe what she did?') — belittles them, driven by the motive of using the implicit comparison to boost oneself. The surest sign of a secure ego is that it has no urge to brag or belittle, and that it speaks rarely about 'me'. Nevertheless, people whose worth is not recognised fittingly may rightly feel that they have suffered an injustice.

The hurt or damaged ego may unleash and direct some horror demons. Judas' ego recognises the existence of one who is better and bigger; who makes it, by comparison, feel vacuous. This is something it cannot bear; so, out of envious rage, it drives to destroy Jesus — who, by the way, was far from modest, as when he asserted, 'Before Abraham was, *I am.*'[5] In fact, Judas suffers from more than slighted ego: the presence of Jesus shows up his deeper being.

Then there are crushed or diminutive egos, perhaps due to a lack of nourishment in childhood, which suffer from timidity, or a low interest in the people and the things around them. Engagement is inhibited, and life rendered dull and depressing, to be gotten through as painlessly as possible.

The ego alone is, of its nature, insecure. Without the soul, it is pathetically weak. Ultimately, this is because of its mortality. How can it be, it asks, that something as great as I am will be snuffed out? 'I die!' Shakespeare formulated its essence when he had Macbeth, a man who is almost solely ego — who only in the face of death begins to feel remorse for all the evil he has done — reflect, early on, that, 'Nothing is but what is not.'[6] Ego alone has to make itself bigger and bigger, or there is nothing. This is Aesop's bullfrog, which had to keep puffing itself up to prove to a real bull that it was just as large as he was. The bullfrog blew and blew until it exploded, and was reduced back to nothing.

Homer's Achilles was the greatest warrior of all, so much bigger than all other men, 'brilliant in his shining', bringing glory to the Greeks.[7] Early in *The Iliad*, his scornful address to King Agamemnon, 'you rule nonentities', reverberates like an earthquake.[8] He can say matter-of-factly to a Trojan youth pleading for his life:

> So, friend, you die also. Why all this clamour about it?
> Patroklos also is dead, who was better by far than you are.
> Do you not see what a man I am, how huge, how splendid
> and born of a great father, and the mother who bore me
> immortal?
> Yet even I have also my death and my strong destiny,
> and there shall be a dawn or an afternoon or a noontime
> when some man in the fighting will take the life from me also.[9]

This is ego, here a formidable sense of self and its unique
presence, of me and my great attributes, the ego of Achilles, fulfilled
in his vocation as warrior and leader—'how huge, how splendid I
am' (*ego kalos te megas te*). Yet there is also soul, and it is because the
ego has lived, not been denied, or cringed in bashful insecurity, that
the great man is no longer driven by its ambitions and anxieties. He
can stand back from his glory and reflect frankly and sorrowfully on
the sense of it all.

*Soul* is the fragment of divinity in all living humans and in many
other creatures and things, if we are to believe in *anima mundi*. Many
religions hold that it enters the body at birth, as we take our first
breath—a view implied in the New Testament Greek, which uses the
word *pneuma* to refer to all of breath, wind, and spirit. Formative in
the West is the Greek word for soul, *psuchē*, which is etymologically
connected with the verb *psuchē*—meaning to blow, or to breathe.[10]
There is some parallel to be seen in the practices of a religiously
musical people, the Hindus, who have developed breathing exercises
as basic to their devotions.

The soul departs at death. The most that can be known in
sceptical modernity about its exit is what Poussin depicted in his
first version of the *Sacrament of the Last Rites*, where he evokes the
soul flying out of the window in a rush of wind as the dying man
expires—again, *pneuma* imagery. Where to, and in what form,
personalised or not, whether or not to be later reincarnated, we
simply cannot know. As the sceptical Socrates put it to his friends,
just before drinking poison, *Either I die and that is it, or at death my
soul departs to join other departed souls.*

Homer, too, had the soul flying away from the body at death,
leaving through the mouth, the chest, or an open wound. One variant
on this is the Augustinian theory that the soul may die before the
body, the body continuing soulless, as may be observed in extreme
cases of brain-stroke, or in accounts from the Nazi concentration

camps of the 'walking dead', those who had given up.[11]

Aristotle's ideal person was magnanimous — 'great of soul'. Aristotle, the more worldly of the two great Greek philosophers, derided the elderly, in contrast, as small of soul *(mikropsuchoi)*, in a passage that is worth quoting at length:

> Because they have lived many years and have been deceived many times and made many mistakes, and because their experience is that most things go badly, they do not insist on anything with confidence, but always less forcefully than is appropriate …
>
> And they are small of soul because they have been humbled by life: for they desire nothing great or excellent, but only what is necessary for survival. And they are ungenerous. For property is one of the necessary things; and in, and through, their experience they know how hard it is to get it and how easy to lose it. And they are cowardly and fear everything beforehand — for they have, in this respect, the opposite character from the young. They are chilly, and the young are hot; so old age prepares the way for cowardice, since fear, too, is a kind of chilling … And they live for advantage and not for the noble, more than is appropriate, because they are self-loving. For the advantageous is good for oneself; the noble is good *simpliciter* … Their desires are gone and they are slaves to profit … And the elderly, too, feel pity, but not for the same reason as the young: for the young feel it through love of humanity, the old through weakness — for they think every suffering is waiting for them, and this inspires pity. For this reason they are given to grieving, and are neither charming nor fond of laughter.[12]

In fact, Aristotle is focusing more on the ego than the soul — the ego rendered gloomy, untrusting, and defeatist, rattled by life experience. His *megalopsuchos,* by contrast, is someone of excellence, who esteems his or her own worth highly, but not with exaggeration (or false modesty); who is not over-excited by success nor much grieved by failure; and who is generous and serves others, but not given to admiration, for nothing is particularly great. Above all, the large of soul are honourable, proud of their own virtue in the practical sense of not allowing any act to compromise it. In modern terms, Aristotle is speaking of a great ego, where 'great' is not simply large, but also high-minded and good.

Aristotle misses the fact that when the old are great, as they can be, they have a presence that is soulful. Others are drawn to them, but not as they are to celebrities, wanting some of the charisma to brush off on them; nor as to sporting champions who have just achieved a great feat. The attraction is rather to a certain aura of depth, of having lived and having been enriched by the experience—just as wisdom is that type of knowledge associated with a minority of the old, a knowledge that is more than theory and information, one steeped in the true mysteries. Such people are ambassadors of the life of the soul. Their example teaches that life lived the right way cultivates the divine essence, nourishes it, and brings it out, in a way that suffuses the whole person.

To go further, it seems that the full life has as one of its natural cycles the retreat of ego in old age, as the spirit dims. The soul fills out commensurately. When this occurs, the fear of death diminishes, and may even disappear altogether. The soul, undistracted by the noise of anxious ego, is then free to prepare for its departure.

There is also *spirit*. It is more than energy; rather, the zing of vitality, as if the blood of life is spirit. Someone who is spirited is full of zest; full of beans. The Homeric assumption about the rampaging warrior is edifying, that a divinity breathes through him—he has such superhuman *esprit*. The modern footballer in form moves around the arena like a god, larger than life, immortal, and the crowd responds to him with awe, religiously, as if he has the magic touch. Just to be in his presence, to be there at this special moment to witness him, is like a revelation that can transform ordinary life and ordinary matter into some enchanted, eternal manifestation. He has that extra spirit, 'oomph', 'pizzazz', that 'it', that 'special something' — the unique, intangible ingredient making life as it can be, should be, 'larger than life'.

When we are *in-spired* we are lifted up by spirit. Its source is obscure. It seems to breathe in through us, coming from the outside, transforming us out of our mundane, material selves. Yet it also seems, simultaneously, to rise from within us.

The opposite is the person who is dispirited. When a person is 'down', he or she is in 'low spirits'. The implication is that without spirit we are dead. When we refer to someone as 'mean-spirited', we imply that they have a stinginess of spirit; again, a lack, which brings out malevolence in them.

Individuals will talk of taking on a task, starting an endeavour, 'when the spirit moves' them. A person described as being in 'good spirits' is bubbling and buoyant, not heavy, limp, or sluggish — not a dead weight, which is a burden on other human spirits. We are in the realm here of pure, everyday metaphysics, where the language of *pneuma* shows no sign of fading.

It is not exactly the language of soul. Nor is it that of ego. Both the soul and the ego bear the individual stamp of the person, whereas the spirit seems more general, belonging to the encompassing sacred cosmos — again, sacred *pneuma* is perhaps as close as we can imagine it. On the other hand, people refer to 'the spirit of a place' as if there is a particular character in the air defining a location. Then there was the Greek *daimon*: in Socrates' case, the spirit watching over him who would whisper advice whenever he was about to do something foolish. The *daimon* was reborn in Catholic Christianity as the Guardian Angel, a personalised spirit helping guide its human protégé through life. But this is a somewhat different usage than that of the animating life-force.

The early Greeks distinguished between *psuchē* and *thumos*, between something like life-soul and breath-soul. The former is located in the head and survives death: a dream phantom flying away. The breath-soul, active in the lungs, is destroyed at death. It has an affinity with what the West came to call 'spirit'.[13]

The spirit has no place in profane modern psychology, Freudian or other, which theorises about instincts and drives, as if humans are animated merely by inherited biological urges, and by food converted into energy, as if genes and environment explain the totality of life. Everyday speech conveys a greater wisdom. There is the fragment of divinity, the soul, present for the mortal span; there is the ego; and there is the life spirit. The spirit ebbs and flows, as is the nature of fluids. In some, it is always at low ebb; in others, mainly at the flood, it is bursting its banks, bubbling over — again, our tendency is to use liquid or gas metaphors to catch its essence. It has one source in the earthy and visceral, its Pan-self located in the instincts, having something of the blood that pulses through arteries and veins. But it is also the sacred spirit, with its other source in the cosmos. In this way, it is more like lightning, joining earth and heaven, although usually with less volatile atmospherics.

Boundary cases help to clarify the three categories. There are the simple of soul, people with unreflective, good natures in harmony with daily life, in whom the ego is unobtrusive. There are pure spirits, like Melville's Billy Budd: a saint so lacking in ego that he goes to his execution joyfully, his last thought for the doomed captain who has condemned him. There are deep souls with low spirits and, in the case of Henry James' Milly Theale, a feeble body; or those nourished by suffering, as in the case of the origins of African-American 'Gospel', 'spiritual', or 'soul' music.

There are the small of soul with high spirits, often talented as salespersons, in whom the spirit is more earthy than divine. Picasso's 'I don't develop; I am!' suggests a big ego with strong native spirits.[14]

Then there are the spiritually gifted with bad characters—people in whom it may be that the soul is large but fractured, or the ego is damaged in a way that triggers malevolent instincts, putting the spirit to spiteful use.

On another front, as James Hillman has argued, individuals bear their own blueprint, a seed within, growing according to its own predetermined logic, controlling the life. This seed cannot be plausibly interpreted as just a combination of inherited genes and environment, for even babies may assert their own particular 'I', their character, their ego.[15] We come into the world with both an ego and a soul. Furthermore, the ego, unlike the soul, is mortal, and it fears its own extinction. When there is too much ego, especially insecure ego, and not enough soul, then the fear of death may eat up the life.

Greek tragedy had its source in *The Iliad*, and its deepest tributaries in Aeschylus' *Agamemnon* and Sophocles' *Oedipus the King*. It explored various forms of the fulfilment, corruption, and annihilation of ego, leading to release from its concerns, so that the soul might rise. Its wisdom centred not on the denial of one or the other, but on a balance of the two. The metaphysical fruit was a cheerfulness of spirit, and a gratitude for life in spite of all.

Calvin's tack was different. On the one hand, his emphasis on activity in the world—work, family, civic duty—carried with it the trappings of fulfilled ego. On the other, his insistence that grace is everything was purely soul-oriented, ego a force for potential corruption. Weber saw in this paradox at the heart of Calvinism the catalyst for the fervid agitation, and restless intellectual self-examination which was sublimated into the systematic disciplined work that produced the industrial revolution, and thereby the modern world.

The Greek balance, formative to Western culture, is always under threat. The trials of the human condition, its woes, misfortunes, and injustices, tend to encourage a withdrawal from the world, an anaesthetising of ego to dull its pains. Or they may provoke the opposite reaction: an attempt to conquer the world, to establish ego triumphant, so powerful as to be immune to suffering. Hence the common metaphor, 'he sold his soul'. But loss of soul in the end means loss of ego, the dark other side of egomania, its shadow, infected with rootless self-consciousness, and a prevailing sense that all is arbitrary and futile. Likewise, matter without soul is dead matter.

Part One

# BATTLEGROUNDS

Chapter One

# WORK

A lot may be learnt about a culture by looking at its heroes. The men and women idealised in the art of the Renaissance were principally religious—Jesus, the Madonna, Mary Magdalene, Moses, and David. There were also figures from classical mythology—Botticelli's Primavera and Venus, Titian's Danaë. And there were images of secular leaders such as Donatello's equestrian warrior, Michelangelo's Lorenzo de Medici, and Titian's Emperor Charles V. The popes were portrayed like worldly potentates. With Vermeer, however, in seventeenth-century Calvinist Holland, there is a cultural sea-change. Seminal portraits of the lacemaker, astronomer, geographer, kitchen maid, and artist show people at their daily work. The individuals are nameless, unknown. It is the work itself that is celebrated.

Take *The Geographer*, today hanging in Frankfurt. The man is alone, standing bent forward over his worktable. His left hand leans on a closed book; the right one lightly balances a pair of dividers. He gazes with fierce concentration into an imaginary distance, his mouth slightly open, his look mixing systematic practical thought with reflective inwardness. Rays descending obliquely through a lead-lighted window play on his figure. In front of him is a nautical parchment map; two other maps lie rolled up on the floor, and a sea chart of Europe is hung on the back wall.

Here is a complete theory of work as central to the good life. Through dedication to a practical task (in this instance, cartography), a life may be both identified and illuminated. A series of balances is established. The man charts the Earth, the domain of matter, but does so through mind—just as, in reverse, the truth seen by intellect is penned onto parchment, where it will endure. The mapping is a tracing of a public and a private world, with the sea chart a projection of the man's inner condition: the ocean of unconscious self is placed, its contours known. He is not a lost soul. The Delphic injunction to 'know thyself' is achieved through work.

The turbulence of emotional life, of intimacy, is mastered, too. Covering the front of the table is a richly woven oriental rug, hanging down to the floor. It is rumpled, symbolising unrest in what is closer to the Earth, in the domain of his instincts and desires, in his personal affairs. Bending forward, he is in part drawn to the disordered rug, weighed down by what it represents. The maps on the floor are another sign of spillage. His task is severe; his failed attempts, discarded. Yet the geographer himself, in spite of a troubled look, is composed. He is robed in blue, edged with red bands—representing blood and passion—running in a V down the front of his body, revealing an abundant white undershirt—representing innocence and virtue. The passion is in harmony with the virtue, their controlled form mirroring the dividers, the tool through which he weighs up the right balance of things.

Work thus has a personal function, as a sort of meditative means for conquering the trials and sufferings inflicted by life. This occurs by gaining a poise whereby the conscience is freed to rule, to see the right way and direct movement along it, or at least to accept what is without complaint.

But there is a further gain, and it is the vital one. The geographer at his work is in a state of prayer, hoping that the spirit will breathe through what he does, making it more than a profane and mundane labour. His is the Protestant seeing God 'through a glass darkly', by means of a central life activity that is pursued with all his heart and mind and virtue. The hoped-for reward is a moment of grace.

The painting is complete. It is, in itself, an order glowing with the sublime — the sublime *in* the world. At its centre is the human individual, whose presence has twin foci. There is the right hand balancing the dividers, body as tool, moving to achieve a three-way harmony, with mind, desire, and the task — which, as we say, is 'at hand'. Vertically above is his face, through which the viewer can sense the power of concentrated mind, a charge between the eyes as hard and clear as diamond. Mind is not just trained intellect. It is also soul. Soul and hand rule the world, and attract the light from beyond. They do so through work.

Above the geographer's broad shoulders, on top of a cupboard, is a globe. His shoulders are bent forward. It is as if he carries the Earth upon them. In this guise, he is Atlas, the ancient titan. The Calvinist allusion is to his responsibility, as an individual, to the world. Everyone is born into that responsibility, which is fulfilled through a vocation. Moreover, the globe is contained in a wooden frame in the shape of a cross. This cross is against the back wall, very much as a crucifix would be positioned in a church. The home, or place of work, is the new church.[1]

The ethos envisioned by Vermeer has shaped modernity. There is a belief — call it faith — that a state of being is accessible in which mind, body, and external world are fused, moving together in harmony as if obeying the same universal law. In sport, the term used is 'form' — the team (or athlete) that strikes form suddenly finds it has almost superhuman powers of movement and control. Form is a state of grace. If modernity has any understanding of the religious category of grace, here is its main expression. Homer knew it, too. In *The Iliad*, when a warrior carries all before him, his enemies assume that some divinity is acting through him.

The Protestant ethic is the belief that such a state may be achieved through work. Vocation is a means of acting in the world so as to make oneself open, receptive to grace. Grace may or may not come — that is beyond human power. Whether the god breathes through the man, as Homer put it, cannot be willed.

The transformation in the attitude to work has made the modern world. Capitalism would not have been possible without a majority of the working population gaining a capacity for methodical application, sustained over long and regulated periods of time. This depended on a change in psychological disposition from the character typical of the European Middle Ages — low self-control, explosive temper, inability to concentrate — with traits, in short, that the modern world would identify as delinquent. It was still the case in Elizabethan England that descriptions of church congregations and theatre crowds convey the impression of widespread restlessness and an inability to sit still, of people with dispositions driven to constant chatter, joking, nudging, shuffling, and spitting — as one historian has put it, like a class of tiresome schoolboys.[2] No modern factory or office would function staffed by such people. The change in attitude to work went with a slow change in character towards a greater capacity for self-discipline, emotional control, and prolonged concentration.[3]

Turning to our own times, and the sociological facts, the question is: what are the signs of the continuing existence of this Protestant work ethic? In particular, is it flourishing, just surviving, or in terminal decline?

There are two dimensions to the question. The first concerns the influence of the ideal itself — the hope that work can be fulfilling in the Vermeer mode — and whether this ideal is being sustained. The second dimension is the practical one that, however powerful the ideal, it may be becoming more difficult to find employment—jobs—with which it is possible to identify in the Protestant-ethic manner.

There is little evidence of a decline in the ideal, however materialist and consumerist the surface social signs may be. On meeting a stranger, the first serious question that is asked is usually, 'What do you do?' This is a Protestant-ethic interest. Identity is charted by occupation—not by rank, school, ancestry, wealth, or leisure associations. Those without work, subject to scorn by others as lazy and parasitical, are hardly ever content with their state. They are likely to be depressed in their idleness, with feelings of guilt and superfluity. Theirs is a Protestant-ethic bad conscience.

The resentment generated by a job badly done is nearly universal—at the hurled spear that does not fly truly, as much as at the replaced window that sticks, or the new car that rattles. However, such outrage is underlined in Protestant-ethic cultures, as illustrated in the greater likelihood in the West, than elsewhere, that a complaint about poor service or faulty goods will have an effect, rather than merely eliciting a shrug of the shoulders. The widespread contemporary cynicism about politicians stems from a suspicion that they are more driven by their own selfish interests than by the public good—in other words, that they are betraying the law of their particular work.

The hard-working professional and managerial elites apply themselves not just because of the money and the status that they acquire. There is pleasure in the job well done: the successfully built enterprise, the well-designed project, the grateful patients and clients, even the precisely and elegantly drafted memorandum. And the pleasure is not like that of a tasty meal or a good wine. It is the satisfaction of having been the agent for contributing something substantial, perhaps lasting, to the world—a microcosm of order somehow echoing the larger order, an instance, a manifestation. That microcosm might be petty, judged on any rational terms — the memorandum might be read by only one other person. Nevertheless, the judgement that counts is the inner knowledge that this was a job well done.

The same elites have difficulty in relaxing. Their holidays are organised like work, with games of tennis and golf that have to be scheduled, books to be read, business projects to be mapped out, and social contacts to be extended. The devil who drives must be kept busy. This is not simply obsessional neurosis. The work ethic never sleeps, insisting that time is precious, that perfection must be constantly worked at, and that idleness is a type of death.

The work ethic was tested in the 1960s by a fashion that emerged for taking up creative hobbies. It drew upon the 'counterculture' of the time, and a new, progressive view of education that saw the teacher as a facilitator for the self-realisation of the child. The utopian assumption was that each person is, in essence, a polymorphously joyful centre of creative potential, cruelly stifled by society. While Rousseau was the patron philosopher, the main influence was the young Marx, and especially an often-quoted passage from *The German Ideology.*[4] Marx had speculated that in a future when there was no more scarcity, division of labour, or competition, a man would be free to hunt in the morning, fish in the afternoon, and rear cattle in the evening, and to be an intellectual critic after dinner.

What happened in practice was a burgeoning in adult-education classes in painting, sculpture, pottery, creative writing, macramé, weaving, and so forth. Most initiates did not sustain their interest for long. The exceptions were those for whom the hobby became serious. In other words, a casual pastime only became fulfilling when it changed into a vocation. The paradigm was, for instance, the middle-aged woman who discovered that she had a talent and a passion for pottery, leading to a rigorous and methodical dedication to her craft, and who, a decade later, was producing objects of fine professional quality. Such is the power of the cultural blueprint—as psychologically binding as any genetic code.

In 1974, a Chicago disk jockey named Studs Terkel published a study of Americans at work. It was based on hundreds of interviews with people from across the country, and across the full range of occupations. It is remarkable for the rich openness of the reflections of ordinary men and women. Terkel is a gifted interviewer. In his introduction, he observes that his study is as much about the search for daily meaning as for daily bread, and that only a happy few find it. The majority are loaded with weariness and discontent. Terkel discovers in all his subjects a deep yearning that their work should give them something more, some 'acknowledgment of man's being'.[5]

There are recurring complaints. A general frustration is caused by work and its quality not being recognised—for example, a steelworker believes that the stones of the Empire State Building should register the names of all the men who helped build it. The jobs are often a curse in themselves, a form of drudgery, reducing the person's goal to simply getting through the day. And there is widespread resentment against close supervision, at being spied upon.

These, however, are superficial compared with two themes that resonate through Terkel's book. The first is a longing for vocation. As an editor of health-care literature puts it:

> I think most of us are looking for a calling, not a job ... Jobs are not big enough for people. It's not just the assembly line worker whose job is too small for his spirit, you know? A job like mine, if you really put your spirit into it, you would sabotage immediately. You don't dare. So you absent your spirit from it ... It's so demeaning to be there and not be challenged. It makes you not at home with

yourself … It's possible for me to sit here and read my books. But then you walk out with no sense of satisfaction, with no sense of legitimacy.[6]

A receptionist lamented, 'A monkey could do what I do.'[7]

The second theme is a distinction between jobs that have intrinsic value and ones that are superfluous to human needs. A fireman puts it thus:

The firemen, you actually see them produce. You see them put out a fire. You see them come out with babies in their hands. You see them give mouth-to-mouth when a guy's dying. You can't get around that shit. That's real. To me, that's what I want to be. I worked in a bank. You know, it's just paper. It's not real. Nine to five and it's shit. You're lookin' at numbers. But I can look back and say, 'I helped put out a fire. I helped save somebody.' It shows something I did on this Earth.[8]

The people most likely to be fulfilled in their work are in the fireman mould, including doctors, nurses, and policemen. Some remark on the pride they felt when their work was admired for its courage, dedication and, above all, for it making a real difference to the lives of others. What is not remarked on is perhaps even more important: the gratitude of those helped. There is vindication—confirmation and recognition—in true gratitude. This is one mode of union with another that transcends ego.

Terkel also records numerous cases of the work ethic in pure form. There is the waitress, for instance, who takes pride in her skill:

When somebody says to me: 'You're great, how come you're *just* a waitress?' *Just* a waitress. I'd say, 'Why, don't you think you deserve to be served by me?' It's implying that he's not worthy, not that I'm not worthy. It makes me irate. I don't feel lowly at all. I myself feel sure. I don't want to change the job. I love it.

When the plate is put down you can hear the sound. I try not to have that sound. I want my hands to be right when I serve. I pick up a glass, I want it to be just right. I get almost Oriental in the serving. I like it to look nice all the way. To be a waitress, it's an art. I feel like a ballerina, too …

If I drop a fork, there is a certain way I pick it up. I know they can see how delicately I do it. I'm on stage …

'cause you're tired. When the night is done, you're tired. You've had so much, there's so much going … You had to get it done. The dread that something wouldn't be right, because you want to please. You hope everyone is satisfied. The night's done, you've done your act. The curtains close.[9]

Likewise, there is a bank-teller who laments that each job, however humble, is not valued as special in itself. A football coach puts it more buoyantly: 'The greatest feeling in life is to take an ordinary job and accomplish something with it.'[10] And to name a few more who love what they do, there is a housewife, a book-binder, a jockey, and a president of a broadcasting corporation.

What conclusions may be drawn from Terkel's study? There is powerful support here for the pervasive influence of the work ethic, in the hopes and aspirations of almost all people in relation to their jobs. From fulfilment to despair, the interviewees' reflections are almost entirely scripted by the ideal of vocation. The modern tragic stage is not set where families starve, plague is rife, or barbarians invade. According to Terkel's life-stories, it is set in the workplace, even more than in family life. What is less clear is whether the likelihood of satisfaction is diminishing—whether the testimony of the waitress is becoming the rare exception.

An Australian study on work in the 1990s, conducted by Belinda Probert, would suggest that Terkel's findings have not dated. It concluded, specifically in relation to the Protestant work ethic, that its hundred lengthy interviews across the occupational spectrum showed 'a quite remarkable degree of commitment to paid work'. The men and women were attached to their work as much for the meaning it gave to their lives as for the income. They responded unanimously in the negative to the question of whether they would give up work if they won a lottery.[11]

Suffering in relation to work is a theme that resonates both softly and loudly through much of popular culture. An example is the *Superman* legend, which held a widespread fascination throughout the twentieth century — in comics, and on radio, television, and film — suggesting that it must have touched a nerve. The story is simple. A bumbling, hardly competent journalist fails to attract his chosen girl, so he compensates by retreating into a dream world in which he is the super-powerful hero, adored by the same girl. The story exploits a central modern anxiety, of failure at work, aggravated in this case by it leading to failure in the other important domain of life: intimacy. It soothes the anxiety by providing a megalomaniac fantasy identification: delusions of grandeur in a withdrawal from reality.

Television has become the principal medium for the communication of human stories. Within it, the most popular genre is the soap-opera. There is no more discerning key to the values of the time. Of enduring appeal are the police-drama series and those centred in medical practices or hospitals, which draw on the moral discourse which is the staple of soap-opera — taking up everyday scenes of human crisis, and querying what is the right and wrong thing to do. They weave the work ethic through this discourse, implying that the best life is one that is led under the star of vocation.[12]

There is the honest cop, who resists corruption, the indifference or even resistance of his superiors, low pay, the trials of family break-up, and world-weariness. He is driven, through all these trials, by one faith: that justice be done. The archetype for him was set in the 1940s by Raymond Chandler's hero, Philip Marlowe, the seedy, dishevelled, and melancholic private detective. Marlowe subjects himself to beatings, the lure of scheming women, binge drinking, near poverty, all to do his job: discovering the truth. Marlowe's world is an anomic Los Angeles—of grimy, sweltering summer heat, dust, and greasy, vicious crooks—in which the weak are unprotected and the powerful are corrupt. The town is without any spirit of community, without any trustworthy bonds between its people, without belief or law, and without hope outside wealth. The wealthy drown in their own listless despair—that of boredom. In this caricature of modernity, the sole anchoring rock is vocation, the integrity of the one just man.

In the medical series, the doctors are not admired for their money or their status—indeed, both are usually understated in a false democratising of the reality. They are looked up to for the reasons identified by Terkel: their work matters, it receives genuine gratitude from those who are healed, and it obeys its own ethic. To serve under the medical oath is an emblem of how all work ought to be, ruled by a self-sacrificing obligation to a universal law.

★★★

The work ethic is not the whole story here. A powerful but quite different argument about modernity was put by Hannah Arendt in her 1958 book, *The Human Condition*. Arendt distinguishes between work and labour. She takes work in the Protestant sense, and extends its logic to that of creating things for use, things which are durable. The paradigm of work is the craftsman.

The paradigm of labour is peasants tilling the fields. Labour is unskilled, routine, repetitious, rhythmical, governed by biology and the seasons, and its produce is consumed. It requires neither imagination nor initiative, and as such was derided by Aristotle as a form of slavery. It is subservient to the tool and to nature—unlike work, which masters both. The collective mass of those who labour may sing (as with sea-shanties) in contrast to the silence—lonely, concentrated, and individual—of those who work. Labour has its own pleasures, earthy ones, including the climax to the first and most painful of all labours, childbirth. Labour is what most adult humans, in most societies, have done, in obedience to necessity and its eternal cycles. One labours in order to eat, to sleep, to labour, and so on; and one procreates, with each generation born into the same cycle. All that is made by labour is consumed—that is, destroyed.[13]

Arendt goes further. Labour establishes a logic that has its end in consumption, while work is linked with production. The two logics lead to quite different psychological dispositions in individuals. As capitalism has progressed, labour has steadily replaced work. This is why the predictions of social critics as different as Karl Marx and John Maynard Keynes have proved wrong: they both assumed that when the economy had created widespread material abundance, as it did in the second half of the twentieth century, humans, freed from necessity, would make creative use of their leisure, and become happy. The contrasting reality has been that abundance has led to consumerism, with one of its temptations to lie in bed gorging chocolates and watching television. Abundance has not produced a society of Michelangelos. For Arendt, this was inevitable, for the ease and comfort of consumerism is the fulfilled dream of those who labour. She suggests that the last person in modernity who works, in the pure sense, is the artist; hence the high regard for his or her vocation.

The argument neglects the existence, perseverance, and force of the work ethic. Consumerism is as much a pained consolation for the failed dream as it is the uncomplicated pleasure of what Arendt terms the *labouring animal*. Consumerism serves, in part, as a nerve-dulling and addictive narcotic. If Arendt were wholly right, modernity would be contented with its state. It clearly is not, and no one needs reminding of the eternal wisdom that we do not live by bread alone. The truth is that there are two cultures entangled here.

To what extent has labour been replacing work? On the one hand, industrial production, and now automated industrial production, has meant that goods are, with few exceptions, manufactured by machines, rather than fashioned by skilled artisans. On the other hand, the modern corporation draws on a widening range of expertise. In 1920, 85 per cent of the cost of manufacturing a car went to factory workers (that is, labourers) and investors. By 1990, more than 40 per cent was going to professionals—executives, engineers, lawyers, advertisers, and so on—who work rather than labour.[14]

Against Arendt, the swathe that automation has cut through employment since 1985 has mainly targeted labour in such low-skilled jobs as bank-tellers, shop assistants, receptionists and secretaries, telephone operators, and service-station attendants, not to mention in factory jobs.[15]

The availability and type of work has always been dependent on the nature and dynamism of the economy, including what Marx termed the 'forces of production'.[16] The latest phase of the industrial revolution is governed by automation, and the threat is that we may see some trend towards what Jeremy Rifkin over-dramatised as *The End of Work* in a 1995 book of that title. In the first phase of capitalism, the introduction of agricultural machinery steadily decimated the need for farm labour—from over 90 per cent of the workforce in the eighteenth century, to less than 5 per cent today. But

new jobs opened up in the manufacturing sector. Towards the end
of the second phase, between roughly 1960 and 1990, employment
in factories declined, but was compensated for by a rapid expansion
of the service industries.

Rifkin's case was that in the third phase — the IT phase —
corporations, banks, insurance companies, retailers, and even
telecommunication giants all shed staff, while this time no new area
of the economy was opening with a high demand for labour. Not
only are we heading towards the farmerless farm, and the workerless
factory, but government and big-company administrations are
shrinking. However, the decade that followed Rifkin's forecast
demonstrated just the opposite in the booming Anglo economies of
the United States, Britain, and Australia. In 2007, Australia achieved
its lowest unemployment rate for thirty years.

More specifically, the 2007 employment profile of Australia
suggests that the opposite of de-skilling has happened. Only 18 per
cent of the workforce was occupied in low-skill areas — elementary
clerical work, sales and service functions, and labouring and related
work. Forty per cent were managers, administrators, professionals,
and associate professionals. In the preceding five years, almost 60
per cent of the new jobs created had been in three skilled major
groups — professionals, associate professionals, and tradespersons
and related workers. Projections for the next five years anticipated
the strongest employment growth in health and community
services, and in mining, followed by personal services, property and
business services, cultural and recreation services, and construction.
The large majority of new jobs will be skilled.[17] All of this suggests
that, however cogent her reflections on the logic of consumerism,
Arendt's prediction about the replacement of work by labour was
wrong.

The rising dominance of the service sector of the economy has
seen a trend towards fluidity of employment: jobs are shorter term,

often casual rather than full-time, and on contract. The earlier norm of a single, full-time career for life is becoming obsolete. The new capitalism demands flexibility, a short-term focus, and employment mobility. Richard Sennett has argued that this flexibility is creating a new form of work alienation. He contends that it is becoming impossible for those who work to build sustained narratives out of what they do. As a result, a stable sense of self is corroded, replaced by a generalised anxiety about identity, and about the future. Individuals find it more difficult to take themselves, and their lives, seriously.[18]

The counter-case is equally compelling. Many people like the greater flexibility. They prefer a more open labour market, which makes it easier to change jobs; the greater choice over work hours; the opportunity of switching to part-time during, say, early motherhood; and the option of working from home. Being 'stuck in the same job for life' does not appeal. New forms of vocation, and its possible narratives, seem to be emerging.[19]

During its two centuries of existence, capitalism has seen a steady procession of prophets of doom, and every time it has proved its resilience, its capacity to invent some new way to detour around what seemed like a fatal crisis—the last major one of which was the Great Depression of the 1930s. It would be a new crisis if a large minority in an affluent modern society become overwhelmingly disenchanted with its life at work. But past experience would suggest that it is foolish to underestimate the vitality of the Western economic system.

***

Let me extend my reflections to the fundamentals of ego and soul. Work is a means to enable the fission of the two. Consider Zen archery. By repute, the master is able, at night, in a pitch-black room, to swing around with his bow and arrow and fire, on the instant, into the dead heart of the target. Let us assume this is true for, as a parable, it fits the concept of vocation. There are parallel images in the Arthurian and Robin Hood legends, and in the modern American Western.

Ego has played a major role in marshalling the archer's ambition over many years — his drive to control, to form, to dominate — into an unremitting repetition of the exercises, focusing his life into one narrow beam of purpose. There is great pride required here, like that of Achilles with his, 'Do you not see what a man I am, how huge, how splendid!' The exercises are of body, training arms, fingers, position of head, smooth turning of torso, handling of bow and arrow, drawing sweetly and, above all, training the eye. They are equally exercises of mind, in the Eastern tradition of meditative devices for ridding it of superfluous thoughts and day-dreams, emptying it so it can be free to focus on the object — shooting the arrow at the target. A mind teeming with thoughts is a restless, useless thing.

The work here, archery, is a means of being taken out of the self, subjecting the self to an independent law — that of the chosen task. The ego must fulfil itself through training, the gaining of mastery, to be able to lose itself in the deed. In its Achillean greatness it bows down before the act, subservient to its objective laws. Indeed, the act is a type of *object*, in the sense of that word's Latin root, meaning to be 'thrown before', or 'thrown out against'. Archery is a throwing of the self, out beyond the self. Only a supremely confident ego *may* do this, free from doubt, from anxiety about itself and its performance, abandoning itself, like the high-trapeze artist flinging herself through space, trusting she will be caught. Then, in the dark, ego is in tune with its task, mind serenely focused and, as the arrow hums towards its goal, there is grace, the self losing its boundaries in a fusion with the greater oneness. The soul has been freed.

The disciple is awed. This man has powers that the very gods might envy. So it is in the West, too. When Michelangelo saw the completed sculpture in the unhewn lump of marble before him, his own task being merely to chip away the concealing superfluous pieces, he had found a similar state of grace. The great sculptor was the obedient servant of the form hidden in the marble.

Or when an architect stands on a site, knowing the functions of his building-to-be and the materials available for it, and in his mind's eye suddenly sees the right form for it, and with it the complete logic of the construction, he too has been graced to learn the plan of what he must make. There is only one right building, and to fail to see it, and thus to build a deformity, is a transgression of the vocation of architect and its eternal laws. The architect who gets the building right has lost himself in objective law, for which he needs quite an ego — an ego that will be enhanced at the end of the day, for his arrow too has flown truly. If his soul is strong, however, it will control his ego, imposing on it the humility of acknowledging that this was not of its own free-will, the great *I* triumphant, but by divine grace. The ego then gets down on its knees in thanks.

Zen has produced an extensive philosophy, much of which plays with aphorisms of loss of self, but in the paradoxical context of all power lying within — the god inside requiring expression through an outer form in order to be realised. The way is through personal experience, acting in the world. This view is very close to the Calvinist stress on individual conscience and this-worldly vocation.

It is important that the activity in itself be useless, for the ego should be given no excuses for praising itself. Even more, individuals must recognise that they do what they do not because of its useful or even moral consequences — that it helps others, even bringing them happiness — but purely with the metaphysical goal in mind, that of the right fusion of ego and soul.

*Work* is a philosophy of 'live your life'. In sport, before a big game, the player is apprehensive: a range of fears of failure disturb the mind in the time before the start, when there is no engagement, when life is in neutral. At a distance from the action, looking on, we are hopelessly vulnerable to fear. Coaches combat this with ritual drills to warm the body up; even more, to occupy the mind. Once the game starts, it is as if there is a birth into the world—indeed, in the grand stadiums, players emerge from underground changing rooms through a dark tunnel into a cosmos of light, colour, and chanting—into a heightened pitch of invigorated existence. Players who then find form lose themselves in the demands of the play, subordinating themselves to its rhythms, servants to its logic. In this state of obedient, selfless ego, they will discover themselves to be instinctively courageous, doing whatever they have to do without fear of injury. Hamlet was always thinking, a symptom of his distance from engaged life; and, it goes without saying, he was unable to move.

The player who is in form, like the Zen master, achieves a state of transcendent balance in which mind, body, and external environment are fused as one, as an undivided harmony. Ego, in spite of the contest, is not differentiated against all the other egos, but diffused into the total movement. This player is capable of superhuman feats, with the mortal self—his ego—metamorphosed.

Players in form are graced. They move with poise, skimming across the turf, cutting and weaving through opposing packs with mesmeric control of the ball. Their presence is breathtaking, charismatic—the word derived from the Greek, *charis,* meaning grace, favour, and charm. They are charmed. And, as is implied in the language, their fulfilment is less that of proud ego than soul in its expansive embrace of the greater all.

This is pictured in the samurai films of Akira Kurosawa, in themselves a celebration of Zen swordsmanship. The climax usually involves the warrior hero meeting his great adversary, the two of them alone in a fight to the death. The two slowly circle each other, an awesome concentration of human spirit, in the vicinity of which anyone else would either be paralysed or would flee. All is quiet; all is still. The environment in which they move is dwarfed by their huge, formidable presence. These are men—this is what it is to be a man. It is a lot.

Then, too fast for the mortal eye to follow, there is the glint of lightning steel, the sword flashes, the blood spurts, the other sinks to the ground, and the samurai turns, his sword already re-sheathed. He shakes his shoulders as if to free them from a light burden, and then he walks away. In the film *Sanjuro*, the only person to tame him is an old woman, who tells him he glistens too much, for the good sword should stay in its scabbard. The power asserts itself through influence, not force. She has seen his prodigious ego showing off its superior excellence. But she has not see that this ego strides in the shadow of the samurai's higher obedience. Kurosawa combines East with the influence of Shakespeare, Dostoevsky, and John Ford's Westerns, in a fusion from which we, on the Western side, may learn.

Work is closely allied with sport in modern cultural forms. Organised sport has played an increasingly important role in the life of modern nations. The world attention devoted to the Olympic Games is indicative of this. So, too, is the celebrity accorded to top sportsmen and sportswomen. They are eclipsing film stars and political leaders as the heroes of our time.

A main reason for this adulation is that today's professional athlete is, contra Arendt's artist, the closest embodiment of the work ethic. The dedication is total, as if some fundamental test and acknowledgment of the individual's being were at stake. It contrasts with the half-heartedness and scepticism with which much modern activity is conducted. Identity is forged in doing, to the pinnacle of a person's best. Excellence is at a premium, and recognised. Training is rigorous, relentless, and exhaustive, requiring at times obsessive commitment, to the exclusion of a personal life—obvious in the Spartan routines of swimmers, gymnasts, and long-distance runners, but not much less the case with golf, tennis, and football.

Competing in a major event, and winning it, is to place a mark in history, that 'something more' which Terkel's subjects sought from their work. Even rank amateurs at their local club may gain a taste of this, for all good clubs have their honour boards. Sport, too, depends on form, the harmony of mind, body, and external task which is a state of grace. If Vermeer were painting today, his geographer might be reborn as a golfer, just as one of the finest surviving statues from the ancient world is of a bronze javelin thrower, capturing the transcendent poise in perfect human balance.

Even the superfluity of sport is a virtue. It is a useless activity—not like baking bread, building homes, or defending the nation. Sport is close to the pure form of the work ethic, which in its Calvinist original had only one significant function, as a non-utilitarian illustration of grace. What matters is not what you do, but how you do it. That sport is at once superfluous and deeply serious places it near to the Calvinist core. Is it not worthy of note that Olympic winners on the dais receiving their gold medal look upwards, at the hoisting of the national flag, then higher? Nevertheless, they have no answer to the fireman's challenge: 'What you do isn't real!'

The example of sport shows the adaptability of the capitalist economy, the vital role of culture in those adaptations, and the abiding centrality of the work ethic to that culture. The wellbeing of modernity will hang, in good part, on the ratios of work to labour, in both imagination and practice, and on their availability. The discontents of work, due to frustrated vocational aspirations, place burdens on the human spirit. The discontents of labour are demoralising in a different way: due no longer, in our era, to the exhaustion of the toiling body, but to the weariness and boredom of the profane repetitions of everyday life, and a certain sense of futility at the eternal recurrence of biological and consumption cycles.

★★★

Work is one path to the truth. It is the modern mode of journeying most likely to reach that destination. Freud held work to be the most successful means of sublimating extreme and unruly passions, and the best way for individuals to attach themselves to reality.[20] In what work enables, transforming ego into its form, yoking it to the task, it removes insecurity of being, freeing the mind to focus—as the high-trapeze artist does, flinging herself out into thin air, letting the soul breathe through the act, and speak its silent words.

Yet the story of work is not just one of inspiration and form. It may equally turn into a graver domain, one where tragedy dwells. Work can make a life; even save a life. John Ford provides the tragic archetype, in his last film, the female Western, *7 Women* (1966).[21]

The central character is a disenchanted, world-weary doctor, a woman equivalent to Philip Marlowe. She believes in only one thing which sustains her—her vocation. Dr Cartwright flees the pain of a failed romance in America to take the job of a doctor in an isolated Christian Mission in China, staffed by celibate women. She arrives wearing jodhpurs and cowboy hat, riding a donkey into the Mission, inside which children are singing, 'Yes, Jesus loves me'. The staid nuns are soon shocked by her smoking, drinking, and swearing, and her earthy realism: 'I never saw God at work in the slums of Boston.'

She is the solitary stranger riding in from nowhere, a lone woman in an alien land, in an alien community, her only possessions a few clothes and a medical bag. She has been stripped of attachment, ambition, and desire, left to shrug her shoulders dismissively at the absurdity of life.

But it is she — a modern, secular Jesus — who redeems things. She saves the Mission from a cholera epidemic; she delivers the baby of a hysterically self-centred, menopausal woman who remains a mental teenager; she inspires the woman's husband to the one act of courage in his life; and she bribes a horde of drunken Mongolian savages who capture the Mission to let the women and baby leave.

She sets the cart right. She finds her own mission, in the midst of a Mission built on inhuman false religion. By the close, those nuns who have retained their sanity shed their wooden Christian doctrines, and come to hold true the spare existential ethos that Cartwright exemplifies. She herself simply acts, in the heat of the moment, as a human being. Yet she holds to nothing, apart from a duty to protect life, even though much of that life is not worth protecting.

Her ransom to free the cart-load of women is to give herself to the Mongol chief. At the finale, she sheds her cowboy outfit, which has served as her medical uniform, thereby freeing herself from her professional oath. She reappears as a woman, dressed in gaudy oriental robes, and proceeds to serve the chief a drink laced with poison. Her last words to him are, 'Farewell, you bastard.' She then drinks poison herself.

Dr Cartwright represents all her modern companions on the vocation path. There is the existential wrestling, trying to stay on her feet, and to extract some meaning from it all. And, drifting through the tense and tangled threads that string the dreams of what might have been, to the prosaic daily concreteness of what usually is, there emerges a fitful, elusive vision of a grander whole.

## Chapter Two

# SPORT

What is it within sport that has made it catch and hold the interest of modern Western societies so much? Those academics who take it seriously, and who do not dismiss it as a vulgar circus for the masses, have tended to see it as yet another victim of the consumer society. They fear that a once-noble pastime is being commercialised—albeit with brilliant success—into mere entertainment.[1]

The argument is that sport used to be a rich part of local community life, providing convincing rituals for the exhibition of such values as skill, courage, and fair play. Big money, which is only interested in profits, has taken it over and is rapidly transforming it into a ragbag of sensational spectacles tailored to mass entertainment. In the process, the rituals are destroyed, the rules are changed, and the standards decline. The players lose their traditional attachments to club, team-mates, and the ethos of good sportsmanship. They themselves become the selfish pursuers of maximum personal gain. Drugs and corruption enter. A new breed of spectator appears, ignorant of traditional codes and standards, whose main interest is in sensational action in the style of the violent taking of vengeance. In short, sport becomes a spectacle that 'mirrors and gratifies the emotional requirements of consumers'.[2]

There can be little doubt that the profit motive is strongly at work in sport, and that it presses in the suggested direction. However, it is countered by a battery of quite different forces. A cultural war is taking place, as in so many other areas of modern society. The contrary forces are deeply rooted and powerful.

The severe weakness of the commercialisation theory — a weakness inherited from the mass of sociology over the last century — is that it grossly underestimates the enduring attachments of the great majority in the modern West. Most people continue to feel strongly moved by such age-old values as trust, nurture, protection of the innocent and helpless, honesty, courage, and patriotism. They do so through their everyday experience of family life and its vicissitudes; of work; and of the life of suburb, city, and nation. Combining with these conservative forces are new explorations for meaning.

Sport sociology suffers equally from a lack of empathy with the fan. It fails to imagine what it is like to stand in his or her shoes. It could learn from Nick Hornby, who, in his multiple award-winning and best-selling book *Fever Pitch* confesses to a life obsessed by soccer — 'nothing ever matters but football'.[3] One of the things Hornby makes clear is how non-consumerist his passion is. The natural state of the fan is 'bitter disappointment'[4]; the typical crowd experience is 'going spare with frustration and worry.'[5]

*** 

Three unconnected experiences set the scene for this chapter. The first was repeated over a number of years in which I taught a university course on Australian culture. The final essay was on a topic of the student's choosing relevant to contemporary values. From the first year, a pattern established itself and then was maintained without exception: the only students who found an Australian group with strongly held beliefs were those males who played football and wrote their essay on the club to which they belonged. The situation of playing together under conditions of common adversity built a deep attachment to the altruistic values of comradeship and self-sacrifice for team-mates. The club came first.

It is not unrelated that national events today that could be called rites are usually sporting ones, like the English FA Cup football final at Wembley. I mean 'rite' in the powerful sociological sense of an activity full of sacred resonances—with an elaborate mythology, which is celebrated on a grand scale with strictly prescribed uniforms, rules of practice, and methods of celebration and lamentation; which is approached with faithful seriousness, anticipated and prepared for weeks in advance, and talked about incessantly; and which provides a common attraction for a population that, for the rest of the year, has extremely diverse and often incompatible interests. This is one area, moreover, in which large parts of the rest of the world have not only followed the West, but have moved ahead of it—Latin America stands out.

The second experience was of trying to comfort myself through a long evening of poker during which I was dealt hardly a winning hand. I tried to work out why I was subjecting myself to such misery. It struck me that the playing of poker, which draws you in with a vicious seriousness whatever your better intentions, is a way of testing whether the gods, the fates, fortune, Madame Chance, or whatever you will, are on your side or not. What is at issue is whether you are in favour. Although it requires great skill to play poker well, the overwhelming factor is whether you are being dealt cards slightly better than those of your fellow gamblers. There is enough skill involved to satisfy our absurd humanist pride—our *ego*—that the human individual is the measure of all things. Luck goes in phases: for a period, things run well and then, inexplicably, for hand after hand, you are punished—at the worst, you are tempted by four good cards, only to be ruined by a vagabond fifth. The truest pleasure of poker comes not in the winning itself, the money, or in the sadistic pleasure of ruining others, but in the sense that fate is on your side—that you are in harmony with the greater forces of destiny.

The third experience has parallels with the poker episode. It was the realisation that in playing golf, the difference between the periods in which one plays well and badly has little to do with skill, coaching, or practice—important as they all are. It is, rather, the case that suddenly mind, body, and the challenges of the environment come into harmony, and the ball inexplicably goes exactly where you want it to go. Above all, during these wonderful and usually short-lived moments, you are able to rid your mind of all superfluous thoughts. The mind, then, in a sort of light, semi-trance state, encompasses the ball, the club, and the distance to the hole, the nature of the terrain and its hazards, and even the wind and the heaviness of the air. It is a state of sublimely relaxed concentration, perhaps better likened to meditation. When the mind achieves this state, the body becomes utterly obedient and works what, in hindsight, seem like miracles. One has no control over this elevated state: it disappears as it once appeared, in an inexorable flash.

In spite of the above references to poker and golf, I shall focus here on team sport and, in particular, on football. In Platonic terms, football is the sport of sports, with all others diverging in one way or another from its ideal. Much of what follows can be generalised to the other sports, even to the individualistic ones such as golf.

What are the motives that draw individuals in, either as competitors or spectators? The major psychological theory—Freud's—has held that sport is a means of sublimating aggression. It provides a context for vigorous and sometimes violent activity in a carefully regulated manner. Aggression may be played out with a good conscience, largely because the controls mean that no one is going to get seriously hurt. Nor is the drive for revenge going to get out of hand. When men do start to get badly injured, the rules are tightened up.

It is hard to over-estimate the therapeutic importance of violent team sport, especially football, for young men. Here is the one approved outlet for that explosive mixture of the multiple frustrations of the transition from boyhood to manhood, and the innate need of the male animal for power. As Freud put it, the fundamental anxiety of the male sex is over castration: that is, over the fear of impotence, emasculation, or powerlessness.[6] Castration anxiety produces a wide range of attempted compensations—some of them dangerous, and some of them criminal—including fast driving, hard drinking and swearing, picking fights, and the sadistic conquest of women. In football, the struggle for power can be waged until exhaustion sets in (that is the full catharsis of the most violent instincts) without there being antisocial consequences.

The deep psychological trouble that young men who have lost the urge to play competitive sport get into is shown by Herbert Hendin in *The Age of Sensation*, a study of American college students in the late 1960s and early 1970s. The study is based on five hundred psychoanalytic interviews conducted by the author, which resulted in a book that stands as a modern Dante's *Inferno*. Hendin portrays the coldness, the joylessness, and the boredom of this youth world in which intimacy is too threatening to be ventured: 'Nothing distinguishes this generation of young men more than the degree to which they are irresistibly drawn to killing feeling as a means of survival'.[7]

Hendin's students no longer played sport. They were haunted by fears of being humiliated if they lost, and of being murderous fighters if they won. The repression of aggression, almost without respite, led to an imaginative life on the brink of madness, in which the whole world, and especially the personal one, had become a minefield of paranoid fantasies. One young man, in talking about intimacy, said, 'If you show your feelings you get your legs cut off!'[8] These students did still want to win prizes, but they expected to do so without competing. Hendin highlights the greater problem that societies, in general, have with the rite of passage of boys, in comparison with girls, into responsible adulthood.[9]

Sport does act successfully as a means for sublimating aggression. This explanation, however, is a polite softening of the older and deeper truth that it is the civilised substitute for war. The deliberate transformation of medieval warfare into the jousting tournament is merely one of the more obvious displacements. It is the warrior drive and the warrior ethos that are resurrected in modern football. The team becomes a band of blood brothers, men who assemble together to undertake dangerous exploits under conditions of duress and threat. The experience creates strong bonds of companionship—ones that often last for life, and certainly long after the team has disbanded. Students who were members of teams wrote unselfconsciously, in a similar vein to returned soldiers,. about their attachment to their mates.

The warrior ethos, stressing courage, tenacity, and self-sacrifice for the higher good of the collectivity, carries over directly into football—with, of course, the one great difference that the greatest sacrifice of all is not asked for. What is involved is 'manliness', with its deepest roots, whatever the humanist niceties of modern civilisation, in the war hero. These roots do not seem to wither. Indeed, I had students who added, without prompting, that if there were a war they and their team-mates would be the first to volunteer, and that, because of their collective morale, they would make an excellent unit. It was the case, in World War I, that English Public School men, writing from the trenches, reflected that fighting for the nation was just like playing for the school.[10] Whether we like it or not, political virtue depends on this—virtue in the Machiavellian sense of the will and the strength of character to defend your own State, when it needs defending.

The language of football draws directly from that of warfare. Sections of the team specialise in defence; others, in attack. The team has a 'spearhead'; there is a 'last line of defence'; a team may 'overrun the opposition', and it may 'cut them to pieces'. In the case of Australian Rules Football, the cultural vitality of the game is illustrated in the linguistic inventiveness of the commentators, their flair for metaphor, and the evocativeness of players' nicknames. Another parallel is the manner in which the coach addresses his team, urging them on, invoking their manliness and their honour. It is exactly the same at many moments in *The Iliad* when the morale of the soldiers is flagging, or, for instance, when Achilles speaks to his troops when they are about to enter battle:

> So he spoke, and stirred the spirit and strength in each man, and their ranks, as they listened to the king, pulled closer together.[11]

Most persuasively, there are musical affinities between warfare and football. There is the ebb and flow in the tempo of waves of men wheeling around the arena looking for a weak front in the opposite defence; the surge forward; the desperate attempts in the heat, speed, and unpredictability of direct exchange to keep cohesion and maintain pressure; the sudden falling-back in fragmented disarray when attack fails; and the stolid struggle to regroup in defence, to halt the enemy's sweep forwards. The music of the play is echoed by the crowd. Anyone living within three kilometres of a major ground hears the extraordinary sound of a sort of deep, primitive chant emanating from tens of thousands of voices, rising and falling like a heaving ocean swell.

There are other psychological factors at work in sport, especially for spectators. First, there is identification with the strong. The team provides an image of the powerful and heroic into whose collective and individual boots onlookers can imaginatively project themselves, for the afternoon, or evening. They can forget whatever failures and insecurities dog their everyday lives. For two hours, they themselves are out there, involved in a 'life or death' contest in which everything seems to be at stake. Nick Hornby goes even further, suggesting that 'players are merely our representatives', and that what we celebrate is our own good fortune, not theirs.[12]

Second, sport allows spectators to 'split the persecutor'.[13] As in fairytales, the world is divided clearly and unambiguously into good and evil. The match allows the fans to identify with the good, their own team, in a war against evil, the opposition. They can project their own inner feelings of good and bad in different directions and attack the latter, which persecute them, with a good conscience. What is occurring is a refinement of the sublimation of aggression, in which aggression is being used by the good against the evil. This is immensely cathartic.

And match culture is so secure that it can tolerate many fans letting go, screaming themselves hoarse with their hatred of the opposition. The venting of such berserk rage can only make their everyday life outside the stadium walls more calm and humane.

Third, there is in sport, and certainly in football, the acting-out of some vestige of tribal life. The supporters behave like members of a pre-modern tribe, dressing in ceremonial warrior colours, holding sacred totems in their hands, and performing ritual dances and chants during the festival. There is something of both the Aboriginal corroboree and the orgiastic Dionysian festival about modern sport, although the eroticism is highly sublimated, and the spectators are civilised to a degree that mob frenzy hardly ever gets out of hand.

\*\*\*

Moving on from psychology, sport fulfils two major *social* functions. First, it works as a moral educator, in the case of football passing on some of the values of the community from one male generation to the next. It does so directly to team members, but also, more diffusely, to supporters, which in some codes includes a significant proportion of women. The three important values it bears are those of excellence, courage, and selflessness. In a society that stresses high achievement, sport celebrates feats of virtuoso skill, of brilliance. It lionises he who, by virtue of character, ability, and training, becomes a champion.

Equally, it celebrates courage, the central trait of manliness, fearlessness in the face of danger; toughness and cool-headedness under conditions that would make the common person quake at the knees. Linked to courage is 'nerve', holding one's concentration and intent in spite of extreme pressure.

Finally, sport encourages selflessness, acting without thought of personal interest — safety, wellbeing, or glory — for the higher good of the team. Here, altruism includes the ancillary virtues of loyalty and fraternity. There is often a fine line separating individual brilliance from selfish showmanship. This is an important focus of moral debate that football highlights. The value of being a good team member will usually be held as superior to individual brilliance.

In football, the crux of the moral testing comes with the violence. For player and spectator alike, the game opens up the sheer sadistic pleasure in annihilating the enemy. It is an invitation to release yourself into an orgy of boasting triumphal power on the rampage, of all-conquering *ego*. Here is the temptation. It is forbidden. The moral code is not to be cast aside. To constrain the rougher players there are both formal rules, enforced by umpire or referee, after the game by tribunals, and the unwritten rules of fair play. A player who flattens an opponent with a forearm jolt to the head will outrage the other team and its supporters—he will be booed for the rest of the match. Nor will he be celebrated by his own supporters: the heroes are the brilliant, the courageous, and the selfless, not the bruisers. The vast majority in even the most partisan crowd will hold in grudging admiration the virtuoso play of fearless little men from the opposite team.

Nevertheless, 'fairness' is charged with tension. Every fan is a little jubilant when one of the opposition's stars is ruthlessly and illegally flattened. It is jubilation with a bad conscience. The importance of football as a moral educator is that it touches the repressed sources of violence, arouses them, and then counters them with civilised interdicts. The moral order is alive here precisely because it is so often at risk, on the edge of being violated.

Against the feverish and arrogant pride aroused by winning, there is the cautioning memory that glory is short-lived, that the next time the boot will be on the other foot. The spoils of victory are soon spent. In addition, the thought sneaks back that we had luck today, things ran well at the vital moments—it could just as easily have gone against us. We should not get too carried away by how good we were, too carried away by *ego*. Football also instructs us that when a team gets too cocky it loses form.

But there is no denying that in football, as in war, to win is everything, and triumph excuses many sins. It is just that, as Agamemnon discovered, after victory in the Trojan War, beware lest in your *pride*—what Aeschylus called 'indecency of mind'—you 'tread down lovely things'.[14]

Football shows the young the working of key values in situations of high emotional and physical duress. It shows them what it means to be a hero, and what is shameful. It teaches a new generation how to act. As a value-asserting rite it, in addition, serves to strengthen the sense of community—that there is a community with obligations to which everyone belongs. As a rite, it strengthens the collective conscience, giving individuals a greater sense of belonging and a greater sense of what to do, that there are things worth doing—a greater sense of purpose. This most important of sociological functions follows on directly from sport being the civilised form of waging war: it integrates the young into the ethos of the warrior tribe.

Sport also provides the profound satisfaction of having acted courageously in a just cause. Although the goal, the team winning, is contrived—being unrelated to the wellbeing of the wider society—within the artificial goal there is the genuine one of the good of the team, and the club. In team sports, participants, spectators, and commentators will sometimes speak of 'the good of the game'. The ultimate loyalty is to something higher than self, even higher than their team.

Also, as already mentioned, there is the fulfilment of vocation, of passionate work, of 'having done a job justice'—the common phrase alludes to the higher purpose, that of justice, framing the endeavour. Fulfilling work, and acting courageously in a just cause, are two of the few human experiences that anchor people in their community. They are experiences that attach them to it with a care for it that will make them want to defend it, believe in it, and take responsibility for its condition. The moral sense, that I shall take a stand on my community's behalf, gains much of its inner strength from precisely this sort of experience.

There is a second, historical factor relevant to the social functions of sport. The organised team game is a product of the English industrial revolution. It developed to satisfy the leisure needs of the working population of the new cities, created in the nineteenth century by the rise of the factory. In its basic form, it has mirrored the history of the industrial workplace: employing elaborate codes of rule which are strictly enforced, quantified scoring, regulation by the clock, and requiring high levels of training for its players—in the end, professionalising them. The industrial, and later bureaucratic, workplace has emphasised greater efficiency and rationalisation.

All of sport's psychological functions need to be understood within this overall context, its provision of a festival symbolically congruent with capitalist organisation. This festival allows some imaginative compensation for the stress of modern work. Sport helps anaesthetise the strains caused by a society that, on the one hand, is highly competitive, placing great weight on individual achievement; and yet, on the other, provides a small proportion of its jobs that are in any grand sense either personally or financially rewarding. Sport gives Clark Kent the chance to identify with his Superman, every weekend.

***

The modern West has created one global cult of mythic force. The modern Olympic Games has become the pre-eminent international institution. It is truly pan-national. Other bodies may lay claim to greater practical consequence — the United Nations, the World Bank, the Group of Eight, or, in part, the European Union. But that would deny the depth of the Olympic impact on the shared conscience of individuals around the world. The Games reflect attachments that transcend nation and tribe — they reflect a common humanity. And, they show that nations can compete without going to war.

No other body commands a fraction of the global attention, ambition, and participation that the Olympics mobilises every four years. In Athens in 2004, 11,000 competitors represented over 200 countries. The global television audience has risen to four billion viewers. In second place, and a long way behind, is the Soccer World Cup — another sporting event.

The modern Olympic Games was initiated in 1896 by the Frenchman Baron Pierre de Coubertin — 1500 years after the ancient

Olympics were closed down, by a Christian Roman emperor, on the grounds that they were pagan. Coubertin sought to recreate the classical Greek ideal of a religious festival in which humans perform athletic and cultural feats at the highest level of excellence.[15]

Coubertin was strongly influenced by the English Public Schools. It was, in particular, the emphasis in Thomas Arnold's Rugby on developing the character of the boys, linked to the neo-Hellenic ideal of 'a sound mind in a healthy body'. For Arnold, sport played a key role, but it was not sport for its own sake. Coubertin's adaptation was to take education out of the school and into the public arena. He then harnessed sport to his pedagogical ends by orchestrating the games within the totality of a brilliantly conceived ritualised drama. He created what would become *the* modern religious festival, dwarfing all others, rising, as if on cue, as the Christian churches began to empty.

Coubertin was quite explicit that his was a religious revival, and that it was pagan. He spoke of new gods to replace the dying old ones. He lamented in the 1930s that the Games were turning into a marketing spectacle; he had intended them as a Temple, in which *religio athletae* was to be practised. He wrote of paganism:

> That is the cult of the human being, of the human body, mind and flesh, feeling and will, instinct and conscience. Sometimes flesh, feeling and instinct have the upper hand, and sometimes mind, will and conscience, for these are the two despots who strive for primacy within us, and whose conflict often rends us cruelly. We have to attain a balance …
>
> It was the immortal glory of Hellenism to imagine the codification of the pursuit of balance and to make it into a prescription for social greatness. Here — at Olympia — we are on the ruins of the first capital of eurhythmy, for eurhythmy does not belong to the art-world alone; there is also a eurhythmy of life.[16]

At the heart of this modern pagan religion, then, is the concept of eurhythmy — 'beautiful rhythm'. Hans Ulrich Gumbrecht, in his book *In Praise of Athletic Beauty*, goes so far as to claim that the main appeal of modern sport to the spectator is aesthetic — the sight of compellingly beautiful performance.

The opening ceremony at the modern Olympics is the feature event. It is even more anticipated than the elite track-and-field contests — which have retained the pre-eminence among the other sports of their ancient Greek models. Seats at the opening ceremony are the most expensive, and the most difficult to get. The ceremony attracts the largest television audience. Here is the cultural dimension of the modern Olympics and, as with the ancient blueprint, it is the case that sport is subordinate to culture, which frames it.

The arena in which the opening ceremony is held has become the new cathedral. The spectacle takes place at night and is choreographed — with lighting, music, special effects, and performance — to create a sort of Midsummer Night's Dream fantasia. This was explicit in Sydney 2000, with a ceremonial retelling of Aboriginal Dreamtime mythology; and in Athens in 2004, with ancient Greek mythology. Fairies, children, heroes, and fantasy creatures descend from the sky to play out fables in a supernatural space in which viewers are invited to join in, abandoning their prosaic everyday selves; invited to enter a semi-divine order, if only for a couple of hours.

There is spectacle. There is also serious ritual. The teams of the nations of the world enter the stadium in procession. An Olympic oath is taken. The Ceremony reaches its climax with the entrance of fire. The Olympic torch is lit in ancient Olympia then travels the world in relay, mimicking the beacons that Queen Clytemnestra had built between Troy and her palace in Mycenae, the chain of fire to inform her that the Trojan War was over.

The last athlete to carry the torch runs through the stadium like a god, or a goddess. Here is *religio athletae*. In Sydney, the athlete was Aboriginal sprinter Cathy Freeman, and she ran through water, then rose out of it, like Venus born from the waves. She ascended a high, celestial staircase to light the Olympic cauldron. Successful modern Olympics, presided over by sacral fire, manage to conjure up some supernatural ambience.

The marathon, the final sporting event held at each Games since 1896, is a modern invention. The closest the ancient Greeks came to an endurance race was 400 metres in full armour. Why did the marathon become the athletic climax? The answer, I suggest, lies in cultural homage. The race recreates the run in 490BC from the battlefield of Marathon to the city of Athens, to convey the news that the Persians had been defeated. That battle was an extraordinary victory against very heavy odds, and against 'barbarians'. More, it marked the rise of the pre-eminent jewel in the cultural crown of the West, fifth-century Athens. The marathon is a tribute to the generative source of so much that was to come.

Coubertin's genius has proved spectacularly successful. There have been other attempts to create new mythology, also pagan—the operas of Richard Wagner, the novels of J. R. R. Tolkien—but it is the Olympics that have triumphed. Success is perhaps due to the closeness of the Modern Olympics to the foundations of the West. The spirit of classical Greek religion has been rekindled. By taking sport, and setting it in a larger metaphysical context, a neo-pagan festival has been recreated that appeals to the religious sensibility of the secular modern West.

***

So far, I have discussed the success of sport in terms of the *psychological* and *social* functions that it fulfils. Sport has, also, become the most prominent Western form of meditation. Its most important function is *religious*. Tim Winton writes in his surfing novel, *Breath* (2008), of the experience of catching the big wave, 'You feel *alive*, completely awake and in your body. Man, it's like you've felt the hand of God.'[17]

Sport is the discipline of body and mind so that the latter may rid itself of superfluous thoughts — the teeming stream of fantasies and day-dreams that occupies the normal life of the waking mind. When the mind succeeds, and the body is trained to a degree of fitness and skill appropriate for the particular match, then brilliant play results. One modern Olympian describes being 'lost in focused intensity'.[18] By the way, a body that is inadequately trained for the challenge at hand will not allow the mind to achieve the necessary state of nonchalant concentration. One of the remarkable qualities of the Western form of meditation is its focus on being and acting *in* the world. It is this-worldly. The body and the ego are both vital.

That sport is a form of meditation is illustrated in the notion of the Personal Best performance, or 'PB'. Olympic swimmers and runners will speak proudly of having achieved their PB time, and even that this is their true mental objective. Sport is a testing of self, against its own inner limits and capacities. The ultimate competition is within. Many golfers are less concerned with beating others and winning trophies than with reducing their handicaps — the yardstick of their level of performance.

How does the mind achieve the state of sustained and yet calm focus needed in sport? Not through the agency of individuals, neither of their will nor their reason. In serious sport, the will to win is always driving; and the degree of reason or calculating intelligence of a particular player, or cumulatively in the team, fits into the category of skill, and does not directly influence the times of inspiration.

Successful meditation is entirely beyond the control of the mind. It happens, or it does not happen. Indeed, the harder the mind is pressed by the will, the less likely it is to succeed. One says, in the case of sport, that a player or a team is in, or out, of *form*. Being out of form is a kind of discord, of inner chaos—literally being at odds with the form. It makes the player frustrated and lonely, not only cut off, but feeling some sort of defilement or pollution. Team-mates have the tendency to respond to one of their number who is out of form as tainted and untouchable, someone to be avoided.

Being in form is a state of grace. It is as if some transcendental power has given the player its blessing. Watching a football team that has suddenly lifted itself, and found its feet, is to observe a collection of individual, fast-running men become one organism. In a sort of state of collective ecstasy, which incorporates the collective mass of cheering fans, they achieve a superhuman level of control. The speeding ball moves as if in total obedience to some hidden law with which they too are now in tune. All the individual egos are as nothing, dissolved into the group hymn. It is as if some unseen hand is guiding things. Or, as Homer puts it in *The Iliad*, in relation to the tired warrior, Hektor:

Apollo ... spoke, and breathed huge strength into the shepherd of the people.
As when some stalled horse who has been corn-fed at the manger breaking free of his rope gallops over the plain in thunder to his accustomed bathing place in a sweet-running river and in the pride of his strength holds high his head and the mane floats over his shoulders; sure of his glorious strength, the quick knees carry him to the loved places and the pasture of horses;
so Hektor moving rapidly his feet and his knees went onward, stirring the horsemen when he heard the god's voice speak.[19]

Tolstoy, who was a master observer of the detailed texture of what humans do, concluded that success in battle never depends on position, or equipment, or even on numbers. As Prince Andrei puts it in *War and Peace,* it depends on the feeling that is in each soldier, the 'firm resolve' to win. He speaks of the coming day's battle, 'A hundred million incalculable contingencies, which will be determined on the instant by whether they run or we do, whether this man or that man is killed.'[20]

What Tolstoy means by 'firm resolve' is not will, for both armies struggle their utmost to win. It is the intangible inspiration of the decisive moment, when the men either run or they do not run. Such inspiration comes from the outside, from on high.

A team that regains its stride experiences regeneration—not by human works or free-will, but by divine grace. There are distant strains of the music of salvation echoing here, of atonement of person with person, with nature, and with the universe.

Sport has come to occupy some intermediary position in modern societies between secular and sacred. I have mentioned the totemic scarves, headgear, colours, and chants. When people today pay homage by visiting the same shrine once a week, it will usually be to a sporting arena not to the local church.[21] They may even talk of the 'hallowed turf', of 'awesome play', and of some players not just moving like divinities, but themselves being gods. Gumbrecht notes an ecstatic communion that develops between spectators and players, one that serves to lift the players' energy.[22] Players will often, at the end of an important match, bow their heads or fall to their knees, and spectators will sweep outstretched arms and heads up and down, in a partly serious imitation of pagan worship of their heroes. We are witnessing the birth of a new type of sacred site. It anchors a new type of religion—Coubertin's *religio athletae.*

It is a religion in which the aesthetic plays a key role—as it does in most religions. The heights of sporting performance exhibit the fully rounded human—body, mind, and soul—achieving a beauty that transcends the normal. To view such 'beautiful rhythm' is exhilarating—awesome. The aesthetic here illustrates the religious category of 'form', to which it is subordinate. But sporting form is not always beautiful to watch. There can be form without beautiful rhythm—as with a football team stuck in defensive strategies, withstanding an onslaught from the opposition, as with a marathon runner, and as with a tennis star struggling through a lull in concentration.

Nick Hornby reflects that football has been his longest and most faithful relationship. He remembers his life by fixtures, and ideally he would like his ashes scattered over the Arsenal pitch. He admits he would not mind spending eternity floating around the ground as a ghost watching reserve games.[23] Golfers joke that after death, when they wake up in heaven, they imagine themselves teeing off on the perfect course. A similar sentiment drove the 1989 American film *Field of Dreams,* in which an Iowa farmer turns a cornfield into a baseball diamond, and succeeds in attracting the ghosts of great past players to compete there. This supernatural game is paradise on Earth.

Nevertheless, sport has no metaphysical language, in the sense that it does not articulate any cosmic vision of the creation of things, or explanation for misfortune and death. It is a secular means for tapping transcendental sources and powers, reviving some fleeting contact with the sacred, testing whether the gods are on your side or not. In the process, it teaches lessons, not directly through language, but indirectly through experience, of the existence of a metaphysical order and of the workings of some of its laws. As such, it is pioneering one of the main ways modern societies seem to like their religion.

The affinity of sport and war is not contradicted by the religious dimensions of the former. The passages from Homer should have made the point. In *The Iliad*, the fortunes of the two armies are made dependent on the will of the gods. The lyrical celebration of a great warrior, like Diomedes, in full flow, resonates with a mystical force—indeed the Trojans assume some god is breathing through him. Even human failings are blamed on the gods. Gods are blamed for war; they are embraced during war.

An Australian soldier, Jo Gullett, reflecting about a battalion ready for action, wrote, 'I am not sure that it is not a state of grace.'[24] Tolstoy describes in Homeric style the battle that his hero walks through, 'happy and with shining eyes':

> Pierre noticed that every ball that hit the redoubt, every man that fell, increased the general elation. The gleams of a hidden burning fire flashed like lightning from an approaching thunder-cloud, brighter and brighter, more and more often in the faces of all these men (as though in defiance of what was taking place). Pierre ... was entirely absorbed in the contemplation of that fire which blazed more fiercely with every moment, and which (so he felt) was flaming in his own soul too.[25]

This Tolstoy passage also implies that it is only in the heat of battle that one is fully alive. If much of our three-score-years-and-ten is like a drifting sleep-walk, then this is the exception: movement, action, valour, and achievement.

Likewise, coursing through the adulation inspired by sporting stars is the sense that here is real blood: these men have got it, whatever it is, that vital spirit, or life-force. With it, they even transcend their own mortality. The expression that he is a 'living legend' is now so common as to be cliché.

War is not a game. While Achilles is a gentleman after the battle, it is not much earlier that, in a torrent of avenging rage, he had mercilessly slaughtered dozens of near helpless Trojans. Human history suggests that war is recurring and inevitable, a terrible necessity that has to be borne gravely and resolutely. Sport, on the other hand, is a game, and although it taps similar drives, calls upon similar talents and strengths of character, it does not entangle with the ultimate authority — that of death. It is the high-trapeze artist who does her balancing over a safety net, and whose hands are not stained by blood-guilt.

There is a superficiality to sport. It does not enter the hallowed underworld of the great archetypes of war. The lives of civilians and especially children, the survival of the community, are not under threat. Supporters walk away miserable from a loss by their team, but essentially unscathed. Tomorrow is another day; next week another game. Moreover, while football is a case in which the surrogate is preferable to the original, the civilised sublimation preferable to plunging too close to the barbarous depths, a game will never produce poems like *The Iliad* or *Agamemnon*.

Football is both the sport of sports and, in its own way, singular. Of its essence are the cultivation of military and political virtues, and the polarisation of male and female. The nurturing female virtues of tenderness and compassion, which emanate from the household, do not belong to it. In reinforcing the masculine persona, it combats one area of intense modern insecurity, the male sense of identity, and it does so on a public stage that allows some detachment from the private, the inhibited, and the introverted.

The singularity of football is in its male exclusivity — although some codes are becoming more mixed in their supporter bases, administration, support staff, and media commentators. The general tendency in sport is for women to participate as frequently and intensively as men, although in segregated performances — the rare exceptions include mixed tennis and equestrian events. This chapter has focused predominantly on men's sport. Women's sport, as it becomes increasingly important, will call for its own interpretation—I assume many of the themes identified here will surface, but there will also be variations. A strength of sport is its variety, its capacity to provide for different inner needs, from the pure masculinity of football to the lithe, feline graces of high-board diving.

The preceding chapter focused on work, but it included sport—a focus determined by today's culture. I suggested that the appeal of sport is to do with the work ethic—its participants subject themselves whole-heartedly to the Calvinist logic of vocation, accepting its rigours and challenges, enjoying its fulfilments. Sport is one of the rare collective activities in which there is no half-heartedness, the day just to be got through, interest fitful, while the mind drifts on to other things. Sport is serious, and with a semi-religious intensity, as demanded by the work ethic.

An illustrative feature is that the rules matter. There is a ferocity with which spectators debate interpretations, protest at umpiring mistakes, express outrage at games lost because of unjust decisions. Most other areas of modern life are quite different, with provisional rules, or wishy-washy sanctions—boundaries that cannot be trusted to hold. Here is another sign of the vitality of sport in a threateningly anomic world.

That we may be redeemed by work gains an extra dimension when that work comes in the form of sport. Glory, celebrity, prestige, and wealth are also showered on those who enter the 'halls of fame'. The work ethic is not the only inducement into sport. Further, as discussed, there is the sublimation of aggression, the search for a tightly knit community—the team and club—and in some cases, led by football, the playing out of a surrogate for war.

Which are the deeper archetypes moving here? Which are the ones that have made sport so compelling to the modern psyche? Comparing different sports, the strongest attachments are to football, in its various codes—this is true for both players and spectators. I note the intensity of despair at loss, the ecstasy at victory, the warmth of reminiscence, the loyalty over decades, and the size of crowds. Soccer is by far the world's most watched sport. There is nothing like the collective euphoria that ignites a football crowd after finals success, the dewy eyes, the charged memories of titanic deeds, and the rolling thunder of triumphal song. It would be incongruous in any other sport to hear fans declaim such grandiloquent sentiments as spoken by Shakespeare's Henry V:

And gentlemen in England now a-bed,
Shall think themselves accurs'd they were not here;
And hold their manhoods cheap, whiles any speaks,
That fought with us upon Saint Crispin's day.[26]

All of this suggests that the dramaturgy of war is central, that the band of blood warrior-brothers taps potent unconscious universals. Those universals are timeless, passing down from the dawn of human experience.

The work ethic is a tandem directing presence in football. In the other sports, it predominates. It manages a unique fusion of the psychological, social, and religious functions discussed in this chapter. In its sport incarnation, deep instinctual passions are engaged, but they end up flowing in harmony with ethical and sacred forces. Sport is thus culturally conserving and creating, and in the two vital spheres, the moral and the religious. Sport is not, at heart, consumerist: not passive, not comfortable and, paradoxically, not ephemeral.

The ancient Roman Coliseum provides the cautionary tale of what sport can degenerate into: a mass orgy of sadism and lust, intoxicated on tearing flesh and blood. There was torture and murder inside the stadium; taverns and brothels, outside. Here is the end-point of the logic of consumption in its pure form, combining

Arendt's picture of garden-of-Eden leisure with Dostoevsky's prophecy that, in the modern Crystal Palace in which all needs are satisfied, we shall start to stick pins into each other, to counter the boredom.[27] Modern football, the spectacle most similar to the Roman sports, has not generally followed this path (although celebrity players are prone to fast cars, drink, drugs, and rampant womanising). Nor have the Olympic Games, in spite of corruption and drug scandals.

English soccer hooliganism is the exception in the West, little matched in Continental Europe, Canada, the United States, or Australasia. Football is saved by its dual underpinning morality: on the one hand, the warrior code of honour; on the other, the work ethic and its constraining associates, especially the solid middle-class family and its values. Here again is the reason the consumerist reading fails.

The preceding chapter concluded that the wellbeing of the modern West will hang, in good part, on the presence of the work ethic, in image and practice. Sport will increasingly have its own lead-role to play.

Chapter Three

# LOVE

That life gains meaning through love is a refrain sounding through almost every segment of modern life. In times of gravity, people commonly reflect that love is the only thing of deep and lasting value. Timeless is the fact that there are three kinds of love, at least, and that the good life depends on a range of their fulfilments. The ancient Greeks used different words in their attempt to catch the essences.

There was *eros*, charged desire, passion for another — its source somewhere in the flesh but, being more than lust, linked with the Greek name for Cupid. Plato described the god of love as a powerful demon spirit plying between Earth and Heaven:

> It has always been his fate to be needy; nor is he delicate and lovely as most of us believe, but harsh and arid, barefoot and homeless, sleeping on the naked earth, in doorways, or in the very streets beneath the stars of heaven ... He is also gallant, impetuous, and energetic, a mighty hunter, and a master of device and artifice — at once desirous and full of wisdom, a lifelong seeker after truth, an adept in sorcery, enchantment and seduction.[1]

Second, there was *philia*, friendship, including the ambience of dear and kindly. Its Latin equivalent, *amicitia*, suggests sympathy and, as with the English 'amicable', a sort of mutual goodwill. It could extend to *philo-sophy*, love of wisdom.

Third, there was *agapē*, sacred love or selfless love, celebrated by Paul:

> Love suffereth long, and is courteous. Love envieth not. Love doth not forwardly, swelleth not, dealeth not dishonestly, seeketh not her own, is not provoked to anger, thinketh not evil, rejoiceth not in iniquity: but rejoiceth in the truth, suffereth all things, believeth all things, hopeth all things, endureth in all things. Though that prophesying fail, or tongues shall cease, or knowledge vanish away, yet love falleth never away.[2]

Let me take *eros* first, for it plays the lead role in the fantasy life of the modern West. It is clothed in the royal finery of Romance, captivating otherwise sceptical adults with the magic of the children's fairytale. Union with the one-true-love is a tune that plays across the culture, from Hollywood to soap-opera to the perennial lyrics of pop music. That leading Hollywood actors are called 'stars' suggests a celestial realm in which their screen personas move — like the ancient Greek gods on Mount Olympus. It is through romance that the lonely, anxious, earth-bound individual is transported into a higher state of being. Here is the one place in modern life where religious language is used unselfconsciously — 'eternal love', 'union made in heaven', 'moments that last forever', 'soul-mate', 'angel', and 'the chosen one'.

I do not want to document the range and intensity of the culture of modern eros — its pervasiveness is obvious.[3] Rather, I will choose three examples from popular culture and explore what they reveal about the role of eros in the search for meaning.

On 9 February 1964, the Beatles first appeared live on American television. It was just two months after president Kennedy had been assassinated. One college student described the experience:

> There had been an item in the paper about a British rock and roll group which was to appear on the Ed Sullivan Show that night. I was curious, so I went down to a common room where there was a TV set, expecting an argument from whoever was there about which channel to watch. Four hundred people sat transfixed as The Beatles sang 'I Want To Hold Your Hand' and when the song was over the crowd exploded. People looked at the faces (and the hair) of John, Paul, George and Ringo and said YES.

One historian later judged that this record's 'joyous energy and invention lifted America out of its gloom, following which, high on gratitude, the country cast itself at the Beatles' feet'.[4] Every American musician, when asked about the song said, in retrospect, much the same thing: it had ushered in a new era, changing their lives. Even Bob Dylan acknowledged the revolutionary spirit animating it. The poet Allen Ginsberg was said to have shocked his intellectual friends by getting up in a New York nightclub when he first heard it, and dancing.

'I Want To Hold Your Hand' is a parable of modern longing, blending fantasy with fear. On the surface, it is a simple love song, underlined in the lyrics, 'When I touch you I feel happy inside' and 'You've got that something'. Here is the eternal flavour of naive love, from Romeo and Juliet to the Hollywood Romance — or, as another early Beatles' title put it, 'All You Need Is Love'.

There are, however, portents of darker things. The words carry an undercurrent, suggestive of a gloomy, dependent child pleading for the distant or absent mother. The title line, repeated three times in the opening, is sung with an edge of hysteria that reaches a climax in the word 'hand', emitted in Paul McCartney falsetto as a restrained scream of hair-raised anguish. What follows is the contrasting mellow sound of 'I feel happy inside'. The phrase is saccharine, depression trying to convince itself that everything is all right. There is the melancholy implication of a cold and empty self — all life comes from the other, Sleeping Beauty awakened from her deathly sleep by the prince's kiss. In 1964, though, it is the mother who is the source of life, and death; it is she who has 'that something'.

A different motif is carried by the John Lennon lead-singing. A nasal carping, almost a rasping snarl of complaint, presses in the music. The 'I wanna' is petulant, with foot-stamping frustration. The full title line, moreover, in its simple pathos is rhetorical, with little expectation of fulfilment. If anything, the protagonist does not even want his hand held; he is more wedded to his own mistreatment, which justifies his rage. At this level, the song indulges in a sort of aggressive self-pity.

There is, nevertheless, a pulsating energy, even euphoria, to the tune, cutting across the discontent — as if to suggest that while you may be frazzled and lonely, our music can transform all that into revitalising love. It chants, with a series of repeated incantations, offering the togetherness of collective song. Moreover, the tones are grainy and unsentimental, their mood honest and direct, implying that this generation's success depends on transcending the sugary pretences and saving lies of its parents.

'I Want To Hold Your Hand' thus beguiles with a complex psychology. It taps into insecurity in intimate relations, the resulting fragility of ego opening up a nervous receptivity to the dark side of the song. Alerted, every nerve jangling, the Beatles then soothe us with the lively beat and the invitation to feel warm inside. Join us, and we will transport you beyond the hurt, our offer combining a triple paradise, that of cuddled child, adored teenager, and successful adult. Be an infant, be a rebellious adolescent, be yourself, open your bruised heart, for the music will set you free.

There are universals running through these strands. The stage set and actors are early 1960s, but the script is from many times and places. Indeed, the lyrics of pop music hardly change, so that the mode of reading 'I Want To Hold Your Hand' could be employed on many songs, almost picked at random from over the last half-century. I have simply chosen the Beatles because of the scale of their impact, and the longevity of their popularity.

The song taps into the highly charged chamber of eros, that sprite which toys with insecure ego, pitching it into a storm of volatile desire and grandiose fantasy —forcing one person backwards in infantile regression; another into self-pitying withdrawal; opening another up to an uncontrollable, desperate clutching; torturing others with explosions of rage, infatuation, vanity, and self-loathing. And, as the song so surreptitiously lets off grenades of anxiety in the unconscious, it carries along with it the intoxicating dream of passion fulfilled. Whereas the beat excites, the lead line, at its more benign, steadies and consolidates, with its three-way evocation of the child walking along happily by its mother's side, the tentative first stage of teenage romance, and a more relaxed adult love, even to the point of a retired couple strolling together.

As Plato intimated, the erotic dream is ultimately one of the loss of self in union with the other, a union which takes both beyond themselves into a greater oneness. There is transcendence and grace here. In the language of the 'soul-mate', there is the hope that it is the fragment of divinity in each which is brought into communion—that, in this union, the eternal incarnate in the mortal flesh awakens by finding its lost other. So eros, which is rooted in the most earth-bound desire, rises up to touch the very heavens.

Modernity has invested much of its hope in the empire of eros.

Widespread scepticism about the value of religious asceticism has helped. There has been a cultural shift away from the belief that purity and, in particular, any form of celibacy, is virtuous. The traditional insistence on virginity at marriage is gone; indeed, if anything, it has drifted into a reverse stigma, of virginity indicating a lack of worldliness, subject to the current abusive retort: 'Get a life!'

Nevertheless, the dominant emphasis on experience, on seizing the day, is less in the hedonistic tradition of pleasure being all, than in the broader pagan classicism according to which immersion in life should be tempered. On the one side, it should be moderated ethically, by acting justly and being a good person; and, on the other, it should be moderated religiously, with reverence, ensuring that the whole is guided by the quest for a higher connection. Apart from the fact that eros has no concern with morality, its enticements are suited to the this-worldly orientation of the West, governed by individual conscience.

The two figures to capture the modern popular imagination as tragic have been stars in the night sky of eros—Marilyn Monroe and Elvis Presley. Marilyn Monroe was known explicitly as sex queen or, more evocatively, as sex goddess. Her presence on the screen, as in her publicity, shimmered with eroticism; flirting, wiggling, using her cool, half-closed eyes and pouting mouth to ever heighten the focus on her erogenous zones.

She challenged the staid 1950s with her flagrant exhibitionism, testing how far she could undress in public. Her film career took a leap after she idled along six studio blocks barefoot, clad merely in a see-through negligee, to attend a photography session in 1951. When she made the return walk, the streets were lined with cheering, leering men. In response to a proposal, on a later occasion, that she join other celebrities by recording her hand prints and foot prints in wet cement, she offered her breasts and buttocks as more fitting.

She died aged thirty-six, in 1962. Her death was almost certainly from sleeping pills, which she had been taking in large doses for years. Many film stars have disappeared young, and some pop-music stars have died early (including John Lennon), all without creating the same kind of legend. So what made her case so tragic?

It is hard to imagine anything more profane than the basic appeal of Marilyn Monroe. She winked straight into the male imagination, whispering, *What a perfect specimen of female sensuality I am, loose and available. Drool over my curves; I would show you more if they'd let me. It's only me, simple and stupid, no threat, interested in just one thing. As one of my titles puts it, some like it hot.* There was not much of Plato's divinity here, except in the sense of climactic pleasure or, rather, the fantasy of its vague accoutrements.

This was but one side of Marilyn. Every time she released a film, she surprised many, including the critics, with the fact that she was far more than a pin-up girl in motion. Her presence was subtle and complicated, even in the modulations of emotion with which she dominated her major works. Lee Strasberg put it, at her funeral:

> She had a luminous quality — a combination of wistfulness, radiance, yearning — that set her apart and yet made everyone wish to be a part of it, to share in the childish naïveté which was at once so shy and so vibrant.[5]

There was the tiny, simpering, baby-doll tinkle of a voice. There was the self-conscious play-acting with her roles, so men knew she was not serious. Her sultry style was a sham. Men could enjoy the dream without the threat of the reality, and she underlined the fact, virtually making it conscious, saying, *Look, I play a vapid, twittering butterfly, but you can see that is pretence, and really I am shrewd, cool, and not at all interested in sex.* Compared to her contemporary Ava Gardner, there was a plastic, desensualised quality to Marilyn on screen, a tendency even towards the antiseptic woodenness of *Playboy* centrefolds. Just as the Beatles were later to explore the ambivalence of live-in-fantasy / don't-engage-in-reality, so had Marilyn a few years earlier.

Her screen performances depended on increasingly tortured trials in gathering her fractured self, her soul so raw and damaged that the slightest false touch by those she worked with would send her over the edge into deep depression, or into a tenacious and malevolent hatred against some man close by—often, the director and, if not him then, over one period, her afflicted third husband, Arthur Miller.

Norman Mailer diagnoses two selves, two souls, in Marilyn. One was a hard, relentless, inhuman machine of cold, calculating ambition, that loved publicity and had a genius for exploiting it. Her other self was like a 'virus-ridden mouse', the eight-year-old girl who had been abandoned to orphanages and foster-homes when her mother collapsed in madness, and was put in an asylum. She could draw on this self for her angelic screen persona: the vulnerable, tender, even large, blonde, and lovely Marilyn. When she wasn't mesmerising the camera, her presence was insignificant, her ego obliterated by insecurities. People who came across her in private were often incredulous that this was *the* Marilyn.

Mailer speculates that it was as if she installed all her victories in the first self, and all her failures in the second. Her life became a series of stops and starts, as one character took over and then faded—as fickle as her loves, which suddenly turned into explosive hates.[6]

Exploiting something like this split meant that she worked best when she had pitched the film-set into chaos. She might turn up two hours late, or four, or six. She might need forty takes, even forgetting a single line like, 'It's me, Sugar.' The director of *Some Like It Hot*, Billy Wilder, confirmed weeks after filming had finished:

I can eat again, sleep again, enjoy life and finally look at my wife without wanting to hit her because she is a woman.[7]

Why then did Marilyn so compel the imagination of the time, and continue to do so? How is it that she became the great tragic heroine of the latter half of the twentieth century—that is, until Princess Diana replaced her, temporarily? The base point is that her realm was that of eros. She conjured up its spirits in her performances, and its demons in her life—which was all too public, given voracious press interest. Her power to captivate any man was the dream of every woman. It was the dream of every man—every Tom, Dick, and Harry—that she was open to seduction, that she could be overwhelmed by even his threadbare veneer of charm.

Then there were the complexities of her screen self. There was the wide-eyed innocent, naive about her body and the hypnotic effect it had on men. This Marilyn offered sex as a child's game, fenced off from the violent passions, from sordidness, and from suffering. The viewer could enjoy looking at her, and enter into a harmless flirtation in which nothing was asked of him—he did not need to be either the urbane French lover or the manly Western hero. He could just be his ordinary bumbling self. In this world, all was light, vibrant, happy, and good fun.

Her act, her put-on persona, never entirely concealed the hurt self from view, seeking love in the displaced form of being the centre of attraction, whether among the actors on screen, or in the wider world that attended her films and devoured the gossip magazines. This Marilyn had those two polar sides: one was cold, detached, and calculating, ensuring that nothing would ever damage her again; the other, sensitive like an open wound. It was as if she bared her flesh as a ruse, to distract from the exposed soul. She did not care about her body: it could not be harmed and, in any case, she was confident about it. Her audience must have somehow grasped all of this unconsciously, for an aspect of her appeal was her invitation to her male audience to escape from crushed nerves, brittle ego, and torn soul—via paradoxical dreams of the flesh as childlike fun, a sort of Disneyland eros.

Her live self showed that the gods charge punitively for giving such prodigious powers. They charge in failed marriages, in lonely and miserable depressions, even in chronic unreliability in her one area of success, her career. In her life, there was very little fun. Her last film was aptly named *The Misfits*. By now, directors loathed her, studios were fed up with her and, this time, even the public didn't respond—although the film, in both its content and her performance, was her most profound work. By now, it was as if her innocent, timid, fragile, vulnerable—indeed, likeable—self had turned demonic. This fairytale princess did not live happily ever after.

Her tragedy offers support to a range of morals, starting with the lower-middle-class belief that it is better to be ordinary and happy. Marilyn had tested the waters of eros to see whether it was possible to live entirely within its domain. Starting with opulent gifts, she had won wealth, and fame to the extreme of world adulation, yet she had paid with her happiness. Live modestly, her life said to others, without excess. This involved making a compact with eros, ensuring that it is sublimated into steady and enduring, if not too-exciting, love—sublimated into family life.

While universal moral themes surface in the Marilyn story, it might be asked whether she has much to contribute to the modern search for meaning. Surely, what we observe is hardly life-affirming? Such a challenge misses the deeper significance of her story: it reasserts the existence and potency of tragedy in the human condition.

It is notable that the *mythos* comes through popular culture, exemplified in Elton John's song tribute to Marilyn:

Goodbye Norma Jean
Though I never knew you at all
You had the grace to hold yourself
While those around you crawled …
And it seems to me you lived your life
Like a candle in the wind
Never knowing who to cling to
When the rain set in.

Elton John adapted the song for the funeral of Princess Diana. It achieved the greatest number of song sales ever. 'Candle in the Wind', in its double life, is steeped in tragic pathos.

To read a life as tragic assumes that there is a higher order to things, and an enduring code for judging what happens, according to which there is success and failure, fulfilment and misery, achievement and waste, and that these categories are not relative or haphazard. It also assumes that there is fate, or its like, and that some people are blessed with good fortune; others, cursed with misfortune. It wrestles with questions of justice, and of whether there are rewards for living virtuously; and of whether misfortune is a form of punishment for wickedness, bad character, evil ancestors, or some past life. Even if it does not find convincing answers, it assumes that these are serious matters.

The tragic imagination encourages a more contemplative orientation to life, a gravity of reflection, opening up the big metaphysical questions. Moreover, it arouses compassion for the victims, and wonder at life and its ineffable mysteries. It induces humility and awe. In all of this, it is central to the human quest for meaning. The Marilyn Monroe films, watched in retrospect, seen as it were through the tragic filter of her biography, deepen with the heroic pathos and mortal completeness that may be apportioned to those born human. Even the floss of her comedy gains poignancy.

In the West, we have a fateful bond to the tragic stand. Pulsing through the culture is Aeschylus' pained utterance, 'grace comes somehow violent'.[8] The ancient Greeks used the same verb, *paschō*, for experience and suffering—the root from which, in English, we derive passion, pathos, sympathy, empathy, and pathology. Passion is suffering, and without it there is no experience. *Paschō* is to live. Moreover, according to this view, it is only through tragedy that we fully awaken to life. A Marilyn Monroe thus helps reconnect us with our deeper mysteries.

Similar attachments and concerns are at the heart of the legend that built up around the life and music of Elvis Presley. The inflections are different, of course. This was the story of a young man with a gift for summoning up the powers of eros for an entire generation through his song and dance. His arrival was sensational; the sound of his voice, the sight of his gyrating body, electric. Teenagers would jive and scream, weep and groan—normally prim middle-class girls would swoon with infatuated self-abandon. The adult generation was so shocked that it censored his dancing on American national television. Elton John credits Elvis with creating the modern revolution in pop music, with the Beatles developing in his wake.

For a time, Elvis had a voice with the Orphic capacity to woo the coldest spirits out of their underworld caves. Then the story gradually turned black, as it became clear that the idol could not cope with stardom and wealth. He became gross, his once-languid, clean features and pouting Pre-Raphaelite mouth puffing up almost beyond recognition. He turned into a bloated, repulsive grotesque, as if drugs, alcohol, junk food, and whatever other perversions he indulged, in his self-created mansion-prison-hell, Graceland, had stifled the soul, like some demonic giant python wringing out the breath.

His later concerts were watched around the world with morbid fascination as this human wreck, his voice largely ruined, managed to summon up momentary flashes of the formidable, charismatic presence of the past. Occasionally, a deep phrase would sink through the weight and the exhaustion to tap the buried reserve of lament, and carry its charge out across the black anonymity of the auditorium and its hushed thousands. Then it would be gone. All that was left on stage was a straining, sweating parody of one for whom it had always been easy.

Since his death in 1977, aged forty-two, his memory has called up some of the weirdest superstitions in a secular age. The man who was known as the King is widely rumoured, in popular culture, to be still alive. There is a booming market in such mountebank articles as phials containing his sweat, sold with the promise that one drop will answer any prayer. There are Elvis look-alike, life-size rubber dolls. Hundreds of Elvis impersonators perform around the Western world—woodenly echoing the legend. His home, Graceland, has become a shrine, the American Lourdes, the best-known home after The White House.

Strains from ancient Greece echo here, not only of Orpheus torn apart by crazed Thracian maidens, who had been aroused by the haunting power of his song. There is Silenus, the drunken old lecher with a red, blotchy face, his bloated belly hanging over sagging genitals, a piece of human blubber lurching around, groping anyone young of either sex—who, at the same time, was attributed with magical powers and wisdom. The Greeks, too, had been drawn to the wildly alternating polarities of beauty and the beast, of seduction and disgust, assuming that proximity to the erotic sources opens doors equally to the squalid and to the sublime, even to the truth. In the legend of the modern King, there are thus not just revisions of the tragic archetype, but encounters with a range of other ancient human essences.

There are Christ motifs, too. Elvis arrives as saviour, a cataclysmic eruption of vital energy. He has 'that something' to peerless royal degree, and what he gives his fans is a metamorphosis out of ordinary life, summoning up powers in them, freeing them to orgiastic dancing, searing their heart strings, transporting their fantasies. His charisma was so powerful that, from local party to large concert and screen audiences, the first strains of his voice would bring *life*. At the same time, there was a sense that his performances were his all, his private world empty—life in Graceland an annihilating tedium, his marriage rumoured to be hardly consummated. He gave his life to his fans, literally in the end, or so it seemed to them. Part of his mystique then draws on guilt: everyone took what he had to give, enjoyed it, consumed it without a second thought, and then saw too late what the sacrifice had done to him.

★★★

An age-old response to the failure of eros is to turn to friendship. In *Casablanca* (1943), the perennial film regularly nominated by critics and audience alike as the greatest of all time, the hero ends up sacrificing the love of his life, Isla. Rick has lived in torment since a brief affair eighteen months earlier in Paris that had been terminated abruptly by her disappearance. Her chance arrival, along with her husband, at Rick's bar in Casablanca pitches him into rapid swings between fury and drunken despair. By the end, she wants to go with him, but he nobly sends her away. The finale, as her plane takes off, is not the dark grief of the hero forsaking the love of his life, but of Rick turning to the captain of police (Claude Rains) and, with some lightness and warmth, uttering the famous line, 'Louis, I think this is the beginning of a beautiful friendship.'

My principal method of investigation, in surveying the modern West, is to try to read the living culture. This means getting down on hands and knees, so to speak, and trying to sniff out the spoors in the dust of everyday life.

In the case of *Casablanca*, there are many attractions: the love story, the brilliant cast led by Humphrey Bogart at his best, the beauty of Ingrid Bergman, and the script. Two leitmotifs of emotion vie for ascendancy. The storm-and-stress of passion between the lovers, the tune of eros, is the predominant key. But there is also, playing breezily through the film, an easy, affectionate urbanity between the two central men, blending wit, casual cynicism, and boyish games dressed up as deals and business. Bogart lets Rains win on the sly at roulette, but takes pleasure in circumventing one of his corruptions—granting exit visas to young couples in return for sleeping with the wives.

Thus the climax, in Bogart's hands, requires him to choose between intimacy and friendship with honour. He may be heartbroken, but he can, nevertheless, choose friendship with some enthusiasm.

In part, it is because he finds that intimacy is too difficult, too painful, not worth the candle. Better not to get involved; for, at its extreme, as Hendin's college student put it, 'If you show your feelings you get your legs cut off.' And, as male and female identities have become less sure in the West—what it is to be a man, what it is to be a woman—relations between the sexes have inevitably grown more strained, and Rick's choice has found an increasingly receptive audience.

There are reverberations in sport. I noted the strong ties within a team, the bonds within a band of blood brothers. This is mateship, and mates are obligated to each other by a code of mutual support—'You can rely on your mates!' They are also united, like warriors, by shared memories of glory, adventure, mishap, and failure—key events, ones that mattered, which have given shape to their life-stories. Mates are friends of a sort. Here is genuine attachment, and a true source of meaning. And yet one of its undercurrents is a regression from adulthood into the carefree, irrepressible circle of boys, free from the emotional tentacles of women. The anxieties that help bind sporting mates show in their put-down jokes about women. These jokes are signs of what Freud called 'masculine protest': a need to display exaggerated manliness on the surface, to compensate for fears of weakness.

For women, the contours of friendship tend to be different. There is more emphasis on talk than on action. Interest is in the story itself, in the intricate tissues of motive and feeling that weave together to form the complete web. Just as Rick and Louis distance themselves through friendship, so women may create a platform together from which to view life as lived, sublimating the pain into the bonds within their own group.

There is companionship, too. Historically, most cultures have regarded it as not a good idea for men and women to spend much time together, the biological differences being too great. Here is a near-universal, which the modern ideal of marriage has cut across with its hope that, at the core, husband and wife will be helpmeets. This cultural transformation followed the Reformation, which replaced the traditional utilitarian focus on marriage as a means of reproduction, sometimes including subsidiary economic functions, with an emphasis on companionship.[9] Husband and wife were to be equals, helping each other along life's way, with shared responsibilities. In the last half-century, as community engagement has lessened, and with it the diffusion of attachment to wider kin through large extended families, bonds of domestic affection have become even more vital to individual wellbeing.

The companion is the person you can be yourself with, at your ease, unguarded—Rick and Louis. This is the hallmark of friendship, in which the ego is unthreatened and therefore not on edge, intrusive, and disruptive. But there is also, behind the scenes, some compatibility of soul, a rapport with at least a trace of the harmony of soul-mates. Here is another case of a balance of ego and soul.

Since the 1960s, there have been further extensions to the companionship ideal—parents and teenage children aspiring to be friends, and among teenagers themselves a shift in relations between boys and girls towards the mateship model, with a commensurate reduction in traditional sexual tensions. The latter itself represents, in part, a defence strategy against eros. Two of the highest-rating TV series of the 1990s, *Seinfeld* (1989–98) and *Friends* (1994–2004), both centred on friendship. All in all, we hear *Casablanca* resounding more loudly through the culture. The fantasy is that of the 'beautiful friendship'.

\*\*\*

When people today reflect that love is the only thing of deep and lasting value, they usually refer to family, and to ties of blood. The practical realm of *agapē*, as almost always and everywhere, is the home. Paul's hymn to a love that suffereth long, and is courteous, remains a favourite reading at wedding ceremonies—phrasing an ideal for the couple and their own anticipated family. Yet the sociology of the contemporary nuclear family indicates a severe weakening in the ties that bind it.

There are three distinct signs of growing instability. First, traditional notions of family cohesiveness are splintering. Since the 1970s, divorce rates have soared. The current Australian estimate is that between 30 and 45 per cent of marriages will end in divorce.[10] One third of American births, and one quarter of Australian births, are to unmarried mothers. The proportion of Australian mothers who are single rose from 4 per cent in 1970 to 14 per cent in 2003.[11]

As a second sign of family instability, parents have less control over their teenage children; this is an indicator of weakening authority, of a radical liberalism eroding family ties.

Third, there has been a long-term trend for families not to take in their grandparents, expecting that the State will provide homes for the aged. This indicates a lower feeling of collective family responsibility, and it goes with the disappearance of veneration for elders, dismissing the notion that grandparents might have something to teach children.

On the other hand, the home remains the haven in a heartless world of equally persuasive sociological analysis.[12] It provides a retreat from coldness and estrangement, from the fickle blows inflicted by the public world. The large majority of children in the West continue to grow up in a nuclear family with both of their biological parents.[13] For most people, former Australian prime minister Robert Menzies' words of 1942 remain true:

> I do not believe that the real life of this nation is to be found either in great luxury hotels and the petty gossip of so-called fashionable suburbs, or in the officialdom of organised masses. It is to be found in the homes of people who are nameless and unadvertised, and who, whatever their individual religious conviction or dogma, see in their children their greatest contribution to the immortality of their race. The home is the foundation of sanity and sobriety; it is the indispensable condition of continuity; its health determines the health of society as a whole.[14]

Modern life centres on the metropolis, which continues to spread in area, population, and density, its major organisations themselves ever growing in size and impersonality — from government and its bureaucracies, to corporations and universities, to sporting arenas and shopping centres. Individuals, confronted by the mounting anomic threat of powerlessness, anonymity, and loneliness, have one place in which they are known, as are all who dwell there, by intimate nicknames and other familiarities. In that haven, everyday ways and things are predictable.

For many, it remains a shock to remember when they were launched in public without parents to hold their hands. The first day at school is one of the modern initiations. Children enter an alien world in which people do not love them. They discover that the cocoon of home is an exception, not a microcosm.

It was the gift of Raphael to draw out the sacred essence of mother and child. His *Madonnas* depict in ideal form the total devotion in love towards the baby that forms the emotional and spiritual circle within which it may grow, supported weightless in her tender hold. Although the mother is strong, whereas the child is weak and dependent, here is the female quintessence of selflessness — contrasting with that of men in battle. It grows out of the most extreme experience of *labour*, of surrender to nature. Out of the climax to the pain not only comes new life, but an explosion of wonder and gratitude. From the most flesh-bound earth, caked in blood and muck, there is union with the highest heaven, in a parallel to Plato's soaring spirit of eros. The experience is, of course, age-old, and continues to pipe an instinctual call.

Old archetypes survive, whatever the complexities that develop in the contemporary West with the blurring of traditional boundaries, due in particular to the increasing proportion of mothers who work, many of them in careers. There may be a general law that mothers are homemakers, and that fathers are providers. Between one-half and two-thirds of contemporary Western women continue to accept that homemaking is their principal life-activity, and that income-earning is men's — that, for wives, going out to work is secondary.[15] A lower commitment to work follows. Nevertheless, an increasing proportion of women, especially upper-middle-class career women, have moved out of the traditional mould.

Furthermore, women are disproportionately satisfied with their jobs, in spite of them being generally of a lower status and less well paid than those of men. Male resistance to doing the housework, recorded in all sociological studies, is not entirely laziness, just as 1990s' men with children still reported the pride they took in 'providing', even when they were only the minor bread-winner.[16] Women, still seeing themselves as mothers and nest-builders, usually feel shame if their house is dirty or untidy—believing it to be their responsibility. This range of archetypes continues to be tapped in television advertisements.

New ambivalences appear. On the one hand, the home increasingly functions as a convenient and efficient service centre, the multiple roles of the various adults and children coinciding with the consumption of takeaway meals and rostered car lifts. On the other hand, the home remains a sacred space. While piety is no longer expressed through religious images on the walls, or rituals of family prayer and the saying of grace before meals, there are enduring forms of reverence.

Once the child begins to make forays into the world, it can only do so with confidence if it emerges from a secure base to which it can flee in retreat when tired or fearful. When it starts to draw, it will soon produce images of its home, usually in the stock form of a simple rectangle, with a path leading straight up to a door set squarely in the middle. These drawings will typically include a chimney, whether the child's own home has one or not, in a further mythic projection of its sense that there is a hearth at the centre—the cosy fire of mother—and a vertical line extending upwards. Psychologists quickly detect disturbances in a child from the variations it builds into this imagery. The home is safe and certain; but, even more for the child, it constitutes right order, inspiring confidence that such a thing exists. It thereby imposes stability on the huge, daunting adult world.

For adults, too, there are higher attachments. It may be an old vase, so familiar as to be unworthy of notice; yet, when from time to time it does come into focus, it is regarded fondly, with warmth, like an old friend, a staple part of one's being. It may be the favourite armchair, ugly and threadbare like a child's teddy bear; but it is loved, and it belongs, carrying some sense of duration, that all is not instant and passing. Then there is the ancestral fruit-bowl, passed down from an earlier generation, to hold in its generous concave lap the fruit, presenting it to be looked at in its glorious ripeness. The rosy peach will come and go while the bowl endures; and we humans belong to both of its domains, temporal and eternal.

The modern home provides a further sphere, that of privacy. In earlier times—from the clan humpy, to the tribal tent, to the Renaissance château—home was open space, with even the sleeping areas unsecluded. Louis XIV's Versailles was so little troubled by physical modesties that the grand courtiers used the corridors as toilets. With the rise of the individual conscience have come various spatial projections. The retreat behind the locked doors of bathroom and toilet is an expression of the victory of conscience over communal shame. Conscience brings a more intense self-consciousness. Modern, private ablutions serve more than a practical, hygienic function. They act as purifications for pressured anxieties and insecurities about the self and its conduct; as a modern form of secular atonement replacing ritual cleansing in public, which used to be carried out through sacrifice, open confession, and acts of penance or other church ceremonies.

In the modern world, individuals want their own special corners, a retreat in which they can be quiet and alone. Here is the new inner sanctum, within the larger temple of the home. 'My room' is a secular reworking of the medieval monk's cell. Now, as then, one may assume that much of the time is spent on prosaic tasks, or is taken up by none-too-spiritual day-dreams. Nevertheless, a higher opportunity is provided in this cosy seclusion, and is felt to be essential to personal wellbeing. It is inconceivable that Vermeer's *Geographer* could sustain his high pitch of *work* concentration in a crowded and noisy room. The needs of the more loosely reflective modes of individual conscience are no less dependent on time and tranquillity—needs that range from meditation on the particulars of the daily doings, to attempts to discern the grander ebb and flow of fate and its trials. Private space enables one to withdraw from the hurly-burly in order to regain balance, even to 'know thyself' in the pure Calvinist sense, orchestrated by conscience.

The ideal of home and family as central to the good life is prominent in popular culture. *Gone with the Wind,* via book and film, was probably the twentieth century's best-known love saga. It ends with the ambivalently likeable/unlikeable heroine, Scarlett O'Hara, finally gaining some wisdom—that she, in her blindness, has been the cause of losing both the men she loved. It is now too late, her husband confronting her indifferently with the renowned line, 'Frankly, my dear, I don't give a damn.' Her response is, as always after crisis, to go back home—to Tara, with its warm memories of childhood, the place where she grew up, the only reliable thing in her life, the only thing she has fought for successfully. There she can always recover her strength. In Tara, she has faith, the one place which under the quakings of mortal life does not move under her feet. Home is Scarlett's sacred site.

The most profound TV drama of the early years of the twenty-first century was *The Sopranos.* Shakespearean in its scripting and dramatisation, it ran for six series, between 1999 and 2007. The story is about a Mafia clan of gangsters who network the state of New Jersey with violent extortion, rackets, gambling, prostitution, and corrupt unions. But the core dynamic of the drama concerns the family of the boss, Tony Soprano.

A backdrop of bloody and ruthless crime, generating a mood of impending doom, serves to intensify the colours in which the family drama plays out. The family itself is typical, with unstable affections between husband and wife; constant trials with a teenage son who is rude, rebellious, and lazy; and a happier narrative following a well-balanced teenage daughter into her life as a young woman. The daughter also provides a moral compass. The central message is that whatever the absorptions of life—here, mateship, riches, brilliant, powerful leadership, grossly immoral egoism, and dangerous adventure—the only thing that truly matters is family love.

'Homeless' has become the term used to refer to people, including children, who live on the streets. The media attention paid to 'homelessness' is hugely out of proportion to its significance as a social problem, which is minor. This suggests that it touches a nerve in the modern imagination. The homeless are perceived to suffer a degradation that, while not as dramatically shocking as that of the vilest perpetrators of crime, is closer to the bone. With them it is possible to identify, for they have lost the key attribute of belonging, even of being human. They are the dispossessed. They are the modern vagabonds, but stripped of any bohemian glamour. The image is of uprooting, spreading beyond the literal, material facts into nightmare fears of individuals being cut loose from all moorings. In these fears, there is recognition that the home today remains the haven in a heartless world. It is where petty and mundane tasks are occasionally illuminated with transcendental significance, and where the overall complexion of a life may find a higher order.

In modernity, the two main areas of life remain those of work and love. The good life depends on fulfilment in both—meaningful belief in their overall shape, and reasonable possibilities of experience, of living them through to some sort of completion. In the sphere of love, the enduring ideal is a union of eros, companionship, and family, of the integration of the three different Greek forms.

The modern tragedies are of failure in one area leading to a complete demoralisation. The *Casablanca* model is one stage better: a promise of a tolerable second best. It is telling that the 1990s saw a major Jane Austen revival, in film and television. What was projected through Austen's very different society and times, faithfully simulated, was a simpler image of love, friendship, and family. The leading young women, of strong and independent character, coming from the milieu of restricted gentry families, typically fall in love with men who are also companions, marry them and, by implication, live happily ever after. In this sphere, the more things change, the more they stay the same.

## Chapter Four

# LOWER-MIDDLE-CLASS CULTURE

Class distinctions survive mainly at the cultural rather than socio-economic level. There are blurrings of economic difference, whereby some low-skilled blue-collar occupations — builders' labourers or miners — earn more than skilled artisans, journalists, architects, and certainly most actors, artists, and writers. There are blurrings of status difference, whereby old money is losing its links with either corporate or political power. In England, the Western country that retained marked class-stratification longest, the rapid fracturing of a closed, homogeneous working-class culture, in which occupation, mode of living, and world-view all cohered, began as early as the 1950s.[1]

The most reliable indicator of class difference has become university education. But the impact of that difference on wealth, status, and power is muffled, and the Marxist reading which held that conflict between the different classes is central to the dynamic of capitalist societies is even less plausible than in the past.

Leaving aside fragments of an under-class, and ethnic enclaves at the margin, modern Western societies divide into two. I am including the traditional working class in with the lower middle class, on grounds of cultural homogeneity — exemplified by them reading the same newspapers and mass-circulation women's magazines, and watching the same television programs. This is not to deny some differences: for instance, more straitlaced staidness in the heirs of the old lower middle class, and greater earthiness in those of the working class.

The seventeenth-century Dutch painter Pieter de Hooch caught, in his simple interiors, the ambience of lower-middle-class life, and within it the vital gene that continues to form this culture today, whatever the greater complexities.[2] De Hooch's milieu is that of domesticity, centring on women carrying out the mundane tasks of the home — the beds are made, the rooms are tidy, the apples are peeled. There is a pleasure in ordinary things. A mood of serenity prevails.

Here is an ideal with two determining foci. There is the hearth, the cosy retreat from the cold of the public world. The wood fire burns, itself an image of life lived, of the consumption by flame which at the same time generates heat, drawing those around it together, warmed by the present, able to gaze into its depths and reflect on timeless things, on generations past and those to come. There is a rocking chair for the old, and a rug in front on which children play.

Second, there is acceptance of finitude. This world is complete in itself, and accepted as such. There is not the generic restlessness of the upper middle class, striving to improve itself and its position, whether in the ethical sense of becoming better, more virtuous people, or in the material sense of becoming richer, more powerful, and more socially esteemed. The high-bourgeois mansion was prone to frigidity in its taste, an anxiety to impress precluding the relaxation necessary for a carefree homeliness.

De Hooch's interiors, while themselves not casual, are modest and plain. In the lower middle class, limits are recognised. They will not be breached. They determine a way of life that will not change in its forms, although children will be born, grow up and, in their time, die. The mundanity of the passing years is not softened by dreams of a higher station. The best has to be made of what is.

The feminist riposte today is that this was successful patriarchy, keeping an obliging and indulgent home for the master to return to in the evening, after his interesting and fulfilled day at work. His wife is kept firmly in her dull place.

The riposte is unfair. It misses the awesome power of the wife and mother. It takes the surface for the real. That power is principally over the husband. Everything else follows from it. He reveals his wife's authority either way, whether it is a fear of women that drives him to keep his spiritual and emotional distance, out of self-preservation, or whether he loves his wife unaffectedly and subjects himself to her rhythms, finding himself bereft if he loses contact.[3]

The acceptance of finitude has its source in the woman. She is more secure in the limited, which she knows from her own body, with its regulating cycles, and its own creative impulse to give birth, suckle, and rear. Her womb creates the particular, an actual child with given character and set needs. The child will itself go through a finite life cycle, including departure from the home into adulthood.

Finitude is harder for the man to accept. His own driving instinct, that of power, has no inherent limit. It relentlessly strives to expand. Even its sublimations are unstable. When the idea of limit is accepted—that there will be no higher position, no greater influence, no better salary, no greater authority at home, the love of no other women—it is often accepted as defeat, his life a failure, and the man deteriorates into a sort of shuffling corpse. Here is another cross to be borne by his wife, just to keep him going, coddling and consoling so that he does not give up completely.

There is a lower-middle-class view of the world, with its own ethic. The home is the centre of life and of what is good. It constitutes the higher purpose, and thereby makes the housework more than a set of dreary routines, and the husband's work more than a job. When the family sits down together on special occasions—at Christmas, on birthdays, or on Mother's Day—for a roast dinner, there is communion. There is the food, which gives strength and vitality. There is the gathering together in a charmed circle that is complete. The cares and doubts are temporarily banished. The table is illuminated by the light of a higher law.

In de Hooch's world, the surrounds are plain. The virtue that emerges from the acceptance of finitude is modesty. There is nothing great or original about what we do. We do not strive to be different or better. Our ambitions are slight. Indeed, we are fearful of aiming too high, for both psychological and ethical reasons. The ancient Greek chorus of Aeschylus said it all, 'Let me attain no envied wealth, let me not plunder cities.'[4]

There is an unadorned honesty to de Hooch's interior spaces. However, a lack of pretence, an openness about what is, does project a pride about rectitude. A rather stoical judgement is imposed on family, on public duty and, above all, on the notion of what is just. There is not much tolerance of human fallibility: it is met by a cool resignation, or stern rebuke, rather than a forgiving urbanity. Decency prevails here, in its double image of a spotless order with things, and a pious engagement with people.

There is time. What that time frees, as the authoritative energy which drives all, is the mother's touch. De Hooch illustrates this in his *Boy Bringing Pomegranates*. A street urchin arrives at the threshold of the inner house. He holds a basket of fruit. The woman of the home greets him. She bends down and, with her left hand, just touches one of the pomegranates. The boy is delighted, as if he, an orphan, has been welcomed into a sacred space. Her touch is that of love, diffused through her world. A cushion to one side is red underneath—passion contained—just as the earthy sexual imagery of the fruit is sublimated into maternal *agapē*. The windows glow with a golden orange-tinged light. An utterly mundane transaction is transformed into a blessing, and everything is right in the world.[5]

The simple joy of the maternal touch is enabled by the overarching Christian ethic of humility, suffusing everyday life. In another of de Hooch's works, *The Courtyard of a House in Delft,* a stone tablet is set over an arch. The painting centres on the tender union of a young girl with a maid going about her chores. The tablet reads:

> This is in St Jerome's vale, if you wish to retire to a realm of patience and meekness. For we must first descend if we wish to be raised.

The source of the credal authority which feeds this culture's vitality is Calvinist. As the English seventeenth-century religious poet George Herbert formulated it:

> Who sweeps a room, as for thy laws,
> Makes that and th' action fine.[6]

Terkel's waitress from Chapter One belongs here.

De Hooch's mapping is, of course, highly idealised. It is idealised even in relation to his own time. In the modern West, it was more true to the 1950s than to the early twenty-first century, in which it is likely that the mother goes out to work, and there is less family stability — the steep rise in divorce rates after the 1970s has included the lower middle class.[7] That we have a tendency to glamorise aspects of the past, imagining the strengths of a certain way of life while excising the deficiencies, suggests that the reality was never unblemished; but it also suggests that, on the other hand, the chosen ideal may have retained more influence than black-and-white caricaturing allows.

From today's standpoint, the ideal would appear nearer to realisation in 1940s' America—as celebrated in Norman Rockwell's homely, sentimental covers for *The Saturday Evening Post*. Yet Rockwell sugared the ideal, raising the suspicion that this was not the whole truth. It is instructive that John Ford's 1941 film of a Welsh mining family, *How Green Was My Valley* (which won six Academy Awards), richly painted the de Hooch ideal, but even then projected it backwards to a time already gone, with a deliberate nostalgic inflection to increase the sense of distance. And while Ford created a model family, the wider mining community was poisoned by a strain of vicious moralism.

In all Western societies today, the cultural, status, wealth, and power elites come predominantly from the upper middle class. That class's own ethic has been under long-term threat: an ethic of hard work and sober piety, of responsible leadership, of economic expansion and civic development tempered by justice and fairness. Philosophy, literature, and art—the forms of high culture—have largely abandoned their traditional mission, as I shall examine in Part II. The key institutions maintaining culture—the churches and the universities—have diminished faith in their own societies. No natural limit, equivalent to fixed social and economic rank, has been there to inhibit the upper middle class. Thus, once the internal restraints reinforced by culture began to slacken, there was little to check its libertine cravings. Christopher Lasch identified this cultural class war in the American case, linking the lower middle class with an 'ethic of limits'.[8]

There is a strain of snobbery in modern high culture that is different from the contempt for the masses sometimes found in Plutarch, Shakespeare, and other pre-nineteenth-century intellectuals. On this, Edmund Burke was notably other: he took it as *noblesse oblige* to defend the good sense and healthy instincts of the common English man and woman. In Nietzsche, the snobbery is still of the old type. The new is represented in a light form by Oscar Wilde; in a dark one by Theodor Adorno. The latter's disdain for American popular culture in the 1940s sat alongside his Leftist revolutionary championing of the theoretical masses.

The lower middle class has remained largely immune to the decadence threatening the more socially privileged. Its own mode, popular culture, has had little in common with such spectacles as Marcel Duchamp presenting a urinal as a serious work of art, and his being lionised for mocking the Old Masters. The popular instinct in the face of modern art has been outrage, or derision. The stock response is familiar: 'My kid can paint as well as Picasso,' a prejudice that, while being false in terms of technique, carries a moral truth that I shall discuss in the next chapter. If anything, it is generous, allowing Picasso the naive virtue of children's art, and its driving assertion that the world is an ordered place.

Picasso was the star of twentieth-century high culture, the exemplar of the highest of all its vocations — that of creative genius. He contributed to the conflation of 'high' and 'popular', the resulting difference merely intellectual snobbery and a certain technical virtuosity (which few of Picasso's heirs have shared). When 'high' was Plato, Poussin, and Henry James, it asserted a hierarchy that made sense. Even in a rare case like that of Shakespeare, who combined the two cultures, it was clear that *Much Ado About Nothing* was popular, and *Hamlet* erudite. For more than a century now, while Western high culture has been largely stagnant, popular culture has retained its vitality. And occasionally, as with *The Sopranos*, a work ostensibly from popular culture manages to incorporate high-culture characteristics.

Illustrations abound. Since the 1950s, the main agent of popular culture has been television. Its own stock-in-trade became soap-opera. The typical soap-opera portrays ordinary people, within their families and communities, thrown into crisis. It then observes their behaviour. It follows the principle that Kant noted as basic to serious conversation: the description and moral evaluation of the action of others. Kant argued that the talk of most enduring interest among humans has the goal of determining right behaviour—what, in a given everyday situation, is the good thing to do.

Soap-opera is a highly moralised reportage of ordinary life. The teenage daughter gets pregnant, for example, arousing discussions about how the individual, the family, and the community should respond—with censure or compassion, urging abortion or marriage, or that she bring up the child on her own. There is anger and fear, embarrassment and confusion, yet practical decisions have to be taken, which themselves depend on assessing the characters involved and their capabilities, as well as the circumstances. Prudent judgement is required about what might work.

Popular culture does contain its nihilistic strains. There is the battering noise of the harder pop music, deliberately drowning out the sublime. As music critic Greil Marcus put it, 1970s Punk was the attempt of people in England to 'live without belief in the future.'[9] There is the pervasiveness of flagrantly erotic music videos directed at teenagers. There is the spread of pornography, now facilitated by the Internet, ever more extreme in sado-masochistic misogyny. And there is the London tabloid press, and the threat that its radical wing may be the way of the future, trumpeting fabricated scandal about celebrities, everything being permitted if it boosts circulation.

The question is whether popular culture is typified by its seamier works. There are some instructive sociological facts. Ratings are published for television viewing—they reveal popular tastes. The lists are dominated by sport, and especially football, soap-opera, police and medical dramas, comedy, sitcom, and 'reality' and chat shows. Apart from sport, most include a strong soap-opera dimension.

In soap-opera, wrong is righted and good prevails, while difficult issues of our time are sometimes aired. The typical program is buoyant, cheerful, and optimistic, without being trite or sugary. It is conservative in the staple sense, in its defence of virtues of character and community. Above all, there is communal vitality and belonging, whether among doctors or nurses in the hospital, or police at the local station.

Some of soap-opera's appeal lies in the ways it compensates for felt absences in real life. The longing for the cosy and complete communities of the past, in which everyone was known and belonged, and someone's shoulder was always there to cry on, finds imaginative satisfaction in the idealised television groups within which there is no agoraphobic loneliness. As remarked, modern societies seem to like their communal life in very small doses, and mainly in the form of fiction that may be switched on and off at will. This does not diminish the moral effect of soap-opera, using a communal voice to remind the individual conscience of universals that it breaks at its peril.

***

Where popular culture is under threat, it is usually as a result of corruption from above—as the old adage put it, the fish starts stinking from the head. The spread of pornography has been made possible by the relaxation of censorship, forced by the liberal cultural elites; and by new technology. Those same elites are responsible for the 'progressive' education that has removed stories about national heroes from school curricula, and has reduced the teaching of basic skills such as grammar and spelling, a reduction that handicaps the lower middle class—where there is a comparatively less-educated home background to compensate for poor schooling.

Popular culture is under pressure from above. But this is not the whole story. There has been the extraordinary appeal of 'reality' shows on television, the most successful example of which, at its height, was *Big Brother*. The United States is an exception, where *Survivor*, the initiator of the genre, had the best ratings in 2000 and 2001. Most nations in the West have screened their local version of *Big Brother*, made to a standard formula, and with record audience ratings. This indicates a major social phenomenon.

*Big Brother* focused exclusively on the petty routines of everyday life. Slouching around drinking coffee became the core life-activity, put on screen, dwelt on hour after hour. It was as if it took its cue, and to the letter, from T. S. Eliot's 1925 image of how the world will end:

> Shape without form, shade without colour,
> Paralysed force, gesture without motion;[10]

Andy Warhol quipped, in 1968, that in the future everybody would be world famous for fifteen minutes. Here is one key to *Big Brother*. The participants were notable for their lack of any exceptional features — of talent, character, or deed. The program used a single dramatic device, periodically evicting one member from the house in which all the 'reality' took place. The method was a vote on unpopularity by the television audience in collaboration with those who remain in the house, the survivors.

The winner was the last one standing — that is, the one not evicted. In the first Australian series it was Ben, whose most notable trait appeared to be that no one disliked him. It was as if he was rewarded for an absence of character — of being 'nobody' with a veneer of amiability. In fact, Ben was kindly, and the audience did use some assessment of character virtues, and their absence, in deciding whom to evict.

*Big Brother* attracted a predominantly young, teenage audience, and it operated within a culture in which stardom might be seen as unattainable. When a Tiger Woods is lionised on the front pages of the newspapers, and in the evening television news, one of the latent messages is dispiriting. It is intimidating: no one can play golf anywhere nearly as well as he can. And he is unassumingly modest about his superhuman talent, while being good looking, pleasant, and mature as well. If Tiger Woods is viewed as unapproachably superior, he can hardly serve as a role model.

On *Big Brother* the subjects become Tiger Woods, or Pamela Anderson, for fifteen minutes, without having to do anything. The millions watching must identify their own ordinariness with that on camera. If the key to the *Superman* story of the twentieth century was psychotic escapism, *Big Brother* has moved one step further. In effect, the mediocre journalist struggling to win the girl of his dreams no longer needs to transform himself into a superstar. He can remain his ordinary old, bumbling, bungling self.

Then, the miracle! For an instant, there is the illusion that I am great, talented, beautiful — the right object of mass adulation. *Big Brother* provides the fame lottery. Its message is to relax, be yourself, and you will miraculously become *somebody*.

But real culture is characterised by providing timeless stories which, when they mysteriously conjoin with the life of the individual, radiate it with significance. In those blessed phases, he or she is transported outside ordinary time, entering an order grander than that of their careworn egos. By contrast, in a profane world in which there is only coffee time, petty emotions tend to take over, if only to lessen the tedium.

*Big Brother* provides titillation. It indulges the impulse to gang together to isolate individuals and then to evict them. It legitimises the sadistic nastiness of the schoolyard, when children pick on one of their number and taunt them, or bully them with mocking exclusion. To lose the big stories is to free baser human emotions to take over. There is a sniff here of the Roman Coliseum.

As a postscript, any high-culture snootiness about reality television should itself take a look in the mirror. *Big Brother* is no different in essence from the art of Marcel Duchamp (to be discussed in the next chapter), the authority presiding over twentieth-century modernism. It does lack the superior wit.

★★★

In any modern Western metropolis, newspapers usually divide along cultural lines, between the upper-middle-class papers, or broadsheets, and the lower-middle-class tabloids. In Melbourne, a city of close to four million, the broadsheet has around 25 per cent of the readership. The breakdown of Australian free-to-air television viewing is similar: three commercial stations geared to popular taste command 80 per cent of the viewers, whereas the two government stations which partly aspire to high culture are doing well if, together, they reach 20 per cent. These figures suggest that the upper middle class, defined in cultural terms, in a modern Western city makes up between 15 per cent and 25 per cent of the population.[11]

The broadsheets claim to be 'serious' or 'quality' newspapers, avoiding sensationalist headlines, including long and considered columns of opinion, often quasi-academic, and featuring arts, computer, epicure, gardening, home, and investment supplements that cater exclusively to contemporary bourgeois interests.[12]

Tabloids are more concerned with personal stories, with which ordinary people can identify: stories of direct emotional impact, of triumph and misfortune, of heroic virtue and cold-blooded wickedness. They tell them in simple, pithy terms. There is much stress on the tears that result, both of joy and of pain. There is outrage at serious crime; a fervour directed against child molesters, swindlers, and corrupt officials; and prejudice against the liberal-utilitarian view that no one is to blame, and that there should be free counselling for all. The tabloid's unconscious drive is to save the family from threat. It is keen on law and order, and on defending the security of the suburbs, doing so through particular tales of suffering. It may counterbalance tragic incidents with anecdotes about pets—how the family dog found the lost child.

Tabloid headlines are often of the 'Jimmy's Crook Knee' variety—colloquial not only in language, but also in the closed reference to the local celebrity, unknown elsewhere, as if he were a relative. This is the idiom of exclusive familiarity, of clan solidarity: a ritual of collective warmth in belonging to the established middle and lower social orders. The newspaper implicitly asserts the superiority of what is ours, and accordingly will take open pleasure in exposing the failings of rival cities and countries. There is not much reserve in flirting with shared prejudice, which is one of the strongest communal glues. This style of journalism achieved its perfect headline many years ago with the announcement of the death of French president Charles de Gaulle: 'Top Frog Croaks'.

However, as the entire print media is coming under increasing pressure from other information outlets, especially the Internet and information technology, the distinctions are blurring: broadsheets are becoming more tabloid, and vice-versa. Both are also borrowing from magazines, in format and content.

The cultural differences between the two classes carries over into taste. The newspapers are laid out according to separate design codes, the logic of which is displayed in a purer form in magazines. An upper-middle-class periodical such as *Vogue* contrasts with lower-middle-class women's publications not only in price. There is a much more generous layout, including wide margins, spacious grids, and extensive white space. Its emphasis is on form rather than subject, often on image rather than text. In its ads, the use of type size, face, and colour—its colour range is restrained—is disciplined, as are its strong, simple, and clear-cut images. It uses studio photography, and higher-quality paper, printing, and binding. In general, the lower-middle-class magazines cram things in, playing on an ethos of value for money. A similar aesthetic is exploited in supermarket design.

Another dimension of the cultural-taste war was illustrated by Tom Wolfe in his book *From Bauhaus to Our House*.[13] Wolfe observed that the 1950s American working class had been free to choose cars it liked—powerful, heavy, vast, with tail fins, and ballooning bumper bars. Yet it was forced to live in high-taste, modernist houses that it hated.

The lower middle class embodies the basic political instinct that craves hierarchy. In America, it is fiercely patriotic when the nation is at war, showing off the flag and proclaiming support for the president and the military. The lower middle class is also unselfconsciously patriotic in celebrating the success of national sporting teams. It warms to collective triumph, thus strengthening the national pulse. It distrusts the cosmopolitanism of the upper middle class, and has little confidence in supra-national bodies such as the United Nations.

In the British and Australian cases, the lower middle class used to be fiercely monarchist, before scandal amongst the Queen's children, and qualms about the way the Queen treated Princess Diana, began to erode the confidence that here was an exemplary family, one which combined the fairytale glamour of hereditary blue blood, and wealth, with the foibles and fallibilities of the average person. Here was a family that, above all, endured across the generations. In fickle times, the Royal Family could be relied upon to provide an example of how to keep going. The proud housewife could day-dream of the Queen visiting her humble spick-and-span abode.

Family is the centre, in this culture. When mothers work, there is little serious conflict over loyalties—the job is merely a means to the family's financial end. Probert's 1990s working-class mothers report that love from their children is enough reward for what they do, and her younger lower-middle-class women see themselves primarily as 'mothers'.[14] Fathers remain important, even when it is acknowledged that real domestic power lies with their wives. The forms matter. If the father is away most of the time, at work, or in male company, and therefore distanced from the emotional cocoon of the brood, he remains essential to security, as if he were the frame structuring one of de Hooch's scenes—in which the men are rarely present.

One consequence is that lower-middle-class parents are appalled by what they perceive as the increasing detachment of their upper-middle-class counterparts, and the world-weary impudence of their teenage children—'spoilt rich kids'. Just as they smell a rat with Picasso, they suspect the urbanity of parents who protest that their children are too adult to punish. If the children turn out to be shifty and spineless, those who are less privileged nod knowingly. Dostoevsky foresaw all this in *The Possessed* (1872), where he had the effete, old liberal father, a cultivated champion of 'progressive' ideas, regularly crying on his young stepson's shoulder, confessing his most intimate troubles.[15] That stepson, Stavrogin, was to become the most nihilistic hero, both debauched and deflated, in the Western novel.

Just as the lower middle class does not aim for the stars, it does not like change. It cherishes things as they are. Its instinct is to be wary of movement, of that footloose insatiability it sees all around it. It mistrusts the television news that replaces its signature tune, or the Westminster Bank when it turns into Natwest, or the airline that changes its tail design. Sound people and institutions are not embarrassed about their shape or their name. It is criminals on the run who have the urge to change their identities.

The lower middle class does have other generic weaknesses. The first Australian to celebrate the suburbs was Barry Humphries, although with satirical ambivalence. In his early *alter ego*, Edna

Everage—her name playing on 'average'—he caught the homely earthiness, the cheerful ordinariness. He also caught the stock banality, the degree to which the speech of everyday life was incantatory cliché, in contrast with the terse flair of tabloid headlines. Things are 'nice'. The greeting, 'How are you?' is rhetorical stammer. Even discussion is almost deliberately stripped of insight—any personal colouring, individuality, or character is suppressed. As a result, language lacks feeling. Conversation is more a ritualised passing of the time, like smoking a peace pipe, passing it from hand to hand. On the rare occasions that there is feeling, it may well be a petty moralism, 'Did you see how Betty Smith is letting her garden go?', or a sugary, 'Isn't she lovely in that dress?' The aesthetics are those of supermarket art.

But is this foolish? There *is* a dulling lack of vitality, but the Socratic belief that understanding is the path to virtue does not apply here, if it does anywhere, with its implied sneer that clichéd speech somehow indicates weakness of character.

The lower middle class also has its forms of rancour. The popular press reports with barely contained glee misfortune and scandal among the rich and famous. At its worst, there is a sort of parasitical, voyeuristic leering. Moreover, moral outrage against bad behaviour in the elites may be charged with spite.

★★★

Family and its home is not the sole foundation of the lower-middle-class ethic. Equally significant is the Calvinist faith in individual conscience.

The 'Dirty Harry' police films of Clint Eastwood were more self-consciously lower-middle-class than most soap-operas. By 1983, when Eastwood was voted America's most popular movie star, he had been in the top ten sixteen times, a record only significantly bettered by John Wayne, his true cultural predecessor—a reliable statistical indicator of lower-middle-class perceptions and values. In the Dirty Harry films, the elite figures—mayors, high-ranking police officers, judges, and senior bureaucrats—are corrupt, as by implication is the entire higher social order. Corruption includes identification with such causes as generous civil rights for criminals; a sexual relativism which assumes men and women are the same, and deviancy legitimate; and a stickling for bureaucratic regulation. The hero is unambiguously manly. He carries out his own ruthless justice, not trusting the softness or corruption of the courts.

In *The Enforcer* (1976), Harry is asked for whom he risks his life, given that the wealthy class that benefits will never invite him in through its doors. The question is itself utilitarian, framed in terms of self-interest, and therein lies its misunderstanding. Harry, like his own class, still believes in universals. One of them is justice, including retribution, and especially in the service of the weak.

Although Clint Eastwood did become the successor to John Wayne, as Wayne himself predicted, there is a difference. Wayne's best films, those directed by John Ford, are works of high art. Ford chose the popular genre of the Western to explore the great metaphysical question of which sacred sites are viable in modernity, if any; ones that might provide some belief to sustain the secular communities of America, the little towns with their hard-working decent families—in other words, lower-middle-class America. Ford projected a spectrum of optimism through to pessimism, most acutely in three films: *Rio Grande* (1950), *The Searchers* (1956), and *The Man who Shot Liberty Valance* (1962).[16]

John Wayne was again voted America's most popular actor in 1995, sixteen years after his death, with Clint Eastwood second, and Mel Gibson a poor third.[17] Understanding Wayne is one key to understanding the culture. That depends on identifying the elements in the character of the Western hero he exemplified that were to so capture the modern imagination, and not just in the United States. The 'West' is the West in the broad sense, the American frontier as a metaphor for the mental terrain across which issues of meaning, hope, moral orientation—indeed, the very justification of the modern world—were all being tested.

As the hero, Wayne is first and foremost the lone, just man. His traits have their roots in Greek stoicism, with elements from the Homeric warrior and his code of honour, and from the Platonic–Aristotelian singling out of universal virtues—courage, justice, and a concept of prudence that includes both judgement and practical reasoning. The one exclusion from the list of the four cardinal virtues is moderation: Wayne sometimes succeeds because of his very excessiveness; although, even at his most violent, in *The Searchers*, there is some harness on himself. The Reformation revived the tradition of the solitary hero, in the form of the Puritan saint or Christian soldier, guided by one authority, the individual's own conscience. It also switched religious emphasis from the contemplative to the active life—to *doing*.

For the twentieth-century Western hero, the Christian theological apparatus had gone, but the Puritan conscience remained, and with it the devotion to a life-long mission, or vocation after a just cause, to which the pilgrim has sworn an implicit oath. The creed is put in *The Alamo*, a film that John Wayne financed, directed, and starred in:

> There's right and there's wrong, you gotta do one or the other. You do the one and you're living, you do the other and you may be walking around but you're as dead as a beaver hat.[18]

What, then, is the secret to the thrall of the Wayne persona? The exaggerated size of the man, and the thickness of the mythic overlay, suggests an extreme need to stoke the charisma. To what end? The modern crisis of meaning is once again directing events. The cinema became, until the end of the Hollywood Golden Age, the new chapel. Whatever the level of church attendance, it was during the weekly night out in front of the silver screen that people's hopes and dreams took flight, where they were moved to tears or euphoria, despair and awe, where their souls breathed. There they reached the 'stars', in a telling comparison with the dulling ritual of the stock Sunday service. And while the 'mere entertainment' tag may have largely fitted the musical, in relation to the serious Western it was a blind misreading.

The Western hero has to be understood in relation to the fateful questions for each individual in a secular age: 'What can I believe in?', 'What sense can I make of my life?', and 'Is there a cause or a mode of engagement that will provide me with a firm place to stand, and still the anxieties of mortality?' Each of those individuals is fundamentally alone, certainly in relation to the issue of faith, with little confidence of securing support from any communities or institutions.

What John Wayne *is* may be gleaned as much from what he is not. Contemporaneous with the heyday of existentialism, and such works as *Waiting for Godot*, Camus' *The Outsider*, and the film *Rebel without a Cause*, he shares the lead players' solitariness, and their estrangement from everyday life, and its ties and customs. However, he does not find life absurd, or nauseous, nor does he spend his days in gloomy introspection, wondering each morning whether he can be bothered getting up. Lack of belief is not his problem. He has a cause and, unlike Hamlet, he can act.

The psychic impact of the screen image relies for its indelibility on his colossal being. It is as if one of the giant, phallic rock formations in Monument Valley, where *The Searchers* was shot, had come to life, and nonchalantly glided down, swaggering into focus. The force of the films, their compelling energy, is centred on him—with other characters, the story, and the direction all serving as little more than a backdrop. He stands for what a human individual can be, a formidable concentration of being, animated by a near-demonic life-force, and out of his very wildness able to conjure up some sort of sacred aura. This is a life with such character and direction that, while stripped of the normal human supports—family, friends, social position, pastimes—it remains indomitable in the face of some of the worst misfortune that may strike.

The message is that it is possible to *be,* even when born into the lawless fluidity of attachment to person, place, and belief typical of the modern world. Wayne is the precise antithesis to the most potent insult coined by contemporary slang, 'You are a waste of space.' The rawest nerve of insecurity in our times is the fear of being nothing, insignificant, a nobody, a non-being, leading a life without sense. Here is the last thing of which John Wayne could be accused.

As a prophet, he stakes his new religion on the individuals' active presence. His is not the humanist ego, served by free-will and reason. Civilisation is not his guiding authority, nor his ideal—he does not aspire to be a creative genius, a builder of cities, a champion of progress, or a great man. He acts, rather, as a broker between civilisation and the wilderness, on the frontier, guided by conscience, obeying universal law. In fact, he knows that civilisation and its cities will destroy what he represents. While he defends community, he himself does not belong within it.

In John Wayne, masculine traits are exaggerated—physical size, strength, and toughness, rugged features and manners, iron will, a devotion to life-quest or work above anything else, and especially women. The *Rio Grande* wife, Kathleen, toasts, 'To my only rival, the United States Cavalry.' In addition, the mythic Wayne is middle-aged or old, the man over forty in 1948, the year of *Red River,* directed by Howard Hawks, the first great film of his maturity. His persona has shed everything boyish and, with it, eagerness, impetuosity, any raw or unsure traits, and much curiosity about or open-mindedness towards what he meets. He is little moved to romance — in most cases, that side of his life having ended, and tragically, years earlier.

The Western is mainly a man's world, often a boys' own community. Relations between men are easy and relaxed; even when violent, a mutual understanding underscores them. Relations with women are rare, and tend to be awkward, usually with the woman forced to make the moves. The Western hero finds a single adult woman who has him in her sights to be far more frightening than rampaging Indians.

The Wayne persona is thus, in part, a fantasy antidote to 'momism', to fears of dominating mothers, punishing wives, or free women and their imagined powers. It appeals to uncertain male identity, which partly explains its return to popularity in the 1990s, with its uncompromising assertion, in the face of the sexual politics of the times, that man is man; woman, woman.

Ultimately, however, the charisma of John Wayne has its source in what holds him to his quest, irrespective of the consequences. His vocation is as *the searcher* — after truth — with faith that it exists, and that he has found his right path. This is the faith that can move mountains, the faith that is everything. His remorselessness, his single and concentrated intent, his 'true grit', demonstrates that there is a powerful demon which drives him, and that there is a higher end, or truth, guiding his — and, by implication, every other — individual life. It is his colossal certainty, and the entire mode of expression incarnate in his formidable *being* and its destiny, that speaks directly to the principal anxiety of the modern world, and to its principal contour of hope.

In relation to the lower middle class, the Wayne character complements and balances the ethos of home. It does so by including the public world, beyond the intimate and privately domestic. It enshrines Thesis Four — the driving cultural blueprint of individual conscience, vocation, and *anima mundi*. And it proclaims Thesis One—a faith in universal laws, and an order governing the human condition.

The threat to the lower middle class is that of the times, the pressure of historical necessity. The Christian creed and practice—whether Protestant or Catholic—that formed its character, has ebbed away. Not much is left, apart from popular culture, to fortify belief, or to steady families under strain. When Nicolas Poussin painted the essentials of a successful community in his *Sacrament of Confirmation* (first version, from 1638), he knew that faith was the key. Once a community is not, at its heart, a sacred community, it cannot last. Families gather together in the church to induct boys and girls into their calling—a faith that commits them to a life working and living for the common weal, defending honour and maintaining piety. The children are being subjected to a higher law, which they shall obey.

Further, in relation to historical necessity, the availability of steady work will play a central role in the continuing wellbeing of the lower middle class. Its way of life depends on owning the family home. Just as young men report a change in attitude to life once they marry, a new sense of responsibility as the 'provider', or one of two providers, the ethical mantle they have put on is dependent for its stitching on some confidence in long-term stability.

Today, the instinct for honour and piety survives. The lower middle class still blushes. A sense for what is right and good endures. But the rites are gone, and the traditional churches are vacant. The turn to the mythic John Wayne figure has arisen out of a need for a charismatic model of conviction and fortitude. But popular culture may not provide strong-enough succour when the slings and arrows of misfortune strike, or when the routines of the everyday become hopelessly dulling.

De Hooch's 'we must first descend if we wish to be raised' is but a whisper. As a result, his domestic interiors are under threat of blurring over into profanity, with the cleaning turning into a demeaning chore. It is becoming more difficult to dwell cosily at home. The liberal dimension to the culture is pervasive, stressing freedom and infinite possibility, clothed in the consumer ethic, and glamorising how good you look, rather than how well you act. It engenders restlessness with what is, driving the children out in the notorious modern flight to nowhere.

There has been no female equivalent to John Wayne. In past times, there was the charismatic Catholic aura surrounding the Virgin Mary, and the French had Joan of Arc. This chapter, readers will recall, opened with the maternal ideal projected by Pieter de Hooch, an ideal still present in 1941 in Ford's *How Green Was My Valley*, and last represented unselfconsciously in American 1950s soap-opera. John Ford's own female counterpart to Wayne, Dr Cartwright (played by Anne Bancroft), dominates a film that sunk, on release, into an obscurity from which it has never emerged.

The death of Princess Diana in 1997 was accompanied by such powerfully mythic symbolism, and world attention, that she seemed destined to endure as one ideal of womanhood, a likely candidate for secular canonisation as the modern, flawed saint. But her legend expired within a couple of years. At the same time, on the male side, the Wayne type continued to reappear, adapted in such major films as *Rocky* (1976, with Sylvester Stallone), *Braveheart* (1995, with Mel Gibson), and *Gladiator* (2000, with Russell Crowe). The one female persona since World War II to claim some enduring mythic presence is far from exemplary: Marilyn Monroe.

The absence of imposing female models for identification may be less of a problem than it seems. Popular culture—and I am thinking primarily of film and television—does continue to tell stories in which characters represent universal strengths and qualities. There is no shortage of heroines who embody the virtues of compassionate warmth, fidelity, courage in sticking to what they believe in, self-honesty, a serious and intense engagement with their own lives, resilience and balance in response to suffering, and cheerfulness in spite of all.

We are witnessing a fateful cultural war, both internally, within the lower middle class, and externally, against demoralising influences from above. The best litmus test of the lower-middle-class condition — popular culture — indicates that the forces of resistance are holding their own, and even that there are some signs of reinvigoration.

Part Two

# NIHILISM AND CONSUMERISM

Chapter Five

# SELF-HATRED IN HIGH CULTURE

I have looked at four central areas of modern life in which the search for meaning has been proceeding with some success. The discussion has made it clear that there are powerful forces acting in the counter direction, pressing towards disintegration. In essence, there are two such forces. They attack with the nihilistic view that human life is without any basic sense; and the consumerist response that, therefore, all that is left is the pursuit of pleasure and comfort. Modern civilisation is uniquely capable of satisfying the need for comfort. Part II focuses firstly on the nihilist influence, and the main paths it has cut; and secondly on consumerism, and two of its leading manifestations—shopping and tourism.

The first part of the story concerns failure of belief—located in the upper middle class. It centres on a crisis in high culture. While the decline of practised Christianity has played an important role, it is rather individual faith, in the full Calvinist sense, which is at issue. I shall examine, in the next two chapters, what happens when individuals lose a fundamental, anchoring belief in themselves and their destiny; lose the feeling that there is some sort of determining order within which they move.

True faith, or knowing, is a sort of poise of being, an ease of self in the world. With it, a person is less likely to complain, hit out, and lament; more likely to face hardship with some higher detachment, with philosophical acceptance that things happen as they do, and to respond to what life has in store with cheerfulness and gratitude. A balance of ego and soul prevails, inducing the unconscious surety that has been celebrated in many different cultures and times, and has little to do with ritual practice or church membership.

Nietzsche's famous Death of God parable asserted that with the loss of faith in a transcendental power, humans would also lose their bearings in the world. In particular, there would be no fixed point by which to determine what was good and what evil. Relativism in morality means no morality. The same theme was to preoccupy Dostoevsky. His telling formulation was that without God, everything will be permitted.[1] Everything permitted means no checks, a world in which the most brutal acts are condoned. In such a world, there is no means of distinguishing a murder from a kiss.

Although Kierkegaard wrote before Nietzsche and Dostoevsky, his work only became known outside Denmark later. His main theme is that life is governed by an ascending hierarchy of levels: the aesthetic, which is the domain of egoism and pleasure, the ethical, and the religious. Kierkegaard attacks modernity for moving in reverse. Having lost the religious domain, it is losing the ethical, and it largely finds itself reduced to the passionless and frivolous pursuit of comfort.

In other words, the three most profound nineteenth-century critics of modern Western society all held that the decline of religion would automatically bring about a collapse of morality and meaning. By the end of their work, two of modern sociology's three founding fathers—Durkheim and Weber—had come to the same conclusion. The third, Marx, thought the opposite.

Much is at stake here. How Western development since the

industrial revolution is read depends on the answer one gives to the religion–morality–meaning question. More explicitly, the entire humanist tradition, with its roots in the Renaissance, and its main branch through the Enlightenment, stands or falls on this issue. Humanism, founded on the axiom that 'man is the measure of all things', assumes that morality is possible without religion. It assumes that a humane, civilised life may be conducted in a metaphysical environment in which the individual ego is the highest end, the goal of existence. Indeed, its main branch points to religion as superstition, a barrier to the achievement of human happiness and virtue.[2]

With some notable exceptions, Western thought since 1920 has neglected this theme (the exceptions include Kafka, Simone Weil, Heidegger, Hannah Arendt, and Philip Rieff).[3] This is nowhere more obvious than within the sociological tradition itself. While Durkheim and Weber have exerted a commanding influence over the discipline, the fundamental question at the root of their work has been repressed.

Durkheim's abiding interest was the pathological consequences in Western society of the decline of community. His most influential concept, 'anomie', describes a state of social breakdown due to a weakening of the force that ties people to each other—their collective conscience, or group mind. In modernity, the enfeeblement of the collective conscience has developed hand-in-hand with rampant individualism. Durkheim's anti-humanist reading is that individualism is a disease. More specifically, individuals who are not integrated into their community, who are not regulated by its superior law, fall victim to an egoistic sense of life being absurd and futile, and an anomic sense of their own natures being chaotic and unruly.

What is the essence of the collective conscience? Durkheim answered: a belief in *sacred* things. Further, it is religion that gives form and practical force to the sacred. There were moments in Durkheim's work when he toyed with the possibility of typically modern forms of association, such as occupational groups, developing their own binding collective ethos.[4] However, such moments were fleeting, and Durkheim reverted to his assumption that religion is the necessary prerequisite for any community's collective conscience. In *The Division of Labour in Society*, he had argued that the collective conscience in traditional societies is based on religion, and it is intense and absolute. In modern societies, without religion, it is weak.[5]

It was in the next major theoretical work, *Suicide,* that he turned the notion of the weakening collective conscience into the central problem of modernity. Soon after completing this work, he said, 'I achieved a clear view of the essential role played by religion in social life.'[6] He went on to devote his last book, *The Elementary Forms of Religious Life,* to searching for religion's staple ingredient — to what is common to all religions, across culture. His discovery was 'sacred force', a universal vitality experienced by all humans in all societies. It is the fuel of religion; therefore it is the fuel of the collective conscience. The implication is that to demolish its cultural representation, the particular religion of a society, is to cut the collective conscience off from its source of energy.[7]

Max Weber, in his major work, *The Protestant Ethic and the Spirit of Capitalism,* defends capitalism against Marx's claim that it was founded on — and driven by — naked self-interest, by greed and exploitation. Weber's counter is that the lust for riches is as old as written history. The secret of capitalism's success is, in fact, the opposite: that it placed ethical checks on the hitherto unscrupulous methods of the merchant and the entrepreneur. The typical capitalist is honest and rational. Weber's lament in the last chapter of *The Protestant Ethic* is that, with the decline of Protestantism in the nineteenth century, the religious goal which directed the work ethic—salvation—had been removed.[8] The modern businessman was left working for the sake of his business, which is in itself an absurdity.

Moreover, the techniques of rationality, which had progressively made business less risky and more efficient, had taken over, and become ends in themselves. The symbol of this is the modern bureaucracy, which is in danger of turning into an 'iron cage', an agent for 'mechanised petrifaction'. In Weber's decisive equation, rationalisation means the *disenchantment* of the world, the creation of a profane world with neither spirit nor sensuality. This is, in effect, a Death-of-God theory. The futility and banality of modern life, in Weber's account, follows from the loss of the tie to the religious goal of salvation. That happened with the decline of Western religion's last vital representative, Protestantism.

***

The surveys already made of the principal cultural battlegrounds make it clear that there has been determined and successful resistance to the pressures of nihilism, and even the winning of new territory. Where the Death-of-God forces have made devastating inroads has been in the upper middle class, and into its own spiritual preserve—high culture.

In the middle of the nineteenth century, Western high culture took an about-turn away from its traditional role of transmitting universal truths. Modern art, literature, philosophy, and music have, in the main, portrayed life as meaningless and absurd; morality as conditional and relative; and truth as an illusion. Through the eyes of the most gifted and perceptive of modern interpreters, life appears as bleak and miserable, a sort of living death. This is the turn to the belief in nothing, to anti-belief—to nihilism.

In painting, Manet's *Olympia* of 1865 was something of a

watershed. It took one of the conventional subjects of Western art, the female nude, and turned it into a frigid and profane object, emptied of all spiritual and moral content. Manet was in explicit rebellion against the masters of the tradition—in particular, Titian—who always set these potentially transgressive subjects within limits, hence preserving the sacred status of the human, and especially the female, body.[9]

One of the greatest exponents of psychological realism in modern art was Edvard Munch. His work is a version of the idea that everything is permitted. In his vision, love means chronically depressed men, and hysterical, icy, and sometimes vampirish women. Passion always metamorphoses into ashes; attraction, into despair. In *The Morning After*, a woman sprawled across a bed is beyond caring for anything. Munch's *Madonna* is without child, herself a martyr to self-obsessed neurosis, not even able to mother herself.

The most brilliant and influential theorist in modern art has been Marcel Duchamp. At the centre of his enterprise was a mocking of the classical tradition—sneering at its technical accomplishments, but even more at its metaphysical core. In entering a urinal as a work of art in a New York exhibition in 1917, he set the most profane act as equal to portraits of courage, pity, and tragedy. The Old Masters had wrestled with the central truths about the human condition and, at their best, had created works which are spaces, like the Gothic cathedrals of Bourges and Amiens, within which even a modern sceptical pilgrim is touched by a sacred breath—sensing that here is an eternal sanctuary where the gods dwell.

Duchamp laughed in disbelief. He questioned by what standards anyone could claim in a materialist world that their great art is any more truthful, beautiful, or good than his piece of porcelain plumbing—which is at least useful. There are no such standards left. That riposte has carried the high-culture day, the art galleries of the West ever since filled with Duchamp derivatives.

In effect, Duchamp states that, for him, the old gods have failed. The traditional European order is riddled with hypocrisy and superstition—with its Christian dogma, its bourgeois rectitude, its sentimental compassion, and its fantasies about truth and goodness. *Let us at least be honest*, challenges Duchamp. *I will show you the truth—here in my urinal. Life is excrement, and at least with me you get witty puns and jokes about the futility of it all.*

But Duchamp was not so honest. He had to go further than cynical detachment. Once there is no faith, the demon of rancour rises. Duchamp was driven by one last belief. Just as Judas was inwardly driven to destroy Jesus, out of envy, and Iago to destroy Othello, so modernist rancour mocks anything that is beautiful, true, or good. It mocks anyone who still believes in such things. Duchamp painted a moustache on the *Mona Lisa,* to make her look ridiculous.

Duchamp's main accomplice in the artistic demolition of Western high culture was Picasso—the man whom twentieth-century high culture celebrated as its quintessential genius and prophet. Behind the playful virtuosity, and the extraordinary talent, lies a complete nihilism. Picasso himself admitted as much, both in his final portrait of himself in the form of a horror-stricken clown skull, and in an interview given late in life:

> When I am alone with myself I haven't got the courage to think of myself as an artist in the grand and ancient sense of the word. Giotto and Titian, Rembrandt and Goya were true painters. I am only a public entertainer who has understood his times and has exploited better than he knew the idiocy, the vanity, and the greed of his contemporaries.[10]

Like Duchamp, Picasso was at least sometimes honest.

In literature, a similar pattern may be observed. Joseph Conrad's *Heart of Darkness* (1899) gave flesh and blood to Nietzsche's insight into modern consciousness: behind the veils of cultural illusion, life is either absurd or horrible. F. Scott Fitzgerald projected the same theme into 1920s America, in *The Great Gatsby* (1925). Kafka portrayed his individuals as tormented by an inexplicable and crushing guilt, evoking a fantasy underworld of bugs, moles, torture camps, and totalitarian bureaucracies. André Gide produced his immoralist hero, and the celebration of gratuitous murder. Dada turned the absurd into the central and single life-principle. The 'theatre of cruelty' followed.

Beckett's *Waiting for Godot* is about the possibility, or impossibility, of life in an amoral world, where everything is permitted. Joyce's *Ulysses* and Musil's *The Man Without Qualities* are works empty of binding belief, as is Camus' *The Outsider*, in which the hero, who is a half-hearted depressive, suffers from a sort of psychotic breakdown during which he murders a quite innocent stranger. The influential early poetry of T. S. Eliot, including his *Wasteland*, echoes the same hollowness.[11]

In philosophy, too, the central thread has been nihilism, with Nietzsche the commanding presence. The Nietzschean view, anticipated by Kierkegaard, and uncontested by the subsequent philosophical mainstream, is that the modern individual is left to pursue comfort, and nothing else. Nietzsche went on to argue in favour of an overthrowing of all morality, in a sort of nihilistic orgy, with the absurd hope that some strength of character might appear on the other side. Conrad had not been so deluded—his Kurtz, who kicks the world to pieces, in taking to a bacchanalia of violent conquest, whispers his dying judgement of what it is all about, the ultimate truth that he has seen: 'The horror, the horror!'[12] The eyes of Picasso's final *Self-Portrait* speak the same message.

The most popular of twentieth-century philosophers, Sartre,

centred his existentialist work on the concept of 'nothingness', borrowed from Heidegger. Sartre's other abiding images were of life as 'nausea' and human action as 'bad faith'.[13] Anglo philosophy in the last century, from Russell through logical positivism, to Wittgenstein, and his Oxford acolytes, in its refusal to discuss ethics, and its retreat into a narrow and pedantic technicality, in effect accepted the nihilistic credo. As Nietzsche put it, logic is like a snake that can merely turn around and bite its own tail.

Then there has been 'post-modernism' and 'deconstruction', further tired and ponderous revamps of Duchamp, explicit in their hatred of 'great works'. The deconstructive paradigm is that a Mickey Mouse comic has as much value as Shakespeare.

The most original and influential theory developed in the twentieth century was the psychology of Sigmund Freud. Behind its sophisticated and powerful interpretations, it too is intellectually nihilistic. Freud's view was that religion is an illusion; in fact, a projection of the father problem. Morality—notions of good and evil—is another projection, an emanation from psychological crisis. Even the incest taboo, posited as universal by Freud, is a utilitarian response to instincts that, without check, would produce a parricidal and fratricidal bloodbath from which no human community could survive. In other words, the small area of morality that is universal is not so because of some absolute law, but because of functional necessity.

Furthermore, in the practice of psychoanalytical therapy, guilt is read as a psychological and not a moral problem. It is to be eradicated by therapy. In short, the force within the individual that enforces morality is interpreted as psychological, deriving from the parental environment. The ethical domain is merely a helpful mask, to be delicately stripped away by the analyst once it becomes troublesome.

Psychoanalysis has contributed to another modern plunge into disenchanted relativism. That is the tendency to redefine acts that are criminal, sinful, or evil in medical terms — in the language of disease. Then the appropriate social response is not punishment, but therapy. Dostoevsky foresaw this: a central theme of *The Brothers Karamazov* is the main character's refusal to be let off a murder charge because of psychological or biological arguments that hold him not to be responsible.

The last century has seen the growing tendency to excuse the criminal because his parents treated him badly in early childhood, or because he came from a poor, underprivileged social background, or because he suffered from a chemically induced psychotic episode. This is the therapeutic model of society — picked up in the Clint Eastwood films as symptomatic of elite decadence.[14] According to its logic, everything *is* permitted, as long as it serves to relieve anxiety. The cultural elites in the West have come to think more and more in therapeutic terms. They have come to find it difficult to call evil acts evil, preferring such descriptions as disturbed, maladjusted, or simply distressed. At this level, they have succeeded far more than Nietzsche would have ever imagined in going 'beyond good and evil'.

The nihilistic world view, which has pervaded high culture, has developed hand-in-hand with the hegemony of science. As much as capitalism, or industrialisation, has been the principal dynamic cause of the rise of a society that is overwhelmingly secular, its own dependence on technological innovation has bestowed unmatched prestige on science. In the principal axiom of *The Communist Manifesto*, Marx asserted that the great revolutionary force in modernity is capitalism itself. This economic system, in its forward march, bulldozes all traditions flat.

The scientific way of thinking has had pervasive cultural consequences. In particular, the Darwinian view has convinced much of the university-educated elite that for the three age-old metaphysical questions, there are complete, materialistic answers:

*Q*: 'Where do we come from?'

*A*: 'A long history of chance, evolutionary mutations, from primitive cells, via the squid, the owl and the pussycat, and on through the great ape.'

*Q*: 'What should we do with our lives?'

*A*: 'Survive, reproduce, seek pleasure, avoid pain.'

*Q*: 'What happens at death?'

*A*: 'Nothing—mere rotting matter, putrefaction, and stench.' (Nobel Laureate Francis Crick put it that the soul is a mere assembly of nerve cells.)

Here is modern nihilism's most authoritative and dispiriting guise. Moreover, its logic, once entered into, is virtually impossible to escape. Anybody who starts to reason scientifically, as is right and necessary in the modern world—such reasoning having proved itself by making us prosperous and comfortable—will find that their moral thinking falters.

Consider the issue of *in vitro* fertilisation. Science can help infertile couples to have children. Surely, it is unambiguously good to fulfil their deepest wish, and it is a fundamental human wish. To do so, experiments must be conducted. As part of this, eggs fertilised in test tubes, which have begun the life process—alive and containing within themselves the complete genetic material to form the full human individual—are frozen, injected, dissected, and killed, just as if they were segments of plant matter. Why not, if the means lead to the higher good?

An issue of the *Australian Journal of Biological Sciences* published, without editorial comment, a report titled, 'Polyethylene glycol-induced Attachment of Human Spermatozoa to Rat Ova *in vitro*'.[15] The experiments were conducted in a hospital in Adelaide—as pretty, civil, and genteel a town as can be found in the Western world. Apart from one or two concerned Catholic commentators picking up the fact that medical science was now cross-breeding humans with rats, the Australian media reacted with a comprehensive lack of interest. It was a nightmare fantasy of the Middle Ages that, in hell, humans are cross-bred with monsters. The paintings of Hieronymous Bosch gave graphic illustration to this fear. The devil did the cross-breeding.

Today, we are not so sure. Once we start to use reason, thinking scientifically, any conviction that this is wrong weakens to the point that almost inevitably we will conclude, with a shrug of the shoulders, 'Why not?' Here is the fruition of what Luther, Nietzsche, and Weber all pointed to as the disenchantment of reason.

★★★

The Death of God has opened the way for radical liberalism. Here is the philosophy that has given legitimacy to upper-middle-class nihilism. Its single guiding belief is in the free individual, with subordinate idealisations of free-will and reason. The assumption is that the best society, the one with the happiest members, will be the one in which the individual is left alone to pursue his or her interests. The liberal inclination is to remove all checks on the individual, to minimise government and the judiciary, and to remove public moral limits such as those that preside over scientific research and censorship. Always, I should be free to choose.

Liberalism's psychological assumption about humans—leave them alone and they will flourish—is naive. It is blind to inclinations to greed, violence, and evil, inclinations that are an inherent part of human egoism. It assumes a capacity for self-restraint that our entire history contradicts. In practice, the upper middle class, without the constraint of culture, has been left with one value—freedom—which has become intoxicating. Liberalism has proven the perfect rationalisation for selfishness.

The great political philosophers have noted, in their different ways, that any institution has to balance liberty and authority if it is to work reasonably well. The balance will vary depending on the institution. Courts, for instance, need more authority than schools, and they in turn need more authority than sporting clubs. Herein lies the clue to where liberalism is socially beneficial: as a leavening influence, freeing up institutions in which there is too much authority. Our civilisation has benefited prodigiously from the liberal impulse, but always in cases in which it has operated in a circumscribed manner, within a securely ordered institutional environment.

Let us consider some examples. The economic boom experienced in Elizabethan England was made possible by the weakening influence of the two huge, monolithic institutions that had dominated the Middle Ages: the nobility — including the monarchy — and the church. Here was a liberalisation that opened up an over-constrained market.[16]

The great period of the English Public School, and its derivatives in other Anglo countries, was roughly between 1920 and 1960. Before this period, the stern patriarchal regimen was too severe, and the enthusiasm for learning inhibited by over-Spartan rituals. A greater liberty, giving more freedom to pupils, and more recognition to their individuality, achieved a better balance.[17] However, the problem with liberalism is that its adherents never know when to stop. Once unleashed, liberalism keeps going until no authority is left; it has no internal principle of restraint. The threat, since 1960, has been of excessive liberalisation rendering schools ineffective in their struggle to keep discipline.

In many ways, the Victorian family and its mores were too strict. To draw upon Freudian terminology, there *was* too much repression. The inhibition of human instincts placed excessive strain on the individual. But again, whereas an initial liberalisation was benign, the process soon got out of hand. The last century has witnessed the irrepressible tide of liberalism surging through marriage bonds and parental authority, and washing away many vital moral restraints on public behaviour.

An idea of the moral condition of a human community can be gauged from its standards of public decency. What is permissible in public? The trend in the modern West has been towards allowing everything in the city streets. Since the *Lady Chatterley's Lover* censorship trial in England in the 1950s, checks over pornography in literature, film, video, satellite television, and now the Internet have rapidly disappeared. In the name of liberalism, pornography has become more widely available and more depraved in content—notably, in a brutalisation of women and children. In Australia in the early twenty-first century, three-quarters of 16-year-old boys admit to having watched an X-rated film, and the same proportion have been exposed accidentally to pornographic websites; 40 per cent of them deliberately seek out those sites.[18]

One dimension is the toleration of filmed perversion. In 1989, an English art film, *The Cook, The Thief, His Wife and Her Lover,* left Western censors quite unperturbed, in spite of it including pictures of a naked man being coated in excrement and urine, the torture of a child, including the cutting out of its navel, the choking to death of a man with pages of a book, and a lengthy and explicit depiction of cannibalism.

Liberalism's fatal flaw is that it obeys nothing; it has no gods. To posit the free individual as a sole locus of meaning in the human condition is akin to a psychotic delusion. The idealisation of Napoleon as the great individual, as the personification of a confident and unimpeded will-to-power conquering the world, was a piece of Romantic liberal megalomania: it conveniently forgot the millions of innocent people who died for nothing during his campaigns. Radical liberalism is continually in danger of letting loose some terrible demons.

The key to understanding the great conservative theorist Edmund Burke lies here. Burke was the first to intuit the enormous destructive potential of modern liberalism. Its major threat in his time was political, in the form of the French Revolution. Burke saw that 'liberty' and 'equality' would not bring to realisation the third ideal, 'fraternity'; rather, it would usher in the Terror and Napoleon. Moreover, he saw that it was not a narrow socialist creed that was doing the damage, but the driving philosophy of modernity: liberalism. It was the ascendancy of liberal principles—freedom, reason, and the omnipotence of the individual—that Burke attacked. He realised that socialism is merely a subspecies of liberalism.[19]

If radical liberalism in politics is the French Revolution, what is it in economics? What would a pure free-market look like? The Wild West frontier of America is the reality, as is gold-mining in the contemporary jungles of Papua New Guinea: no government, no law, no sheriffs—no restraint. In this world without rules, there is one inevitable rule, that of the gun. The general point is that any society is a tight web of discriminations, interventions, and controls, and necessarily so. Any radical freeing move is fraught with the danger of unforeseen consequences.

Since the 1970s, the Anglo economies have prospered, due to a systematic application of free-market principles, leading to a reduction in the bureaucratic control of markets, the elimination of tariff barriers to imports, the deregulation of labour markets, and a general opening-up of nations to international competition. European economies—notably French and German—that have resisted this trend have declined. But this Anglo success has only been possible because it has taken place within a strong and stable framework of governmental, legal, and financial institutions, largely free of corruption. The best free-market theorists acknowledge this.[20] Again, it is an issue of balance.

The nihilism of high culture, and the spread of radical liberalism, has served to erode the upper-middle-class's traditional sense of social obligation. In return for its privileged position—its wealth, status, and power—it used to believe that it had a duty to act in the wider public interest. There is a code of *noblesse oblige* under which elites should govern. They are required to obey the injunction, 'Be just!'

Weber singled out the business domain as the locus of the capitalist revolution in morals. Capitalism depends on rationality and trust. However, the ethos of trust is regularly under threat. The 1980s saw an outbreak of crooked dealing on a large scale in the big-business sector of Western societies. The leading practices were creative accounting and insider trading. The spread of fraudulent accountancy, rationalised with some unintended wit as 'creative', meant that any company could shop around for an accountancy firm that was willing to cook its books. Reports from the highest sources indicated that such a company would not have to look very far.

There are two quite different sides to the weakening of social conscience implied here. First, there is the return of robber-baron capitalism, where everything is permitted in the pursuit of profit. Second, one of the professions—accountancy—was shown to have many practitioners holding none of the scruples that form the inviolable conditions of entry into membership of the guild. Accountants are well rewarded in money and prestige for their position of responsibility, and they abused the public's confidence.

Numerous members of that older profession, the law, which at least in modern times might have been expected to have deeper traditions binding it, were involved in the same practices. Here was reflected a general deterioration in the ethical standards of the legal profession. For many, the choice of a career in law, via elite schools and universities, has been driven by the pursuit of wealth. It has produced a cadre of senior barristers who brag unashamedly, among themselves, of the fees they charge and the shady clients they represent. Legal practices have sprung up which meretriciously tout for business, encouraging citizens to sue others, however trivial the offence. In 2007, an American judge sued a family dry-cleaning business for $65 million for losing a pair of his trousers.

The legal profession's diminishing sense of social responsibility has had a range of bad effects. For example, pregnant women have had to pay sharply higher prices for gynaecological and obstetric consultations because their doctors are forced to pay radically accelerating medical insurance charges, due to the threat of litigation for malpractice. Many organisations, such as local councils and small-business operators, face sky-rocketing insurance premiums that can often send them out of business—for example, many US ice-skating rinks have had to close because novice skaters are encouraged to sue for damages if they fall over and sprain their wrists.

However, the most blatant sign, in the Anglo countries, of upper-middle-class greed has been the astronomical salaries that corporate chief executives have paid themselves, with ever-increasing increments, since the 1980s. In 2006, the average chief executive officer in the top-500 listed American companies was earning $15 million a year. That year, two CEOs, leaving companies that had underperformed under their leadership, received exit packages of $200 million each. Between 1980 and 2005 in the United States, the ratio of what the average CEO earned to what the average worker earned rose ten-fold—from a multiple of 40, to one of 400. Chief executives now earn four hundred times what their employees, on average, take home.

There was no more flagrant example in the public mind of the corruption of the elites, which had been caricatured in the Clint Eastwood films. It was as if the upper stratum of the corporate world was sticking its tongue out at the rest of society. The excuses were framed in liberal terms: the free market determined salary levels, obeying the laws of open competition, which have nothing to do with morality. Even the most sober and worldly of publications, *The Economist,* used this language to rationalise executive greed. In the post-war Golden Age, there had been a strong civic ethos among senior businessmen, which both restrained their own remuneration and led many to devote their spare time to honorary public duties.[21]

A general case against upper-middle-class selfishness needs qualifying. In America today, college graduates are twice as likely as others to do volunteer work and to donate blood.[22] It may be that there is a difference between the wealthiest in the upper middle class and the rest.

In the final quarter of the twentieth century, there grew a mistrust of political elites. Perhaps it was due to particular examples, like president Nixon's Watergate, or president Clinton's sex scandals, or the behaviour of the British Queen's children—all of them seeming to have little capacity for accepting the constraints of *noblesse oblige* that went with their privilege. Perhaps it was television series like the BBC's *Yes Minister,* showing top civil servants and ministers alike, driven entirely by selfish motives, creating a climate in which everyday politics was reported, at times, with a like cynicism. Perhaps it was a sense that the ship of state is no longer run in the interests of most, as had seemed the case in the Golden Age of the 1950s and 1960s. The result, whatever the combination of influences, was a popular perception of leaders who are out for themselves, free from conscience in relation to financial double-dealing, sexual promiscuity, and bare-faced lying.

While some, perhaps much, of this perception is unfair, the case remains that an era appears to have gone in which Australia's longest-serving prime minister, Sir Robert Menzies, could leave office in 1966 with so little accumulated wealth that a group of Melbourne businessmen had to pass around a hat to buy him a house for his retirement. His example may well be exceptional to any time. It still symbolises a world that has been largely lost.

***

Rampant liberalism is the cultural vanguard of upper-middle-class nihilism. It has two effects on the character of individuals. One is self-absorption, the philosophy of *me, me, me*. I examine more of its effects in the chapters on shopping and tourism.

The other consequence of the ebbing of belief, and the rise of the radical liberal view, is *rancour*. Nietzsche saw rancour as the prototypical modern disease. It manifests itself in resentment against another person, another group or party, or another body of ideas. Nietzsche saw its psychological roots in an individual's need to blame someone else for how bad he or she felt. Nietzsche also linked it with *moralism*, the disposition to indignation and moral righteousness, and to explosive dogmatism. He read moralism as the revenge of the spiritually limited. No one lies as much as the indignant do.[23]

The turn of high culture to nihilism has had its own rancorous edge. There is a rage against what came before and, especially, against the creative foundations of Western culture. Duchamp hates Raphael and all he represents — above all, his belief that there are deep and binding truths that it is his duty as an artist to try to represent. Duchamp hates Raphael's belief in beauty. Duchamp's rancour strives to destroy the authority of the Old Masters, through mockery. Here is the paradigm of self-hatred in Western high culture.

The same rancorous impulse feeds a more generalised upper-middle-class resentment against its own culture and civilisation. This exploded in the 1960s student revolution, which read all Western figures of authority as corrupt and evil — whether they were presidents and prime ministers, business executives, bishops, chancellors and vice-chancellors, or even fathers. The totalitarian mass-murderer Mao Tse-tung was celebrated as a hero simply because he was an anti-Western leader. *My enemy's enemy is my friend.*

In the case of cultural nihilism, self-hatred is displaced outwards. It is projected onto extensions of the self. Whereas the lower middle class is patriotic, and proudly so, the rancorous upper middle class is hostile to its own nation—to its history, to its foreign policy, to its treatment of immigrants. Another 1960s effect has been the reading of the national story in negative terms. What used to be a narrative of achievement, heroism, progress, and character—often one-sidedly utopian—became inverted into a tale of barbarous conquest, exploitation, racism, patriarchal oppression, rampant greed, and corruption. In the Australian case, this was dubbed the 'black-armband' view of history.[24] The past was turned into a subject of shame.

This moved into schools, with a radical revamping of curricula. Where the teaching of history has not been removed altogether, its content has shifted into the black-armband mode, stressing past injustices meted out, and spotlighting the most disadvantaged groups—for example, native peoples—as martyrs, and glorifying their original ways as radiated by primal virtue.

Politicised curricula have combined with the radical liberal view, again inherited from the 1960s counter-culture, that schooling should be democratically non-repressive. The task of the teacher then becomes to act as an equal, one who facilitates the innate creativity of the child, helping a process of self-realisation. This corrodes a sense that there are standards of achievement, universal moral laws, and important truths. There has been the further cost, especially to the lower middle class, in producing inadequate levels of numeracy and literacy, because of the consequent failure of the education system to teach the basics of arithmetic, reading, grammar, and spelling.

The same culture has excused Islamic terrorism since September 11, 2001, on the grounds that Western cities ought to be attacked: it is our own wickedness, our own mistreatment of others, which warrants punishment.[25] Noam Chomsky argued that America deserved what it got because it had a morally corrupt government. The assumption is that anyone who is not us is good—and this includes Islamo-fascists who killed three thousand innocent civilians on September 11, and who would have been unreservedly more jubilant if the figure had been 300,000. The German composer Stockhausen celebrated the destruction of the Twin Towers as the greatest modern work of art. This is radical cultural paranoia, and just as demented as the narrower psychiatric condition.

Upper-middle-class rancour displays a kind of civilisational masochism. Which other society in history has had segments of its elites supporting the nation's enemies, wanting their country to lose the wars it fights?[26] Since the Vietnam War in the 1960s, significant numbers of the most socially privileged have taken pleasure in their own country's soldiers being killed in action—soldiers inevitably coming from the ranks of the lower middle class. Students gathered at Monash University in Melbourne on the morning after September 11 to cheer. While these students represent a lunatic fringe, their virulent anti-Americanism finds widespread echoes throughout the upper middle classes of Western Europe and, to a lesser degree, in Australia and even in America itself. To be deeply hostile to the leader of your own geo-political side discloses a failure of nerve, twisted by rancorous self-hatred.

The workings of this entire scrum of cultural forces may be seen in clear relief in the case of Anthony Blunt, who had a golden career as an art historian and connoisseur, and reached the inner sanctum of the British Establishment. Knighted in 1956, he was appointed

Slade Professor of Fine Art in turn at Oxford and Cambridge, and was elected a Fellow of the British Academy in 1950, and a Fellow of the Society of Antiquaries in 1960. He was appointed Surveyor of the Queen's Pictures from 1952, and Adviser for the Queen's Pictures and Drawings from 1972.[27] The world fraternity of art historians regarded him as a master, perhaps without equal. As George Steiner notes, his reception by royalty underlined the judgement of his profession, that in Sir Anthony Blunt the qualities of intellectual and moral integrity united at the highest level.

And yet, some time in the late 1920s or early 1930s, while at Cambridge (he became a Fellow of Trinity College in 1932), Blunt had been recruited by Soviet security; he acted mainly as a talent spotter and primary agent in the Cambridge circle of spies. Later, he worked within the British intelligence organisation MI5 as a Russian agent, during the period of World War II in which Stalin and Hitler were allies. He could have lost Britain the war, by leaking the vital decrypts of German communications at a time when the Germans had cracked the Russian codes. He passed the secret of D-Day to Moscow, again risking the whole enterprise.[28] He sent untold numbers of east European activists hostile to Stalin to their deaths. In 1951, it was Blunt who orchestrated the escape of the Russian moles Burgess and Maclean to Moscow. In other words, over a long career, Anthony Blunt was repeatedly guilty of high treason.

That Blunt, who was known from the 1930s to have views sympathetic to communism, was not only taken into MI5, but survived until his confession in 1963, suggests that he benefited from protection in high places. In part, it was because Blunt was a gentleman—he belonged. He also used sexual blackmail, and extensive homosexual contacts through the British Establishment.[29]

In 1979, when the scandal became public, it was the popular press in London that came out and called treason by its name. Not only did *The Times* fail to express any outrage; it invited Sir Anthony to lunch and served him salmon sandwiches. 'Top people' rallied to his support. One Cambridge academic commented, 'Certainly nothing has happened that would make him less of a friend.'[30]

Oxford did not ask him to resign the honorary doctorate it had awarded him. University College, London, immediately offered him lectures, as a visiting professor. One of his publishers spent two minutes in an editorial meeting joking about the case, then decided to take no notice. *The Times Literary Supplement* continued to publish reviews by Blunt.[31]

The Blunt case does have at least one perplexing complication. Sir Anthony's major publications as an art historian were on Nicolas Poussin, a painter singular for the integration of formal neo-classical construction in his canvasses with a profound spiritual content. Blunt's work on Poussin is not marred either by pedantic academicism or by narrow connoisseurship. Indeed, his 1958 Mellon Lectures remain the most perceptive philosophical and iconographic overview of Poussin's art.[32] His teaching is reported to have sustained a similar rigour. There is true virtue in Blunt's scholarship, yet this scholar was also a political man. Poussin, who had venerated civic duty and fidelity in a number of paintings, would have judged his admirer severely.[33]

Jung's hypothesis was that when the gods are killed, they are reborn as diseases.[34] He was referring to the degree to which individuals without belief, in order to give shape to what they do and how they live, will find themselves trapped in self-absorbed compulsions, depressions, and anxieties. Psychopathology is *the* modern form of illness. Indeed, the very term 'psycho-pathology' means, in the original Greek, suffering of the soul. Jung interprets neurosis as the suffering of a soul that has not discovered its meaning.[35]

In the modern usage of *psyche*, soul has been dropped in favour of personality—in effect, *ego*. Ego detached from soul loses contact with the healing spirits, and becomes deranged. It is then misdiagnosed as sick in itself.

Radical liberalism and upper-middle-class rancour are cultural pathologies spawned by an absence of meaning. When the old gods are not replaced by compelling new ones, a condition of spiritual failure paralyses the individual. A rancorous metaphysics arises as a false god, providing counterfeit meaning. That this meaning is itself stagnant is indicated by its self-destructive focus. Anthony Blunt's rancorous betrayal of his own country was matched in his later years by a total lack of remorse.[36]

Chapter Six

# THE MODERN
# UNIVERSITY

The causes of the slump in upper-middle-class morale have not been trivial or ephemeral. Moreover, their impact has been overwhelming on the institution that has come, in the modern West, to serve as the training centre and incubator for elite culture — the university. It is within the walls of the academy that the slow and sharp corrosions of the Death of God and radical liberalism have etched most deeply into the steel of inherited belief. Indeed, the steps in the advance of nihilistic high culture are most clearly to be observed in the history of changes to the university.

The Western university as we know it today was founded in the Middle Ages as a Christian institution. It was predicated on unquestioned and unifying faith. Within the faith, its central task was theological — to explain the works of God to man — and to train minds for that interpretative work. The university was transformed by the Renaissance, and later the Enlightenment, into a humanist institution. In this, its second phase, culture replaced God as the transcendental force that welded the unifying vision. We are now well into a third phase, in which the university has a confused idea of itself; in as much as it has direction, it is to be found in pockets

143

still under the influence of the ghosts of the old beliefs.

This history is best clarified by a closer look at the humanist era. The humanist university drew its life-blood from three related ideals. One was aristocratic, that of the gentleman—a character ideal. The assumption was that the good society depends on a social hierarchy led by a cultivated elite, based on inherited wealth and status, with a strong sense of civic duty. That elite is defined by its individuals, men of character. In the nineteenth century, the conception expanded to include the upper middle class, and the gentleman ethos was consolidated in the Anglo world in the English Public Schools. The education of the gentleman culminated in university studies.

The second ideal was that of 'civilisation'. Civilisation was imagined as the pinnacle of human achievement. It depended on the most intellectually and imaginatively gifted, in trained application, producing great works. Civilisation has created the Gothic cathedral and the steam engine, *Hamlet,* and the Sistine ceiling, graceful town-planning, hygiene, and codified law. The works of civilisation show humans at their highest, transcending mundane everyday life; making of themselves something immortal and godlike; and creating powerful tools for the conquest of necessity, and objects of supreme and edifying beauty.

The third ideal was a utilitarian one—that culture and knowledge are useful. In Matthew Arnold's formulation, deriving from Socrates, knowledge will make a person better and happier. Ignorance is the source of misery and evil.[1] Humans who have knowledge will find it more difficult—in the extreme version, impossible—to do ill. They will be more rational about their lives, which will therefore become more pleasurable and fulfilling. These qualities applied to society will result in it, too, being reformed and improved.

The humanist ideals were combined in John Henry Newman's 1852 lectures on *The Idea of a University.* Newman focused on what he called 'the culture of the intellect', by which he meant:

the force, the steadiness, the comprehensiveness and the versatility of the intellect, the command over our own powers, the instinctive just estimate of things as they pass before us, which sometimes indeed is a natural gift, but commonly is not gained without much effort and the exercise of years. This is real cultivation of mind.[2]

Apart from the training of the intellect, the main function of the Newman university was to transmit universal knowledge — albeit, given the time and the social hierarchy, only to upper-class males. The goal was a boy with a disciplined mind who was knowledgeable and who had good judgement. This is not directly utilitarian: cultivation of the mind is, like health, good in itself.

While Newman's explicit task was to set the rules for a Catholic university, the reality is that he expounded the humanist ideal of his times. Literature is the centre of his university; theology, merely one branch of knowledge. But the tone of The Idea of a University, read today, lacks gravity, religious or other. Its mood is buoyant with Victorian upper-class optimism. Newman is secure within his class and his institution, Oxford, and in knowing that he addresses a captive, like-minded audience which believes in the cultivated gentleman as the lynch-pin of the social and political elite, which believes in civilisation, and is confident about the complementarity of knowledge and progress. The Newman ethos was echoed soon after in Matthew Arnold's highly influential book Culture and Anarchy (1869).

The optimism had gone by the end of the First World War, as Max Weber reflected in a 1918 lecture titled, 'Knowledge as a Vocation'. Weber's question was whether the university was possible in a godless and prophetless time, a time in which the traditional ultimate values had lapsed, and no new ones had appeared. Weber observed that many were looking to the university to provide the meaning that had gone out of a disenchanted world. However, knowledge cannot provide meaning, in the ultimate sense of answering Tolstoy's questions: 'What should we do and how shall we live?'³ Nor, according to Weber, should it try. Prophecy does not belong in the lecture halls.

What then remains? Weber finds three functions for the university: the advancement of knowledge, the teaching of methods of thinking, and the imposition on students of a clarity and consistency of thought, within the framework of already-given ultimate values. At this point, Weber's defence of the university collapses in unacknowledged contradiction. The one function that preoccupies him is the third, but it depends on already given ultimate values, the lack of which is the problem that stimulated his lecture in the first place.

Weber concludes with a piece of vintage Calvinism, defending the virtue of intellectual integrity, founded on the individual teacher's own conscience. The implication is that rigorously disciplined scholars dedicated to their own branches of knowledge will communicate enough moral authority to their students to fill the metaphysical void. Behind this flattering absurdity, Weber has described the modern university: where there is authority, it is in individuals obeying their own consciences, usually in isolation—an odd dispersion of one-person sects to be found sprinkled thinly through a sluggish bureaucracy.

The last serious attempt to revitalise the humanist university was undertaken by the Cambridge literary critic F. R. Leavis. In *Education and the University* (1943), Leavis argued for the university as the most important social institution, for only it could preserve culture and humanity from the barbarism of the modern world. Culture is the core, he says, and it has its highest representation in literature. Culture is moral, humane, and intelligent, and the last defence against the material and philistine juggernaut of modernity.

Culture is the continuity of a nation, its moral centre, preserved in its literature. The task of the university is to keep it alive.

Leavis, echoing Matthew Arnold, goes on to advocate reading and thinking in a disciplined manner. The goal is to stimulate intelligence and sensibility. Leavis and his school did manage to put these principles into practice for a generation. Yet, in spite of their success in instilling a real seriousness and discipline, Leavisite English departments at their zenith, in the 1960s, were notorious for internal ructions. Far from being centres of humanity and virtue, they were typified by self-righteousness, pettiness, and malice.

Some of the modern practices of the Western universities, before the 1960s, continued on the assumption of the humanist model. Michael Oakeshott, in his essay 'The Study of Politics in a University', theorised this practice, arguing that the functions of the institution were to preserve the intellectual capital of a civilisation, to set up a conversation across the disciplines, and to teach.[4] In other words, the 'civilisation' part of the humanist ideal is accentuated. But Oakeshott in 1961 failed to see what Max Weber had seen in 1918.

In the United States, there were similar examples of the survival of the old education, especially in the liberal arts colleges, often centring on courses teaching the great books of Western culture. Chicago and Columbia were notable cases.

In the twentieth-century wake of the humanist university, there was one quite different strategy: to create a politically active institution. In the ashes of the last 'idea' grew the university as training camp for political and social reformers. Here, the university again followed the church, in compensating for a lack of belief in itself with political activism. Weber knew the phenomenon in the German universities of the 1890s. It reappeared in the 1930s with the sacking of Jewish professors, the burning of books, and Heidegger's Rectorial Address at Freiburg in which the eminent philosopher urged a commitment to Hitler.[5]

In the 1930s, it also appeared in other countries—in England, for instance, where a Marxist socialism became the fashion amongst intellectuals. The political motivation returned in the 1960s, this time pioneered by Leftist students demanding that radical social reform replace learning as the main activity of the university. Typical of behaviour in the politicised institution was the stigmatising of Goethe by German students as a reactionary: they refused to read his work, and turned to Brecht as the master of their own culture.

No less political has been the recurring utilitarian attempt to turn the university into a polytechnic, or a technical high school, to use the apt German term. The university is then a collection of guild schools for social engineers and applied scientists, devoted to those specialist branches of knowledge that are relevant to the short-run social and economic problems of the day. There has been widespread government pressure in Western countries since the 1980s to make the universities more narrowly vocational.

The political cell and utilitarian notions of the university have never been theorised. Leaving aside the systems of Bentham and Comte for their positivist banality, there is no serious treatise defending them. There is, however, a powerful antecedent. That is Plato's *Republic*.

In Plato's totalitarian utopia, designed from scratch by philosopher-kings, the university is the key social institution. The rulers undergo a forty-year education, from ages ten to fifty, before taking over the state. The state arranges marriages, censors literature to the point of banning all poetry (including that of Homer), and it keeps control over a strict social hierarchy. This formative work of Western philosophy gave authority to political idealism, to the belief that the best human intellects, with appropriate training, could set about designing and building the perfect human society.

★★★

The sequence of modern defences of the university, from Newman to Leavis, and the alternative moves at politicisation, have occurred not only because of the failure of the humanist ideal. They have also had to contend with a profound attack on the university.

That attack was launched by Friedrich Nietzsche in a castigation of intellectuals, and indeed of the entire Western ascetic tradition of scholars and priests. Nietzsche develops an argument that has roots in Romanticism, and deeper ones in the Reformation and further back in the pre-Socratic Greeks, and elaborates it into a general theory of the decline of European culture. Sorel, Spengler, Benda, and other later critics of intellectuals have been much under his influence, although their work is pale by comparison.[6] Max Weber's 1918 lecture is troubled precisely because it accepts Nietzsche's case, and cannot get around it.

Nietzsche's argument contrasts instinct and knowledge. The history of civilisation is the history of increasing repression, of steadily proliferating checks on the instincts. This development is against nature. Healthy, strong, admirable human individuals are decisive, they see things clearly, and can act on what they see—their instincts are good, and they obey them. The high level of repression concomitant with civilisation produces people, by contrast, whose passions are tepid, who dither, who are ineffectual, and who take to moralising in compensation for their inability to decide and to act. In their inhibition, they turn to thinking, to the pursuit of knowledge as a rationalisation for their own weak characters and drab lives.

Hamlet is the literary exemplar. He lost the instinctive sense of what is good and bad, what is worth doing and what not, and lived under the delusion that he could reason himself into action. It follows that the celebration of knowledge, epitomised in the philosopher and the university, is not a mark of progress, not the banner under which human life will be made better and happier. It is rather a neurotic symptom of bad character and decadent culture.

For Nietzsche, the devil in all of this was Socrates, the man of knowledge who hated instinct. The West has followed Socrates and what he represents.[7]

In effect, Nietzsche makes two points. One is about the human types who pursue knowledge; the other, about the function of knowledge itself. The first point is that it is the worst people who become intellectuals, slave types who are devious, inhibited, and rancorous. Not only is repressed emotion sublimated into thinking, but the overcharged intellectual faculty is then commandeered to manufacture tortuous justifications of bad motives as good ones, of bad acts as reasonable ones. Such people are the last that any community should look to for example. In other words, the university is not a place for the training of character, or the development of virtue.

Nietzsche's second point is that knowledge has helped us become more comfortable, not better or happier. The best societies have strong cultures. Culture is rooted in myth, not knowledge. Indeed, the pursuit of knowledge is a sure sign that the sacred myths have lost their authority. In particular, academic history is an abstract endeavour, and only appears once real ties to the past have withered—family ties, tribal ties, and communal ties. History is a futile attempt to replace this loss, to find new roots. The quintessence of strong culture, the tragedy of Aeschylus and Sophocles, posited that wisdom is a crime against nature. That tragedy, in its turn, was regarded by the messiah of knowledge, Socrates, as barbaric, as a bad influence on children.

Nietzsche here posits a distinction between 'civilisation' and 'culture' that was to assume great significance in later Western thought. Through civilisation, the West has developed science and technology, and it has become more rational, more refined, more cultivated and, above all, more comfortable. It has also become weaker and more mediocre, more frustrated, and more resentful.

Great culture is not the product of civilisation; indeed, it is incompatible with it. It appears at rare and unpredictable moments in human history — fifth-century Athens and Renaissance Italy — and is the product of individuals with strong and wilful characters. Such people are more likely in hard times and in harsh environments. Greatness among humans, in myth, and through culture, is born out of suffering, not comfort.

The last part of the argument is that the increasing repression of the active individual, combined with the canonisation of knowledge, has killed God. There are no transcendental powers left in a rational world. Where comfort is the highest value, it is the stomach, not the sacred, that rules. However, human life becomes meaningless, losing purpose and direction, without belief in a higher order. Hence the modern problem of nihilism, as theorised by its most insightful prophet. The pursuit of knowledge, with the philosopher as hero, and the university as Olympus, has emptied the world of meaning.

Nietzsche's work succeeded in undermining the naive confidence about knowledge that had been axiomatic to the humanist tradition. Newman's 1852 lectures on *The Idea of a University* lost their plausibility a mere twenty years later, when Nietzsche published his first book, *The Birth of Tragedy* — although it was to take several decades for his attack to strike home. After 1872, it was no longer possible to take knowledge for granted, to assume that it was a good thing; or that the pursuit of knowledge was one of the highest human vocations; or that 'civilisation' was pure achievement. Nietzsche turned the philosopher into the intellectual — a term full of pejorative insinuations.

Weber's defence of the university is against the forces of modern culture as interpreted by Nietzsche. The task of the university is not to restore the spirit, or to revive the heart. In any case, Weber is too pessimistic to believe in that possibility. His modest claim is that the university allows specialist disciplines, and that they have a virtue as long as their practitioners obey their ethos: that of intellectual integrity.

Leavis, in effect also accepting Nietzsche, takes a different line. Yes, the task is to restore culture, which is the moral heart of a society. The university has the central role here, for it keeps culture alive by teaching the highest literature of a people. Taught in the right way, this literature will make a student not only more sensitive and intelligent, but also more moral. Thereby it trains a cultural elite strong enough to counter the profanity of the epoch. Nietzsche would not have been persuaded by this optimism.

There is one further contribution of significance to the university saga. That is Philip Rieff's book, *Fellow Teachers*, first published in essay form in 1972. Rieff, unlike other modern critics, provides a view of what the university ought to be, and it is not a rehash of the humanist ideal.

Rieff would agree with Leavis that the defence and maintenance of culture is the task of the university, and that this task is vital for any society's wellbeing. The difference is in the concept of culture. Culture, for Rieff, is interdictory: it commands, it has authority. It is what stops people doing what they should not do. It is the 'thou shalt nots' of a society charged in such a way that breaking them will hurt.

Culture is 'privileged knowledge'. The job of the university is to pass on this privileged knowledge, through the most objective, personal, closest re-cognitions of the great texts and theories. Thereby the related benefits and penalties of inherited culture are conserved. The vocation of teacher is 'to probe the workings of reverence and justice, and by an exemplary presence (that of the teacher himself) preserve both'. Teachers are the policemen of culture, through their interdictory schools. Finally, a university is, for Rieff, of necessity, a 'credal institution'. It is predicated on faith, without which it is nothing, lacking either authority or mission.[8]

This view is that of the old Plato, in his last work, the *Laws*. The task of Platonic education was to teach virtue. Two quotations from Book II give the essence of Plato's final vision:

> Education is the drawing and leading of children to the rule which has been pronounced right by the voice of the law, and approved as truly right by the concordant experience of the best and oldest men.

> Education is the rightly disciplined state of pleasures and pains whereby a man, from his first beginnings on, will abhor what he should abhor and relish what he should relish.[9]

Teachers themselves must be of exemplary virtue, for it is pedagogically vital to have contact with people better than oneself. Plato's picture is completed in Book V, 'We should leave our children rich, not in gold but in reverence.'[10]

For Plato, there is an eternally given law, decreeing the rules that govern human life. Education is the teaching of those rules, so that individuals can learn to control their impulses in obedience to them. In another phrase from the *Laws*, an individual must know what to fear. 'Right fear' is the key to the virtuous life.[11] Moreover, when individuals fear what should be feared, they will be modest, they will be courageous, and they will be under the influence of the highest mood, that of reverence. Education is the instilling of right fear before the law.

\*\*\*

We know, at the start of the twenty-first century, that Max Weber's uncertain defence of the university does not work—as a conglomerate of specialist disciplines vaguely unified at the individual level by an ethic of intellectual integrity.

Nor is a polytechnic a university—and, in any case, it only suits the natural sciences, and perhaps such in-between studies as business and the various professions. A university draws its sustenance from the ultimate questions about the human condition, and therefore it centres on the humanities (including the social sciences). It always has.

The university requires a unifying vision. Experience in the last century proves that without such a vision, it becomes demoralised, and that those teachers who are not completely listless in their vocations tend to become rancorous, teaching against the authorities and truths of the inherited culture, in what they themselves often celebrate as a 'critical' or 'radical' manner. This is not criticism in the sense of open-minded scrutiny of a text, in order to gain access to some truth, but the drive to deny all universals. University rancour has also commonly surfaced in a condescending disparagement of ordinary people and popular culture—for cheap taste, crass materialism, jingoism, xenophobia, and syrupy values.

A good part of the reason that students turned to politics in the 1960s was out of frustration with teachers who had little authority and no mission: teachers, in other words, who had nothing to teach.

Plato failed to recognise that the moral law is taught in many ways. High culture, the mode of the university, is but one of many pathways. Popular culture teaches the law, too, and in modern times more reliably. It does so through its moral tales told in such forms as television soap-opera. It does so through sport. It does so through the popular newspapers and their morally charged coverage of everyday drama and crime. The law is taught, above all, by the example of obedient and reverent individuals, whoever they may be, and in whichever walks of life.

High culture itself has organs other than the universities. The great imaginings of our culture hang on art-gallery walls, while others may be witnessed at the opera, ballet, concert, and cinema, and others again quietly read at home. However, it remains the case that much, but not all, of this needs teaching, if a person is going to approach a true reading of one of the great works.

In spite of the Nietzschean shadow, the humanist university in the last century still had some fine moments, and not only in the sciences. As one example, there is the Denniston–Page commentary on Aeschylus' *Agamemnon*, published in 1957.[12] Two Oxbridge classicists wrestle with the 'decayed and patched foundations' of various later manuscript versions of the play, all corrupt, and the *scholia*, or annotations by the unknown ancient scholars who copied them. They draw painstaking comparisons with other early Greek texts to reconstruct doubtful words and their multiple potential endings. They project Aeschylean metre for the same purpose. The commentary itself has philosophical depth, drawing out the textual implications for fate, divine intervention, justice, free-will, and meaning. The work is steeped in the sense that what we do here matters, that there are fundamental truths in this great classical work, and that it is our job to make access as clear as possible, given the flawed materials available.

The humanist university has run down. The Christian university, founded in medieval form, is too culturally alien to the contemporary West to be revived. Likewise the church, the one institution that could replace the university as the master teacher of eternal truths, is in a state of hopeless disrepair. Yet the university is here to stay, for a bureaucratically·organised society will, of its nature, maintain an educational hierarchy with the universities at the pinnacle.

Reinvigorating the university will not be easy. The first problem is one of faith. The entire story of the failure of upper-middle-class nerve in modernity is one of the loss of a place to stand. Nietzsche saw this, with his Death of God parable, but then himself became a part of the problem by denying the existence of any absolute truths.

Nietzsche saw that cultural demolition will start with ascetic individuals, ones subject to high levels of instinctual repression and to complexity of psychological disposition, and also given to thinking—those very individuals who fill the ranks of the priesthood, the academy, and the caste of artists, writers, and musicians. When they begin to lose their faith, they turn on the gods that have failed them. It is commonplace that the most virulent critics of the Pope and the Church of Rome are priests with faltering belief, or laity in the process of defection. There is a sense of betrayal, a rage against the sacred walls that have crumbled, against the past authorities that still roam around in the individual unconscious, but no longer command.

There is a second problem, likely to prove just as formidable. Nietzsche's critique, at its deepest level, put a question mark against all intellectual production, asserting that, until proven otherwise, it should be taken as a deceit—a fantasy compensation or rationalisation for what the creator is not. Here is an extrapolation from the central thesis of La Rochefoucauld (the French moralist admired by Nietzsche), that precariousness of self-esteem—insecure ego—is a motivational despot amongst us humans. Thus painters create beautiful pictures to disguise the ugliness that they fear in their own souls, inwardly driven to protest that, if their creation is so sublime, so truthful, and so good, they must be, too. Likewise for novelists who write insightfully, musicians who compose sensitively, and moral philosophers who theorise judiciously.

Kierkegaard had put the same point in the form of a query about who had ever managed to think in the categories in which they actually lived—that is, honestly. He must have suspected the degree to which his writing about the ethical and the religious was an attempt at self-justification. Similarly, Nietzsche must have suspected that his repeated disparaging of the sentiment of pity had one source: his dread of his own compassionate nature. These two theorists served to place a red light over the palace of knowledge, flashing, 'Beware!'

High culture, in its entirety, hereby received a body blow from which it has not recovered. With the Death of God, it had become detached from the domain of soul and its quest for grace. When the soul fails to find its meaning, the self and its kingdom fall sick.

The humanities, confined to the pursuit of knowledge, but with diminished confidence and self-respect, were in danger of becoming enslaved to ego, to boosting the individual egos of its many practitioners or, alternatively, to consoling them for their dispiritedness. From time to time, they would still launch new ideals; but, as these were no more than repainted masks for either deflated humanism or its nihilistic shadow, they never convinced for long.

The story of the modern university is more one of fateful inevitability than of irresponsible teachers who could have chosen differently. The combination of the Calvinist emphasis on individual conscience driving the culture, with the increasing prestige of science, meant that any simple religious faith, with or without supporting church ritual, was doomed.

New ways are struggling to be born. The Rieff view misses the mark, for the moral law is taught through many other social institutions, starting with families. And the times have passed in which authoritative creeds, delivered from on high, persuade many. As Thesis Three puts it, the crisis of meaning in the modern West is an issue of culture, not of morals.

The issue of culture for the university equates with the need to subordinate knowledge to a sense of higher mission. How we live now, in a modern secular democracy, determines the method. The tissues of meaning that may be drawn out from everyday life constitute the material. Those tissues of meaning may be teased out directly in university courses through sociology, politics, and history; and through literature, art, music, and film. Or they may be reflected in grander narratives from the full sweep of Western culture. Both pathways are vital.

Central to this idea of the university is a retelling of the human story as a kind of epic, with gravity and dignity, following the diverse ways it plays out its fateful tragedies. This requires interpretations of the story which reveal that life is more than an egoistic performance governed by biological necessity. Today's students crave just this sort of education.

There is a reality principle: to tell stories of how things are, getting at the nature of human life, in categories that reflect honestly the forces that govern it. There is equally an aspirational principle: to project exemplars of individual character, group, institution, and national culture, showing how life might be. Plato's educational ideal has not dated: we still need to leave our youth rich, not in gold but in reverence.

Chapter Seven

# SHOPPING

The search for meaning is predicated on some kind of knowing of the mystery of things beyond. The last two chapters have outlined the consequences of loss of contact with the gods. They have exposed disenchantment and pathology, and the rise of rancorous, life-denying forces. I turn now to the cultural form that has found free licence to spread, given the lack of resistance from the centre, and to the question of whether consumerism is itself a disease.

Nietzsche caricatured the typical inhabitant of the modern world, after the Death of God, as the 'last man':

> Alas! The time is coming when humans will no longer shoot the arrows of their longing beyond themselves, and the strings of their bows will have forgotten how to whir! ...
>
> One still works, for work is a form of entertainment. But one is careful lest the entertainment be too harrowing.
>
> One no longer becomes poor or rich any more: both require too much exertion. Who still wants to rule? Who obey? Both require too much exertion ...
>
> One is clever and knows everything that has ever happened:

so there is no end of derision. One still quarrels, but one is soon reconciled—else it might spoil the digestion.

One has one's little pleasure for the day and one's little pleasure for the night: but one has a regard for health.[1]

So runs the cast of consumerism's stereotype. We may go further. The ethos of this society proclaims, 'If you feel bad, eat!' Here is the antidote to the stoicism of the past, which, in response to distress, advised, 'Pull yourself together.' It assumed that strong character and control are the keys to wellbeing; that we are as responsible for our state of mind as for what we do. The consumerist reflex is an inherently melancholic response to a malaise that takes the form of feeling empty, cold, and flat—it can be remedied by being filled up with warm, rich, and vital things. The solution need not be food, as in what made the Beatles 'feel happy inside'. Gorging is the path to salvation: consume, and feel good.

Two other consumerist traits follow. A cure comes not through action, doing, and making, but through taking it easy. There is passivity, and there is, equally, restlessness, a mania for constant change, movement, and difference: to sit still is to die. The two combine into an aimless drifting, as through a department store, sluggishly eying these goods—but only half-seeing them, the mind in weary distraction—then over to those, this window, those people, and on, all without sense, apart from passing the time. Consumerism is the social analogue to the psychopathology of depression, with its twin, clashing symptoms of enervation and an inability to sleep.

But is this the whole truth? Is it even the essential truth? How right was Nietzsche? Clues to the essential logic of a consumer society must lie within the walls of the institutions that service its buying. So let us enter the portals of one of the modern emporiums of consumption.

***

They come for their groceries, for their clothing, for their DVDs, and to eat. They also come eager for excitement. It is a large, unremarkable building about the height of St Paul's Cathedral in London, with its own dome, and covering ten times the ground space. It is set in the middle of a plateau of asphalt jammed with rows of parked cars, the whole strangely out of scale with the miles of sedate suburbs in which it is set. The sun shines, there is a slight breeze, one can see the low mountains in the distance, and the mood is of a quiet, carefree tranquillity, with people here and there going about their afternoon business, in no great hurry, paying no great attention to anything beyond the path in front of them. A large neon sign over the entrance we approach reads, SHOPPING WORLD.[2]

Crossing the threshold, we falter in astonishment at the exotic new world that confronts us. We have entered a long gallery, skirted by two storeys of upper balconies, connected by staircases and spiral walks. The entire space, as far as the eye can see, is draped with fairy lights, neon signs, and richly coloured hangings, interspersed with fountains, split-levels, kiosks, and merry-go-rounds. The soothing, gently exciting throb of pop-music fills the air, picking up the warm, ochre tones that back the kaleidoscope of bright lights and that determine the visual fabric of the surfaces. Then there are the people — thousands of them — crowding, milling, walking, loitering, some hanging over the balustrades, watching, daydreaming; altogether forming another dimension of shapes, movements, and colours.

Shops flank the gallery and the balconies. They open directly onto the central space, without doors or, in most cases, windows, forming a line of elaborately decorated alcoves, each with its specialised textures of posters, signs, hangings, and goods. People seem to wander in and out of them, as a diversion from the central parade, as one catches their fancy, or if they feel like withdrawing momentarily.

In Melbourne, each week, 350,000 people pass through the city's largest Shopping World, which boasts 9,000 car-parking spaces, 130,000 square metres of trading space, and 400 specialty shops, as well as half-a-dozen large stores and supermarkets. The trend is towards bigger, grander, and more extravagant Shopping Worlds. They are now planned with twenty-year build-ups to full capacity.

In this particular one, we could be in any metropolis of the Western world. It is the city of the present, and of the future; coming developments will see some centring on airports, others incorporating Disneyland and Las Vegas themes. The business editor of the *Atlanta Journal* nominated shopping malls as the leading candidate for what typified American civilisation in the twentieth century.[3]

Most of the reasons for the success of Shopping World are straightforward. Compared to the local shopping street, a greater variety of shops is provided; in fact, everything you could imagine you might want, and more, is here. There is plentiful car-parking space, which is safe, and of easy access. The whole centre is enclosed and kept at a constant temperature, thus providing insulation from climatic variation, and protection from the nuisance and danger of car traffic. Compared to city shopping, it has the advantage of being relatively close to the homes of most who use it. And it is open seven days and evenings a week. In short, Shopping World is convenient.

Yet the key to Shopping World's triumph is not to do with convenience. The overwhelming impression on entry is of a bustle of purposeful human activity set in a bright, cheerful palace, so vast as to seem like the very universe. And the heavens are always there to be seen, as the central stretch of every gallery is roofed high above in convex glass. The height and the light, channelled through simple architectural forms, which contrast with the cornucopia of look, sound, and smell closer to ground, combine to give to the spaces an airy exhilaration. Here is London's Crystal Palace of 1851 recreated for new times and new functions.

One gallery leads into another, traversed by a third; the points of intersection are deep, open spaces, at the base of which may be fountains, stages for performances, or cafés. Where a gallery ends, the walk will dive into a satellite world, a fruit and vegetable hall, a gourmet-delicatessen complex, a toy supermarket, a circle of computer and telecommunication shops, a food court offering twenty different national cuisines. At one extremity is a battery of sixteen cinemas; even there, at this time of day, people are queuing—mainly, retired couples. The ground-plan seems deliberately random, almost maze-like, as if to encourage abandon, losing oneself, throwing away the normal need for control and direction. There are no public clocks.

Four of the main galleries converge on an amphitheatre under a huge dome, itself glass, opening far above to a wide expanse of sky. Spectators may view the scene from balconies that encircle the space, or wander in and out at ground level. This vast cylinder of vertical expanse, bathed in light, is flanked by four baroque columns rising three stories and on, up a similar distance again, to the base of the cupola. Four elegantly thin palm trees rise from the floor to the same height, giving a tropical feel. Looking down from the upper balcony, it feels like a piazza below, centring on a Roman fountain, spraying billows of water generously out over four sculpted horses—lions might be seen as too imperial for a democratic age. The rest of the space is covered in small tables and chairs. The aroma of fresh coffee and warm croissants drifts upwards.

The ambience is strongly, almost rigorously, European. The core is Paris café society, as painted by Renoir, or photographed in the Boulevard Saint-Germain. The set of this fantasia is stylish. The physical forms, from the structural lines to the details, are elegant and of quality craftsmanship: the balustrades are made of brass; the floor of the amphitheatre, marble, as are its tables; and its serving counters are panelled in mahogany. The casual dress of the people might seem out of place, were it not for the brightness of the natural light, which endows the scene with a relaxed vitality. And there is the heightening contrast with the shabbiness and decay of many local shopping streets as they continue to run down.

Moving along, one may happen upon a staged event. It could be a fashion parade, a quiz, a boys' choir, or a cosmetic or cooking demonstration. A car is on display, reiterating its demand for attention with advertising that announces it is the first prize in a lottery. On again, past a newsstand, a passer-by might stop in front of a furniture shop inviting her into any of its simulated living rooms, one of which is guaranteed to suit her individual taste.

What then is Shopping World? What is really going on here? In this, the modern market-place, the ratio in size and importance between the public space and that occupied by stalls or shops has been inverted. The galleries, promenades, and the open-theatre piazzas are what enthral: they are the focus of activity and attention. The shops are subsidiary, rather like the side-chapels in a Gothic cathedral. The change in the use of space indicates a change in the priorities of the shoppers. Shopping has become of secondary importance. Shoppers are drawn, by and large, to Shopping World by the promise of consumption more metaphysical, more quixotic, than the purchase of soap and socks. Indeed, it is as if, in those moments that they spend in the side booths filling their shopping bags, they are purchasing their entrance tickets.

To what world, offering what metaphysical allures, have they bought tickets? Shopping World is a fairground, a carnival. As at the fairground, visitors stroll around, alternating at will, or on whim, between being spectators and performers. They are always a part of the performance, but sometimes they merge with the crowd, or disappear through a tent door to watch the bearded lady. At other times, they become a more prominent part of the play, throwing balls at coconuts, or driving dodgem-cars. Then it is the performance that matters. It counts for little whether they carry off a coconut or lap the other dodgems: what is important to them is that, for a moment, they have been at the centre of the action, absorbed in handling the challenges of their act. As they step out of the car and return to being spectators, they can relax a little, daydream about their time at the wheel, and walk on while watching others, seeking new absorptions, and day-dreaming further.

Shopping World is much the same. The performances might seem less defined, but in fact there are merry-go-rounds, there are clothes to try on, and furniture displays to occupy, and there are market surveyors who interview, and wine salesmen who tempt. This domain is not as passive as the consumerism stereotype assumes.

What Shopping World is not, in spite of the emphasis on convenience, is 'rationalised' to any great degree. Max Weber coined the term to refer to the capitalist principle of making economic processes ever more standardised and subject to calculation, thus reducing risk and unpredictability.[4] The contemporary paradigm is McDonald's, where assembly-line production combines with heavily routinised consumption.[5] At Shopping World, there are elements of rationalisation, in that chain shops will be represented (including McDonald's) and, when they are, their windows, internal décor, and layout will obey strict formulae — the familiarity putting shoppers at their ease. But so much else here invites spontaneity.

The fairground/grand-café is popular not merely because it provides a hubbub of show and activity. Within its walls we may witness some of the lineaments of contemporary hope. Here, some of the wishes unfulfilled within the frame of the incipiently aimless and monotonous stability of suburban life leave traces as to their ultimate purposes.

That hope, and those wishes, are not directed towards consumption — or, at least, not the consumption of material goods. Buying is something to do on the way. It is the way that is important to the shopper, and for us to concentrate on the shopping-bag would be to take the person merely at face value.

Maybe there was a brief period in the history of capitalism that was more obsessional, when the sociologist had reason to identify 'commodity fetishism' as a central passion, and to see self-esteem linked directly to social status, which in turn gained its most secure demonstration from the ownership and conspicuous consumption of material goods.[6] Possessions have always been, and will continue to be, taken, in part, as emblems of power and prestige. And, in a few cases — for instance, deprivation in early childhood, or living through economic depression — they may satisfy a deep need. But, in general, they do not answer any essential wish. This is clear today at Shopping World.

Material consumption offers, in part, a substitute satisfaction, a palliative to the wish to possess a thing of ultimate importance. The redeeming possession that is the true object of consumer desire may take the form of a beautiful moment; a taste in the mouth that awakens all the senses; a feeling of self-containment, of increasing pleasure in the person's self; or, finally, at the end of the aisle, the possession of love.

Gratified desire, the goal of so much human endeavour, is tantalisingly elusive: the formative childhood image of it comes from the mood in which fairytales end. There are moments when everybody achieves that longed-for state, and those moments cast some of the lines of hope that govern life through the in-betweens. They pattern the way that struggling individuals will, at once, compromise their deepest desires, and console themselves for the discontent that the compromises cause them. Consumption has taken over from religious ritual as the main source of compromise and consolation.

Emile Zola has provided a benchmark for measuring the degree to which the nature of consumption has changed. In his richly sociological novel *Au Bonheur des Dames,* written in 1882, he described the advent of the great department store.[7] The new emporiums were eclipsing all the small, traditional shops in their neighbourhoods. Zola attributed their success to two factors. First, they exploited the 'bargain', seducing women into buying things that they did not need by making them seem so cheap that the customer imagined, every time she bought one, that she was bringing off an economic coup. The stores created a frenzy of buying.

Second, because of their size, the stores could offer an unprecedented range of merchandise. The important thing for my purposes here is that the commodity itself remained the focus of attention in the department store. Although the director of Zola's store knew that his success depended on him capturing the imagination of the bourgeois ladies of Paris, playing with their fantasies, and drawing them in at just the right moment, he did so purely through his goods. The shopper's mind was concentrated on the articles of consumption. It was yet to stray into more abstract fields.

People do, of course, buy things at Shopping World. Moreover, not all their shopping takes the form of an incidental dropping into an alcove as a relief from the central parade. There is some serious shopping done, carried out with matter-of-fact efficiency. It is common to proceed, on arrival, to the supermarket section and to speedily purchase the week's groceries—or, in more recent differentiations, to go to the fish market, the delicatessen complex, and the greengrocer. The full bags are then deposited, to be collected later, when the shopper finally leaves. Her duty done, she can throw herself with a good conscience into the pure pleasure of being here.

Indeed, it is essential to the success of Shopping World that it cater to the guilt of a Puritan culture—a culture in which women report being too busy to have time for leisure.[8] Women can pretend to themselves that their motive for coming here is to do something useful, even necessary—an obligation that, in reality, they choose to get out of the way first. Once they have done their serious shopping, and thereby absolved their guilt, they can relax, having successfully rationalised an hour or two at leisure in the fair.

Shopping World is also a meeting-place. The cafés are full. Occasionally, even lone shoppers meet friends. They stop to gossip, stand together, and wistfully gaze around, or sit down for coffee and cakes. However, such meetings are generally not sought or planned, and the shopper is likely to get impatient fairly quickly with such collisions with familiarity. If it were familiarity that she desired, she would stick to her local butcher, who knows her personally, and likes to chat with her. She comes here to escape her private suburban circle of known people and predictable situations. If it is a meeting she seeks, it is one of those surprise intersections of fate, here conjured up by the image of the fairground or the café—illustrated most poignantly in the French classic *Les Enfants du Paradis* (1944), a film that could stand as the fantasy blueprint for Shopping World.

Shopping World represents a significant change in the history of consumption. Its design recognises the all-too-human reality that experience is usually more exciting and gratifying in the anticipation than in the fact. It exploits the wide gap that usually exists between the wish and the commodity. It fills that gap with activity that is more conducive than basic shopping to arouse the wish, to clothe it in a whole range of exotic guises, and to carry it into the realm of possibility.

Shopping World tries to play the role of the eternal seducer: it arouses extravagant expectations, and then keeps just enough interest in itself, and just enough distance from itself, not to break the spell. It offers neither total consummation nor total rejection. Although its sole motive is to increase sales, the temple of consumption supplies many activities to keep its captive's wish alive. Buying is merely one of those activities, and consequently the shopper does not expect too much from it. As a result, she is less likely to be disappointed. The history of consumption has now advanced to the point at which the commodity's main function is to serve as a background ritual, and as an excuse.

If we choose to retain the term 'consumption', we have to disregard the Marxist emphasis on commodities. In a sense, what the shopper wants, as Max Stirner would have put it, is to consume herself.[9] She wants to be eaten up, absorbed by a larger universe than that of her solitary self. She wants to be consumed by a captivating moment, a moment that resonates with past fantasies and that may imply a future quite different from the mundane present. What she seeks to purchase is experience, a release from what she knows, into something larger and richer. The mall trade-magazines in the United States openly refer to the 'retail drama', and talk about centres 'casting' their stores.[10]

In its first decade, the 1970s, well over 80 per cent of the people buying at Shopping World were suburban wives. They still predominate; nevertheless, changes are underway, with increasing numbers to be seen of those who have retired early, and who are living longer. There are young married couples, too, sometimes with an infant or a small child. Then, in the late afternoon or evening, there are groups of teenagers lounging around—Shopping World is their street-corner meeting-place. But, more and more, it is everyone who comes here to taste of the *cosmos* of our times.

Clothing shops, especially women's boutiques, predominate at Shopping World. So let us follow one of the suburban wives inside, where there is sheer sensuous pleasure to be found in the dimmed and perfumed boutique chapel. Touch enriches look. She glides around in a reverie, caressing the gorgeous silks, feeling the contours of the Milanese sandals, slipping into a sleek dress that shows her off to stunning perfection.

There may be moments when a new pair of shoes catches her fancy to the degree that she feels that the gods have blessed her with one of their finest gifts. A purchase — the pair of shoes — may serve as its own type of icon. The brand name itself is more than just a marketing device. It is charged with some of the magic of Italian style and the glamorous world that these beautifully designed and crafted shoes represent. The shoes are, in their own special way, an emblem of transcendence.

The ideal commodity has to be suggestive — suggestive enough for her to believe in the fantasy. She does not want compromise, although that is, in fact, what she usually gets. She may not have gained a momentous experience, one that lasts in the memory; but she has at least been taken out of herself for a while, and she may take away with her a memento to keep the dream alive, as it was for Cinderella transformed by her fairy godmother.

And her dream may gain added lustre once she is outside in the passing throng again, and comes across a fashion parade, as she becomes intoxicated by the glamour of the lights and music, the beautiful clothes, and what she imagines to be international models, close enough to touch. Here, she is at the centre of the world, not some suburb in the middle of nowhere.

If the shopper were able to confess, and to clarify those vague metaphysical longings that have driven her here, the shadow of some stranger might be made out beckoning to her. She is protected enough at Shopping World by the deliberateness of the space, the anonymity of the people, and the concreteness of her own motive for having come, to dare the unfamiliar, to loosen slightly the halter on her most deeply unconscious intention. Is she not, in fact, flirting with the fancy of a mysterious and enthralling encounter, the passage to an alternative life? Is there not a wayward impulse in her that she is indulging this afternoon? Yves Saint Laurent observed, 'People don't want to be elegant any more; they want to be seductive.'[11]

Were some real opportunity to confront her (which is unlikely, because most of the people here are either other suburban wives or retirees), she would probably flee in agitation. But living out a fantasy is not everything. The experience she is in search of is a feat of the imagination; if she can live through it for even an hour, she will return home satisfied. Shopping World provides her with the props that allow her to stage herself in this play of her imagination—an experience that releases her, if only temporarily, from the carefully defined finite surfaces of her life.

Maybe it is even more ethereal, the wish that Shopping World alerts. Maybe it signals to a long-subdued childhood, or an adolescent dream of adult omnipotence—of having the power to attract, at the right moment, in the right place, the people and the circumstances that would make of her life something royal, that would draw her into a mystery of exquisite splendour and significance. Where better than here, where there is the atmosphere, the crowds of strangers, and dancing models who stimulate dreams of stardom, of elegance, and of influence?

So she wanders around, gazing through a veil of reverie at the particular goings-on. After an hour, she begins to feel pains in her legs, the large space and the crowd now look alien, and she remembers the chores that await her at home. With the charm of Shopping World fading fast, she heads off to collect her groceries.

\*\*\*

What may we conclude about consumerism? Our story is surely complicated. The capitalist economic system continually evolves, forcing radical changes to the material conditions within which humans live. It has created, in its last phase, new levels of abundance, and simultaneously left production increasingly to machines, themselves directed by computers. It has geared human energies to consumption, including to jobs that service consumption. Two quite opposite tendencies have been induced by these conditions: one, in alliance with the quest for meaning; the other, strengthening nihilistic currents.

Let me first consider the positives. Hannah Arendt argued that the logic of consumption, according to which the ideal life is to sleep, eat, drink, and be merry, is a direct and necessary consequence of labour—the mode of the 'labouring animal'.[12] This argument exaggerates the animal component and, in relation to modern society, neglects the driving Calvinism, as already discussed in the cases of work and sport. It also neglects the need for fantasy, as exhibited in Shopping World consumerism. We humans are dependent on our hopes and our dreams.

Many of the people here (exactly what proportion could never be known) live within the lower-middle-class ethos of the acceptance of finitude and ordinariness. Reasonably content with their state, they take an uncomplicated pleasure in buying new things. They enjoy Shopping World for itself, as an addition to their everyday activities. Arendt's labour/consumption applies, but with the major qualification that it is governed by a strict cultural ethos.

The fun of the fairground, a labour derivative, has been reborn at Shopping World, even if in a moderate, understated form. It is most marked in the light buzz of excitement in the crowds. Here is perhaps as much fun as may be found in a modern Calvinist culture.

Modern consumption is not all about chocolate and instant gratification. There are goods that appeal for longer than an hour or a day—notably, cars and personal computers, whose more serious call is to do with their linking with the work ethic and democracy, as I shall examine in Part III. Also, the commodities that contribute to the beautifully furnished home will likely be transformed into more than the profanely useful, as time and familiarity integrate them into the sacred haven.

Clothing is more difficult to place. Although it may be worn for a time, and even on rare occasions will be repaired, its appeal seems largely ephemeral. Bought on the crest of the wave of bubbling images of the triumphant ego, of the metamorphosis of everyday, ordinary self into shimmering beauty, it is the intoxicated day-dream of power that commands — to be a super-model for an hour. At the same time, it is a basic human pleasure to look good. And there is genuine satisfaction in presenting oneself out in public looking one's best, exhibiting taste and aesthetic judgement.

Then there is practical shopping. Daniel Miller has shown, in a study of shoppers in a North London supermarket, how remote it is, in reality, from consumerist stereotypes — more like a religious ritual than drudgery or mindless materialism. The women whom Miller observes express their care for those they love through shopping, even when it comes to seemingly profane necessities. And the strategies they employ are thoughtful and skilled. Miller concludes, about one of his typical subjects:

> When all these complexities of her situation are considered — nostalgia for the old; excitement of the new; responsibility for her relationships; acknowledging their autonomy; moral and financial considerations, and many more such concerns — when one tries to empathetically follow the logics of these internal arguments, then it becomes possible to tease out the specifics of the goods she chooses, why a brand item here and a value label there, why her own taste here and something she loathes there.[13]

The fantasy encouraged by shopping is partly escapist. Its invitation is to withdraw from reality, with its tarnished hopes, its gruelling routines, the way in which most things are unrewarding, and certainly less than ideal. In reverie, one may find perfection. This was the Superman solution. The potential negatives of consumerism feed here, so let me pause to consider them.

First, the escape into fantasy is part of a general middle-class retreat from active public life. The agora of the classical Greek city was similar to Shopping World in being the market-place of its day, and yet it served as much more—indeed, as the most important public space available. When a citizen left the privacy of his home, wishing to engage in public life, most likely he went to the agora.

The Greek agora was surrounded by civic buildings and temples. It served as the daily centre not only of commerce, but also of religious, political, judicial, and indeed general social life. To be engaged in public activities in ancient Athens meant to be a citizen and, often, to be engaged in civic duties. In modern life, though, the areas of direct political action are remote. Being in public has become abstracted from having power over the commanding political, legal, and economic institutions. It has been focused back on private life. Shopping World is designed to encourage narcissistic fantasies about the future of the least political of all interests, those of the personal and the intimate. That the principal Shopping World in Melbourne titles its information brochure *Citizen's Guide* suggests some bad conscience about its civic role.[14]

This argument is easily pushed too far, as modern democracy has a different logic to that of classical Athens. Shopping World answers to one of the most basic of human needs: for social interaction in a defined space, among other people, in which to see and be seen, in which to move and to meet, to linger and to evade; and for a space, at the same time, in which to conduct some of life's important business. Consider a bunch of girls who regularly meet together to go shopping. They are treating themselves. If their shopping does function as an escape from the rest of their lives, so what? They have a lot of fun together.[15]

A second potential negative is that there is the promise of absolution from guilt, without the need for either remorse or penance. As with medieval papal indulgences, grace may be bought.

A series of Nike television advertisements serves as an example. These ads profiled half-a-dozen ordinary people from different walks of life, throwing themselves with Spartan rigour into their sports, from jogging to backyard basketball. Filmed in severe, grainy black-and white, set in asphalt and concrete urban landscapes, the subjects strain, their sweaty faces grimacing with pain — there is no glory, no comfort, nor any sublimity here. The ethos is hard-core Calvinist work, fitting the Nike slogan, 'Just do it.' And everybody can *do it*. These ads could themselves serve as a condensed guide to modern Western culture.

The ads succeed by means of a stock anxiety arousal-and-release psychology. The opening gambit triggers a Puritan guilt that viewers are slovenly and half-hearted in their endeavours, in comparison with these profiles. Viewers cannot excuse themselves on the grounds that these are champions — they are ordinary people like them. A nerve has been touched, one central in modern Calvinist sport-as-vocation culture.

The two-stage absolution follows. Viewers can identify with the cast in their frenetic striving, imaginatively accompanying them. And they can buy Nike, thus confirming the identification, and the satisfied release when the game is done. The ads cleverly leave out the fulfilment and relaxation, planting the implied fantasy that relief comes through consumption. And it is serious consumption, as the shoes themselves broadcast, with an anti-aesthetic, raw, utilitarian look. Mind you, the crude shape is counterbalanced by the fine, simple line of the Nike signature: its graceful 'swoosh'. Shops acknowledge that 90 per cent of Nike sales are for image rather than for sport. The high price of the items, given what consumers actually get for their feet, may be indicative of the levels of guilt mobilised.

This example needs reading carefully for its ambivalences. Nike as a brand-name is a secular icon. It represents a way of life, intimating a range of ideals. The icon heralds a sporting culture to identify with, and to live up to. Here is generalised the fact that people sometimes go shopping in order to cheer themselves up — after a car accident, an injury, or a setback at work. The Nike running shoes may take the mind beyond the cocoon of the anxious self.

A third negative of consumerism is that while the shopping ritual is not fundamentally materialistic, the dreams it conjures up fail to engage with higher forces. At the most, ego is fulfilled for a moment, as when the new dress metamorphoses its buyer into a princess. There is fun, there is fancy, there is magic, and even enchantment, but it is not that of the flight of the soul into union with another, or with a grander order.

Consumerism does induce restlessness. It offers so much, almost everything in terms of fantasy, encouraging the need for sacred engagement. Yet there is no serenity in Shopping World. Where everything is colour, movement, distraction, and enticement, the atmosphere can convey no sense of a sanctuary, of a sacred place. No wind is here that 'bloweth where it wills, and thou hearest its sound; but canst not tell whence it cometh, and whither it goeth'.[16]

Thus, when there is consumer pathology here, it is that of a passive, irritable meandering, an aimless trudging along the walks, amidst millions of alluring goods, none of which really appeal. Being taken out of everyday life increases the risk of feeling permanently uprooted. Psychic homelessness shadows a world that is everywhere, and nowhere.

There is an anti-metaphysical pressure, too, but not that of commodity fetishism. It is through shopping that the Western world's cult of freedom may be indulged. Here, there is free choice.

Here, you can believe you control your own destiny, make yourself whomever you want to be and, thereby, transform your life.

Gilles Lipovetsky has gone so far as to claim that fashion is a major weapon in the service of democracy, freeing people from the constraints of class, tradition, and indeed all social constraint, enhancing their individual autonomy.[17] The cost is the feeding of the insecure ego with the escapist illusion that it can change its spots, and even correct the foundations of its being.

What we are not seeing in modern consumerism is the ancient Roman saturnalia — everything permitted in the pursuit of pleasure. That was a culture of gorging: sadism at the Coliseum, followed in the elites by gargantuan orgiastic feasts, including licit vomiting, in order to be able to continue eating and drinking. Radical freedom in ancient Rome led to ever more extreme licence to stave off the boredom. The modern West is more Calvinist.

Signs of loss of control are appearing at some of the margins, notably in an ever-escalating trade in pornography. Obesity levels are rising around the Western world, but this has more to do with poor-quality food, and lack of exercise, than Roman gluttony. In contrast, long-term statistics on average alcohol intake show a modest trend downwards, and the West is reducing its consumption of tobacco.

In Shopping World, except for the occasional sales frenzy, we do not observe manic buying. Indeed, the norm is more the controlled behaviour of look a lot, buy a little. Even with fashion clothing, the tendency is to buy more small things more often, in a parsimony of pleasure.[18] In other words, the pathology of consumerism is not Roman excess. It is the behaviour, instead, of Nietzsche's last man, petty in his 'little pleasures', and hypochondriac.

Where there is excess, it occurs when the dreams take over, as in the case of Superman. The life as lived is no longer central, but sidelined into something to be evaded. Then the last man will have arrived, with his frail ego, his diseases, and his lost soul. As yet, he has been kept at bay, the mood at Shopping World too bright and cheerful to include much of his baleful presence.

The negatives of consumerism are readily exaggerated. There is nothing wrong with indulging in a few escapist dreams. Consolations are healthy and necessary. Likewise, a glass of cold beer after a hard day's work is part of the good life, a sane means of relaxation. The problem comes with a loss of balance, when more is asked of these little distractions, these small pleasures, and these mild narcotics than they are up to—when they are asked to give meaning to life.

## Chapter Eight

# TOURISM

The threat of consumerism is that it will infect the whole culture. If the old gods lose their power, in a rising tide of nihilism, it is there to fill the vacuum. Its method is to take over traditional activities and convert them to its own logic. I have looked at major areas of modern activity and interest, like sport, in which it has failed. In others, it has succeeded. Package-tourism is the leading case-study.

Zygmunt Bauman has gone so far as to nominate the tourist, along with his *alter ego*, the vagabond, as the metaphor of contemporary life. The argument is that freedom of choice has become the most seminal of stratifying factors — the more choice you have, the higher you rank. This is exemplified in tourism.[1]

The restless striving that drove Westerners through their industrial revolution, and hurled them forward into a dizzy rate of social change, finally, in the last half-century, came to focus much of its energy on the search for the sight of some physical landmark that might put restless pilgrims at their ease. At their best, today, they rove the globe after that experience, or revelation, that eludes them at home, and whose absence unsettles their domesticity.

The ultimate offerings of the consumer society, beyond homes and cars, are dining out and travelling. Tourism is the big brother of the two, and is growing to such an extent that it has become the most important sector of world trade.[2] The facts tell us that its appeal is extraordinary, like no other form of modern consumption. It must offer a main path to the inner chamber of the new culture. It does so, first and foremost, because it invites us to a quest, awakening the age-old belief in a journey that will lead, by the end, to the fundamental truth.

Tourism has succeeded by stimulating a range of fantasies in the mind of the modern citizen. It has brought to the many an experience imagined to be the privilege of the few. I shall concentrate here on the side of tourism that offers the journey of a lifetime, and which has nothing to do with relaxation as a goal. My main interest is in the package-tour. The package-tour is tourism in caricature — a caricature that illustrates in exaggerated form many of the characteristics of other modes of travel.[3]

Let us look first at the dream, and then enquire into the reality. Tourists see themselves as adventurers. In this guise, they dream of the pioneer, the explorer, the great voyager, or the conquering emperor. They leave the security of home far behind and set out beyond the perimeters of the known world for fame, fortune, and excitement. They want to take on the minotaur, scale the Matterhorn, discover a lost Amazonian tribe, or sample Thai nightlife. Their heroes are Marco Polo, Dr Livingstone, Ernest Hemingway, and modern high-life celebrities of film, music, and modelling.

Tourists also see themselves as aristocrats. As soon as they leave home, they become persons of distinction. They stay in first-class hotels; they employ porters, guides, and interpreters. In short, they are served: their every whim may be instantly satisfied by a grateful and deferential servant. Their pleasure is the goal of all those around them. They have the authority and power of medieval lords and ladies.

The identification with the upper class carries over into the glamorous image of travel. Wealthy celebrities move at will from one international playground to another; billionaires cruise the Mediterranean in their luxury yachts. Now, mere tourists can take a step into this world. On the terrace of the Oriental Hotel in Bangkok, they can sip cocktails and gaze across the river just as Joseph Conrad, Somerset Maugham, and Noel Coward would have done from exactly the same spot.

Tourists may also dream of themselves as aesthetes, travelling in search of the beautiful, and of knowledge about the finest of human or natural creations. Through knowledge of other cultures, and other epochs, they gain a sense of the richness of human achievement, and of the range of human refinement. For tourists in this role, cities are museums in which they hope for inspiration and enlightenment. They seek cultivation, or to become connoisseurs in some special field. They become cosmopolitan—that is, people of the world.

Tourists may simply want to escape cold weather and, at the same time, to go in search of a grander vision—that of the tropical paradise. They imagine themselves in Tahiti or Barbados, suntanned, lazing on golden beaches under palm trees, gazing out across azure lagoons, with sultry, dark, sensual women or handsome, bronzed demigods strolling past. Or they may be lonely and in search of company. They travel in order to meet fellow tourists, to become part of a group, or in the hope of romance. Then there is tourism as an escape from the constraints of home—to the nightclubs of Bali, say, into a bacchanalia of drink, drugs, and sex.

The haunting melody that seduces tourists leads them on with the cry of freedom, the compelling central ideal of modern culture. In a society that endorses mobility—of status, income, and power; of domicile, relationship, and experience—here is the ultimate in individual autonomy. To travel is to be free, like a bird, to cast off all normal inhibitions — to move as they will, how they will. In new places, they will be new people; in finding sites of historical moment, they will find themselves.

But modern tourists have been duped. If consumer culture has victims, helpless in its sometimes-powerful grip, it is they.

Travelling is an art. The word 'travel' derives from the French word *travail*, meaning both work and suffering. Some people unwisely travel to escape from a difficult period in their lives, or to patch up fraying relationships. Travelling brings with it an inordinate level of strain. Day after day has to be filled from scratch with different activities, testing both concentration and interest, let alone the feet. Tourists without an organised tour are confronted by a constant sequence of petty worries. *Where shall we stay tomorrow? Where shall we have lunch? Do we have enough money? How do I ask for antacid tablets? Where is that museum, and is it worth the effort? If we are exhausted this afternoon, what shall we do?* The strain of touring often dims the eyes — meaning that tourists lose their main resource, their desire to see new things and to experience strange situations.

Whatever their fantasies, not many could take on adventure as the Victorian explorer knew it. Modern tourist adventurers suffer from a great deal of common nervousness. They are constantly threatened by the unexpected. It is not simply knowledge of other societies that they lack; in a more general sense, they have no traditions, no skills — in short, no culture — to prepare them for new places, new languages, and new customs. It is little wonder that they become so attached to their castle, and demand that it not vary too much from Manila to Salzburg. At least they are able to master the workings of the international hotel.

The tour is the greatest of modern 'saving lies' — Ibsen's term for illusions that people hold about themselves and their lives which give them the hope to keep going. The dream promises action, excitement, and revelation. There is no action. Tourism in its purest modern form, that of the package-tour, has been fitted strictly into the model of consumption. The itinerary is planned down to the last detail: the consumer should ideally just sit back and enjoy it, leaving all the worrying to the agent. The battery of brochures and magazine articles become an extension of the instruction manual for the latest domestic appliance — even though they are mainly gloss, not providing much practical advice.

The consumption model, with its excision of action, is obvious in the sphere of service. Tourists may be attended like aristocrats, but they have none of the power and responsibility that went with the manor. In effect, it is the guide who orders them around, leads them by the nose, and advises them what to see and where to eat. If London catches their fancy and they would like to stay longer, or if they are bored by Munich and would like to cut short their visit, they will have no power to follow their desire.

Daniel Boorstin, in an essay titled, 'The Lost Art of Travel', demonstrates the historical development in which the traveller turned into the tourist.[4] He illustrates the old world of travellers: individuals who prepared themselves, for whom things were not easy, and who acted. Theirs was the logic of work, not that of labour/consumption.

Albert Camus wrote of travelling as a playing with fear, with no pleasure involved, a tearing of oneself out of the familiar in order to expose oneself, a sort of 'spiritual testing'.[5] Michael Crichton put it:

Often I feel I go to some distant region of the world to be reminded of who I really am. There is no mystery about why this should be so. Stripped of your ordinary surroundings, your friends, your daily routines ... you are forced into direct experience. Such direct experience inevitably makes you aware of who it is that is having the experience. That is not always comfortable, but it is always invigorating.[6]

If modern tourists could articulate their unconscious longings, they might say something like this. Their problem is that they choose a path which systematically closes off any such possibility.

To see how few of the rigours of vocation remain, let us accompany package-tourists visiting the Forum in Rome. Most of them are unprepared in any way for what stretches in front of them. As studies show, they will not have done any preparatory reading—any *work*—about ancient Rome or its many rebirths. They are ignorant about the Forum, about what type of buildings stood here and of their function, or even of the fact that the great Julius Caesar was murdered just over there, on what would have been the steps to the Senate. They cannot feel moved that from this small, insignificant wasteland, most of the known world was ruled for five hundred years.

What they do see is rubble, and grass growing unkemptly over piles of old stones. If they were to pause, and reflect honestly, they would ask themselves what they are doing here, half-way around the world, at great expense and hardship, in the heat and the dust, anxious, in an alien city in which they do not understand the language, the food is unfamiliar, and stalked by people who look like they are after their wallets or handbags. And what is the climax to all this pain and effort? A dirty heap of stones—no beauty, no grandeur, and no sense.

That tourists have traded the forms of work for those of consumption appears in many ways. They want to spend extravagantly, royally—to use up all of their budgets. One of their leading interests is in shops, bargains, and trophies. At another level, one of their favourite topics of conversation is the relative price of things—how cheap pineapples are in Hong Kong. Like everybody, they carry their interests with them, as essential a part of their luggage as their underwear, and it is the weaknesses of their old selves that surface, not the strengths of any new and more robust ones.

The excitement they gain is not that of the fulfilment of challenging tasks, but that of apprehensive worry. This is borne out in the stories that are told, and re-told, with animation to relatives, friends, and colleagues back home. It is virtually never what has been seen that is recounted with enthusiasm. When the sites are described, it is in the form of ritualised clichés: the Eiffel Tower really is a wonder—we went up it, and you get such a nice view. It is rather the personal moments of the tour, moments of near-crisis, that in retrospect were exciting: when one of the suitcases failed to arrive off the luggage chute at Frankfurt Airport. This signals the true nature of the experience.

Touring has itself been turned into a routine, restricting adventure to those moments when the programme breaks down. But, again, what sort of excitement is this? Tourists might as well be confined to a repeating sequence of jumbo-jet flights, international airport interludes, air-conditioned taxi rides, and International Hilton stops. For what they remember, and therefore for what in fact they see, there is no point in stepping outside this carefully controlled and secured touring capsule. Moreover, the fact that so much fuss can be made about a minor inconvenience suggests the underlying level of free-floating anxiety, which finds outlet only here, exaggerating the banality of the event.

Because touring is consumption, there can be no revelation—only repletion. Tourism is imagined as the largest and richest dessert at the end of the meal of modern life. Virtually all consumers want to taste it. All of the electronic and print media give a strong boost to the assembly of influences that build the tour up as a grand event. Consumers get seduced into trying it. Receptive to the dream, they are swindled into believing that it can be bought and consumed, rather than earned. They are deceived, too, in believing that their work ends with the saving-up to afford it. They are subject to the most common and profound case of cultural fraud in the modern

West. Their fellow victims are, in the main, the hapless denizens of popular culture.

The saving lie of tourism is often in danger of straining credibility to breaking-point. Above all, there is the shock of what the tour is like, in reality—how far from its publicised ideal. The tension between dream and reality builds up to a crisis of legitimacy. To this, a range of defences is provided, the most important of which is the camera. The photograph is an aid to authenticity, and not just for package-tourists. We really were there: see us photographed in the Forum. It really was great: see these famous places, so widely written and spoken about—don't they look exciting here in colour? A bit of the magnificence has brushed off onto us—like seeing or, even better, touching a celebrity. This magnificence extends a hand to we who have witnessed it; we who have now walked amongst titanic ruins. The colour photograph, emailed to family and friends, makes it seem real. Those moments when we were tired and irritated, wondering what the fuss surrounding these lumps of stone was all about, are forgotten.

Clicking the camera also gives tourists something to do. It is a duty that adds definition to their role, and makes them feel less at sea. Moreover, this duty takes their minds off whether or not they are inspired or even interested. They can at least enjoy the action of getting it on camera, even if they have little idea of what the 'it' is.

When not being sure of what to do threatens to paralyse them, they can fall back on the role of tourist; for this, they are provided with the props, the costume, and the make-up. They also have a reliable prompt constantly in the wings. Guides themselves prefer tourists to stick to their role: that way, they are easier to organise. When things are running smoothly, tourists do not have to worry about whether they are living up to their own expectations. Their task is to recognise the famous sites, with cues from the brochures and the guide, and then to photograph them. The job done, they can move on to the next, or retire for a well-earned dinner and rest.

There are complementary aids to authenticity. The string of postcards launched at those back home serve a number of purposes. They confirm the umbilical cord, the ties to a familiar place where they can relax and know what is happening, where things are not alien and forbidding, where they belong and shall return. These missives affirm the importance of where they are, and what they are doing and seeing: they are sent not from one anonymous suburb amongst thousands, but from a great and unique cultural site. One of the advantages of the postcard is that there is so little writing space that tourists can cover up their insecurities with a good conscience.

The postcard—like the snaps shown off two months later, like the presents bought near the pyramids and, indeed, like the entire tour—may serve as an act of aggression against those at home. Again, the cultural fraud brings out the worst self, not the hoped-for reborn one. After all, it was, in part, envy of others who had already gone, stimulated by stories and glamorous advertisements, which had sent these tourists off in the first place. They can at least have the pleasure of revenge, through encouraging the same illusion, and stimulating in the next generation of potential tour consumers the same urges that had driven them.

There is likely some universal fantasy in the Prodigal Son theme that involves the one who goes out and travels, whose travels are by and large a misery, eventually returning home to be welcomed by the father as the favoured son. Meanwhile, the son who dutifully stayed at home was eaten up by envy. Modern Western tourists carry this age-old theme of recognition upon their return from great and difficult adventures with them, and may well suffer deeply when there is no father to welcome them home with understanding and forgiveness. At least there are plenty of brothers to envy them.

Insecurity serves to further reinforce the need to keep up

appearances. The first worry of tourists when it dawns on them that they are not enjoying themselves is directed against themselves: *What am I doing wrong?* Their deepest anxiety is that they are bungling it — they are failing to live up to their appointed role. Their worries about legitimacy increase.

One defence is to convince those back home that it *is* working, that they *are* having a great time. Indeed, the number of postcards sent may be in proportion to the level of insecurity. If those at home believe in us and our tour, we can have a little more confidence ourselves.

Worries may readily be turned against the tourist agency. Tourists, because of underlying insecurity about their role, tend to fear that they are not really being treated like aristocrats, that the service should be better, that maybe the hotel they are in is not really first-class, and that they are being duped. Package-tourists are notorious for kicking up an enormous stink if the most minor of visits listed in the brochure is omitted. Here is a sign of the degree to which they have been reduced to the narrow obsession of ticking off items — getting their money's worth — while they see nothing.

Much of the paraphernalia of tourism is designed to help tourists keep up appearances. There are the stickers for the back window of the car to indicate which towns have been visited. There are hotel matchboxes and sundry other knickknacks that vary from place to place, the contemporary replacements for the tusks and tiger-skins displayed by the big-game hunters. Tourists are primarily keeping up their own morale, and this means keeping up the image of the tour.

It is significant to note what is photographed. The hotel itself may be the main focus, as if to boast of the magnificent building in which they stayed. Some tourists have even been known to immortalise on camera the bedroom in which they slept for one night. Is this not an unconscious confession that the hotel bedroom was the part of the tour that was the most enjoyed, a refuge in which the weary couple could retreat into privacy, and relax a little because they were no longer on show? The bedroom served as the private dressing-room where they could step out of their role and regain a semblance of their ordinary selves. Moreover, there was some novelty in this hotel bedroom, in its luxury, in the services that were provided, allowing them to indulge in the fantasy of being a lord for a day and, at the same time, letting them take it easy.

In spite of all this, the tour may have been important. It was indeed an adventure, and they were treated royally — to the degree of being able to enjoy criticising the hotel service in Florence, if only to fellow tour members. It was an adventure because they were pitching themselves into the unknown. Actually, the things they saw, and the way they saw them, were far from unknown: in fact, they went where they did because it was so well known. They travelled in a secure manner. They were never in the slightest danger. They knew exactly where they would be at noon the next day, or noon in seven days' time.

But, in their own modest ways, they were daring to travel in uncharted waters. Even if their favourite topics of conversation, when they return, are the six-hour delay at Athens airport, or the stifling heat on the bus from Avignon to Paris, or the price of beer in Madrid, they did leave the routines of their normal lives behind. They did go on a serious journey, and they did subject themselves to constant and acute nervous strain. They did take some initiative to go on this tour. There was a type of action involved in making the decision.

Above all, they went in hope: they entered that very human cycle of taking on something different in great eagerness, of experiencing it, of finding that, in many ways, it proved to be a trial rather than a joy and, finally, of returning home tired and wanting only to relax and regather their strength. This is the Prodigal Son syndrome.

Dean MacCannell has argued that 'touristic consciousness is motivated by its desire for authentic experiences.'[7] It is getting at how the natives really live that is of first importance for the tourist. I doubt this. Certainly, there is a corner of the tourist mind that searches out the real thing, and does not want to be faced with substitutes. However, the desire for the authentic is subordinate to the deeper tourist goals.

What tourists do get is staged authenticity. It may well be that they get what they want. They do not want things to be too authentic. How many Anglo tourists in France have any desire to eat frogs' legs or snails? There may be occasional high-culture aesthetes hot in pursuit of the natives; but even in most of their cases, they prefer the natives tidied up a little, and visited with prior instruction of what to see, what to avoid, and how to proceed in such dangerously unfamiliar territory.

Modern package-tourists are terrified of standing still. When they travel they cannot linger, such is their anxiety; they have to keep pushing on. Some tours visit five European countries and ten cities in two weeks. Nothing really engages them. Nothing so arrests their attention that they want to stop and spend a few hours in its presence, meditating, losing themselves in its beauty, releasing themselves to the rhythms of its symmetries. There are no moments of joy; no moments of humility. They are not carried away, out of themselves.

In the midst of the grand beauty of St Mark's in Venice, the tourist reality is dozens of groups packed into the Piazza, with guides screaming out to corral their flustered charges, waving the flag that indicates the rallying-point of 'Trumpi Tour Group 15'. This is a universe away from Michael Crichton's being reminded of who you are. As with Shopping World, there is no serenity here, and nothing sublime.

Tourists have lost all resemblance to their noble ancestor, the religious pilgrim. Compare Western tourists, staggering up the long dragon staircase to the Buddhist temple of Doy Sutep near Chaing Mai, with the devout Thai making a pilgrimage to this very important religious site. The Westerners know it is a temple, and have been told that they ought not to miss it while they are in Chaing Mai. They climb the hill, take off their shoes, enter the building, speed around photographing the gold Buddhas, take a quick look at the view, and then descend and return to their hotel.

The Thais are highly self-possessed and do not seem to mind the intrusion of these busy Westerners. They offer prayers, burn candles, and stick gold foil onto some part of one of the icons. A priest says a prayer for them. The visit to Doy Sutep is of special significance in their lives. They, too, presumably, have their worries once they are away from home—are their fields being properly tended in their absence, have they brought all their medicaments with them, is their son keeping up his religious duties? But they are in contact with greater-than-human forces at Doy Sutep, and they are humbled by the experience. Also, the temple is alive with historical importance. In marked contrast to the Western tourists, the Thais find a confirmation of their deepest beliefs, and their lives gain a greater placement and poise.

The tourist quest fails religiously—it is a pilgrimage to nowhere—although it might claim other contours of belief. One instructive model of journeying in the Western tradition, alternative to that of the pilgrimage, is Don Quixote's. His faith was in the more pagan ideal of chivalry, predicated on a code of honour. Quixote, in spite of being under the sway of wild fantasies and hallucinations, was a man of action—killing monsters, saving damsels in distress, defending the poor and helpless. His axiom for living is that you have to dream in order to move. Tourists have the same hope, but they mistake consuming for doing.

Henry James provided a high-culture ancestor to modern tourists in Isabel Archer, the tragic heroine of *The Portrait of a Lady*

(1881). She strides into the novel as an attractive twenty-three-year-old woman 'affronting her destiny'. She is spirited, intelligent, perceptive, confident, and everyone is fascinated by her, intrigued to see what she makes of her life—especially once she inherits a fortune. A New England industrialist and a rich English lord both propose, but she turns them down, cherishing her freedom, and wanting to live. But what does that *living* involve? It involves falling for cultivated Europe in the form of a passionless aesthete who is after her money.

Isabel delays marriage for a year to give herself a chance to experience the world. She tours, with the implication, when she returns, that all she has done is indulge her defence against living. She has looked at things, rather than engaged with them—this is what her 'freedom' means in practice. She learns all about the Forum, being a sophisticated tourist, but her knowledge does not help. Having gained nothing except a certain panic at the emptiness of freedom, she then enchains the rest of her life to a marriage that is all contrivance and cold hatred.

Tourism serves as a rich parable of the central conflict and challenge in the modern West. Camus was right to imply that travelling is nothing if it is not a spiritual testing. It is so cruel to its victims precisely because the tune it plays is to the soul, arousing longings that, if not addressed, pitch the ego into despondency. It is thus quite different from Shopping World, which is basically honest, not pretending to be what it is not, and as a result provides pleasures and consolations that tend to be in harmony with its music. The tourist, to amend Bauman, is the cautionary metaphor of contemporary life. The package-tourist is consumerism gone wrong.

Travel, as spiritual testing, is an art, and has to be worked at in the mode of a vocation. Travellers, because they lived, were story-tellers. We are reminded yet again that the Calvinist cultural form of work is the royal road to meaning in the modern West. Lose that path, and you will be condemned to endless laboured wandering over the lone plains of nihilism.

***

In any discussion of consumerism and tourism today, there must be a place for Las Vegas. It is phenomenal—simply extraordinary. It has become the favourite site for American tourists, and increasingly popular, also, for those from the rest of the world.[8] It provides an alternative model to that of the package-tour.

There is a restaurant situated half-way up an imitation Eiffel Tower that highlights the casino named 'Paris Las Vegas'. Inside, it is obvious to tourists that the waiter is an American faking a French accent and French gestures, in accordance with the stereotype familiar to them from television comedians. They like the familiarity. They prefer the fake to the real French waiter they might encounter if they strayed off the tourist track in Paris, France: a waiter whose alien customs and expectations would only make them nervous.

Americans are happier to bring the rest of the world that interests them to the United States, and to radically transform it into forms that suit their own tastes. The giant casinos are modern palaces, built like Cecille B. de Mille Hollywood sets, recreating Paris and Venice, ancient Rome and ancient Egypt; or putting together variants on Disneyland, such as *Treasure Island*, *Excalibur* (for medieval Arthurian pageantry), and *The New Frontier*.

In Las Vegas, there is scale and extravagance, with spectacular recreations—simulated Paris streets with vernacular shops and cafés, set under a vast, painted night sky. Tourists can ride in a gondola, serenaded by tunes from Italian opera, sung in high tenor by a suitably costumed gondolier, on a canal running through the centre of *The Venetian*. Las Vegas succeeds because of a blend: there is enough authenticity and enough familiarity to make the experience exciting, amusing, and yet relaxing. Here, there is little of the obsessional anxiety that swamps the package-tour.

Most who visit are having fun. And the sets, while grandiose, are unpretentious: tourists know that they are all cardboard imitations, and they like it that way. The setting and the mood are playful. Tourists here don't take themselves, or the experience, too seriously. Moreover, the presentation is clean and cheerful. There is little sign for the casual visitor of the dark side of the city: compulsive gambling, strip shows, and prostitution.

Here is popular culture's simulacrum of high culture. In the grandest of all the casinos, *Caesar's Palace*, much is monumental, with little subtlety or fine taste. The modern United States does the ancient Roman Empire well. Yet 'bad taste' would be the wrong description. The hotel rooms at *Caesar's Palace* are tasteful and restrained, in deliberate contrast with the extravaganza outside. *Paris Las Vegas* recreates the ambience of St Germain dès Pres with warmth and some conviction. Here and there, in the main Vegas casinos, there are public spaces and intimate bars designed with flair, high taste, and originality.

The town boasts that, in it, none of the normal rules apply—'what you do in Las Vegas stays in Las Vegas'. The surface meaning alludes to the town's nickname:'Sin City'. The subtler meaning is that here you step out of normal life for a day or a week. The true holiday is a fantasia in which tourism and consumption blend into a cornucopia of entertainment, amusement, wandering around at one's whim, buying, eating, and drinking—all titillated with a little gambling.

Las Vegas shows off the extraordinary inventiveness of American society. In it, Western popular culture is hard at work devising new ways to tour and to consume—ones that defy any easy rush to judgement.

Part Three

# NEW DYNAMISM

Chapter Nine

# DEMOCRACY

In Part I, I explored the four principal battlegrounds across which the struggle for meaning is being fought, largely with success. In Part II, I examined the opposing forces, those of nihilism and consumerism, and their leading battalions. Now, in Part III, I turn to five significant spheres of modern life in which, in quite different ways, there have been strategic gains.

Democracy is one of the main sources of vitality and resilience that has saved modern Western societies from decline. It has successfully resisted the nihilism of high culture, in spite of its own affinity with doctrines of radical freedom. In part, democracy has become a way of life in the modern West. Through it, the majority can impose its will on reluctant elites.

The great nineteenth and early-twentieth-century theorists who foresaw the cultural consequences of the union of nihilism with radical liberalism prophesied a general decline of the West. The most insightful of the pessimists were Tocqueville, Kierkegaard, Nietzsche, Dostoevsky, and Weber. What they predicted has not come to pass, in spite of the fact that segments of modern life do seem to bear out the fear that a decline in religion would lead to a pleasure-centred individualism, lost in the present, with comfort as its one remaining value, and with no deep and binding attachments left, to anyone or to anything.

Key institutions, starting with political and legal ones, have retained an authority and legitimacy that defies the theories of cultural decline. Most Western societies today are, in any realistic historical terms, prosperous, orderly, civil, and relatively free from violence. Weber's projection of a disenchanted, over-bureaucratised world of 'specialists without spirit' has proved, at most, a part-truth. Tocqueville's warning of a 'new despotism', in which restless individuals, swamped by petty desires, cede more and more power to the state, may be traced out as a tendency, but one with powerful counter-movements. The linked fear of 'mass society', with the withering away of all institutions intermediary between the state and a wide scatter of atomised individuals, has also not eventuated.

Secularisation has not had the pervasively dire consequences predicted. The collapse of religion, as a significant check on human temptations and selfishness, has failed to unleash a condition of Hobbesean anarchy in which everything is permitted.

That democracy has retained its vitality needs to be examined at two levels. There is the institutional level—that of parliamentary democracy—and there is democracy as a collective orientation to public life generalised across the society. Parliamentary democracy has achieved a remarkable stability that, if anything, has strengthened during the last century. Its form, pioneered slowly over centuries in England, has spread throughout the West, and has even been adopted in Germany and France, where it finally brought political stability. It is better than Churchill's famous quip allows: 'the worst form of Government except all those other forms that have been tried from time to time.' Parliamentary democracy has something of the essence of a Platonic form.

The popular legitimacy that liberal democracy has attained is illustrated in the Australian case. In the electorate, while there is often widespread discontent with the party in power, and with the character and performance of the prime minister, any move to question the system as a whole receives negligible support. Moves to make minor changes to the Constitution, at referenda, are almost always overwhelmingly rejected. This central pillar of modern society does not shake. It is fitting that the new Parliament House in Canberra, opened in 1988, has become the building in the country that Australians themselves most visit. There is a similarity here to the role that the House of Congress has played in the American national imagination.[1]

Democracy is not just parliament or congress. To proceed with examining its lower reaches takes us into the argument proper, and into questions of what are the factors that make democracy work. The one enduring classic on the subject, Alexis de Tocqueville's two-volume *Democracy in America* (volume 1, 1835; volume 2, 1840), continues to provide most of the cues.

★★★

Robert Putnam, in a study of modern Italy, compared regional governments that prospered in the two decades after 1970—characterised by initiative, development, and municipal order—with those that were inefficient, slothful, and corrupt.[2] He found that what distinguished success from failure was not wealth, levels of education, urbanisation, or the degree of Catholic or communist influence in politics; it was, rather, whether there was a flourishing local culture of choral societies.

It was not that prosperity produced civic associations, but the other way around. In a town in which a significant proportion of the citizens join together in voluntary organisations, they learn the values of trust, reciprocity, and engagement. This builds an active climate of civic responsibility, which flows out into a general attitude that the condition of the community in which we live is our business, not to be left to the state. In such a society, there is an accumulation of 'social capital', which is far more important to long-term wellbeing than the financial type.[3] Putnam argues that the key is 'horizontal collaboration between equals'.[4]

This study gives powerful vindication to the stress that Tocqueville placed on free associations in democracy. Tocqueville argued that such associations, which he observed in abundance in America, served to check the excessive individualism encouraged by democracy—encouraged once the aristocratic bonds of family honour, social hierarchy, and *noblesse oblige* had been loosened. Associations also served to check the power of the central government, and thereby countered fears of a new despotism. Putnam has added a further important consideration: the building-up of civic habits and conscience.

What is democratic about the experience of belonging to clubs, societies, or cooperative ventures? For the active members, it means getting together in a spirit of mutual help to build, maintain, and finance an organisation, thereby ensuring that it works.

In the case of a golf club, there are three main areas of management. There is the maintenance of the course itself—a vast landscape of sculpted nature. This includes the employment of staff, the purchasing of machinery and chemicals and, above all, a constant vigilance over the art of keeping tees, fairways, bunkers, and greens in immaculate condition. Second, there is the planning and running of tournaments. Third, there is the operation of the clubhouse, usually including a bar and eating facilities.

An elected, honorary committee is responsible for all of this, including its financing. The committee reflects the wider membership and, in part, responds to its opinion. In the Australian clubs with which I am familiar, most members have a deep love for their clubs, which means that they take a special and intense interest in how they are run. There is an ever-present communal hubbub of commentary, opinion, praise, and complaint. Usually there is pride, and the immensely rewarding experience, in good times, felt by a group of citizens banding together to work for a club they love, and making improvements that may be enjoyed by others. In the process, an atmosphere of fellowship and bonhomie arises. The annual general meeting is exemplary — as a democratic ideal of citizens gathering together to debate issues of mutual interest, and to reach collective decisions.

It is worth noting that this kind of club follows the same political model, in miniature, as the central government in a parliamentary democracy. An elected executive deals with the practical management, builds up expertise, and is served by a permanently employed secretariat. It reports to the membership, which is analogous to the ordinary members of parliament. Clubs also have constitutions, which specify the responsibilities of committees and members, any breach of which may ultimately be referred to the courts of law.

Civic associations also include businesses, trade unions, schools, local councils, churches, charities, and many others. One and all may provide some of the democratic experience. A small minority, including fanatical religious or ethnic sects, will press in the opposite direction.

The democratic experience transmits standards — of what good management looks like, of efficiency and its benefits, and of the morale and spirit that pervades, say, a good school. These are standards by which to judge other civic bodies. This experience also breeds confidence, and the knowledge that it is not only especially talented people who are capable — a small and remote elite with charismatic gifts, or long and exacting training — but that, to organise most things, it is quite sufficient to have commitment, good will, common sense, and an open mind. By contrast, the production and understanding of high art is not democratic; that is, available to the untutored majority. The world of clubs and societies is.

Theorists of mass society in the 1950s feared that voluntary societies were dying out. This has not happened. The suburbs of the towns and cities of the West remain dotted with small organisations. But, since about 1970, there has been a steady decline in social capital. There has been a general trend, in some areas very strong, for people in the West to socialise less frequently with others, to be less likely to join associations and clubs, and to be less generous in donating money to needy causes. Opinion polling shows that people trust each other considerably less than they did a generation ago. The definitive work on this subject is again by Robert Putnam, in his book *Bowling Alone: the collapse and revival of American community* (2000).

Putnam provides telling data. Between 1973 and 1994, the proportion of Americans who served on a committee of some club or local organisation halved, from 10 per cent to 5 per cent. The attendance at club meetings dropped from a mean of 12 per annum to four. Union membership dropped from 30 per cent of the non-agricultural workforce to 14 per cent. In the same period, the average number of times that Americans entertained others at home dropped from 14 to eight per annum. The amount of time that families spent together declined by a fifth. Outside the home, bowling is America's most popular participant sport: but, while participation has increased, membership of bowling teams has declined precipitously, to a quarter of the figures in the 1960s.[5]

Putnum sums up:

[A]cross a very wide range of activities, the last several decades have witnessed a striking diminution of regular contacts with our friends and neighbours. We spend less time in conversation over meals, we exchange visits less often, we engage less often in leisure activities that encourage casual social interaction, we spend more time watching (admittedly, some of it in the presence of others) and less time doing. We know our neighbours less well, and we see old friends less often. In short, it is not merely 'do good' civic activities that engage us less, but also informal connecting.[6]

Sporting clubs in Australia are subject to the same trend. Club membership in all of the major participant sports — tennis, lawn bowls, cricket, local suburban and country football, and golf — is in decline. The surf life-saving clubs are a rare example of expansion.

Golf is the country's largest participant sport, with the possible exception of fishing and cycling: 8 per cent of the population play it. The sport is also enjoying remarkable success at the highest professional level; in 2007, eleven Australian male golfers were ranked in the top 80 in the world, and two were in the top ten. Geoff Ogilvy won the 2006 US Open — one of the four 'majors', and Carrie Webb was ranked number-one female golfer in the world in 2000. More and more people are playing — in other words, social participation is increasing. Yet club membership has begun a steady decline.[7]

The club golfer is being replaced by the 'social golfer'. Social golfers don't join clubs, preferring to pay fees for each individual round at the public or semi-public courses where they play. This gives them the flexibility of trying a variety of courses. In many parts of Australia, they can now gain access to the best courses. Thirty years ago, they would have been limited to the very inferior standard public course — unchallenging, poorly designed, and scruffily kept.

Golfers in their twenties, thirties, and forties prefer the 'social' mode. This means that clubs are in the process of becoming the preserve of older members. And, in Australia, they have been comparatively weak at attracting juniors: juniors make up only 8 per cent of male golfers and only 3 per cent of female ones.[8] With too few juniors being inducted into the virtues of club culture, and social golfers oblivious to what they are missing, warning bells are ringing. The threat is the loss of club culture altogether.

What, precisely, is in danger of being lost? Golf-club life achieves its zenith in the 'Saturday Comp'. Men and women—in segregated playing groups—subject themselves to four hours of mental and physical toil in the hope of recapturing one of the rare moments of sublime harmony. After this long, masochistic ordeal, most gather in the clubhouse to drink off the pain. For an hour or so, they enjoy the conviviality of shared stories of what might have been, of notable happenings such as the tiger snake on the seventh ladies tee, or Jack's calamitous five-putt on the tenth. The camaraderie climaxes in a spinning-wheel raffle and trophy presentations by the captain—including his own amused, self-deprecatory reflections on the day's absurdities. Whatever the frustrations of the afternoon, members depart in a spirit of exuberant, if weary, wellbeing.

*** 

The first essential characteristic of democracy, noted by Tocqueville, is a flourishing network of free associations. The second is an independent legal system. Institutionalised law counters an inherent contempt for forms. Social order depends, in good part, on established rules of procedure and behaviour: on traditions, customs, and manners. Social forms also serve to protect the weak from exploitation by the powerful. The democratic spirit encourages in individuals a concentration on their own passing pleasures, making them irritated with constraints—in short, hostile to forms.

From a constitution, at one end of the legal spectrum, to the centuries-old accumulation and application of the 'common law' at the other, the body of laws is a powerful form in itself, resistant to major or rapid change. Tocqueville saw lawyers in America as the single remaining aristocracy. Their training and their practice cultivated in them a focus on the past, a working with precedents — with what previous generations in their vocational family had done with similar cases, their interpretations and their judgements, and even their habits of mind. They developed a method of thinking which respects ancestors and their wisdom. They were the single body in a democracy free from the fashions and impulses of the moment. In fact, to this day, the practice of the English common-law tradition is to judge acts in the present in terms of universal laws codified, interpreted, and applied by generations of learned predecessors.

The argument may be taken further, by drawing on Walter Bagehot's observation that a main function of the monarchy in the English Constitution is to provide dignity, with an authority aloof from the affairs of the day, shrouded in some mystery.[9] Judges, in heavy black gowns and wigs, sitting high above their courts, the individual virtually faceless and subordinate to his or her role and its forms, give to the proceedings a sense of the majesty and gravity of the law, and the cool, impersonal objectivity of justice. So does the sight of similarly dressed barristers consulting thick, leather-bound tomes of statutes and cases. It was a mistake, I think, for American lawyers to democratise the forms of dress in their courts.

Nearly two centuries on from Tocqueville, we have grounds to be even more concerned that the judiciary remain independent of government, and true to its own conservative traditions. The need to have the highest court in the land (whether it is the Supreme Court in the United States, the Privy Council in Britain, or the High Court in Australia) act as a defender of the Constitution and, above all, of the people against illegitimate seizures of power by government, is greater today — simply because the reach of the state has extended.

There is also special importance in the judiciary as a whole retaining its prestige and authority, as an anchoring symbol of stable forms and universal laws, in the context of a wider culture that has sceptical and relativist inclinations. As Tocqueville predicted, the radical liberal view (which he identified with 'equality' rather than 'liberty') vies for ascendancy.[10]

The judiciary is also a check on the tendency in modern thought to redefine crime and transgression in medical terms. The criminal courts still treat crime as crime, judge it by the law, and hand down punishments. There remains high public interest in serious crime, and concern that there be appropriate punishment for it. This interest demonstrates that the instincts of the average citizen are anti-relativist; it reflects the need in every human community for a steady dialogue on morality. The legal system, with the judiciary at its apex, provides a stable context for this vital human activity.

There are threatening signs, though. The highest judicial offices, notably in the United States, became more politicised in the latter half of the twentieth century, with campaigns run for and against candidates.[11] To have the best proven legal mind is no longer the single criterion for appointment. The courts themselves are straying into making law, rather than merely interpreting it. High Court judgements in Australia have even cited the need to take account of contemporary public opinion, implying that a part of the justices' role now is that of legal reform. Some top lawyers are becoming celebrities, because of star performances, at huge fees, in highly publicised trials. In Tocqueville's terms, we are witnessing here signs of the democratic destruction of the judiciary, with the dignity of the lawyer sliding towards that of the used-car-salesman.

***

The third of Tocqueville's institutions that save democracy from itself is a free press (which we would now call 'free media'). The press checks the state. In its capacity to investigate and expose corruption and bad management, it influences public opinion to force reform, or to change the government. It can also help protect the individual from injustice at the hands of any group or institution. An example is the television program that investigates investment fraud, defective products, and crooked builders.

The press has become the main communal organ for moral discourse. Newspapers have swung their main focus from news to opinion. Talk-back radio and television chat-shows cater, in part, to a similar need. From the great public issues of the time, to the petty challenges of everyday life, there is discussion of what is right and wrong. In a time in which the grey area between incontestable goodness and serious crime and transgression has spread, when there is less surety about right conduct, this open forum for the canvassing of practical ethics has come to fulfil a vital democratic function.

A related service is the airing of public-policy options, such as where to build a new airport or freeway, whether to increase immigration, or at what level to pitch welfare payments. The press reports the issues, provides a range of its own opinions, including in editorials, opens space to experts and interested citizens and, through letters pages and talk-back radio, allows a further opportunity for debate. Politics is, in part, informed by the press.

Politicians increasingly test public opinion on talkback radio, where they engage in direct discussion with citizens who ring in. This is one way in which they can get a feel for which issues are hotly topical, and for the drift of majority opinion. What we are witnessing here is the creative adaptability and vitality of liberal democracy.[12] A new civil sphere is being built. Old forms of political participation are in decline — membership of political parties, attendance at party conferences, and the holding of public meetings. Concurrently, new ones are emerging.

Public opinion is powerfully influenced by the press. Tocqueville warned that a weakness of democracy is that the desire to be equal, and free, breeds uniformity. In aristocracies, individuals were more confident and varied in their character and views. Democracy fosters an insecurity that makes its citizens more dependent on a communal consensus, and more vulnerable to fashionable opinion. This gives the press an influence with high potential civic costs. It can easily become an unwitting ally of a strong central state, contributing to an oligarchy of power and culture. Here is the new despotism feared by Tocqueville, rooted in tyranny by the majority.

While the free press is crucial to the wellbeing of democracy, it has shown signs of losing the sense of responsibility that is necessary if it is to curb its own potential excesses. The popular press has applied the sound values of the lower middle class to stories of crime and misfortune. At the same time, it has been vulnerable to the vices of prurience and sensationalism. The British tabloid newspapers, in the latter decades of the twentieth century, dropped most scruples in their reporting of the royal family, and thereby played a key role in undermining the dignity and authority of that central political institution. Moreover, their own immorality of practice—in the fabrication of stories, the deliberate whipping-up of public hysteria, and gross invasions of privacy—has catered to the lowest democratic vices of salaciousness, titillation, petty righteousness, and rancour against the privileged.

During the 1990s, the American press exploited the past private life of president Clinton with relentless vigour, abandoning its own traditions of judging public figures by their public acts, oblivious to the damage that it caused to the authority of the highest political office in the country. The press seemed driven to prove that it was more powerful than the president—free to use any means to create and apply a new public morality and, at the same time, to satisfy the prurience of its audience. It is as if it ran the ancient Roman

Coliseum, with the climax of the show taking place when it tossed the emperor to the lions.

The moral is obvious. On the one hand, the press is vital to democracy. On the other, it is vulnerable to the temptations of power, to turning itself into a vain and wilful potentate, hostile to criticism, with a sweet tooth for causing political anarchy. In Tocqueville's terms, its respect for forms is shaky.

The outside checks on the press are weak. The defamation laws are of value for ordinary citizens, but they were of no use to the English royal family, or to president Clinton. There is competition, with rival newspapers exposing each other's lack of veracity, but this seems more to entertain journalists than to inhibit malpractice. Overall, the only constraint likely to work is an ethic of responsibility in the press itself: a vivid-enough sense of its own public duty to restrain the temptation to show off its power to topple kings, and to resist the money that can be made in the scoop-reporting of scandal. This depends on journalists with a sense of the gravity of their vocation. We are back to Thesis Four: the central role in the modern West of vocation informed by individual conscience.

The rise of the Internet will see seismic shifts in the democratic role of the media. Newspapers, and especially the broadsheets, are undergoing a steady decline in their sales and influence. Media consumers are becoming more fragmented. But a democracy needs independent information, investigative journalism, a range of opinion (some of it informed and expert), outlets for public comment, and widely shared sites of news. These needs will drive the new media to satisfy them.

★★★

One defender of forms not recognised by Tocqueville is popular culture. Its main expressions are through television, the 'non-quality' press (including magazines), sport, popular music, and the bric-a-brac of consumerism. Its locus is the home; its values are domestic, conservative, and sentimental. Tocqueville had observed that the home is the centre of order in a democracy, and that the ownership of private property is a major stabilising factor.

The nineteenth-century cultural pessimists had predicted that the Death of God would lead to cultural nihilism and institutional anarchy. The empirical fact is that a further century of secularisation, during which the various churches have become marginal to Western life and belief, has not ushered in the sort of political chaos portrayed by Dostoevsky in his novel *The Possessed*, nor that intimated by Max Weber in his 1918 lecture 'Politics as a Vocation.'[13] In part, this is due to the enduring character and influence of popular culture.

Moreover, there have been exceptions to the general rule about modern high culture, some of which have contributed to democracy. Science does not fit the Death-of-God model: it has continued to produce work, both inside and outside the universities, of the first rank—its procedures, innovations, and morale not the lesser than in its great past epochs. The continuing success of capitalism as an economic system depends on scientific discovery and technological innovation.

There are also disciplines within the humanities that have retained a seriousness and professionalism that contributes to the management of a democracy—the study of international relations, political economy, and the theory of the state, and some areas of history and sociology. It may be that disciplines which grapple with practical politics at close hand are subjected to a reality principle that saves them from becoming too abstract, fanciful, doctrinaire, or pedantic; and that discriminates in favour of those whose analysis and judgement are vindicated by what actually happens.

Tocqueville saw religion as essential to democracy. He argued that only faith in a metaphysical order could lift the mind of democratic individuals above material self-interest, saving them from a restless existence buffeted by petty desires and instant gratifications. Religion was necessary to provide some long-term vision, and insulation from current pains, making possible a calm concentration on achieving great and permanent designs. Prosperity depends on such non-material aims.

What Tocqueville identified with religion has not been satisfied by church membership, which has shrunk in all Western countries, with the partial exception of the United States, to that of a very small minority.[14] It has rather been satisfied by individual conscience tutored by everyday experience, illustrated in popular culture, and reinforced by various communities—the most important of which, by far, is the family. Tocqueville, like the extreme cultural pessimists, had too little confidence in human nature, in its instinctive law-abiding, order-craving proclivities—its innate respect for forms.

Democracy facilitates the living-out of this unconscious sense of law, thus giving it greater visibility and authority. The best civil education—which clubs and societies provide—is the opportunity to act as a citizen. Indeed, the more conventional form of civics classes are usually counterproductive, casting a pall of dullness over images of polity and nation; a case in which proper teaching does not belong in the school-room or the academy. A rare exception to this rule is the gifted teacher who introduces senior pupils to, say, Shakespeare's *Richard II*, a play in which deep political issues are projected with mythic resonance. Once upon a time, the West had a high culture that believed in doing precisely this.

At a practical level, universal respect is felt for a job well done, and reciprocal contempt for shoddy workmanship. The spear that does not fly truly, the new roof that leaks, or the jumbled memorandum all draw our condemnation, for we feel that a law has been broken. The English language puts it beautifully: one has to 'do a job justice'. For justice—that is, law—is at stake. Experience in clubs and societies brings with it a realism of judgements about the larger political stage: high offices have their own laws; poor management lowers such offices; and something needs to be done to remedy civic transgression. It brings with it a feeling of responsibility for public forms.

★★★

There is a range of virtues that may be called democratic—in that they are cultivated in a society in which there is not too much social distance, and there exists the possibility of mobility up and down a hierarchy that is not too vertical. They include consideration for the rights of others, whatever their station, which is a practical working-out of the Kantian injunction to treat all human individuals as an ends in themselves, not as a means to an end—and to so act as you would judge anyone else in your situation should act. Linked to this are a tolerance of diversity, an inclination towards inclusiveness, a sense of fair play, of equality before the law, of appointment by merit, and a basic, humane provision of welfare for the underprivileged. This democratic ethos is guarded by an independent judiciary, a free press and, above all, the practical experience of cooperative associations.

Democracy has produced societies in which individuals have less to fear than their ancestors, or than those who live under different political orders. They are free from the fear of poverty, due to capitalist prosperity; and they are free from the fear of persecution by those in power. As a consequence, they are freer to practice a universal moral code.

Democracy, in its complete modern form, hinges on the moral principle that all humans are equal, irrespective of race, creed, age, sex, station, or physical and mental capacity. They all have universal rights, which means that there is a standard of justice—with particular tenets such as not striking another without due cause — which is timeless and valid across culture. Furthermore, these rights override every other attachment and creed.

While the generative source of this view was the Gospels — 'love thy neighbour as thyself' and the 'do as ye would be done by' which Kant was to take up — it sits awkwardly with the exclusivity of church Christianity. In fact, it was only with the eighteenth-century European Enlightenment that the belief in universal rights began to take political hold, and it was only during the second half of the twentieth century that it became orthodoxy in the West. It is this historical development that makes Thesis Three possible — holding that the crisis of meaning in the modern West is an issue of culture, not of morals.

The doctrine of universal rights has conquered, at least for the moment, the tribalism that held sway in virtually every previous human society. Attachment to it is precarious, depending on the conscience of the individual, under the countervailing pressure of ties of blood and prejudice. The knowledge that justice is a categorical imperative is constantly under threat. After all, it was in Kant's own country that the most barbaric Western tribalism broke out, legitimating a virulent and triumphal anti-Semitism which swept through almost the entire population.[15] This episode hangs over the head of the modern West, an ever-present spur to keep the democratic system and temper strong. Here is a domain in which individual conscience needs reinforcement from the collective conscience, as long as it is a democratic one.

This is particularly the case with the lower middle class and its popular culture. For all its strengths, whenever it feels its life-forms under threat — whether due to economic insecurity, rapid cultural change, or war — it tends to retreat into xenophobic hostility towards those who are different. It has its own tribal fundamentalism: a narrow creed of us, our own, and what we believe.

The importance of democracy is to encourage public discourse, and the sense of equality and inclusion that binds the lower-middle-class ethos. Properly functioning democracy checks prejudice by appealing to popular culture's better instincts — its respect for fairplay, tolerance, and the rights of others. Democratic vehicles of expression — especially television — have a unique ability to put the individual in the shoes of others, however different they are, to experience their humanity sympathetically.

Democracy plays an important fortifying role in all of the principal battlegrounds. There is a mutually supporting affinity with sport, as anyone with the right attitude and discipline may join in. In the modern West, discussion of sport has increasingly cut across race, class, age, and sex barriers and, indeed, shows signs of becoming the common language. Sport has provided one of the main avenues for underprivileged minorities to successfully integrate — for example, African Americans in the United States, and Aborigines in Australia. And some sports, like Australian Rules football, have played a pioneering role in attacking racial prejudice.

Sport has also played a decisive role in democratising clothing fashions: it is so powerful that it has even conquered Parisian *haute couture* with the mode of the casual and out-of-door. As Lipovetsky puts it, women now dress to be modern, not classy.[16] In the modern democracy, you are not judged primarily by wealth, status, or style, but by your own individual self and its fitness, by your incarnation of the Calvinist ethic as sublimated through sport and its satellites. Furthermore, the very existence of a large sporting crowd — of, say, one hundred thousand people of all ages, and from all walks of life, packed in at very close quarters, moved to extremes of euphoria, anger, and despair, in a peaceful and orderly assembly for mutual enjoyment — stands in itself as a great democratic achievement.

Sport serves to check the democratic tendency to over-generalise equality. That people are equal before the law, and that they may associate cooperatively with success, does not imply that they have the same abilities, nor that hierarchies may be entirely done away with. Every sport is an anti-relativist lesson in ranking. It focuses attention on who is the better player, on which is the better team. An individual who plays for the thirds is simply and categorically not as good as one who plays for the firsts. Sport amplifies the Platonic law that people have their different places in a hierarchy, suited to their temperament and talents, and that they should accept this fact, for their own wellbeing and for the larger good of their society.

Work, too, shares interests with democracy. The choral society and the golf club are conducted along work lines—just as, historically, artisan groups were active in seventeenth-century English-revolutionary moves to make parliament more democratic. *Work* breeds an independence of mind and spirit and, with it, an intolerance of despotism, and a natural inclination towards democracy. Indeed, Rousseau based his theory of the ideal polity of self-governing equals on his observation of a Swiss village of watchmakers.

A work culture is a necessary check on the democratic vice of stressing rights at the expense of responsibilities. In its rigorous accent on individual conscience as the sole ultimate authority, it makes everybody responsible for whatever happens in their political environment. The major threat in democracy is that the liberal rhetoric of freedom gains over the Calvinist conscience, and that the insecure ego is freed to scream like the spoilt child, *Me ... me ... me*—the unhappy conjunction of liberty and consumerism.

The domain of love requires a degree of autonomy from the public sphere, so that individual beings are left alone to live how they please. Again, it is democracy that best allows this freedom from political interference, which used to come, in the monarchical or aristocratic past, in the form of controls over behaviour and belief mobilised by a powerful social and clerical elite.

Democracy permits almost total privacy, as long as the citizen obeys the law when out in public. It has even questioned its own enforcement of universal rights in the private domain. It has become a genuine question as to whether, for instance, parents should be permitted to smack their young children. Should the authority and judgement of the family be respected, or should the wider collectivity attribute a dissenting individual conscience to the minor?

Democracy in the broad, from parliament or congress to local associations, with a free press, an independent judiciary, a flourishing popular culture, and a respect for universal rights can create an ideal balance of involvement and delegation, of trusting elected representatives with power, and yet being able to check them. This order depends on a sizeable minority taking on the active role of a citizen. It is a different order from that governing a hierarchical society, which may have its own strengths, but is notably vulnerable to weakness and corruption in the ruling class.

We have observed threats to democracy in all of its constitutive elements. Levels of sociability and communal engagement have been declining for several decades—social capital is diminishing. In both the legal profession and the free press there are signs of a weakening sense of the professional responsibility that is vital to their integrity. Popular culture plunges, at times, into tribal prejudice.

On the other hand, democracy encourages self-correcting mechanisms. When institutions that are vital to its wellbeing lose balance, public opinion intervenes. A press that is narrow or biased in its reporting of important events stimulates new media—in recent times, this has come to include blogs and freelance news-and-opinion websites. When judges without merit are appointed, their flawed judgements are checked by being overturned in courts of appeal, and publicly shamed in the press. The weakening of political associations—declining party and trade-union membership—has been balanced by the increasing political influence of public opinion through blogs and talk-back radio.

The vitality of democracy lies in good part in its capacity to engender a civic consciousness of its own forms. The key to its future lies here. The radical liberal decadence that has grown in Western elites would have been far more corrosive of the polity, and of other central institutions, as predicted by the cultural pessimists, had it not been for democracy.

Chapter Ten

# THE MOTOR CAR

The motor car has changed the world. Since World War II, it has transformed how people live, and the spaces in which they dwell and move. The 'dream machine' has given families unprecedented mobility, freed up teenage sex, revolutionised tourism, and opened up new opportunities for work, friendship, and leisure. It has made travel a common part of everyday life.

The modern city is relentlessly and continuously reconfigured to suit the car. Freeways have cut swathes through suburbs and parks, swept over neighbourhoods, and tunnelled under rivers. Drive-in shopping centres, service stations, and motels have come to dot the urban landscape. 'A visitor from a different planet would have no trouble in describing the car as the central feature of an almost universal religion.'[1]

That cars pollute the air, fill cities with noise, and carve up suburbs, and that they maim and kill a significant proportion of those who use them—all of this is quite clear. It is also a commonplace that some male owners project onto their beloved machines their unfulfilled ambitions of power, adventure, and even of sexual release, expressing their frustrated egos on the road.

Less well recognised is quite a different development. The main opportunity for most people to demonstrate mature citizenship comes with the driving of a motor car. Democracy and the car move forward hand in hand.

When people buy a car, they gain a range of powers. They have gained mobility: they can travel farther, faster, by their own routes, and when they choose. They have gained access to remote landscapes, to golf clubs, and to the houses of all their acquaintances who live within a couple of hundred kilometres. They have also gained access, in the quite-distinct moral sphere, to the major social arena in which they will be tested against public laws, and the judgement of their fellow citizens.

Modern citizens are never less self-conscious in their obedience, never less hesitant in their responses, than when faced by a red traffic-light. Automatically, they stop. The same holds for much of the traffic code. Driving becomes a ritualised sequence of responses to an almost entirely predictable sequence of events, governed by a set of laws and conventions that are so well internalised by drivers that they are second nature.

Out in public, driving, modern citizens are unwittingly soothing all those latent fears that they are alone, disconnected from other people, from other groups, and even from their own purposes. They have introduced themselves into a central social ritual, as surely and with as much faith as their ancestors stood humbly in churches singing hymns. They have relaxed in the sea of social life, and now alternately swim and drift with the ebb and flow of its currents—no longer fighting against it, no longer in fear of sinking or of having to flee to the beach. They are in harmony with their community and its collective conscience, cooperating, understanding intuitively the movement of things—moving with them, being part of that movement—recognised, and respected as such. In a modest and covert way, they belong; and, through such belonging, they find that their lives a little more meaningful.

Today, the village green is asphalted; shopping centres are of Coliseum size and anonymity; politics is conducted at a great distance, and by inscrutable giant bureaucracies; and privacies are guarded by the family home. The main experience that people have of being out in public in an active communal way — in other words, in the great classical sense of the term — is driving on the roads. Here, their society as a collectivity is alive for them, with a real tension existing between themselves, others, and the legal code.

The fact that fellow drivers will, in their own ways, assert that code, if it is infringed, further illustrates communal vitality in this sphere of its life. It is not merely state bureaucracies that serve as the watchdogs of motoring conduct. The car-horn is a weapon for expressing an opinion, for voicing a public judgement.

Driving is action. The routine motor-activity of working pedals and steering is cathartic and, linked with the concentration required, draws drivers out of introspection and indecision. Certainly, if they drive well, they will day-dream at the wheel and rely on their trained reflexes. But light daydreaming is quite different from nervous introspection — on the road, it gains the rhythmical quality of reverie.

At the wheel, the world is ordered. Decisions are made according to specific rules and reasonably exact predictions. There is an informal science at work here, one that includes knowledge of the car's performance: how quickly it can stop, how well it corners, its capacity to overtake if necessary. Drivers have to gauge the different factors influencing the situation they are in.

Driving is a ritual that requires the exercise of active responsibility. It is an experience of risk, of the testing of competence. To be proved able is satisfying. The more capable the driver, the more relaxed he or she is, and the more the automatic ritualistic routines in the experience predominate. The skill of drivers is something like the courage of soldiers: most of the time it lies dormant, as routine processes are followed. Then it is needed, at an instant's notice, and it is decisive. In driving, responsibility depends on competence, and it is the duty of those who lack the ability or the temperament for this civic ritual to renounce the wheel.

Families find it difficult to suggest to their aged kin that they ought, for the safety of all, to retire from driving. This would be tantamount to depriving them of their citizenship. That such a fundamental notion is involved is confirmed by the fact that, at the other threshold of maturity, modern youth attaches far more importance to reaching the driver's licence age than on becoming old enough to vote. Young boys play at driving cars. Those who lose their licence, because of dangerous or drunken driving, feel they have been deprived of one of their key rights. They have been rendered immobile—physically and psychologically. Even back in the 1920s, Robert and Helen Lynd, in their classic study *Middletown*, reported that the average American was asserting that he would go without food rather than give up his car.[2]

Over the years, the automobile has undergone a certain demotion in the palace of consumption, as indicated by the car industry having lost its glamour, first to plastics and television, and then to information technology, and by the fact that consumers are more likely to spend their marginal dollars on new electronic gadgetry, air travel, or dining out. In recent times, it has been hit harder by the rising cost of petrol.

Yet while the motor car may have lost its monopoly as the emblem of consumerism, it has retained its importance in modern life. From the VIP Rolls Royce to the contemporary limousine, it serves as a leading signifier of status, wealth, and power. The limo masquerades as the royal carriage in lavish contemporary wedding rituals, especially among the lower middle class. More importantly, the car satisfies genuine human needs.

The car remains, apart from the house or apartment, the largest expenditure item for most families. It is needed, first of all, because it provides mobility in the consumer society—a society that has mobility as part of its essence (apart from the rare exceptions of environments less dependent on the motor car, such as the central areas of old cities like Paris and Florence). Those who do not drive remove themselves one significant pace from the social world in which they live, and on which they are dependent for work, for regular supplies of food, clothing, and shelter, and for culture in its widest sense. The car is crucial to the versatility of consumption. And, as we have seen, consumption has become the means through which fantasies are stimulated, and wishes induced.

In this guise, the car is at the service of *freedom*—for good and for bad. On the one hand, it is an aid to conscience, the means by which friends may be visited, work and sport may be facilitated, and lakes, oceans, and mountains may be sought out for their timeless serenity. On the other, it can become the vehicle of rootlessness, of avoiding sitting still, dwelling, and concentrating.

Most consumer items are bought for the house, for the enjoyment of privacy from society at large. The car fulfils a similar and yet different function, extending the virtues of the home out into public. It offers comfort and isolation from others, compared, above all, with buses and trains. In this, it is antisocial. Yet it takes consumption beyond a self-contained egoism into the realm of morals, thereby giving it a dignity, and attaching it to a deeper, more troubling, and more absorbing level of the human condition. As passive consumers, modern individuals are granted no more responsibility than a child; their freedom is restricted to asking for more, or for this rather than that. As the possessors and drivers of a motor car, they find themselves treated as adults.

There is a further dimension of a truly democratic society that is preserved on the road. Drivers form a community of equals. They have equal rights, and they are equal before the law as practised—unlike some other areas of justice in which wealth provides an undeniable advantage, buying access to the best legal representation.

On the road, individual responsibility is not token. This may be important psychologically as well as morally. Drivers may experience the most significant other parts of their lives, whether in their offices or at home in their families, as a subordinate, or a superordinate. The road then provides the balance of a longed-for responsibility, or a salutary constraint of their power. Here again, car-culture serves as an important practical model for a democratic society.

The decline of respect for the authority of individual public figures, whether bishops, business heads, or civic and political leaders, and the complementary increased power of institutions, particularly large corporations and governments, has been accompanied by the social and psychological importance gained by consumption. The motor car is a bulwark against the dimension of passivity that threatens to follow these developments.

In the case of public transport, one of the signs of the presence of the maternal state, in caring for its child dependants, is the safety of the transport it provides. Private transport has always been dangerous—from the horse, or the horse and carriage, to the automobile. Ironically, it may be a mistake of the advocates of public transport to stress safety. To take a risk requires a kind of individual choice; and in a world that overvalues comfort, it may be necessary to keep alive the choice to be reckless, and to retain the motor car not only as a vehicle for exercising personal responsibility, but also as one for experiencing adventure.

Offering a type of adventure, the motor car is violent. Whatever images may recur in modern nightmares, the real contact that individuals have with objects and situations powerful enough to maim them will almost entirely involve motor cars. They may turn pale when their jumbo jet takes off, or swim with trepidation because of the thought of sharks. But if they die violently, it will almost certainly be in a car. If they see seriously injured bodies in the flesh, it will be near car wreckage that is strewn across a highway. If they are tortured by loud noises or dense fumes, these will surely emanate from motor vehicles. As a consequence, the important civic discussion of how, and in which situations, the law and its agents ought to protect citizens against violence ought to take a special interest in automobile traffic and its movement.

Cars have been made safer than they were. They are better engineered, and the innovation of seatbelts, airbags, and ABS-braking has reduced the risk of accidents and of serious injury to those involved in accidents. Police breath-testing for alcohol and drugs, and more severe penalties for dangerous driving, have also contributed to reducing the toll of road accidents. Hoons have their cars impounded. Nevertheless, this is risk-reduction at the margins, and does not change the fundamental car-culture.

Drivers imagine that they are insulated from the potential violence that surrounds them. Their car shields them, and this shielding is one of the factors contributing to the relaxation that they experience at the wheel, in their air-conditioned cabin, listening to music. A sudden blow from the side is utterly unexpected, like a sharp knock in the middle of the back when walking along the footpath. Peace of mind is shattered; personal space has been violated.

But the shock is not simply that of one individual intruding upon another. Suddenly, the driver is really in public, and something has gone wrong. In fact, a crime may have been committed, and they find that they have to leave their car where it is, awkwardly placed in the middle of the road, blocking traffic. They have to get out of their cocoon to face the other driver. They see themselves becoming the centre of a public event, surrounded by spectators and the growing number of irate drivers who are being held up, some of them eager to intrude their judgements of the accident. As the panic intensifies, they have to calm themselves and think quickly. *Was I in the wrong, wholly or partly? What should my approach be? Don't I need witnesses? Should I call the police? I had better first examine the damage. I really am going to be late.*

The anxiety over lateness cloaks the real source of unrest—that their so-comfortable, so smoothly running, ritual has been exploded. It is like waking from a deep and very peaceful sleep to face an interrogation, instantly in need of all your wits. Moreover, this public event is highly unpredictable. *Will the other driver be aggressive? Is he drunk? Will he have insurance?* Someone has been irresponsible. Maybe they were both partly to blame. All drivers are at times lazy, careless, impetuous, off their guard. *Now I have been selected as the one to suffer, the one to be punished.* To possess a motor car means, inevitably, to become a law-breaker during a driving career.

The worries pile one on top of the other, in the seconds that tick by as the drivers collect themselves to get out of their cars. They step out into the public spotlight that is turned on a crime which so many passers-by identify with; but for the grace of God, they themselves would have been in the same predicament many times. As a corollary to the linking of violence with automobiles, it may be that the crowds which form around an accident are the modern equivalent of the masses that used to be drawn to watch public hangings.

For some, a dent is punishment enough for a lapse on the road: the car's perfect surface has been flawed, thus atoning for the black streak across the driver's virtue. These are the happy ones, those sane enough to recognise that, because of their own mistake, or bad luck, a price has to be paid—but a price that, like the dent, is easily repaired, and then may be forgotten.

For others, ego is much more deeply involved: punishment

comes in a severe and inscrutable form as intensified guilt, flowing from the suspicion that there was a moment in which the driver's self-control must have weakened, resulting in violence. The damage done to the car is like the body being disfigured—here is the punishment in the bruising, puffy skin, and the loss of shape. The panel-beater becomes a substitute for the plastic surgeon who has the expertise to repair the driver's own flaws.

For such drivers, the sense of guilt commands them to exercise much more control in the future—or else some catastrophe will result. It attacks their sense of their own competence, of their worthiness to pretend to be mature citizens. It makes them more hesitant, more indecisive, and less controlled on the roads. It may induce a trough of depression.

The moral centrality of the car, its potential violence, and the responsibility or irresponsibility with which it is handled, are themes that converge in the question of automobile suicide. Some doctors in Houston, Texas, conducted 'psychological autopsies' on people killed in crashes, and concluded that one in seven road deaths should properly be called suicide. This would mean that one-quarter of American suicides are carried out on the roads.[3]

Without taking these figures literally, there is little reason to doubt their implications. It would be surprising if some of those drawn towards the ultimate act of violence did not find themselves tempted by the sphere of modern life in which the ordinary citizen has power—instant power. This is taking to a grotesque and tragic extreme the boast of Harley Earl, General Motors' first stylist: 'You can design a car so that every time you get in it, it's a relief.'[4] Suicidal depression can be metamorphosed into an act of bravado. In a carefree, careless fit, they who have lost the will to live can hurtle along a highway, testing how much fate is on their side: whether or not it is intended that they survive.

The act, from every point of view other than that of the driver, is damningly irresponsible. How many innocent victims are created by all those automobile suicides? Leaving aside brutal and deliberate crime, there is hardly anyone more deserving of the condemnation of modern society than reckless drivers. Caring little for themselves, they are careless towards others. Their action contravenes the first liberal-democratic principle: everyone is free, as long as their freedom does not intrude on that of someone else.

Yet the very fact that reckless drivers are allowed the means to be so effectively irresponsible is one of Western society's great remaining freedoms—a real one, in contrast with many illusory liberties. If these drivers were restricted to trains, or to some futuristic compromise such as an electronically controlled bubble car, there would be one less sphere of social life in which they found themselves thrust together with their fellow citizens in situations in which their own authority counted for something. For individual liberty to be a reality, there must exist situations in which that liberty is in peril, and even withdrawn by free individuals.

This chapter has argued that we have come to belong to an automobile culture in a more profound sense than we commonly recognise. Even so, I have disregarded some aspects of car-culture. There is the image of the car salesman as the businessman that Westerners most distrust; there is the role that the car came to play in teenage courting; there is the adoring care that some young men lavish on their dream machine; and there is the rise of 'road rage', and the question of whether it is a symptom of a general decline in public civility.

I have also bypassed the automobile's contribution to the uniformity, rootlessness, and anonymity of modern life. On the other side of the judgement scales, I have left unmentioned the contribution it has made to family life, confirming the nuclear family as the fundamental social unit in modern society, offsetting some of that society's incipient individualism.

Marshall McLuhan is one who prophesied the demise of the car.[5] More recent predictions of its end have usually centred on traffic congestion, pollution, and oil dependency. Modern cities like Los Angeles are becoming choked-up with traffic. Congestion gets progressively worse, travel-time longer, grid-locked freeway systems more common. There is a space limit to how far old freeways may be widened, and how many new ones can be built. Car-culture as it exists now cannot expand for ever.

But is this true? People love their cars; they love to travel by car. If oil becomes scarce or prohibitively expensive, capitalism will quickly engineer cars powered by other forms of energy. The pollution emanating from petrol and diesel engines is being steadily reduced. The average car may become much smaller, as in Europe. If Los Angeles becomes so clogged up with traffic that its citizens revolt, it is more likely that the car will win, stopping the expansion of the city—rather than that alternative train, tram, and bus networks will develop. Satellite towns will then rise around Los Angeles, connected by multi-lane fast freeways. This is already happening.

And love for the car is complemented by the deeper fact that it has become, to modern consumers, one of the most vital, effective elements in their struggle to keep their liberty intact.

## Chapter Eleven

# THE DO-IT-YOURSELF HOME

This book is about the quest for meaning. The search centres on the individual. Inevitably, it orbits around the question of *being*. 'What should I do with my life?' is inextricably tied in with, 'Who am I?' and 'What is the essence of my self?'

The *doing* question, 'What should I do?' is directed by the *being* question, 'Who am I?' Doing is a projection of being; reciprocally, being may be glimpsed through doing. In relation to the theme of vocation, when the waitress puts the fork down 'just right', she has found a method of being at ease in herself; in a way, she has found herself. Dr Cartwright discovers that by doing what she has to do, as a doctor, she sheds her old skin of disenchanted cynicism. She becomes such a forceful centre of what it is to be human that a charisma of being emanates from her, charging those in her vicinity. The footballer who strikes form finds himself in an inspired and exalted state of self-possession. Michael Crichton, as a traveller, puts it literally, 'I go to some distant region of the world to be reminded of who I really am.'

The quest for the deeper *I* shadows much of modern activity. As an example, let's consider a relatively new and fast-growing activity:

Do-It-Yourself home building and renovation.

The Australian indicators are striking. In a city newsagency, about 200 different magazines are for sale that relate directly or indirectly to DIY—from the TV-show-linked *Better Homes and Gardens*, through *Australian House and Garden* and *Australian Home Beautiful*, to the international *Marie Claire Home* and *Vogue Home*, to *Real Living* and *Family Handyman*. They include traditional magazines featuring architectural and interior design; ideas for home beautification, from décor to furniture; and a specialist focus on kitchens, bathrooms, and gardens. All of these feed into designing the home as the reader wants it. The traditional hardware-shop catering to the home handyman has expanded into a major industry serviced by DIY megastores—led in Australia by Bunnings Warehouse.[1] Around a million magazines in the specific DIY category sell monthly, engaging 5 per cent of the total population. The free-to-air TV DIY show *Better Homes and Gardens* rates in the top ten regularly, drawing an audience of 1.5 million.

***

It all starts with the child decorating its own room. This is 'my space', with images of favourite things on the walls, and favourite toys, books, dolls, and teddy bears in their set places. Children can be fussy about where things belong.

Let us take the example of a newly married couple who have just bought their first home. All they can afford is a shabby, unrenovated house with a 1950s' room layout. The main structural problem is the rear section, which should open out onto a veranda extending into a potentially large and charming garden. But it is an ugly clutter—it comprises a small, poky bathroom, an undersized kitchen, and an awkward L-shaped living room.

The couple make their plans. They watch *Better Homes and*

*Gardens* with religious devotion; they buy DIY magazines. They visit showrooms, and tour model homes on new housing estates. He begins to haunt DIY shops, and slowly assembles an array of tools. He benefits from prices that are unprecedentedly low, due to Chinese mass production. The cheapness of DIY tools seems to move in inverse proportion to the expense of hiring tradesmen.

Soon after moving in, they assault the house's bad cosmetics. At weekends, they repaint the two bedrooms and the study, one by one. This is not as simple as they assumed: they learn through trial and error, consulting interior décor magazines, and using sample colours from the local paint shop until they get colour schemes they like.

They discover that, under the grubby and mite-infested wall-to-wall carpet, there is hardboard flooring. The carpet is ripped out and, with it, the foul and dusty underfelt—the lot dumped down the back of the garden. With hammer, chisel, and pliers they remove the strips of plywood and tacks around the wall edges that have held the carpet down. After advice from more knowledgeable friends, they decide that they can get away without sanding the floor-boards. So they simply paint on two coats of heavy varnish with walnut stain mixed in.

They have enough furniture, some good pieces given to them by family members, and some adequate ones—the latter they will slowly replace over time, as they can afford it. All that remains is light fittings: they will dive into second-hand shops over the next six months to find 1920s' art-deco replacements that suit their three very pleasing, stylish new rooms.

Meanwhile, they have been rethinking the back of the house. What to do becomes obvious: it needs gutting. They can save money by keeping the kitchen sink, stove, and cupboards for the time being. The back wall needs opening up with a lintel across three-quarters of its width, and new French doors in the centre flanked by floor-to-ceiling plate-glass windows. A new bathroom needs building internally, opposite the study. This will leave a large, almost square general living area, including an open kitchen.

The big question is how much of it they can do on their own. The more they can do themselves, the more money they will save, and the more extensive the renovations they can afford. After broad consultation, they conclude that they need tradesmen for the electrical wiring, the structural plumbing in the bathroom, and the constructing and plastering of the new bathroom walls. They can handle all the demolition work themselves. They will employ a carpenter to direct the insertion of the lintel, and the installation of windows and French doors that they themselves have had made.

For the bathroom, they visit a demolition yard and find themselves a matching 1920s' cast-iron bath and washbasin. They will reuse the existing toilet. They also find a thickly painted nineteenth-century cedar door that fits the bathroom; they have it stripped back to the wood, which they satin varnish.

The demolition weekend arrives. Two male friends are there to help. Fortunately, the internal walls are made of plasterboard over timber, and are not load-bearing. The electricity is turned off. Doors are unscrewed from their hinges, then they get to work with sledge-hammers. The three men take to slamming the hammers, with increasing zeal, into shattering plaster, screeching nails, and groaning beams. By mid-morning the walls are gone. With the gleam of destruction-frenzy in their eyes, they decide to knock out the ceiling plaster, so as to give the new living area much greater height and expansiveness. Two of them climb through the manhole into the roof cavity, and start to bash the plaster away. It comes down in a fog of fifty years of accumulated thick black dust.

The carpenter arrives at two o'clock to oversee the installation of a 6-metre lintel in the rear brick wall. Under his instruction, they bash away a section of bricks, then help him install windows and doors in the yawning cavity. By the time he leaves, at six, they are dizzy with exhaustion. Their bodies covered in sweat-congealed grime, they are still coughing up, and sneezing out, plaster particles and black gunk from the ceiling dust. They use their last energy to shovel up remaining debris in the vast open living space, then sweep and vacuum as best they can. The women then tell them grimly that, in spite of sealing off the front rooms, everything through the house is coated in a thick layer of dust.

That night, over an improvised barbecue in the back garden, with plenty of beer and wine, they joke and groan about their day. All agree that this sort of demolition is so filthy and foul that no sane person would do it more than once. But the result is spectacular: they regularly go into the house to admire the grand open room with its high, cavernous roof space. A weary self-satisfaction and camaraderie settles over them.

Throughout the next week, tradesmen build the bathroom. Once the couple has their new shell, it will take them a year to complete the renovation. They enjoy this greatly, as they finish one detail at a time to their satisfaction, under no deadline pressure. They learn tiling; minor plumbing; brick-and-cement infilling and bagging; serviceable carpentry; and insulating and lining the inside of the roof — they have replaced the previous slim roof joists with a few heavy beams. The drop-saw becomes the male's favourite tool. They make some mistakes, but always manage to redo work that looks shoddy.

They love their renovated house. It gives them pleasure whenever they walk around in it — a pleasure that hardly dims with the passing of time. This is strange, given that the delight in most things human wears off with familiarity. In some deep sense, this couple feels that they are at home. Here is where they fit; here fits them.

They fantasise about entertaining friends in their new spaces, showing off what they have done; they imagine preparing food in the new kitchen, and that eventually children will arrive and they will play here, and in the garden. The couple see themselves coming home from work to relax, potter around, and lounge about watching films.

It helps that they have done it themselves. They have discovered that, as confident individuals proclaiming *I can do this* — using their own judgement, even if hesitantly and with some trepidation — they can indeed do it. The most private and intimate spaces, those of home, are not spaces in which they have to force themselves to fit the given — thus inhibiting and distorting themselves. They can make their world suit who they are; use it to find a little more about who they are. It is as if, in some small way (and maybe not so small), they are creating themselves through their haven. Here, they are not 'out of sorts', restless, or ill at ease — precisely what people feel when they are inhabiting spaces that they instinctively feel are wrong.

A bad space— one that is out of proportion, in which the colour scheme clashes, or the furniture is ugly and clumsily arranged — is jarring. There are strict laws governing space, Platonic forms. The perfection of spatial form strikes almost everybody, whether from the balanced grandeur of the Parthenon or the interior of one of the great Gothic cathedrals; or an eighteenth-century, neo-classical English garden; or a living room in which those who have just entered murmur, 'This is a fine room, a beautiful room, a good room.' The deep satisfaction our couple takes in their DIY-renovated home allows each of them to affirm something like, *This house is me — anchored!*

DIY is one mode of sublimated vocation (sport is another). It stands as a further bulwark against passive consumerism. DIY allows our couple to become Arendt's artist. As with the artist, there is creation, but not out of nothing. There are influences, and there are predecessors. There is copying, and partial imitation, and the adaptation of forms that take their fancy. But, in the end, they create what they want, how they want it.

Of course, doing something, on its own, is not enough. It is possible to get things wrong, to bungle. The world is full of mediocre paintings and bad buildings. Making it means little unless the maker gets it right. The pleasure in doing something on its own is a childhood pleasure — affectionately satirised in the film *The Castle*, in the naively unworldly, grown-up son coming in from the backyard to boast to his father, 'Dad, I dug a hole!'[2] Adult doings may create things of permanence — ones that are worth preserving. Our couple's home is not merely a hole to be filled in, or a sandcastle to be washed away by the next high tide.

Vocation, in the case of DIY, means that *I made it*. The notion of 'possession' is deepened. The individual owns it in a more profound sense than that the title deed is his or hers. The motto of *The Castle* is about richer possession: 'A house is not a home.' The father builds a patio and puts on a fake chimney, 'to add a bit of charm'. Whether outsiders share his taste is of no concern to him: he is a case of someone who does not care about Platonic aesthetic forms.

A dwelling, as a place where one dwells, allows an ease of inhabiting without rush or fervour. The Biblical 'abide with me' draws on the evocation of abiding as a harmonious, right relationship to what matters — with the allusion that this happens in an *abode*. An abode is a place in which I feel most at ease in myself. It is a home.

★★★

The evolution of DIY has moved in parallel with an adapted form of TV show and a new type of celebrity expert. On *Better Homes and Gardens*, the experts are ordinary people who happen to be tradesmen. They give instructions to the viewer on how to imitate what they do. They are ordinary *and* expert, which gives viewers confidence that they, too, can renovate like this.[3]

Television DIY does produce celebrities. In America, they are led by Martha Stewart—a one-woman industry in herself. Through her website, television shows, radio shows, and magazines, she has created advice and products to cover the full sweep of DIY lifestyle, from home renovation, to sewing, cooking, and planning holidays. Her magazines include *Martha Stewart Living, Everyday Food, Weddings, Body + Soul, Blueprint,* and *Good Things for the Home.* Under her own brand name, she markets crafts, colours, floor designs, homes, furniture, lighting, rugs, and so on—it is the 'Martha Stewart Collection'. Her TV shows are led by the top-rating *Martha Stewart Show.* Martha Stewart is a new type of celebrity, helping the viewer to become a little bit like her, by learning from her taste and her methods.

A variant is the English cooking celebrity Nigella Lawson. She is an exemplar on a narrower scale. There is how she looks and dresses—an earthy, sensual, coquettish mode of femininity, but one centred squarely in the kitchen, with the practical end of feeding people. There is her kitchen itself, its design, her range of equipment, and how she operates in it—blending the graceful and practical. And there is what and how she cooks. She presents an aesthetic whole for the viewer to admire, and attempt to emulate. The aesthetic whole integrates home, kitchen, family, entertaining, lifestyle, and self. Again, this is not the world of passive adulation, and the fantasy identification of, *If only I was like her, and could do what she does.* The viewer is invited to act on what she sees: *I can do this myself, creating a functional and stylish kitchen, just as I want it to be.*

DIY shares an affinity with democracy. It extends democratic practices. A new form of participatory citizenship is emerging. It bridges the gulf between mass-audience television and, dotted all around the country, individual citizens in their homes. Interaction grows. As with club membership, individuals are encouraged to fashion their world. They are responsible.

In most of the contexts examined in this book, ambivalences emerge. The DIY house is not different. There are potential negatives. There is the risk of excessive self-centred individualism. While the couple may fantasise about entertaining friends, sociability beyond the bounds of the nuclear family is not a major goal of the DIY home. The fact is that, throughout the West, less and less entertaining is being done at home.[4]

And there are status dimensions: the home may be for showing off, the renovation a means of boasting to friends and to imaginary others. *Home Beautiful* gleams with the polish of high style, projecting images of social prestige. Some model display-homes in Melbourne include a banquet room, which is a ludicrous bloating of ambition. Virtually nobody who occupies one of these houses will ever hold a banquet. It calls to mind the palatial mansion Xanadu, built by Citizen Kane.[5] Xanadu was haunted by Kane's own solitary, lonely, power-obsessed self, and no one else. Nigella, too, is unabashedly narcissistic.

In all areas of human creativity there is an overwhelming degree of conformism: very little appears that is original. Those who renovate and decorate their homes are not exempt from the pressure of fashion: *We chose this, and did it that way, because it's fashionable.* To follow fashion slavishly displays an insecurity of being; it signals an absent self: *I like it, not because it's me—indeed, I don't know or trust who I am. I like it because the people I admire, and the celebrities in the magazines, do it this way.* Model homes in new housing estates, like ads for cosmetics, contribute to a type of false consciousness. They provide a modish mask to hide behind. What is masked is the self-conscious person. The expression 'self-conscious'—English usage at its most subtle—highlights an embarrassment with self, not a better knowledge of it.

Martha Stewart has a coercive manner, with the threatening undertone, *Don't you dare stray from my taste, or else* (here is perhaps the reason she has not succeeded outside America). By implication, everybody else is foolish, clumsy, and misguided; they have little or no vision. Martha provides a megalomaniacal model of how to live—just like *me*. Likewise, the IKEA home-furnishing emporium invites insecure individuals to use it to fit out the complete apartment. The message is, *You don't have to think, you don't have to choose, you don't have to worry about whether it is stylish. Because your apartment is wall-to-wall IKEA, it is stylish.*[6] Mind you, IKEA itself gestures towards DIY—many of its goods come as kits to be assembled at home, cheaper than the fully finished item.

These negatives only threaten DIY culture at the margins. In any age, it is only a minority of people who display significant originality in building and decorating. Most buildings and interiors replicate others. At the most, there are some personal touches—in the furniture arrangements and the choice of rugs, in the photographs on the living-room walls, and in the flowers on the dining-table.

The DIY age is different in offering new and wider opportunities to stretch the net of conformism, and even to break free, snipping some of its binding threads. Many more are doing it themselves. Likewise, truer to this age's democratic temper is the ordinary tradesman on *Better Homes and Gardens*, and not Nigella Lawson or Martha Stewart. In any case, most American viewers will take what they want from Martha's advice, and from her collection. They will leave the rest.

There is a new and wider opportunity to fulfil the age-old desire to provide a home as a personal place where visitors are looked after, put at their ease, and fed. The hosts will be able to make other people feel welcome the more they are proud of their spaces as bearing their own imprint—the more they themselves feel at home.

For modern individuals in search of meaning, DIY offers a new, practical domain. Like our married couple renovating their shabby 1950s house, they have been provided with an increasingly popular way of finding some bearings in relation to *being*.

## Chapter Twelve

# THE PERSONAL COMPUTER

One of the dual tensions running through this book involves work and labour/consumption, and their competing logics, as they weave through the everyday life of the modern West. In sport, the inner need for 'work' has taken over an old area of life, and transformed and amplified it, turning it into a central activity. The case of tourism is the opposite: consumerism has replaced the dynamics of work that were essential to its integrity.

I extend the argument now to the personal computer. Its development has been as important as sport in opening new opportunities for the expression of a Calvinist work ethos.

The vanguard emblem of capitalism in the second quarter of the twentieth century was the motor car; television and the jumbo jet, in the third. The personal computer has played this role since the 1980s. In fact, its influence may prove to be the most significant of all.

In the 1990s, Bill Gates, the then head of Microsoft, became what Henry Ford had been to the 1920s: the pioneering entrepreneur of the time, a business hero whose aura glowed across the culture. Gates also became the world's richest man, and it is instructive that his fortune was not made out of computer hardware — the functioning physical parts, the keyboards, the screen monitors, or the discs and drives. Manufacturing has been reduced to a marginal corner of the economy, with most factories exported to less-developed parts of the world, especially China. The Gates' fortune was made from knowledge-intensive software, the intellectual programs that constitute the new power.

The full ramifications of the automation revolution are still to be seen, although two major transformations may be delineated so far. One is to the forms of production and the range of employment. The car-assembly line has gone, replaced by computerised robots overseen by a handful of technicians. In general, the West is tending towards the workerless factory. In the service sector, from banks to airline-booking offices and welfare bureaucracies, clerical employment has been decimated; at the same time, automation has increased exponentially the power, volume, and speed — in sum, the efficiency — of transactions.

We are, furthermore, moving inexorably towards the utopia of the hi-tech home — with houses becoming ever larger, in spite of shrinking family sizes. Inside, modern citizens can conduct virtually their entire life and work, if they so choose. This includes speaking or writing to anyone, anywhere, on the instant, buying goods from around the world, doing their local shopping and their banking, booking air flights and hotels, paying their bills, playing a simulated game of golf, finding out where the fish are biting, checking radar and satellite images of coming weather, and entertaining themselves with virtually any film, or piece of music, ever created — all through their personal computers. In the process, a vast sweep of service jobs is being abolished. This may seem like the hellish endpoint of passive consumerism, with all living done in the abstract. I want here to suggest otherwise, at least in some key regards.

The other transformation is to have opened up to each individual an entirely new opportunity for 'work'. One of the characteristics that Hannah Arendt attributes to work is that the tool becomes the agent of the hand; unlike labour, in which the person becomes the servant of the tool, the machine, and indeed nature herself.[1] Never have human individuals had such a powerful tool as the personal computer in their hands (the giant crane driver, the jumbo-jet pilot, and the aircraft-carrier captain are not essentially in the craftsman mould, for a vehicle is not a tool, except in an oblique sense).

Travel agents have fingertip access to all of the Western world's flights, and may book their clients here and there at will. Architects can tap into basic design modules and freely adapt them to their creative visions. Advertising designers, photographers, and newspaper layout technicians can reshape and adapt images, including the figure of a fashion model, the features of a fictitious hero, or the scene of a crime, to suit their own concepts. The writer, the journalist, and the student can not only draft their work rapidly; they can edit, add, cut and polish with facility, and they can design their page layouts, their contents, their diagrams, and illustrations. They have a power that hundreds of generations of their ancestors could only have dreamed of, all because of the new work-tool responsive to their touch.

Anyone, in any household, may now compose and design letters and memoranda to a professional level of presentation, such that not even the most competent and experienced secretary in 1980 could have produced. They may buy a software package that enables them to keep their own financial records, which they only need hand over to a professional accountant once a year, replacing all but a final checking part of his function.

Furthermore, individuals sitting at their computers are like Vermeer's geographer in openly manifesting the other characteristics of vocation. There is the solitariness, the quiet, and the concentration to the point of total absorption, intolerant of interruption. The mind and tool are as one, with the special bond of having the eyes focused on the screen, while the hands work the keyboard and mouse—placed as mechanical intermediaries—the body with its function, but subordinate to the union of mind with text, and the text itself merely the vehicle for the ideas.

There is the stamp of the Protestant ethic here, with individuals fashioning their world through a concentrated mind guided by conscience, creating a particular order which, in its concreteness, may stand as an instance of a grander scheme. The process of creation may involve acts of intense and relentless persistence, of constant wrestling to improve, so that the final product is excellent. The computer acts not only as an enabling tool, but serves to found a work domain in which there is an almost-hypnotic call to the individual: here is your place and what you have to do. The workbench is all set up for you. Only sit down and you will find a relaxed state of focus, almost a meditative level of mental control, as in a Zen practice, and in that trance-state your ideas will flow through the machine, and be registered.

Take a retiree, incensed that the local authority has savagely pruned an old tree in his street. He sits down to write his complaint. He types his address and the date, that of the authority, and a title line for the letter. Then he works at positioning them all, tries different fonts and font sizes, and experiments with bold, italics, and capitalisation. Finally, it is just as he wants it. So he starts his letter. He is very angry, but by now he is under control, thanks to the computer, channelling the rage into his work—the letter. Not usually very fluent, he finds the words just come: the sentences flow, accompanied by a taut, withering pitch of cold invective. He tells them what he thinks of them, and puts an argument about what they have done. This will hurt; it may even have an effect. He finishes, inserts, 'Yours sincerely' with a wry smile, and then spends another half-hour polishing his prose.

After previewing how the whole page will appear in print, and making some final adjustments to the gaps between the paragraphs, he clicks the 'save' icon, pauses and, with a slight twitch of decisiveness, as if to affirm to himself that this is it, he clicks the print icon. The printer immediately begins to emit its operating groans, and he listens with a certain apprehension as it prints: there is always the fear that something will go wrong, that the system will collapse, although it hardly ever does.

Then, there it is—his letter. He takes it, and stares at it with pride. It does look professional. He made this. It bears his stamp, and that of no one else. It is his design, these are his words, it is his tone and force, it is his creation, and it does look good. It may not be very grand in the scheme of human creations. It may not have any effect. But he has proved something: he has made out of himself a complete, pleasing, and independent thing. Here is a sort of vindication of his existence. He looks at the computer with a new attachment and affection, like the carpenter of old toying with his favourite chisel. He is a typical representative of the modern West: once he has taken on an absorbing task in the mode of *vocation*, he enjoys it, finding it deeply fulfilling.

Even the manias that typically afflict personal computer users take the Calvinist form—that of work obsession. There is the common addiction, whereby individuals excuse themselves hurriedly from the dinner table and return to their computer (or to more recent hi-tech evolutions such as the Blackberry and the iPhone), where much of their spare time, through long evenings or over weekends, is spent glued to the monitor. It may involve work. If not, with males it is more likely to be computer games; with females, email, MySpace, or Facebook.[2]

For some, the personal computer becomes a principal love-object, the ties to it like an umbilical cord through which life's vital fluids flow. An electricity failure may throw such compulsive devotees into a state of panic, or even derangement. If men used to love their cars, and find sublimation of their need for power by driving them hard and fast, many of them now turn to the computer for fulfilment of their imperial phallic fantasies of conquest and control.

There is a singular feeling of impotence when the computer will not respond: when users have made an error that they cannot correct, or they fail to understand a function that has suddenly become indispensable, or the program has developed a flaw, or they face the even-worse horror of having caught a virus. The feeling is not like the frustration of the last biro running out of ink, of the car breaking down, or even of suddenly being struck by an enervating flu. It is as if the power has been switched off, a parallel to the Homeric description of the dying warrior being unstrung at the knees. A panic sets in, often leading to the random hitting of keys in a stupid flailing-around; or a tantrum while searching for non-existent files. It is as if an intimacy has been severed without any warning, with the unsuspecting lover left out to freeze.

There are wider cultural implications. The Calvinist dynamic, instating the individual conscience as the one presiding authority in the modern West, encourages new levels of individual autonomy. The personal computer has become a vital aid. One of its revolutionary effects has been to begin the reversal of a major economic trend since the industrial revolution, one underlined by both Adam Smith and Karl Marx: the increasing division of labour, and the specialisation of tasks. For instance, the twentieth-century family progressively abandoned its general tasks to specialists—growing its vegetables, keeping its hens, cooking its meals, cleaning its houses, making and mending its clothes, and using its own sense in caring for its members' health, diet, pre-school instruction, and old-age infirmities.

With the personal computer, the individual is again becoming a generalist, replacing many of the intermediary specialists such as secretaries, bank clerks, ticket agents, and telephonists, as well as some teachers, lawyers, doctors, and consultants.

That the personal computer gives power to the people can be observed on a number of fronts. The job of typist was largely a low-skill, mechanical *labour* function, performed under instructions from the boss. That function has been transformed into *work*, because the computer requires much higher levels of skill. Nor is the personal computer restricted to the upper middle class. All schools have introduced it into the basic curriculum, so that literacy has come to include an assumed computer literacy. Some people will remain illiterate; but it will be a minority, not the large demographic sweep of the lower middle class.

At the same time, science-fiction terrors, which were so common in the 1960s, of a world taken over by robots, have largely disappeared. The reality of the computer—while itself even more powerful than earlier imagined—is to have given strength to individuals, not enslaved them. The robot fear derived from the logic of labour, and then disappeared because of the work capacities of the new tool.

Worldwide access to information through the Internet also enhances individual autonomy. Anyone can now read the *New York Times*, shop at Harrods, consult an encyclopaedia, or check Austrian chalet design. The terminology 'surfing the Net' indicates that this is not passive consumerism, at least in its potential. It may, on the other hand, encourage the idling-away of time, as individuals dart from item to item and skim hundreds of sources of random facts, like aimlessly flicking through a gossip or fashion magazine. In this mode, the computer does feed consumerist nihilism and undermine concentration spans.

The main threat posed by the personal computer is to aggravate a chronic individualism: of withdrawal not only from the community, but from all except for the most transient, and ephemeral, personal relations. Here is a general vice to which *work* culture has always been vulnerable; because, according to its logic, the principal psychic engagements are with the abstract task at hand. Great care is taken with the task; not so much with actual people. The tool and the work become the loved objects.

★★★

What may we conclude about the impact of information technology? Obviously, it has profoundly changed the conduct of everyday life. The Internet has inaugurated a *communication* revolution. But it is too early to tell whether the impact is more than one of convenience, an extension of what we did previously, or whether the West is undergoing a transformation in the way it experiences and understands the way it lives.

It is worth recalling that the telephone changed the nature of communication in the twentieth century. But social historian Daniel Boorstin summed up the telephone as 'only a convenience, permitting Americans to do more casually and with less effort what they had already been doing before'.[3]

The most obvious, and uncomplicated, 'convenience' function of the Internet is the access it provides to information and knowledge, with the aid of search engines led by Google. Most homes in the Western world have gained instant digital access to encyclopaedias, books, scholarly articles, the world's newspapers, magazines, and journals, government and business reports, and a world history of information.

The Internet already seems to be more than just a convenience, although to what degree is unclear. New modes of civic engagement are appearing. The emergence of blogs gives every citizen the opportunity to create a public space for discussion, commentary, and debate. Blog sites have developed that complement and extend

the important democratic function of the press — to investigate
fraud and corruption. They are free from the constraints imposed
by the financial interests that own the major media corporations.
Blog sites also facilitate and encourage community action groups,
thereby adding to social capital.[4]

Websites and blogs provide unprecedented democratic access to
information and power. They reduce the secrecy and inaccessibility
of traditional hierarchies of expertise, power, and wealth. In the
realm of recreation, for example, any golfer who is interested in
golf-course layout and quality may visit golfclubatlas.com to chat
with Tom Doak, the most successful designer in the world since
the legendary Alistair Mackenzie in the 1920s. Doak will respond
personally with carefully considered opinions.

Then there is Wikipedia. By 2007, it had a range 20 times greater
than the 17-volume *Encyclopaedia Britannica*. At peak times, it was
receiving 15,000 hits a second. It is a collaborative effort: a 'Wiki
community' has grown around it. Anyone can volunteer and jump
in, supplying background articles or editing others — to the extent
that several hundred thousand people have contributed to it. This is
an altruistic community: one 'Wikipedian' says of his motivation, 'I
may only be providing a small amount, but I know that every time
I edit an article, I've made a difference in someone else's learning
experience.' And Wikipedia's accuracy, at least in science areas, is
not far short of that of *Encyclopaedia Britannica*, as tested by the
journal *Nature*.[5]

The principal mode of Internet communication has been email.
It provides smooth, easy contact, removing the inhibitions and
time delays of traditional post — as well as removing the bother of
having to use paper, ink, envelopes, and stamps, and of having to
drop off mail to the post-box or post office. Yet technological change
has become so rapid that email is already becoming obsolete for a
younger generation, who communicate with their friends by text

messaging on their mobile phones, and through social-networking sites.[6]

Email has the great strength of connecting people who are isolated, or who feel isolated. This is even more the case when email is complemented, and succeeded, by websites (including MySpace and Facebook), and by free Skype-type person-to-person video-communication. This includes those in small, remote communities, or those just feeling alone in their suburban bedrooms; friends and members of families living in different places, countries, and continents; migrants and expatriates; and members of the military stationed overseas. The US military has been the most dedicated user of the Internet.[7] In all of this, email has hugely amplified the convenience of the telephone.

Websites continue to extend creative freedom. MySpace provides everybody with the opportunity to gather together their own personal running autobiography, and to post it on the World Wide Web for everybody to see (the same is true for the more sophisticated Facebook site, which has attracted an upper-middle-class, university-educated market). Andy Warhol's future of everybody being famous for fifteen minutes has been superseded.

The MySpace site is public and permanent. Personal details are posted, and made visual in photos and videos; as are hopes and ambitions, and personal tastes in music, bands, reading, clothing, and those admired and despised. A running commentary is provided of what the subject has done today, who she met, and how she felt, and in an open site for chatting with friends, or whomever. This may seem indiscreet to an older generation — a rash blurring of traditional boundaries between public and private. But the MySpace identity is carefully constructed, and excludes whatever the individual prefers to keep private.

The opportunity here is to build one's own identikit self. With MySpace, the surface facts are drawn from the life as lived, the 'reality', and then woven into the chosen form. In fact, the Internet provides powerful openings to create a largely fictitious self. This was true from the early days, with meetings via email leading to virtual romance. On the other hand, the 1998 film *You've Got Mail* showed a man and a woman in a virtual romance being more honest with each other than they would have been normally.

Players in computer games can now build their own characters—with freedom of choice to project parts of themselves (real, idealised, or feared) into a construct, a sort of simulacrum. The game may then take the form of a story, which the player enters as his or her other self. The player becomes an active participant, using imagination to create a fantasy narrative. The originating author of the game supplies the narrative thread; the players improvise within it.[8]

Here is play with 'work' characteristics—not the passive consumerism of television-watching. Yet these virtual selves and virtual relationships flirt with the Superman pathology. There is the escape from reality into a fantasy *Super-me*. The *Super-me* is power and beauty—fantasy power—and is never tested in personal contact with other living humans.

Real human relations are governed by an enigmatic chemistry, beating at the heart of what is personal. There is the vast repertoire of cues that feed personal chemistry—visual ones of eye contact, movements of the mouth, posture, and hand gestures; auditory ones of tone of voice, and orchestration of words; and touch and smell cues. Above all, there is the dynamic interaction between fantasy projections of the other and the real person opposite, with a greater familiarity usually leading to a steady reduction in the gap. And this happens over time, in different situations together, and is modulated by changing moods.

In virtual relationships, most people may try to be their natural selves, but the medium deletes the face-to-face chemistry. The name

'Facebook' may deliberately attempt to counter the deeper fear that what it offers is *face-less*, and therefore lifeless, contact. The danger here is what was highlighted in the social-capital argument: the concern that sociability provides the antidote to the self-absorbed madness of Superman. Experience in genuine personal relations is crucial to every individual *I*, and its sense both of itself and of a meaningful human existence.

Balance is key, as expressed in the Delphic injunction, 'Nothing in excess.' The more life is conducted through the personal computer, the more fear of the domain of the personal and intimate may inflate, becoming a self-fulfilling prophecy. The end of this road is the paranoia of Hendin's student from Chapter Two: 'If you show your feelings you get your legs cut off.' So, you don't get involved.

Virtual relationships, in excess, will aggravate the inability to sit still. The consumerist reflex is to fill the emptiness inside—and to evade plunging into life experience, out of fear of the pain—by losing oneself in being busy. The automation revolution services the evasion. There is the impatient rush to the computer game, the manic stream of text messages, and the compulsive panic to check email. Also lost in the hurry is the time needed to sit still and reflect on oneself and one's life. Every life is a story which, to have coherence and gravity, needs to be brought into an imaginative focus, and not forgotten in the rush.

Perhaps the crowning symbol of this new frenzy—of constant movement on the surface of life—is the intrusive noise of the mobile phone. Every social and work situation is under threat from these exploding aural landmines. And to what purpose, apart from the banality of a family member, or friend, or partner ringing to say that they have just arrived at work, or finished their first coffee, or visited the toilet? Here is technology-facilitated regression to the security of childhood, with mother always close by, there to soothe every frustrated impulse. The umbilical cord has been restored digitally.

Is it the case, then, that 'virtual social capital' is a contradiction in terms? Robert Putnam himself concluded that 'computer-mediated communication will turn out to *complement*, not *replace* face-to-face communities'.[9] While this is almost certainly true, it underplays the pathological side-effects — the implosion into self-absorption, the withdrawal from life into a capsule populated by fantasies and fears, with relationships electronically controlled. And it underplays the opportunities for *vocation* — serious creative engagement, at work and in leisure.

Chapter Thirteen

# NATURE

The beach is Australia's most important social space. It is also fundamental to the nation's culture.

A ring of semi-sacred sites circles the vast continent, making its edge vital to the country's modern sense of self. It is an edge that faces out, into the eternity that is evoked by the ocean. Humans are writ tiny here, something they seem to cherish. The atmosphere is spiced by the roar of the waves, the whip and tang of salt air, the tread of hot sand, the radiance of turquoise vistas, and the ever-present dangers of undertows, rips, crocodiles, and sharks. But volunteers make the beach secure.

The Australian surf life-saving clubs have, for a century, been national talismans in their own right, representing an ideal of beautiful youth. That youth is suntanned, virile, and professionally skilled. It gives its time freely to protect and save lives. It is casual yet alert. These club members are like secular priests and priestesses officiating in nature's grand sand-and-surf cathedral—Australia's favourite place of worship. They contribute to the cult of beach worship and its distinctive values of inclusiveness, constrained freedom, hedonistic fun, and safety. Surf life-saving clubs are voluntary associations that are expanding in number and membership.[1]

While the culture of the beach is particular to Australia, the fantasy it expresses is general to the modern West. Northern Europeans flock to beach resorts on the Spanish coast or in the Greek islands, just as Americans holiday in Hawaii, Florida, and the West Indies.

As the churches have emptied in the West, it has been in nature that most have sought the divine. The ways are many: going to the country, picnicking by a river, fishing, walking in forests, bicycling, camping in the bush, climbing mountains, skiing, boating on lakes, sitting on beaches, standing on cliff-tops while gazing out over the oceans, even favouring life in suburbia, where each home has its own back-garden. So many modern ways of retreat from the metropolis have been found, in search of some peace and serenity, some inspiration, some release from self into union with the All. From the great Romantic poetry and painting of two centuries ago, to television advertisements today, the sublime vision has persuaded many that the sacred is to be discovered out in the natural world, under its heavenly canopy.

Implicit here is a theological revolution, the most radical in the history of the Christian West. The Lord God who appears in the Old Testament as Yahweh, and then is personified in the Gospels as the Father, the principal figure in the Trinity, has faded away. The vast majority of people instinctively (and consciously, if they reflect on these matters) have come to find implausible the image of a single omnipotent God, who determines all things that happen; and who sits up above watching and judging every move, totting up rewards and punishments; a God who may be appealed to through prayer. The projection of a providential and merciful Father has lost cultural hold. Here is a way in which the Death of God has been a liberation, but not as Nietzsche postulated it.

There are rational, historical reasons for this. The scepticism of the West, reinforced by science, which tends only to trust experience, has been based on the observation that the human story is not a well-balanced morality play. Often, the wicked prosper, while the good suffer bewildering misfortune. Luther had already acknowledged that God's Earth is not a just place. It would be an outrageous presumption to claim that the millions of victims of torture and death in the Holocaust, including young children, suffered what they did in response to a merciful divine plan. Humans can merely look on, agape at such horrors, with nothing to say. Whatever metaphysical forces influence events, they do not appear to do so benevolently, or in the interests of justice. The ancient Greek picture of the gods as vain, spiteful, and fickle seems a far more credible imagining of the higher workings of destiny.

There are also deeper cultural shifts involved in the distancing from the God of old. With the continuing development of the West, under the dual influence of the Renaissance and the Reformation, individuals have gained a stronger sense of themselves, both in their worldly capacities and in their sense that the path to salvation lies within.

The history of art illustrates this, and in depth. Let me choose three exemplary moments. As early as 1450, Donatello sculpted a Christ who was fully human for the High Altar in St Anthony's Basilica in Padua. Here is the doubting Jesus of Mark's Gospel, whose last words were, 'My God, my God, why hast thou forsaken me?' There is no heavenly father waiting to spirit away this man, dying a tortured and anguished death.

Second, at the height of the Renaissance, Raphael consummated his genius with completely human Madonna and Childs, figures caught up in their very this-worldly tragic destinies.

Third, the extension into landscape was carried out by Nicolas Poussin, with all the theological transformations included. His vision remains unsurpassed. The formative work is *St Matthew and the Angel* from 1640, now in Berlin — the first and, in many ways, the purest of his 'ideal landscapes'.[2]

Poussin sets his scene on the bank of a river winding away towards ruins and distant hills. A light-blue sky with bright clouds casts an airy mood. By the river sits a very ordinary-looking Matthew. His hair and beard are thick, muddy brown in colour, streaked with grey. His skin is dark; his features, unrefined. This man is almost sub-human, with allusions to Pan, the dark god of lust and animal appetite.

Matthew holds pen and paper, but he is vacant, lacking any inspiration. Suddenly, an angel in white is standing beside him. The pair are positioned among the ruins of ancient temples — the greatest creations of human civilisation, the best of the past, now rendered as nothing, mere rubble next to the gift of truth. They are of no worth compared with being called to write *the* story.

The angel is everywhere. Grey clouds scud across the sky, backed by swirling white ones; an assembly that mimics the wings, bright white in sunlight, light grey in shadow, in a projection of their recent flight. White cloud is mirrored in the river, and the shape is that of enlarged wings. The river winds, suggesting the spiral path of the flight in, around the trees, to Matthew. In wind, in cloud, in distant hills and near trees, in the cast of the river, breathes the divinity and its sure presence: this sublime angel.

Poussin integrates the principal figures into nature. In *Matthew*, there is a still serenity that glows through the canvas. No threatening storm, no moving animal, and no rustle of wind disturb the moment. Even the ruins speak of a divine harmony composing the natural world within which we humans dwell.

Matthew is weak with love and gratitude. He gazes joyfully up into the eyes of the angel, who is close to him, relaxed, smiling benevolently down, as he lightly takes hold of the top of the page, and shows where the first word will appear. Matthew is a lucid shimmer, seized by divine illumination, now as if weightless on his stone block, freed from the Earth, in awe of this purity of white and gold: the closed white wings vibrant, the pale, chubby skin soft enough to swoon into, the sweet face friendly without any trace of human reserve, and the golden hair aglow.

Matthew's entire world is concentrated in this still, small space next to the river. Here is everywhere, his inspiration taking him out of the boundaries of his meagre individual self, and uniting him with the Whole that is existence. Suddenly, he *is* river, plains, hills, and sky, as the earthy goat-god of the woods is infused with an angelic presence. Such is Matthew's call. His pen will fly across the page, without him even knowing what he is writing. The Word will speak through him; he is merely its enchanted mouthpiece. Such is grace.

Poussin has been called a neo-classical painter. His works, planned down to the least detail with intellectual rigour, are structured in obedience to classical forms and proportions, like a Palladian church. Also, he drew extensively on ancient Greek and Roman mythology, and Stoicism weaves through his philosophy.[3] But the deepest bite of his neo-classicism has not been recognised by scholars. It is to have returned to a Greco–Roman metaphysics in which there are two clear manifestations of the divine. The first is inspired individual humans, finding a state of grace through their work, or through their intimacies. The second is serenity in nature. Moreover, the highest state of human experience is to be in harmony with a mystical, real landscape — often with a city, and its people integrated into it.

God has gone. In fact, the mature Poussin did paint God once, in *Spring,* the first of his final cycle of works, the *Four Seasons.* It is a waggish God departing the human world, with a disgusted wave of goodbye to Adam and Eve; in part, satirising Michelangelo's Sistine Almighty, who touches life into Adam. Symbolically, it is not the first humans whom Poussin is banishing from earthly paradise, but the Creator, whom he cannot take seriously anymore.[4]

Poussin's last masterpiece, *Winter*, is a death landscape in which all things human are shown as futile, including the finest embodiments of family and friendship. The divinity comes in the form of a haunting light from beyond a disastrous flood that is drowning the Earth and everything on it. A Zeus-like shaft of lightning slashes through the black gloom of the human condition, casting a glowing, grey lustre across the scene—making of the whole, in spite of the dispiriting detail, an awesomely beautiful order. There is no saving God, no church, and no redemptive Jesus but, simply, in Poussin's final vision, a higher order, mediated through the grandeur of Nature, welcoming the departing soul.

Poussin was a forerunner, an intellectual pioneer, of the West's turn eastwards in its theology. God is being replaced by the *sacred cosmos*.[5] A quite different sense of the divine emerges, as a sort of ether diffused through the world. As we have seen, the classical Greek word *pneuma* expresses it well, meaning 'breath', 'wind', and 'spirit'. We are bathed, as it were, in sacred *pneuma*. It is not something at a distance, concentrated in one entity—alien, directing, and judging—typical of church religion.

Here is the main reason for the scale of contemporary Western interest in Buddhism. Buddhism is a god-less religion, driven by a theology of the divine dwelling within each individual, waiting to be freed through exercises, or other techniques that extinguish the ego. In the achieved state of freedom, or enlightenment, the individual joins with all other sentient beings in the world, sharing a common identity of universal love. Buddhism is the quintessential *sacred cosmos* religion—which is not to suggest that it is particularly suited to the modern West. It is too hostile to the ego, and too other-worldly for that.

The West has its own parallels with Buddhism, and not just the modern Calvinist ones. There was the ancient doctrine of *anima mundi*—'the soul of the world'—according to which, all things have their own spirit, their own metaphysical essence. In the original Latin, to be *animate* was, by definition, to be 'of soul'. There is a fragment of divinity in all things, the human soul being the apex, the means by which we may engage with the sacred *pneuma* all around us. The West is heading rapidly back to this pagan view.

Nature has been the main vehicle, with Romanticism the accompanying philosophical movement. Wordsworth put the credo in his poem *Tintern Abbey* (1798):

> And I have felt
> A presence that disturbs me with the joy
> Of elevated thoughts; a sense sublime
> Of something far more deeply interfused,
> Whose dwelling is the light of setting suns,
> And the round ocean and the living air,
> And the blue sky, and in the mind of man;
> A motion and a spirit, that impels
> All thinking things, all objects of all thought,
> And rolls through all things. Therefore am I still
>    …well pleased to recognise
> In nature and the language of the sense
> The anchor of my purest thoughts, the nurse,
> The guide, the guardian of my heart, and soul
> Of all my moral being.

The Jesuit poet Gerard Manley Hopkins later strove to integrate God into the Romantic conception:

> The world is charged with the grandeur of God.
> It will flame out, like shining from shook foil;

It gathers to a greatness, like the ooze of oil
Crushed. Why do men then now not reck his rod?
Generations have trod, have trod, have trod;
And all is seared with trade; bleared, smeared with toil;
And wears man's smudge and shares man's smell: the soil
Is bare now, nor can foot feel, being shod.[6]

The energy in this poem is that of love of the world, of the everyday human. The focus is the earth, the language so rich that one can almost feel the sods; in the English canon, only Shakespeare has had such evocative powers. This is not poetry of the beyond. Its effect is rather *anima mundi*. It is *pneuma* inspiring the Earthly — not the calling forth of a distant Lord. Hopkins may not have liked the irony that he provided the concrete imagery for Wordsworth's abstractly articulated theory.

There is also the great German tradition of Romantic poetry, from Goethe to Hölderlin, taken up in the songs of Schubert, and feeding into the twentieth century through Rilke. Rilke wove a metaphysics of love and distant angelic forces through the awkward sense felt by humans of not belonging in the world that they find themselves driven to interpret. Rilke wrote that the theme and purpose of art is the 'reconciliation of the Individual and the All', but had doubts about how successfully this dream could ever be realised.[7] His first *Duino Elegy* puts it:

Oh, and there's Night, there's Night, when wind full of cosmic
    space
feeds on our faces: for whom would she not remain,
longed for, mild disenchantress, painfully there
for the lonely heart to achieve? Is she lighter for lovers?
Alas, with each other they only conceal their lot!
Don't you know yet? — Fling the emptiness out of your arms

to broaden the spaces we breathe — maybe that the birds
will feel the extended air in more fervent flight.

Yes, the Springs had need of you. Many a star
was waiting for you to perceive it. Many a wave
would rise in the past towards you; ...[8]

The Romantic poets were the founding philosophers of the
new archetype, leaving aside precursors such as Poussin. Poussin,
incidentally, was closer to Rilke, in counterpoising ego and nature,
than the more passive Wordsworth, who posits ego submerging
itself in nature.

High culture led the way, with the imagery and the underlying
theory, and then popular culture followed, if slowly. Art illustrates
this movement. The Impressionists were nineteenth-century
cultural radicals who removed the human narrative from painting,
and flirted with abstraction. Since World War II, they have become
widely popular, with reproductions of their works commonly to be
seen on lower-middle-class living-room walls. Their dreamily blurred
landscapes, painted in rich, pleasant colours, invite a withdrawal
from the pains of the human drama, into soothing fantasies bathed
in sunny nature. Their works are not too abstract for popular taste
and, more importantly, they portray the world as an ordered and
beautiful place.

However, once the full onslaught of Modernism took hold
(following Cezanne, in his late period, and then Cubism), the lower
middle class recoiled from what they rightly suspected was nihilistic.
Their favourite art remains Monet and Renoir — art that is vivid,
sentimental, and suggestive of a divinity with which they feel some
affinity — one that breathes through nature.

The Romantic archetype has flourished for two centuries,
steadily spreading into new areas of life. The more that the West

has found time for leisure, the more it has spent it away from the cities, in nature, with the aid of the motor car and the jumbo jet. Its individuals fancy the sheer pleasure of being at the wheel of their own cars, liberated from the cares of the city, speeding along open roads through rolling hills, or along coasts, inhaling the view. Here is a recurring modern image of autonomy, power, and freedom — often used in television advertisements, in which the car may be open, the driver's hair blowing in the wind.

The popularity of the Western film genre has depended heavily on its setting, on the frontier. The frontier inherits the Romantic tradition's belief in salvation in nature. The city is viewed as, at the least, profane and dulling; at the worst, a cage of hypocrisy, effeteness, and immorality. It is out in the wild, beyond human society, under the stars, perhaps battling with savage Indians or stampeding cattle, or around a camp-fire, that life may gain a purpose. In the untamed wilderness, one imbibes the sense that there are grander forces within which life is cast and programmed to play its role; and, moreover, that that role matters. John Wayne states explicitly in his valedictory film, *The Shootist* (1976), 'My church has been the mountains and solitude.'

With the shrinking of mainstream church attendance, couples have turned away from holding their marriage ceremonies in buildings in which they feel awkward, following rites that they do not hold to be true. Their preferred alternative, where the climate permits, is in grand parks and botanical gardens, or in the cultivated nature of great homes, once private but now publicly owned, and used for such quasi-sacred functions.

Here is a perfect symbol for the new theology. The new church, within which the most important life-commitment takes place, is nature. More particularly, it is an artistically designed blend of the cultivated and the wild, with its origins in the English landscape garden of the eighteenth century — in itself, heavily influenced by

Poussin, many of whose greatest works were bought by the British aristocracy.⁹ Where once God's priests consecrated matrimony, the human role in the ritual is now downplayed, the ceremony conducted by a secular functionary called a marriage celebrant. Today, the sacred cosmos stands as witness, and blesses the plighting of the troth.

During the course of the past century, the suntan became a mark of beauty and distinction, reversing the traditional view that to be dark is sign of a menial status — of those forced to labour all day out of doors. In part, there was a simple inversion, because the Western lower classes now worked long hours in factories and offices and, as a result, were pasty pale of skin. So it became a contrasting signature of wealth and leisure to sport a suntan, following the example of the jet-set who skied at St Moritz, and summered on the French Riviera.

The sport ethos became increasingly influential here, and in the last quarter of the twentieth century it drove out of fashion much of the preceding stratification by class. Sport provided its own rationale for the fit and well-tanned body. The jet-set disappeared as heroes of the time, and film stars were joined by elite sportsmen and women, and by 'supermodels'. The supermodels projected a new female ideal. What they showed off was a super-slim body, long and lean-legged, and they were often photographed in bright outdoor light, wearing sunglasses.

The appeal of sport, in its turn, draws on the Romantic archetype. In fact, it is *work in nature*, a cultural fusion that could stand as the symbol of the modern West. The most popular participant sports for adults — fishing, bicycling, boating, skiing, golf, tennis, and bowls — all belong out-of-doors, except in extreme climates.¹⁰ Fishing, yachting, skiing, and golf all have as a fundamental component the union of self, through the sport, with one of the grand expanses of nature. It is not far-fetched to say that the fisherman worships the sea, meditating for hours, gazing into its depths.

For the serious fisherman, what he does is an art. To learn to
know the habits of river trout, especially their feeding and breathing,
takes years of patient study. Then there are the hours of concentrated
stalking, creeping while camouflaged along banks and through
shallows, casting with deft precision. Yet fishermen, whatever their
specialty, seem to agree that the pleasure is not principally in the
catch, but in the act and the environment:

> You come out here on a sunny day; there's no rushing around,
> and you've got the beach to yourself. It's just like a little piece of
> heaven.[11]

The golfing sublime is to strike form, a state of grace in
which there is a perfect union of mind, body, and natural
environment—which, in turn, includes terrain, trees, hazards, and
condition of the turf, wind, light, and rain. It is telling that as the
new major economies (first of Japan, and then of China) started to
boom, so did the building of golf courses.

Golf was dreamed up and developed in Calvinist Scotland: in
particular, in and around the home of the Presbyterian Church in
Edinburgh.[12] Golf is *the* Calvinist sport, a fact of significance to one
of the main themes of this book: the continuing imperial drive of
the cultural blueprint, ever commanding new territory in the West,
and now beyond. China looks like becoming the next country to be
obsessed by golf.

Golf is a mental exercise—more so than any other active sport.
Most of the three-to-five hours it takes to complete a round is spent
in walking and thinking; very little time is spent in playing shots.
As a result, it takes a formidable level of concentration, as one is
often forced to struggle, Zen-like, to free the mind from racing
anxieties, to calm it down, to empty it. Almost always, for a period,

the concentration lapses, leaving the golfer struggling and inept, out of sorts and clumsy, feeling wretched—as if damned. The Calvinist notion of vocation fits golf: it requires relentless dedication, a superhuman rigour of trained and disciplined application, and an impossible perfectionism. In golf, you almost always fail. Only a guilt-hounded masochist with a fatalist obsession would persevere. In its essence, it is hard to conceive of any popular human activity that is less consumerist in spirit.

Also, golf teaches its practitioners, more acutely than any other sport, the doctrine of *sola fide*: grace is everything, and it cannot be willed. Grace comes from beyond. One moment, one is suddenly in form, the hands moving sweetly in tune with the club, the mind assessing length, wind, and trajectory—the mind at ease, not rushing, but quiet and focused—and the ball speeds to the distant target. The ego is fulfilled; the soul is in flight. This is both Poussin's Matthew, and Hopkins' world, full of the grandeur of God. The next minute, doing exactly the same things, everything falls apart. The swing jerks, the club jars in the hands, the ball slices into dense trees, and the head is dizzy with panic. One minute there is a serenity, as if one has been chosen, welcomed into the company of the elect; the next moment, perdition. The elusive dream is caught in the title of Michael Murphy's book: *Golf in the Kingdom*.[13]

*** 

In recent decades, the new political movement that has shown the most resilience has been 'environmentalism'. It has taken over the leading role in the domain of ideas about what is wrong with the world, and what is in urgent need of reforming political action. A precondition for this rise has been the prosperity of the West—the emancipation from concern with basic economic necessities—and diminishing military threats.

Environmentalism is not merely a fad of affluence, however. It partly represents a response to a real problem of an overpopulated world that is rapidly using up some of the Earth's natural resources—notably trees, forests and jungle, but also threatening the stock of fish, and of some of the larger wild-life species, such as tigers. There is the real problem of the pollution of air, land, rivers, and seas. And there is global warming.

Notwithstanding this, the generative passion behind the Green movement has its source in the Romantic archetype. The fundamental belief of this culture is that God dwells in nature. It follows that to damage the environment is sacrilege, a desecration of our church: the place we go to worship, once we free ourselves from the materialistic profanities of capitalism. The language is steeped in religious symbols and metaphors. Moreover, the fanatics of the movement offer themselves as martyrs to their god, flinging themselves in front of bulldozers, chaining themselves to trees, and challenging warships in rubber dinghies. Press photographs of green heroics are often reminiscent of Christian paintings of the early martyrs. A recurring image throughout the West is the young devotee embracing a tree, as if it were the one true cross, willing to die rather than have one of its precious branches lopped.

Here is a return to *anima mundi* with a Puritan fervour unreported in ancient Greco–Roman times. The mainstream Christian churches would gasp with thanks were they to find a congregation with one-tenth of this enthusiasm—another sign of the shifting Calvinist perception of the sacred into the world.

Furthermore, while the young, from teenagers at school to university students, are in the main cynical and detached from the mainstream political parties in their countries, they take with charged and unsceptical enthusiasm to environmentalist causes. They are, in effect, converts to the new religion. In their eyes, the victims of **modernity** are not the underprivileged, the focus of the socialists of old—their creed formed by Marxism. The new 'wretched of the Earth' are the Earth itself and its non-human creatures. This youth's intellectual fathers were the Romantic poets.

The strengthening sense of universal rights has also contributed. It has been extended, Buddhist style, to include animals—predominantly but not exclusively mammals, such as in successful 'Save the Whale' campaigns. One theme has been that we humans have a responsibility to the natural world we inhabit because of our privileged position at the top of the evolutionary tree, and our history of ruthless and immoral exploitation of our planet.

We transgress an absolute law when we violate nature. We may even be on the threshold of the attitude found in some simpler societies: before cutting down a tree, a rite of propitiation should be performed. It may include asking the tree for forgiveness: *I have to do this ... I need your wood ... You are in the way ... Please understand.* So it is that *anima mundi* as a pagan religious philosophy is returning to the West.

Green politics is itself a fusion of *work* and *nature*. At its best, it belongs within the perspective of Poussin and Rilke, and of sport-in-nature. The dynamic human ego strives to integrate itself, through action, into the sublime natural environment. This perspective is Calvinist. Poussin's Matthew is desperate to begin his vocational task, to write the story of the man who changed his life; but it is only once he has received grace, and begun his work, that he feels himself at home in the landscape. His inspiration does not come from nature, from passively contemplating its distant and external beauties, but from within—once the angel has breathed saving life into the man. Individuals, through carrying out their chosen mission, their egos fulfilled rather than extinguished, may find their eyes opening to the wonder of the sacred cosmos.

The contrasting Wordsworth view has also maintained its influence in the West. Its paradigm is travelling to the countryside, the mountains, or the seas, preferably alone, and quietly contemplating the scene. In one variant, the nocturne—at night, under the moon and stars, with the trees as sculpted silhouettes, surrounded by mysterious shadows and rustlings—the seeker hopes to be jolted out of his or her normal inhibitions into a state of alertness in which the deepest communion with the beyond is possible.

There are psychological intimations here of the child drinking in the inspirational milk at the breast of Mother Nature. Wordsworth's own biography suggests that he held a deep longing for his mother, who died when he was only seven.[14] It is not just spirit, but also vitality, which dwells in the visible beyond. To be detached is to sink into a depressive lethargy.

The German Romantic painter Caspar David Friedrich, in one of his most powerful works, *Monk by the Sea* (1809), has a still, black figure, his back to the viewer, gazing out into a grim, dark sea overhung by brooding storm-clouds. All the force is in nature, with the human projected as a lifeless blank—that is, a vertical corpse, if he fails to connect himself with the saving passion around him. Casting the anonymous figure as a monk underlines the sense that this domain is religious, that here is the new church. In that a monk has an ascetic vocation, Friedrich anticipates the more dynamic, Calvinist interaction of nature with work.

In the dynamic mode is the Byronic emphasis on *sturm und drang,* the individual galloping wildly through gales and driving rain, sailing small boats during storms—as painted by Turner. The Byronic is picked up today in the public fascination with extreme sports, such as climbing the Himalayas or sailing solo around the world.

Poussin's primary focus, in his landscapes, is on the human narrative. Occasionally, it is on one man like Matthew; more commonly, a collective drama, such as the widow of Phocion illegally tending her husband's ashes outside the walls of Athens.[15] It was a weakness in Romanticism to reject the notion of community.

Indeed, in many indicative works, from Goethe's *The Sorrows of Young Werther* (1774) to Keats' 'Ode to a Nightingale' (1819), the dream is to escape life altogether—the lonely individual withdrawing into nature or, ultimately, to his or her death in nature. An explicit example is Millais' Pre-Raphaelite painting of *Ophelia* (1851). Ophelia's corpse floats serenely in an intimate corner of a stream, enclosed by brilliantly vivid greens, the flowers glowing like jewels—the whole effect being an attempt at creating an enchanted coffin. Millais is trying to convince us that death in nature is sublimely beautiful: that it is not death.

A similar escapism is marked in the Impressionists, although without the dark side. They exclude human stories, as if to repress the pain, and offer the soothing, cheerful fantasy of another world within this world: one without shadows. The contrasting ego-assertive drive in the West is a more positive sign, choosing to experience landscape in active ways, especially through sport.

Of course, there is something to the stock complaint of the non-golfer, 'Why don't you relax and enjoy the view, instead of compulsively swiping at that little white ball?' Here is the weakness of vocation in nature: it is vulnerable to the *work* neuroses. Its virtue is the concentration through work so as to free the inner eye to sense the surrounds, expanding the ego beyond the self into union with the soul, itself diffused, *anima* through *mundi*. This strategy is quite different from that of Friedrich's monk, or of Wordsworth, whose first move is to look with the outer eye, the mind quietly focused so as to still the rest of the human organism, and to hypnotise the ego to sleep. By means of this meditative technique—for that is what it is, if un-formalised—the aim is to become as one with the elements, breathing in their spirit.

★★★

What can we conclude, in surveying the modern West and its search for meaning, when we focus on 'holydays'? The question targets the weekend, the annual vacation, or more random periods of leisure — what people choose to do when freed from economic necessity. On the one side, there is the depressive consumerism of television viewing, gobbling junk food; or of long hours spent playing computer games and surfing the Internet; or failed attempts to break free, like the package-tour.

On the other, there is the widespread urge to be out in nature. The flight to the country during three or four-day long-weekends has become a notorious cause of traffic congestion. Once having arrived at the holiday site, unselfconsciously, and usually in small, modest ways, modern individuals will find themselves worshipping the sacred cosmos — a picnic or a barbecue, a stroll along a beach, a drive through hills, a ferry ride, or a game of tennis or golf.

Because this is a taken-for-granted part of their mundane lives, they approach it without any of the self-importance with which their ancestors attended Sunday church. There is, as a result, a natural humility to their devotions. Indeed, if one were to describe to them what they do in religious language, they would likely scoff at such airy-fairy pretensions. They seek out their preferred landscapes by instinct, unknowingly, and by choosing one or other of the two modes discussed in this chapter. An unstated passion and faith moves here — one which speaks of the degree to which the Western religious impulse has been dechurched.

Part Four

# THE FUTURE

Chapter Fourteen

# THE NIGHTMARE — IF IT
# ALL GOES WRONG

Part IV of this book queries the future. It is structured in the form of a debate, conducted over two chapters. One side is put in this chapter: the dystopia, if all goes wrong. The next chapter puts the affirmative case.

A Hollywood classic sets the scene. In his last great Western, *The Man Who Shot Liberty Valance* (1962), John Ford tells the story of Hallie. She is everywoman, and everyman, who inhabits the modern West.

The young Hallie lives in the old West. It is wild, violent, but full of vitality, exuberance, and cheerfulness. The community, a frontier town called Shinbone, is strong. Hallie's parents run the main diner, feeding the community. Hallie is unofficially betrothed to Tom Doniphon (played by John Wayne), the big man who keeps rough order by checking the excesses of Liberty Valance, the town's rampaging, explosively violent baddie. The law of the gun rules the old West.

Ransom Stoddard (played by James Stewart) arrives, carried bleeding into Hallie's place before dawn, having been robbed and brutally beaten by Liberty Valance. Ransom is a young lawyer from

Puritan New England. He champions law, democracy, education, freedom, and technological progress in the explicit forms of railways and irrigation. Tom nicknames him 'pilgrim'. Hallie falls in love with the pilgrim from the east, and his ideals—the new ideals that underpin the modern world. She is fed up with the violence of the old West, and its lack of order, and she wants to learn to read and write; soon, she even becomes the schoolteacher. Also, part of her prefers a less manly man, one whom she can mother. And she is restless, preferring a vision of a more adventurous future that is glowing with idealism, compared with the predictability of settling down with Tom, on his small farm, to raise a family.

The story opens with Hallie, as an old woman, returning to Shinbone with Ransom to attend the funeral of Tom Doniphon. Shinbone is now modern. The town is prosperous and orderly: there is a train station and irrigation, and there is democracy. But the streets of the new Shinbone are dead. The earlier communal warmth has gone. The only thing left that Hallie cares for is the body of Tom, a now-forgotten relic of the past, lying in a crude coffin in a cheap backstreet undertaker's room. When she first sees the coffin, through an open door, she reels back in shock. Tom's hidden corpse becomes the authority that rules the story. Shinbone has turned into a farce of a place signalled by its name.

Ransom, the once-idealistic lawyer, has turned into Senator Stoddard, a powerful political figure in Washington. But he is a caricature of his younger self, now given to long, pompous monologues and grandly affected gestures. While he tells the story of the old West in the newspaper office, Hallie grieves beside Tom. She goes off to fetch a cactus rose from the desert, which she puts unpotted—plant, roots, and soil—on top of the coffin. It is as if she has attempted to replant the spirit of the old West, and its earthy energy, on top of the one vital thing left from the past: Tom's dead body.

The story ends with Hallie and Ransom leaving Shinbone by train. Ransom asks whether she put the cactus rose on Tom's coffin. He slumps at her affirmation, realising that she has loved Tom all along. The conductor then appears, boasting that everything is arranged for the senator's speedy connections back to Washington, as '[n]othing's too good for the man who shot Liberty Valance'. Ransom, who has lit a match for his pipe, snuffs it out. The light is extinguished. His wife, sitting beside him, is ashen and frail, little more than a shade that has overstayed its welcome on Earth.

Ransom and Hallie are both tragic figures. The senator is the ransom paid by modernity to get its way. His political career was founded on his reputation as the man of courage who shot Liberty Valance, thereby purging the old West of barbarism by killing it off. But his reputation as a hero is fraudulent, as he knows — because it was Tom who shot Liberty Valance. The pilgrim who champions the high ideals of honesty, integrity, and selfless service has built his career on a lie. The modern world is founded on a lie. Law, education, and freedom carry no gravity. This is what Hallie fell for.

The hero of the old West, its representative, is the real man of honour. Tom is ruled by duty, doing what he has to do because it is right. He is the least free of all the characters in the story — he is *not-Liberty*. In doing his duty, and saving Ransom's life, saving it for Hallie, he ruins his own. He knows perfectly well what he is doing. He also knows that his way of life is rapidly coming to an end — both historically, in that progress is inevitable, and personally, in that he is middle-aged and wants to hang up his gun and settle down on his farm.

But what is the point of the modern world that Hallie has been inwardly driven to choose? She was seduced by its redemptive illusion of her becoming literate and knowledgeable, a woman of the world, helping her husband build a modern, democratic America of prosperous small towns, full of decent, hard-working citizens, bringing up and educating their families. Her illusion needed Tom, the man of the old West, to bring it to fruition. Yet, while under the thrall of the illusion, she had no place for Tom—just as the modern West that he has made possible has no role for him. The man of exemplary honour, the man with gravity in his character, is now superfluous.

The dream that drove Hallie to change direction has left her stranded in a sterile life; returning, at the end, to the place she once loved, only to find it barren. She comes to realise that what she cherishes is dead. Her last act of nurture is to lovingly place wild cactus in raw earth on top of his cold remains.

Everyone who inhabits the modern West, man or woman, finding themselves in Hallie's shoes, would have made the same decision. Guided by reason and the rosy illusions of freedom and progress, they would have overruled their deeper instincts. They would have chosen comfort and order, education and democracy, over Tom Doniphon and the wild frontier.

★★★

Stavrogin is the shadow self of everyman, and everywoman, who inhabits the modern West. Dostoevsky tells the story in his novel *The Possessed*. Indeed, Stavrogin is the most interesting character in all of Dostoevsky's fiction—the nineteenth century's Hamlet.

Stavrogin is a Russian prince in his mid-to-late twenties. He is extremely handsome: tall, black-haired, a pale complexion, elegant, well-dressed, and with fine manners. He is intelligent, and physically powerful. He is well travelled, having visited the cultural sites of Europe, and the esoteric and religious sites of Egypt and Jerusalem, and having taken a course of lectures at a German university. Yet there is something hideous about the look of this 'paragon of beauty'. His face reminds people of a mask.

He returns to the provincial town he came from. Rumours precede him — of wild debauchery, of seducing wives and then fighting duels with their husbands and killing them. He commits acts of outrageous rudeness. In the local club, he goes up to an elderly gentleman who is in the habit of blustering, 'No, sir, they won't lead me by the nose!' and seizes him by the nose, dragging him across the room. When the governor, a relative, chastises Stavrogin mildly, the young prince bends down to whisper in his ear. Instead of speaking, however, Stavrogin bites the governor's ear.

All of the young women in the town fall in love with Stavrogin, and so do the men. Most of the latter have been disciples. Shatov gives some sense of the profundity of the prince's earlier philosophical reflections. He reminds Stavrogin that he once claimed that if it could be mathematically proven that truth was independent of Christ, he would choose Christ over truth. He taught that a society, or a people, is the body of its particular God, and that nations decay when they begin to have common gods. But Stavrogin has changed. Shatov challenges the current-day Stavrogin, asking whether it is true that he believes that brutish acts of debauchery can be as beautiful as sacrifices for the good of humanity. Stavrogin evades the question. There is a story circulating of him having seduced a 12-year-old girl, and then having sat by idly as she killed herself.

Shatov cries out that he himself is without talent, 'Stavrogin, why am I condemned to believe in you forever?' Another disciple calmly and fearlessly commits suicide, in order to prove that he has free-will, and therefore that all humans are gods, being free — ideas fed to him by Stavrogin. A third disciple builds a revolutionary cell, desperately trying to persuade Stavrogin to become its leader, only to receive the bored dismissal, 'What for?'

All of the town's young women have been seduced, at some time or other, by Stavrogin. Shatov's wife is pregnant with his child. In a last attempt to raise some feeling in himself, he spends a whole night with Lisa, the town beauty. The night is all talk. Stavrogin is by now impotent, with the implication that he belongs in a sect of castrati that practices in the neighbourhood. In his case, he is sexually, morally, and spiritually emasculated. The morning after, Lisa runs off, hysterically demented, only to be seized by an enraged crowd, and murdered. Stavrogin hangs himself, citing in a suicide note his lack of passion: 'You can cross a river on a tree-trunk, not on a chip.'

This man has extraordinary charisma. Given the sordid and evil facts of his life, how can this be? What is the source of such demonic charm?

Dostoevsky portrays a human world without meaning. God is dead; the new liberal, humanist, and scientific ideals are hollow; the older generation, including the mothers and fathers of the town's younger generation, is lost, enfeebled, and irresponsible. This world without meaning is desperate for a new Christ—a new teacher and a new leader to show it the way. 'Stavros' means 'cross' in Greek.

Stavrogin has the right credentials. He is intelligent, perceptive, original, and free. He fears no man—not suffering from the insecurities that dog normal human beings. Because he has studied and travelled, he knows things. He has personal style and intellectual substance. He thumbs his nose at conventional society, disgusted by the effeteness of the older generation. He creates his own moral law. He is detached and aloof, beholden to nobody and no thing. He has experienced life to the full, including testing the limits of human depravity, although he admits that debauchery brought him no pleasure. The stories of his violence are titillating to a generation that is aimless, tepid, and disgruntled—especially titillating to its women. And he is mysterious: no one can read him. Stavrogin has seized the day. If anyone has found the answer, it is he. He is precisely the hero whom modern times need.

But the man who has tried everything is left, at the end of his life pilgrimage, listless and empty. He has sought limits, something that might check him — whether in the form of social conventions, moral laws, or some inner conscience. His descent into gratuitous violence and depravity has been driven by a despairing need to find something to stop him. But no inner voice has spoken, 'No, don't dare do that!' If only it had, for that would have meant he had found something to believe in. If only he could conjure up some sense of shame in himself. He learns instead, like his next literary descendent, Joseph Conrad's Kurtz, that he has kicked the world to pieces. There is nothing for him to obey: nothing above, and nothing below. Stavrogin is a soul gone mad. All that remains is his lust for destruction. The last wish of this soul-mate of Hamlet is for death.

So what can we conclude about a generation, and a time, that adores Stavrogin? Out of its own failure to find a convincing answer to the metaphysical question, 'What should I do with my life?' it is charmed by the beautiful mask. In an earlier epoch, this would have been called Satanism. Today, we use terms such as 'nihilism', 'rancour', and 'pneumaphobia'. This generation is unconsciously — not knowing what it is doing — drawn to death-worship.

There has been a procession of humanist Christs in the West. Hamlet was the first, the pioneer. Stavrogin comes second, and he incorporates a strain of Mephistopheles — of satanic genius. Then follow, to name some leading examples, Conrad's Kurtz; the legend of Che Guevara; and, finally, right at the end of the twentieth century, *Fight Club's* Tyler Durden. (Scott Fitzgerald's Great Gatsby is a variant — in him, naive idealism replaces violence.) Each of these humanist Christs fails. One by one, they inexorably metamorphose into the anti-Christ. Here is the fundamental metaphysical *either–or*. Charisma turns demonic. If the human soul fails to discover its meaning, it goes mad and, in its dementia, loses authority over the ego. The unhinged ego becomes possessed by a mania for destruction—which ultimately means self-destruction. Freud termed something like this the 'death instinct'.

\*\*\*

If the West is heading steadily downwards into dystopia, J. G. Ballard's futuristic novel *Super-Cannes* (2000) traces some of the contours. The setting is 'Eden-Olympia': part business park, part luxury housing estate, and part self-contained rural compound serviced by hi-tech communications, top medical research and practice facilities, and luxury shopping. Eden-Olympia is secured by an intricate complex of video surveillance and security guards. The inhabitants are multi-national, and run global businesses, science laboratories, and hi-tech enterprises. The new elite of the smartest and most ambitious live together in a 'suburb of paradise', set on the French Riviera, bathed in benign Mediterranean sunshine.

For the talented and the ambitious, the future is here, and it means work, not play. They devote themselves to their offices and laboratories twelve hours a day, seven days a week—by choice. Their leisure is reduced to exhausted evenings at home, consuming pre-prepared meals and adult movie entertainment. They watch hard-core pornography, with nostalgia for a world they have lost—having little energy left for actual sex. These denizens of paradise live by a mixture of duty and caution, with emotion leached out of their lives.

In an earlier time at Eden-Olympia, the inhabitants were all becoming sick and paranoid. Their immune levels had declined; internal stress had reached screaming pitch. Creativity dropped. Then a cure was engineered by the visionary psychiatrist who still runs Super-Cannes. The breakthrough came from a recognition that his highly talented and productive professionals had dream fantasies of extreme rage and violent revenge. He decided to experiment with therapeutic violence: he designed a new order that openly and shamelessly ran on psychopathology, calling his method 'homeopathic madness'.

The psychiatrist set up self-help groups in the form of gangs, involving almost all the senior executives. The gangs would launch night expeditions into the local towns to start brawls, beat up pimps and petty criminals, and stage daring robberies. The result: immune levels recovered, insomnia and depression disappeared, and respiratory infections became a thing of the past. Innovation rose, as did profit levels.

A thirst for dramatic risk and violence steadily grew. Sado-masochistic sexual orgies were introduced, themselves increasingly dependent on drug-induced excitement. An Eden-Olympia doctor set up a paedophile ring, exploiting girls from the nearby Arab slums. Voyeurism was common, the psychiatrist noting dispassionately that when men watch their wives having sex with strangers, it confronts them with the basic truth that they are totally alone.

Ballard's *Super-Cannes* explores themes that are neither new, nor unique to it. A virtually identical psychology appears in the 1999 film (and earlier book), *Fight Club*. Men discover that violent fights with each other get the blood flowing, bringing them deep satisfaction and the new experience of masculine self-esteem, and a zest for life. But the Fight Clubs inexorably turn into fascist gangs. And Dostoevsky, already in his 1864 book, *Notes from Underground*, had predicted that in the future technological paradise, where comfort and order prevail, people would start sticking gold pins into each other out of boredom.

★★★

Let me chart the worst future by taking negative Western trends, and extrapolating from them. To put such a prophecy into perspective, these trends have been running for over a century and a half. My three exemplars have come from 1872, 1962, and 2000.

In the Western metropolis of today, traces of *Super-Cannes* appear more broadly and more deeply etched by the day. The new celebrity elite — film, television, and music idols, supermodels, and sporting mega-stars — live increasingly like the inhabitants of Eden-Olympia. Drug scandals among Olympic athletes are commonplace, as they are in cycling's Tour de France and, increasingly, among footballers. Top-ranked tennis and golf professionals withdraw to live in security-protected luxury housing compounds in Florida and Arizona. Rich professionals — in law, medicine, accountancy, and the upper management strata of the corporations — are turning to cocaine and the methamphetamines, speed and ice.

The emerging metropolis is Neurotic City. New suburbs grow, carpeted by larger and larger houses, containing smaller and smaller families. Levels of household debt soar to pay for them and for the consumer cornucopia that fills them, with families gorging heedlessly beyond their means, ditching the prudence that inclined their parents and grandparents to build up nest-eggs for rainy days.[1] Gardens disappear, as new generations appear for whom play is not the physical fun of games out-of-doors, but sedentary and solitary hours of computer games, Internet browsing, and fabricating fantasy identities on the Web. Obesity is at epidemic levels in the Anglo countries: in the worst case, America, the proportion of adults who are overweight is six out of every ten, and rising.[2] Teenage eating disorders have become common. And, as in Eden-Olympia, pornography is becoming a pastime stimulant for the majority.[3] Paedophilia is being surreptitiously and unwittingly facilitated in the mainstream culture with the sexualisation of children: scantily clad, made-up children in erotically suggestive poses appear in television, billboard, and department-store advertising. Stavrogin would be at home in this world — and even more disgusted with himself.

Teenagers compensate for their unnaturally sedentary and mind-centred lives with drugs and binge drinking at weekends. Parents have so little dynamic engagement with the hurly-burly of everyday life that they are haunted by their own paranoid fantasies—about safety, and especially that of their children. False fear takes over, with wild, delusional imaginings of paedophilia and traffic dangers making them harness their days to chauffeuring their children, making them wear tracking devices, and infecting them with their own red-alert anxiety levels.[4] The reality is that, in spite of the constant, confronting imagery of sex and violence in the public media, Western societies have never run as smoothly, nor have they been as safe.

Meanwhile, depression rates have risen tenfold in the West over the last two generations.[5] In Australia, well over a million people—5 per cent of the population—are medicated daily for depression. In 2004, anti-depressant prescriptions were written for 15 per cent of young people aged sixteen to twenty.[6] In these souls that have lost their meaning, the mania for destruction turns inwards, attacking the self as worthless and unlovable.

The emergency services that dot the urban landscape are no longer the old, practical ones—the policeman, the ambulance, and the fire-engine—but therapy agencies, ranging across a broad spectrum from doctors to counsellors to peddlers of quack new-age cures. A child who sees a cat torturing a mouse in the school play-yard is rushed off for psychological counselling. Neurotic City is all busyness on the surface, but melancholia and bleached emotion behind the scenes.

Neither Hallie nor Stavrogin had children—Mary Shatov's baby died. *Barrenness* was their signature tune. In the traditional heartland of the West, continental Europe, the birth-rate is calamitously low—as it is in Russia, China, and Japan. Germany is steadily turning into one vast retirement village, with the birth-rate having halved between 1965 and 2002 to little more than half the replacement rate — which means that the generic German population will halve in the next thirty years. The Italian and Spanish birth-rates are even lower.

The French birth-rate is marginally higher, but only because of the 15 per cent of the population that is Muslim — a reality that in itself is feeding gang rioting in outer-urban Islamic ghettoes and, in reaction, right-wing nationalist movements campaigning against the threat of 'Eurabia'.[7] In Holland, the same trend has led to predictions that by the second decade of the century the large cities of Amsterdam, Rotterdam, The Hague, and Utrecht will have Muslim majorities; Rotterdam is already 40 per cent Muslim. The fear of an imminent bi-cultural schism has transformed the Dutch, in one generation, from the most liberal and tolerant people in Europe to one of the most xenophobic.[8] A society that has lost the will to reproduce itself has, in the most basic sense, lost the will to live.

The other major indicator of a society's loss of will to live is already manifest in continental Europe. This is the will to defend its security interests. In the 1990s, Europe could only talk and dither while genocidal mass murder was conducted on its own soil, in Bosnia. Finally, the Unites States intervened. France and Germany generally oppose American initiatives against radical Islam, while under mounting civilisational threat from within their own borders. Under the increasing pressure of Europe turning into Eurabia, it is perhaps just as likely that the indigenous French will, step by small step, capitulate to the alien ideology from the east, as that they will fight back in defence of their traditions.[9]

As Europe fades into obscurity, except as a museum, its coming Eden-Olympias will be retirement compounds, managed by head therapists and security chiefs. They will be oases of luxury, inhabited by a gerontocracy that prolongs its passing of the time with gene-replacement and cosmetic surgery, while under increasing threat from the society beyond the perimeter walls — with its population becoming more impoverished, and more religiously and ethnically riven. One institutional bastion of the West for over two millennia, the Vatican, will have moved, in every practical sense, to the non-developed world, to either Africa or Latin America. And the two nations that are not committing demographic suicide, both Anglo — the United States and Australia — will switch their focus to the Asia-Pacific region, integrating Asian cultural forms.[10]

## Chapter Fifteen

# RESILIENCE

I have put forward one side of the debate about the future — the dystopia, if everything goes wrong. This chapter puts the affirmative case.

The nightmare future projected in the last chapter needs to be treated with a dose of scepticism. Dystopias, like their opposites (utopias), are a rationalist conceit. Human reason is adept at building logical systems, models that are elegant and internally consistent. It enjoys doing this, just as it enjoys solving mathematical puzzles: it gains a sense of power — above all, the power to create and restore order in the world. It is reason in this triumphalist mode that Luther dubbed 'the devil's whore'. He meant that it will sell itself to any bidder. Because reason cannot create values, it has no judgement.

When it comes to individuals and their societies, reason needs to stay modest. The human world is extraordinarily complex, its processes governed by myriad variables. This unfathomable complexity makes nonsense of any rational model that seeks to predict future workings. Edmund Burke argued that any great institution takes the cumulative wisdom of many generations to develop, after a lot of trial and error; here was the basis of his conservatism. He believed that any attempt to build a society from scratch, based on a rational utopian model, is, like the French Revolution, bound to fail. It fails because of consequences unforeseen in the plan.

It is the same with futurology. Predicting the social future is dependent on two dubious assumptions. The first is that current trends will continue in the same pattern as they have in the recent past; this means that major trends will remain major, significant ones will stay significant, and minor ones will neither gain in importance nor disappear. The second assumption is that nothing new will emerge; that, in other words, human behaviour will not surprise us. But human history is a narrative of surprises: the new and unforeseen is exactly what characterises much of it.

We humans are resilient. We are a notably adaptable species. And at work in our collectivities, there are antibodies — capacities that resist the social pathologies which develop. To change the metaphor, our societies contain dynamic self-correcting mechanisms. This is generally the case, but not inevitably. And all societies do, at some point in time, go into a terminal decline.[1]

What follows is a reflection on the main themes in this book, on the strength of the positive currents, and on the likelihood of them flowing through into the future.

★★★

I have used the polarity of *ego* and *soul* as an aid in helping us comprehend modern ways, and the sense that people make of what they do. These categories remain alive and rich in the West, helping give form to timeless universals.

As Thesis Five puts it, the strength of the Western tradition has been founded on a balance of the two: the fulfilment of the ego and the freedom of the soul to speak. Each needs the other; to a surprising degree, contemporary activity is directed to casting lines into the transcendent in the hope of a catch.

We glimpse the ego and the soul in the shadows, but beyond them there is scant religious language of any gravity that has survived in modern times. Living with uncertainty has become the norm. Not only are the mainstream churches near empty, but Christian doctrine is largely bygone. On the one hand, the West has a richness of practice, in its discovery of ways—some new, some remade—of acting in the world so as to maintain contact with the beyond. On the other, it has little theology to describe what it does, little metaphysical imagery to make sense of its quest. Most find themselves in the shoes of the fisherman, deep in contemplation, acting as if he worships the sea, simply doing what he does, without linking it with the rest of his life, or having any higher conception of the meaning of things.

There is no sign of a return to monastic asceticism of any type, which would be at odds with the whole Calvinist tendency of Thesis Four. Modern society is founded on the worldly ethic of 'seize the day': develop yourself and your talents, your imagination, and your intellect, in order to make a contribution, build something, become a success, leave a mark, make your social world a better place than the one you inherited. Such a celebration of the ego shows no sign of waning. Indeed, the last Christian injunctions against taking pride in achievement have lapsed.

Nevertheless, the Calvinist gearing of the work-ego to the soul, making the ideal of vocation central to a sense of individual wellbeing, continues to compel the West. Terkel's waitress throws herself 'heart and soul' into her work, and she would be ashamed to do a mediocre job. The sanctioning presence of the threat of shame is a sure sign that a higher spirit moves here. This is not a mundane job; she is not a slave to necessity. Moreover, those who are served by her, those who witness her waitressing, are moved: they know instinctively that she is virtuous and, moreover, that she is a living teacher of a central universal law, that of vocation. As a teacher, she points the finger at them in relation to their own different modes of work, as if to say, *If you do not approach it as I do, with everything at stake, my whole being engaged, then you are transgressing.* In this way, she too 'makes a difference', just as surely as does the fireman.

The waitress embodies the lower-middle-class ethos that while what we do may not be grand or prestigious, celebrated or influential — indeed, it is probably utterly mundane, like setting a table — the way that we do it counts. This Calvinist emphasis has extended in the modern West, with widespread exhortations to take care in ordinary, everyday life, to make the most of that life, to look after the little things, and to be open and generous in personal encounters. For here is the pursuit of vocation, available to everyone — indeed, required of everyone. The waitress has the special something that Hallie lacks, and it makes all the difference.

An effective teacher of this secular theology is television soap-opera. Its dwelling on average lives, and their daily ups-and-downs, provides a continuous conversation about the right and wrong things to do. Above all, it voices a driving undercurrent which asserts that this is your life, it is the only one you have got, and it is important; make sure that you take its seemingly trivial incidents seriously, or else. Here is 'seize the day' made concrete, within a moral structure, with a higher end mediated by the generalised ideal of vocation. Even *The Sopranos* explores stock soap-opera moral themes through the lives of the Mafia boss's two families — that of the gang and that of his own nuclear family.

This is the cultural terrain across which the modern parables sound. *Casablanca* is a trial of suffering for Rick, alone, following the thread of his solitary life-story. He voyages blind and groaning, like the exiled Oedipus, except for moments guided by his conscience. There is no family or community to soothe his pain; only friendship, all feeding into a dry, urbane, world-weary sarcasm, but one in which the bitterness is softened by a faith under the surface, where conscience still rules. Rick, it turns out, is a compassionate and just man. He has intense personal reasons for punishing a young married woman willing to sell herself for an exit visa, but he saves her, in spite of his tragic reflection: 'No one ever loved *me* that much.'

Here is no brash ego, affronting its destiny, yet it is not one to be tangled with. There is warmth in the distant, rumbling snarl of the old lion. There is warmth, too, in the way that his own young, innocent romance, once thwarted and now returning to torment him — mixed up with a live drama of political good and evil, through rages and drunkenness — transmutes in him into a soulfulness that casts an otherworldly charm over the events.

*Gone with the Wind* has a different inflection. The heroine, again, is a solitary figure with no communal attachments. She is cast in harsh times with a formidable ego and animal spirits — extraordinary vitality, but very little conscience. The story implies that her lack of conscience feeds a coldness of character, and this ruins any possibility of happiness. It is contrasted with the soulfulness of the saintly Melanie, who is, however, too selflessly good to be true. Scarlett's one genuine attachment is to the home in which she grew up, to which she retreats at the end. The implication is that home is the only place in which her soul might find some space to breathe.

The tragedy of Marilyn Monroe is also to do with the failed pursuit of happiness. With the natural gift of a beauty and character that appealed to the times, an ambitious and manipulative ego that could exploit her fortune and which shone magnetically in front of the camera, she was ruined by her other self, a helplessly crushed ego. In addition, even her effervescent moods on screen were accompanied by dead-cold eyes that told of some sort of absence of soul.

Philip Marlowe had occupied the same anomic Los Angeles as Marilyn — seedy, corrupt, and with no communal bonds. He was himself in his withering aloneness, and in his indifference to any but the most fleeting romantic attachment, given to regular drunken escapes. But Marlowe had faith. It got him up in the mornings. His faith animated his conscience, and they together were his only worldly possessions. There was a strong ego, too, but it was under their strict orders to do a good job, to make sure he finished it — whatever the personal risk — to not overcharge, to not get involved with his attractive female clients (at least while a case was on), and to ensure that the truth came out. He was unmoved by social eminence, political clout, and physical intimidation, and was unembarrassed by his own shabby circumstances.

Justice in modernity is no longer tribal, maintained by elders and ministers. Its true judiciary has been democratised into each individual conscience. Marlowe is one of its exemplars, with film and television police and detective dramas ever since populated by his descendants, an increasing number of whom are women.

Dr Cartwright belongs to the same lineage. Her ego has been battered by the afflictions that curse Aristotle's 'small of soul'. She is dispirited, almost past caring about her life. Yet she is *megalopsuchē*, great of soul. Her conscience, shaped by her medical oath, steadies her, and she takes charge of the world into which she has been cast, redeeming it.

Marlowe, Rick, and Dr Cartwright stand as the counter to Stavrogin. Their ultimate appeal is a certain charisma of soul. It is not, oddly enough, so different from that of Raphael's great Madonnas — Sistine, Grand Duke, and *La Belle Jardinière*. All cases live in the thick of worldly mayhem, advancing slowly into their own tragic destinies, open and defenceless to the blows, the slashes across the eyes, alert and aware yet resigned, under no illusions. It is not shining hopes that draw them forwards. Yet all have their pleasures — like the Madonna in her motherhood enjoying her little boy. They do not turn away, denying, retreating into some busyness. They do not need to test boundaries, to see whether they exist; they know the limits all too well. They take their fate, face on, past caring about being something big themselves — in them, the ego has become mellow and retiring. They gain gravity, becoming a presence in the world in the vicinity of which others appear ephemeral, blowing around like autumn leaves. It is a presence steeped in spirit, as if the battered ego embraces the soul, letting it take over and occupy the whole self. These are the modern saints. Where they dwell is the modern sacred site.

We learn by example. As always, there remains the need for exemplars — for heroes — and morality tales about ambition, striving, greatness, and success and failure. As we have seen, sport has come to provide many of these, especially as a consequence of its conversion to the work ethic. At its highest, it is a lesson about the harmony of ego and soul.

When the samurai's sword finally breaks its poised immobility and, with a single spare *flash,* too fast for the eye to follow, executes its task, it moves under the authority of soul. The ego has overseen the years of hard discipline, demanded the steady and remorseless perfecting of technique. It has turned the delinquent mind into a steel band of spotlit concentration, so that it itself at the testing moment, huge and splendid, yet simultaneously at ease, can lose itself, surrendering to the soul. Soul knows the moment to move, its movement obedient to the divine form, as if guided by Matthew's angel. With such grace there is no failure.

So it is when one hundred thousand fans move as one, in speechless awe, with the godlike footballer striding the arena. They, too, learn of the exhilaration of the fusion of ego and soul. They learn that what they watch is not just a game. They are right to make this the site of their pilgrimages, true to themselves and to their culture. This is *religio athletae,* centring on the 'beautiful rhythm'. Conversely, the tourist, packaged into the Roman Forum, gets it wrong.

In search of exemplars, it has become more important to include nature. When it is the sacred cosmos rather than a personalised God that calls, the angels of the beyond—those spirits which carry the messages—are most likely to disguise themselves as forests and bush, hills and mountains, seas and oceans and, of course, skies in their own manifold splendour.

The West started here, with the ancient Greeks and their river gods, their tree nymphs, Zeus of thunder and lightning, Apollo of the sun, Poseidon of the sea, and Artemis of the uncultivated earth and fertility. The neo-classical Poussin draws on their authority when he places his Matthew in landscape. The inspiring angel comes from distant hills and skies, its language that of clouds and trees and river. It is only once Matthew is in tune with that language, able to hear, to breathe in its spirit, that he who is nothing—a combination of a fearful tramp ego and mute soul—is freed to begin his story. Strangely, it is a story entirely about humans and what they do to each other, what drives them, in what they may believe and how. By the end of that story, it has turned into the ultimate Western tragedy.

Modernity has revolutionised its relationship to nature. It no longer labours in the fields, ruled by the climate and the seasons. For a long time, it romanticised the old ways, imagining some sort of uplifting union in ploughing, harvesting, and herding—blind to the reality that, through the long European winters, digging turnips out of frozen ground in driving sleet in order not to starve must have been a bitter drudgery, a slave-animal subsistence.

The modern West has gradually found its own way of building bridges to nature, largely through sport. These bridges are not restricted to a small elite—no longer just to upper-class English poets in the Lake District. Its method has been through leisure vocations, drawing on the logic of work, but adapting one aspect. In its sport mode, it no longer seeks to dominate nature—to mine it, hunt it, fell it, carve it, or smelt it. It now seeks to find a harmonious integration, for one treads reverently in a sanctuary. Here is a return to the pagan worship of the Earth, as a goddess infinite in her beauty: the new incarnation of transcendent order. As individuals today seek to balance ego and soul, many of them include nature, to make a three-way equation.

The modern search for meaning depends on finding a way of living with metaphysical uncertainty. Confidence has dissipated in response to the big questions — why I am here, which god or other mysterious force governs my life, and what happens to me when I die. Dogmatic religious creeds no longer convince most people in asserting that God's in his heaven, looking down and listening, rewarding the pious and the good. Kierkegaard, in the 1840s, had already dismissed such a creedal orientation as religion for children. Moreover, all the signs suggest that the West has passed the point of no return in relation to a clear and distinct metaphysical doctrine. There is no going back.

In the face of uncertainty, it is down to the individual. One and all are engaged in a life quest, drawn to the mystery, trying to find ways into its domain. The goal is to find traces of the self within the enigma.

The Protestant principles enumerated in Thesis Four continue to guide the Western dynamic. Individual conscience presides, overseeing a this-worldly vocation, including work and sport, and providing the underpinning laws for conversation in popular culture about what constitutes right conduct. These principles are wedded to a philosophy of live your life, seize the day, but take care of the little things shaping daily practice. Their spirit infuses new activities such as DIY home-renovation and personal computers, integrating them with the work ethic; and motor car driving, uniting it to personal responsibility. The implicit theology of grace has extended one way into everyday life; the other, into finding signals of transcendence in nature. This theology has placed its stamp on the private sphere — whether of eros, philia, or *agapē* — weakening communal and tribal bonds, but strengthening individual ones. Again, the individual conscience is the master. Overall, this modern world-view has been supported and invigorated by democracy.

In short, this book has vindicated Thesis One: all humans, unconsciously, know the true and the good, and are inwardly compelled to find what they know, through their lives and what they see. They sense that there is some higher order framing their existence. The West continues to grope for the frayed metaphysical tissues.

This book has vindicated Thesis One by employing Thesis Two. Thesis Two proposes that culture is those myths, stories, images, rhythms, and conversations that voice the eternal and difficult truths on which deep knowing, and therefore wellbeing, is dependent.

Here are universals that endure, and that continue to frame the way people live. Everyday life, of its nature, tests individual morale with its routines and disappointments. Suffering — whether of tedium, hardship, sickness, or loss — brings the question of meaning to the surface. With no certain answers, the grinning mask of nihilism appears from the shadows, leering, and jeering that life, boiled down to its essence, when it is not merely absurd, is horrible. The temptations of orgiastic consumption offer an escape, and the illusion that a person affluent in his or her comforts shall be secure from the dread that there is nothing.

Through all of this, an instinctual knowing prevails, seeking meaningful shape in cultural forms. It does so for almost all, and for most of the time. It signals that there is beauty and goodness, and an order beyond the everyday, affirming why we are here.

# BIBLIOGRAPHY

Aeschylus, *Agamemnon*, trans. Richmond Lattimore, University of
  Chicago Press, Chicago, 1953
Alexander, Jeffrey, *The Civil Sphere*, Oxford University Press, New York,
  2006
Arendt, Hannah, *The Human Condition*, University of Chicago Press,
  Chicago, 1958
——, *On Revolution*, Faber and Faber, London, 1964
Aristotle, *Nichomachean Ethics*, trans. H. Rackham, Heinemann, London,
  1934
——, *Rhetoric*, trans. H.C. Lawson-Tancred, Penguin, London, 1991
Augustine, *The City of God*, trans. J. Healey, Dent, London, 1945
Bagehot, Walter, *The English Constitution*, intro. Richard Crossman,
  Fontana, London, 1993
Baudrillard, Jean, *Selected Writings*, trans. J. Mourrain, Polity, Cambridge,
  1988
Bauman, Zygmunt, *Liquid Fear*, Polity, Cambridge, 2006
——, *Postmodernity and its Discontents*, Polity, Cambridge, 1996
Bell, Daniel, *The Cultural Contradictions of Capitalism*, Heinemann,
  London, 1976
Berger, Peter, *A Rumor of Angels*, Anchor, New York, 1970
—— *The Sacred Canopy*, Anchor, New York, 1969
Bloom, Allan, *The Closing of the American Mind*, Simon and Schuster, New
  York, 1987
Bloom, Harold, *The American Religion*, Chu Hartley, New York, 2006

Boorstin, Daniel J., *The Image*, Atheneum, New York, 1962

Bork, Robert H., *The Tempting of America: the political seduction of the law*, Free Press, New York, 1990

Bouma, Gary, *Australian Soul*, Cambridge University Press, Melbourne, 2006

Bourdieu, Pierre, *Distinction: a social critique of the judgement of taste*, trans. R. Nice, Routledge & Kegan Paul, London, 1984

Bremmer, Jan, *The Early Greek Concept of the Soul*, Princeton University Press, Princeton, 1983

Burke, Edmund, *Reflections on the Revolution in France*, Dodsley, London, 1790

Calasso, Roberto, *The Marriage of Cadmus and Harmony*, trans. Tim Parks, Knopf, New York, 1993

Campbell, Joseph, *The Power of Myth*, Doubleday, New York, 1988

Carroll, John, *Guilt: the grey eminence behind character, history, and culture*, Routledge & Kegan Paul, London, 1985

——, *The Western Dreaming*, HarperCollins, Sydney, 2001

——, *The Wreck of Western Culture: humanism revisited*, Scribe, Melbourne, 2004

Carter, Miranda, *Anthony Blunt, His Lives*, Picador, New York, 2003

*Catechism of the Catholic Church*, St Pauls, Sydney, 1994

Claus, David, *Toward the Soul*, Yale University Press, New Haven, 1981

Costello, John, *Mask of Treachery*, Collins, London, 1988

Davison, Graeme, *Car Wars: how the car won our hearts and conquered our cities*, Allen & Unwin, Sydney, 2004

De Vaus, David, *Diversity and Change in Australian Families: statistical profiles*, Australian Institute of Family Studies, Melbourne, 2004

Durkheim, Emile, *The Elementary Forms of Religious Life*, trans. J.W. Swain, Free Press, New York, 1965

——, *Suicide: a study in sociology*, trans. J.A. Spaulding and G. Simpson, Routledge & Kegan Paul, London, 1952

Eliot, T.S., *Notes towards the Definition of Culture*, Faber and Faber, London, 1962

Freud, Sigmund, *Civilization and its Discontents*, trans. Joan Riviere, Hogarth, London, 1963

Furedi, Frank, *Culture of Fear*, Continuum, London, 2002

Gathorne-Hardy, Jonathan, *The Public School Phenomenon*, Penguin, London, 1979

Green, Martin, *Children of the Sun*, Basic Books, New York, 1976

Gumbrecht, Hans Ulrich, *In Praise of Athletic Beauty*, Harvard University Press, Cambridge, Mass., 2006

Heidegger, Martin, *Vorträge und Aufsätze*, Neske, Pfullingen, 1954

Hendin, Herbert, *The Age of Sensation*, Norton, New York, 1975

Hill, Christopher, *Reformation to Industrial Revolution*, Penguin, London, 1969

Hillman, James, *The Soul's Code*, Random House, New York, 1996

Himmelfarb, Gertrude, *Marriage and Morals among the Victorians*, Knopf, New York, 1985

Hobsbawm, Eric, *Age of Extremes: the short twentieth century, 1914–1991*, Abacus, London, 1995

Homer, *The Iliad*, trans. Richmond Lattimore, Chicago University Press, Chicago, 1951

Hornby, Nick, *Fever Pitch*, Indigo, London, 1996

Huffington, Arianna Stassinopoulos, *Picasso*, Weidenfeld & Nicolson, London, 1988

James, William, *The Varieties of Religious Experience*, Fontana, London, 1960

Kant, Immanuel, *Critique of Practical Reason*, trans. L.W. Beck, Macmillan, New York, 1985

——, *Groundwork of the Metaphysic of Morals*, trans. H.J. Paton, Harper & Row, New York, 1964

Kapleau, Philip, *The Three Pillars of Zen*, Anchor, New York, 1980

Kemp, C.D., *Big Businessmen*, Institute of Public Affairs, Melbourne, 1964

Kierkegaard, Soren, *Concluding Unscientific Postscript*, trans. D.F. Swenson, Princeton University Press, Princeton, 1968

——, *Either–Or*, trans. D.F. & L.M. Swenson, Princeton University Press, Princeton, 1959

——, *Fear and Trembling*, trans. W. Lowrie, Princeton University Press, Princeton, 1954

Kowinski, William Severini, *The Malling of America*, Morrow, New York, 1985

Lasch, Christopher, *Haven in a Heartless World*, Basic Books, New York, 1979

—— *The True and Only Heaven*, Norton, New York, 1991

Leavis, F.R., *Education and the University*, Chatto and Windus, London, 1948

Leed, Eric J., *The Mind of the Traveller*, Basic Books, New York, 1991

Levi, Primo, *If This Is a Man*, trans. S. Woolf, Sphere, London, 1987

Lewis, Tania, *Smart Living: lifestyle media and popular expertise*, Peter Lang, New York, 2008

Lilla, Mark, *The Stillborn God*, Knopf, New York, 2007

Lipovetsky, Gilles, *The Empire of Fashion*, Princeton University Press, Princeton, 1994

Lukács, Georg, *Soul and Form*, trans. A. Bostock, Merlin, London, 1974

MacDonald, Ian, *Revolution in the Head: The Beatles' records and the sixties*, Fourth Estate, London, 1994

Mailer, Norman, *Marilyn: a biography*, Grosset & Dunlap, New York, 1974

Marcus, Greil, *In the Fascist Bathroom*, Penguin, London, 1993

Marx, Karl, *Capital*, trans. E. & C. Paul, Dent, London, 1933

Marx, Karl & Engels, Frederick, *The Communist Manifesto*, Progress, Moscow, 1952

——, *The German Ideology*, trans. S. Ryazanskaya, Progress, Moscow, 1964

McLuhan, Marshall, *Understanding Media*, Sphere, London, 1967

Mérot, Alain, *Nicolas Poussin*, Thames & Hudson, London, 1990

Miller, Daniel, *A Theory of Shopping*, Polity, Cambridge, 1998

Newman, John Henry, *The Idea of a University*, Oxford University Press, Oxford, 1976

Nietzsche, Friedrich, *Basic Writings*, trans. Walter Kaufmann, Modern Library, New York, 1968

——, *Thus Spoke Zarathustra*, trans. Walter Kaufmann, Viking, New York, 1954

Novak, Michael, *The Joy of Sports*, Basic Books, New York, 1976

Oakeshott, Michael, *Rationalism in Politics and other Essays*, Methuen, London, 1962

O'Brien, Conor Cruise, *The Great Melody: a thematic biography of Edmund Burke*, Minerva, London, 1993

Onians, R.B., *The Origins of European Thought*, Cambridge University Press, Cambridge, 1951

Paglia, Camille, *Sexual Personae*, Yale University Press, New Haven, 1990

Plato, *The Collected Dialogues*, ed., Princeton University Press, Princeton, 1963

Probert, Belinda, *The Work Generation*, Brotherhood of St Laurence, Melbourne, 1996

Putnam, Robert D., *Bowling Alone: the collapse and revival of American community*, Simon & Schuster, New York, 2000

Putnam, Robert D., Leonardi, Robert, & Nanetti, Raffaella, *Making Democracy Work: civic traditions in modern Italy*, Princeton University Press, Princeton, 1993

Richardson, John, *A Life of Picasso, vol. II, 1907–1917*, Random House, New York, 1996

Rieff, Philip, *Fellow Teachers*, University of Chicago Press, Chicago, 1985

——, *The Triumph of the Therapeutic*, Harper & Row, New York, 1966

Rifkin, Jeremy, *The End of Work*, Putnam, New York, 1995

Rochefoucauld, Duc de la, *Maximes et Réflexions*, Gallimard, Paris, 1965

Rosenberg, Pierre, *Nicolas Poussin*, Réunion des Musées Nationaux, Paris, 1994

Rothschild, Emma, *Paradise Lost: the decline of the auto-industrial age*, Random House, New York, 1973

Ruprecht, Louis A., *Was Greek Thought Religious?* Palgrave, New York, 2002

Sartre, Jean-Paul, *Being and Nothingness*, trans. H.E. Barnes, Methuen, London, 1969

Schumpeter, Joseph, *Capitalism, Socialism and Democracy*, Allen & Unwin, London, 1976

Sennett, Richard, *The Corrosion of Character*, Norton, New York, 1998

Shorter, Edward, *The Making of the Modern Family*, Fontana, London, 1977

Sophocles, *Oedipus the King*, trans. R. Grene, Chicago University Press, Chicago, 1954

Steiner, George, *In Bluebeard's Castle: some notes towards the redefinition of culture*, Faber and Faber, London, 1971

——, *No Passion Spent*, Faber and Faber, London, 1996

——, *A Reader*, Penguin, London, 1984

Steyn, Mark, *America Alone: the end of the world as we know it*, Regnery, Washington, 2006

Stone, Lawrence, *The Causes of the English Revolution, 1529–1642*, Routledge & Kegan Paul, London, 1972

——, *The Family, Sex and Marriage in England 1500–1800*, Penguin, London, 1979

Tacey, David, *Edge of the Sacred: transformation in Australia*, HarperCollins, Melbourne, 1995

——, *Jung*, Granta, London, 2006

Terkel, Studs, *Working*, Peregrine, London, 1977

Tocqueville, Alexis de, *Democracy in America*, trans. H. Reeve, Colonial Press, 1900

Weber, Max, *From Max Weber*, trans. H.H. Gerth & C.W. Mills, Routledge & Kegan Paul, London, 1948

——, *The Protestant Ethic and the Spirit of Capitalism*, trans. Talcott Parsons, Unwin, London, 1930

Wilson, William Julius, *When Work Disappears*, Knopf, New York, 1996

Wolf, Martin, *Why Globalization Works*, Yale University Press, New Haven, 2004

# NOTES

## Five Theses

1  Nietzsche, *The Birth of Tragedy, Basic Writings*, p. 137.
2  Weber, *The Protestant Ethic and the Spirit of Capitalism*, p. 182.
3  La Rochefoucauld, *Maximes*, no. 4.
4  Aristotle, *Rhetoric,* chapter 2.2, pp. 142–6.
5  John 8: 58.
6  Shakespeare, *Macbeth,* act I, scene II, lines 141–2.
7  Homer, *The Iliad,* book 19, lines 362–4.
8  Homer, *The Iliad,* book 1, line 231.
9  Homer, *The Iliad,* book 21, lines 106–12.
10  Bremmer, *The City of God,* pp. 21–2.
11  Augustine, *The Early Greek Concept of the Soul,* vol. 2, book 13, chapters 2–4, pp. 1–4. Primo Levi refers, in his accounts of the Nazi Concentration Camps, to the *Muselmänner,* those who had given up, as the drowned, 'non-men' already too empty to really suffer (pp. 93–106).
12  Aristotle, *Rhetoric,* book 2, chapter 2. 13, pp. 174–6. This translation is by Martha C. Nussbaum, *The Fragility of Goodness,* Cambridge University Press, Cambridge, 1986, p. 338.
13  Onians, *The Origins of European Thought,* pp. 93–6. David Claus has traced the psychologising of the Greek concept of the soul, from Homer, for whom it is a sort of immortal life-force, completely without

personality, to Plato, for whom it has a comprehensive personal self, part immortal and part mortal, with moral, rational, and emotional components—it is responsive to both education and therapy.

14 Hillman, *The Soul's Code*, p. ix.

15 Hillman, *The Soul's Code*, pp. 63–91.

## 1. Work

1 Vermeer had been raised as a Protestant, but he married a Catholic and converted. Whatever his own explicit religious views—and there seem to have been ties with the Jesuits—the cultural ethos he painted was rigorously Protestant. His own town of Delft had close links with the House of Orange in The Hague. Max Weber, in whose shadow this chapter was conceived, would have found Vermeer particularly suited to illustrating his Protestant Ethic thesis.

2 Keith Thomas, *Religion and the Decline of Magic*, Penguin, London, 1978, p. 192.

3 I have explored at some length the characteristics of this change in disposition, its psychological preconditions, and some of the historical evolution in the case of England, in 'The Role of Guilt in the Formation of Modern Society: England 1350–1800', *The British Journal of Sociology*, vol. 32, no. 4, Dec. 1981; and in *Guilt*, pp. 97–122.

4 Marx & Engels, *The German Ideology*, p. 45.

5 Terkel, *Working*, pp. 1, 3.

6 Terkel, *Working*, pp. 421–4.

7 Terkel, *Working*, p. 61.

8 Terkel, *Working*, p. 479.

9 Terkel, *Working*, pp. 249–53.

10 Terkel, *Working*, p. 324.

11 Probert, *The Work Generation*, pp. 72–3.

12 There is so much overlap in the categories of television genre that I will use 'soap-opera' in the broader rather than the narrower sense. Hal Himmelstein addresses the same problem by using the term 'television melodrama' to include soap-opera, police shows, frontier drama, TV westerns, and murder and private detective mysteries. See his *Television Myth and the American Mind*, 2nd edn, Praeger, Westport, 1994, pp. 197–245.

13 Arendt, *The Human Condition*, pp. 79–174.

14 Rifkin, *The End of Work*, p. 175.

15  Rifkin, *The End of Work*, pp. 141–62.

16  See, for example, Marx & Engels, *Manifesto of the Communist Party*, pp. 47–59.

17  *Australian Jobs 2007*, Department of Employment and Workplace Relations, Canberra, 2007, especially pp. 9, 19.

18  Sennett, *The Corrosion of Character*, for example, pp. 122, 116.

19  Michael Pusey is finding, in a current study of young Australians aged 20 to 24, that they like the challenge of the new economy. They see themselves as 'entrepreneurs of the self', approaching their lives with a strong commitment to having a 'positive attitude', and to the need to move out of their 'comfort zones'.

    Sara James, in a PhD dissertation, written under my supervision, is discovering similar attitudes. Interviewing Australians, in the Terkel mode, across a broad range of 25 occupational groups about their reflections on their experience of work, she is encountering the same need to find meaning.

20  Freud, *Civilization and its Discontents*, pp. 16–17.

21  The film did very poorly at the box office, and is, today, very difficult to find. Ford critics polarise on its merit. One who recognises its high place in the canon is Tag Gallagher (*John Ford*, University of California Press, Berkeley, 1986). Joseph McBride and Michael Wilmington devote the final chapter of their book, *John Ford*, entirely to 7 *Women* (Da Capo Press, New York, 1975).

## 2. Sport

1  See, as an example, John Alt, 'Sport and Cultural Reification: from ritual to mass consumption', *Theory, Culture and Society*, vol. 1, no. 3, 1983, pp. 93–107. George Orwell, in 'The Sporting Spirit', *Collected Essays, Journalism and Letters*, vol. IV, Secker & Warburg, London, 1968. pp. 40–4, was more of the old school, finding crudity, violence and xenophobia. On the other side, Michael Novak, in *The Joy of Sports*, provides many American examples that contradict the commercialisation thesis. And Gumbrecht's *In Praise of Athletic Beauty* celebrates sport for its aesthetic appeal.

2  Alt, 'Sport and Cultural Reification: from ritual to mass consumption', p. 98.

3  Hornby, *Fever Pitch*, p. 225.

4  Hornby, *Fever Pitch*, p. 20.

5   Hornby, *Fever Pitch*, p. 198.

6   Sigmund Freud, *Dictionary of Psychoanalysis*, ed. N. B. F. Gaynor, Premier, New York, 1963, pp. 22–3.

7   Hendin, *The Age of Sensation*, p. 103.

8   Hendin, *The Age of Sensation*, p. 294.

9   This was the main reason that the Australian Aborigines, in their quite different type of society, traditionally subjected only their boys to initiation, a rite that was of greater cultural importance than any other. See Robert Tonkinson, *The Mardu Aborigines*, Holt, Rinehart and Winston, Fortworth, Texas, 1993, ch. 4.

10  Gathorne-Hardy, *The Public School Phenomenon*, pp. 213–18.

11  Homer, *The Iliad*, book 16, lines 210–11.

12  Hornby, *Fever Pitch*, p. 187.

13  Carroll, *Guilt*, pp. 37–8.

14  Aeschylus, *Agamemnon*, lines 925–6.

15  Louis A. Ruprecht, 'Greek Exercises: The Modern Olympics as Hellenic Appropriation and Reinvention', *Thesis Eleven*, 93, May 2008. Also, Ruprecht, *Was Greek Thought Religious?*, ch. 9. Ruprecht stresses the degree to which Olympic games, both ancient and modern, have been essentially religious.

16  Quoted by Ruprecht, *Was Greek Thought Religious?* p. 143.

17  Tim Winton, *Breath*, Penguin, Melbourne, 2008, p. 76.

18  Quoted by Gumbrecht, *In Praise of Athletic Beauty*, p. 51.

19  Homer, *The Iliad*, book 15, lines 262–70.

20  Leo Tolstoy, *War and Peace*, trans. Rosemary Edmonds, Penguin, London, 1957, vol. II, p. 919.

21  This is the case if the symbolic attendance of watching games on television is taken into account. Australian statistics help to give some sense of the comparison. In 2005, around 7 per cent of the population attended church regularly, which comes to 1.5 million people. In the six months of the year in which football is played, the most attended code by a large margin is Australian Rules. On average, 300,000 fans attend matches every weekend in the major national competition. In addition, there are minor competitions, country football, two codes of rugby (the dominant game played in the states of New South Wales and Queensland), and national and local soccer competitions. Football attendance per weekend aggregates to something like 600,000. This is less than half the number of people who attend church.

However, football also attracts a huge television audience. Four million watch Australian Rules Football every weekend on television. In 2005, four million watched the Australian Rules Grand Final, the largest television audience for any program for the year. Around one-third of Australians regularly watch football, one way or another.

22  Gumbrecht, *In Praise of Athletic Beauty*, p. 216.

23  Hornby, *Fever Pitch*, p. 72.

24  Henry Gullett, *Not As a Duty Only*, Melbourne University Press, Melbourne, 1976, p. 1.

25  Tolstoy, *War and Peace*, p. 945.

26  Shakespeare, *Henry V*, act IV, scene III, lines 64–7.

27  Fyodor Dostoevsky, *Notes from Underground*, trans. A. A. MacAndrew, Signet, New York, 1961, p. 108.

## 3. Love

1  Plato, *Symposium*, in *The Collected Dialogues of Plato*, 202e–203e.

2  William Tyndale translation of Paul's Letter to the Corinthians, I: 13 (in *Tyndale's New Testament*, Yale University Press, New Haven, 1989).

3  I have done this, in part, in a chapter on 'Soul-Mate Love' in *The Western Dreaming*.

4  MacDonald, *Revolution in the Head*, pp. 76–8.

5  Mailer, *Marilyn: a biography*, p. 245. Mailer's biography is a rare reminder of the light which may be shed by a writer of judgement who wrestles with his subject. His book is not the random accumulation of lifeless facts simulating a portrait.

6  Mailer, *Marilyn*, pp. 97, 226.

7  Mailer, *Marilyn*, p. 178.

8  Aeschylus, *Agamemnon*, line 183.

9  Stone, *The Family, Sex and Marriage in England*, pp. 217–99.

10  De Vaus, *Diversity and Change in Australian Families*, p. 232.

11  De Vaus, *Diversity and Change*, p. 135.

12  Christopher Lasch, *Haven in a Heartless World*.

13  In Australia, 77 per cent of children born in 1981–85 spent all of their first 15 years living with their biological parents (De Vaus, *Diversity and Change*, p. 140).

14  R. G. Menzies, *The Forgotten People*, Robertson & Mullens, Melbourne, 1942, pp. 4–5.

15  Catherine Hakim, 'Grateful Slaves and Self-made Women: fact and

fantasy in women's work orientations', *European Sociological Review*, vol. 7, no. 2, Sept. 1991, pp. 101–21. See also, Hakim, 'The Sexual Division of Labour and Women's Heterogeneity', *The British Journal of Sociology*, vol. 47, no. 1, March 1996, pp. 178–88; preceded by her article, 'Five Feminist Myths about Women's Employment', *The British Journal of Sociology*, vol. 46, no. 3, Sept. 1995, pp 429–55. A 1997 Australian study based on large-sample national surveys found that an even higher 76 per cent of women agreed that if a woman works, her main responsibility is still to home and children (David de Vaus, 'Family Values in the Nineties', *Family Matters*, Australian Institute of Family Studies, no. 48, Spring/Summer 1997, pp. 4–10).

At the same time, a 2007 study of Australian working mothers carried out by Peter Brown of Griffith University's *Centre for Work, Organisation and Wellbeing* found a high proportion of young mothers complaining that caring for the children was stressful and boring.

16  Probert, *The Work Generation*, p. 19.

## 4. Lower-Middle-Class Culture

1  Peter Willmott and Michael Young, *Family and Kinship in East London*, Penguin, London, 1962.

2  My argument in this chapter has some affinity with Georg Lukács' 1909 essay 'The Bourgeois Way of Life', which uses the short stories of Theodor Storm to explore 'a lyrical description of a quiet, warm, simple life-mood' (Georg Lukács, *Soul and Form*). It needs to be stressed that the Lukács of 1909 portrays a different bourgeois than the one of his later work, focused on Thomas Mann. The former is lower middle class, the latter high bourgeois. Agnes Heller and Ferenc Fehér informed me that Lukács had a great liking for de Hooch.

3  Durkheim, in his pioneering study *Suicide* (1897), found that after the loss of a spouse, to either death or separation, men are twice as likely to kill themselves as women—suggesting their greater dependency. Today in Australia, after divorce, men are twice as likely to report being unhappy as women (De Vaus, *Diversity and Change*, p. 228).

4  Aeschylus, *Agamemnon*, lines 471–2.

5  Many of de Hooch's scenes depict what is in strict socio-economic terms the middle middle class. There is a certain prosperity but it is not the milieu of the affluent and worldly seventeenth-century Dutch burgher shown in some works by de Keyser and Rembrandt. While

the woman blessing the pomegranates has some of the poise, and the dress, of higher social station, her ethic is that of meekness. Above all, de Hooch's prevailing mood, of an unambitious piety and modesty, speaks in cultural terms of the lower middle class.

6 George Herbert, *The Elixer*, *The Complete English Poems*, ed. J. Tobin, Penguin, London, 1991, p. 174.

7 In Australia in 2001, 10.3 per cent of men from the managerial and administrative occupational group were separated or divorced; compared with 18.6 of labouring men (De Vaus, *Diversity and Change*, p. 218). The former may be more likely to remarry. Nevertheless, this is one indicator of a greater vulnerability in the lower middle class to divorce. Amongst employed women there was negligible correlation between occupational grouping and divorce.

8 Christopher Lasch, *The True and Only Heaven*, pp. 476–532. One of Lasch's examples of the cultural class war that has developed was the civic elite of Boston forcing the busing of black pupils into schools in poorer white — predominantly Irish — suburbs, in spite of furious resistance from locals.

9 Marcus, *In the Fascist Bathroom*, p. 22.

10 T. S. Eliot, 'The Hollow Men', 1925.

11 The Sydney newspaper figures are closer — the broadsheet gaining 33 per cent of average weekly sales in 2007 — due to poorer performance by the tabloid. I am assuming that a smaller proportion of the lower middle class read newspapers, partly compensated by huge sales of women's magazines: in Australia, the top three gossip magazines sell in total over 1.5 million copies a week to a total population of 22 million.

12 While the Melbourne *Herald Sun* is a far more responsible and sober paper than its London tabloid counterparts, the Australian 'serious' press is of generally lower quality than its best British, or American equivalents.

13 Tom Wolfe, *From Bauhaus to Our House*, Farrar Straus Giroux, New York, 1981, pp.67–71.

14 Probert, *The Work Generation*, pp. 31, 47.

15 Fyodor Dostoevsky, *The Possessed*, trans. Constance Garnett, Modern Library, New York, 1963, p. 37.

16 For an extended analysis of Ford's films see my *The Wreck of Western Culture*, ch. 13, and 'John Wayne's West', *Quadrant*, vol. 41, no. 11, November 1997, pp. 26–30.

17 Gary Wills, *John Wayne*, Faber and Faber, London, 1997, p. 11.

18 Davy Crockett (John Wayne), *The Alamo*, directed by John Wayne, 1960.

## 5. Self-Hatred in High Culture

1 Friedrich Nietzsche, *The Gay Science*, trans, W. Kaufman, Vintage Books, 1974 (1887), section 125. 'Everything is permitted' is used first in Dostoevsky's major fiction in *Crime and Punishment*, trans. D. Magarshack, Penguin, London, 1951 (1866), p. 291, and then the argument is developed more fully in *The Possessed* (1872) and *The Brothers Karamazov* (1880). The same connections had been anticipated with a brilliant vividness by the painter, Holbein, in the early sixteenth century. I argue in *The Wreck of Western Culture*, ch. 3, that works such as *The Ambassadors*, *The Corpse of Christ*, and the *London Merchant* already equate humanism with a deathly nihilism. Dostoevsky thought the painting of *The Corpse of Christ* in Basel the most horrible thing he had ever seen.

2 I put this argument at some length in *The Wreck*.

3 It is implicit throughout Kafka's work, and most obvious in such parables as 'Before the Law' (*The Trial*, Penguin, London, 1953, pp. 235–44). It is central in Heidegger's late work, especially *Vorträge und Aufsätze*. Hannah Arendt, *On Revolution*, and Philip Rieff, *Fellow Teachers*, are the final references. T. S. Eliot's *Notes Towards the Definition of Culture* takes as central the mutual dependence of religion and culture.

4 Durkheim, *Suicide*, pp. 378–84.

5 Emile Durkheim, *The Division of Labour in Society*, trans. G. Simpson, Free Press, New York, 1933.

6 Steven Lukes, *Emile Durkheim*, Lane, London, 1973, p. 237.

7 Emile Durkheim, *The Elementary Forms of Religions Life*, pp. 53, 466.

8 Weber, *The Protestant Ethic and the Spirit of Capitalism*, pp. 174–83.

9 The explicit reference made by Manet is to Titian's *Venus of Urbino* and *Venus and Cupid*, both in the Uffizi. Goya had in part anticipated Manet in his *Maja Nude*.

10 Reported by Giovanni Papini, *Prose Morale*. Mondadori, Milan, 1959, pp. 724–26. On Picasso's nihilism in life and work see Arianna Stassinopoulos Huffington's *Picasso*; or for a more sympathetic view, John Richardson, *A Life of Picasso. vol. II, 1907–1917*.

11 George Steiner surveys the same scene as 'The Great Ennui', *In Bluebeard's Castle*, pp. 13–27.

12 Joseph Conrad, *Heart of Darkness*, Heritage, New York, 1969, p. 105.

13 Sartre, *Being and Nothingness*, pp. 44, 47–70.

14 On the therapeutic model of culture, Rieff, *The Triumph of the Therapeutic*.

15 *Australian Journal of Biological Sciences*, vol. 35, no. 2, 1982, pp. 179–86.

16 This is the Christopher Hill view, found in *Reformation to Industrial Revolution*, pp. 169–89. It was largely endorsed by Lawrence Stone in *The Causes of the English Revolution, 1529–1642*, pp. 47–147.

17 Gathorne-Hardy, *The Public School Phenomenon*, pp. 332–54.

18 Michael Flood, 'Exposure to Pornography among Youth in Australia', *Journal of Sociology*, vol. 43 (1), March 2007, p. 45.

19 The main reference is Edmund Burke, *Reflections on the Revolution in France*. On Burke in general, see Conor Cruise O'Brien, *The Great Melody*.

20 For example, Wolf, *Why Globalization Works*.

21 As an example, see Kemp, *Big Businessmen*.

22 Putnam, *Bowling Alone*, pp. 118–19.

23 Nietzsche, *The Genealogy of Morals*, third essay, section 15; and *Beyond Good and Evil*, sections 219, 26 (both included in *Basic Writings*).

24 The phrase was coined by historian Geoffrey Blainey.

25 Susan Sontag, in *The New Yorker*, praised the terrorists as courageous.

26 This is Peter Murphy's formulation.

27 Most of the material used here comes from an essay by George Steiner, 'The Cleric of Treason', *The New Yorker*, 8 December 1980; reprinted in Steiner, *A Reader*, pp. 178–204.

28 Carter, *Anthony Blunt, His Lives*, pp. 288, 301.

29 Costello, *Mask of Treachery*, p. 41. Costello painstakingly documents Blunt's whole career as a spy.

30 Steiner, *A Reader*, p. 202.

31 On the decadence of the English upper class in the twentieth century there is excellent material — see, for example, Gertrude Himmelfarb, 'From Clapham to Bloomsbury', *Marriage and Morals Among the Victorians,*; and Martin Green, *Children of the Sun*.

32 Anthony Blunt, *Nicolas Poussin*, vols. 1 and 2, Pantheon, New York, 1967.

33 Notably in his pair of Phocion paintings. See my essay interpreting the second of the pair, 'What Poussin Knew', *Quadrant*, vol. 41, no. 7–8, July 1997.

34 Tacey, *Jung*, p. 101. Tacey's book provides a profound insight into Jung's religious philosophy, presenting it in a language that is often more

plausible and succinct than Jung's own. It is a work of interpretation in the highest sense, drawing out often-latent meaning to present a reading of the psyche and the sacred that is of particular relevance to the contemporary West.

35  Tacey, *Jung*, p. 85.
36  Carter, p. 489.

## 6. The Modern University

1   Matthew Arnold, *Culture and Anarchy*, Cambridge University Press, Cambridge, 1932, pp. 43–71.
2   Newman, *The Idea of a University*, p. 10.
3   Weber, 'Science as a Vocation', *From Max Weber*, p. 243. The first word of the title of the lecture has usually been translated into English as 'science' — 'knowledge' is closer to Weber's meaning.
4   Michael Oakeshott, 'The Study of "Politics" in a University', *Rationalism in Politics and Other Essays*, pp. 301–33.
5   On Heidegger's Rectorial Address and his links with National Socialism, see Hugo Ott, *Martin Heidegger*, trans. A. Blunden, HarperCollins, London, 1993, pp. 131–260.
6   Georges Sorel, *Reflections on Violence* (1908); Oswald Spengler, *The Decline of the West* (1923); Julien Benda, *The Treason of the Intellectuals* (1928); and more recently Allan Bloom, *The Closing of the American Mind* (1987).
7   The principal works in which the argument is put are *The Birth of Tragedy* (1872), *Beyond Good and Evil* (1886) and *The Genealogy of Morals* (1887). Freud will continue the argument linking the rise of civilisation with increasing repression.
8   Rieff, *Fellow Teachers*, pp. 124, 94.
9   Plato, *The Laws*, in *The Collected Dialogues of Plato*, book II, 659 d and 653 b–c.
10  Plato, *Laws*, book V, 729b.
11  Plato, *Laws*, book I, 647 a–d.
12  J.D. Denniston and D.L. Page, *Aeschylus' Agamemnon*, Oxford University Press, Oxford, 1957.

## 7. Shopping

1   Nietzsche, *Thus Spoke Zarathustra*, part I, prologue, section 5, pp. 129–30.
2   'Shopping World' as described here is, in sociological parlance, an *ideal-*

*type*. It is based mainly on the largest shopping mall in Melbourne, but draws on elements from others. I am after the defining logic of the mega-shopping complex, its essential characteristics.

3  Kowinski, *The Malling of America*, p. 26.

4  Weber, 'Science as a Vocation', *From Max Weber*, pp. 134–9.

5  For a laboured exposition of the elements of rationalisation in this case, see George Ritzer, *The McDonaldization of Society*, Pine Forge, Thousand Oaks, California, 1996.

6  The term 'commodity fetish' comes from Marx, from the first volume of *Capital* (1867), pp. 43–50. In a way, it typifies his emphasis that capitalism is materialistic, focusing on commodities, turning people into objects, treating them merely as *means* to monetary ends. The assumption that consumerism is entirely profane has its origins here.

The notion of 'conspicuous consumption', the urge to buy in order to show off one's wealth and status, was coined by Thorstein Veblen, in his *The Theory of the Leisure Class* (1917).

A different neo-Marxist interpretation is that of Jean Baudrillard, who sees the consumer as a slave of the productive system, a 'labourer of consumption', in 'Consumer Society', *Selected Writings*, pp. 29–56. Baudrillard shares with the current reading a view that consumerism is more puritanical than hedonistic, although his assertion that it has nothing to do with pleasure goes too far.

7  Emile Zola, *Au Bonheur des Dames, Oeuvres Complètes*, vol. 4, Cercle du Livre Précieux, Paris, 1967.

8  Miller observed that the women he studied claimed to be so busy they viewed shopping as more like work than leisure (p. 69).

9  Max Stirner, *The Ego and His Own*, ed. John Carroll, Harper & Row, New York, 1971 (1844)—the German title translating more literally as 'The Unique One and his Properties'.

10 Kowinski, *The Malling of America*, p. 75.

11 Lipovetsky, *The Empire of Fashion*, p. 101. Lipovetsky's work is nearly definitive as a sociology of fashion.

12 Arendt, *The Human Condition*, pp. 126–35.

13 Miller, *A Theory of Shopping*, ch.1 and pp. 145–6, 150.

14 The *Citizen's Guide* is rigorously practical, presented in high aesthetic mode. It comprises a cover featuring a *Vogue* style black-and-white photo of female model and secondary male, a page with contact details and trading hours, and a ten-page list of shops and services according

to category, with telephone numbers and referencing to a double-page map.

15 Miller, *A Theory of Shopping*, p. 47.

16 John 3:8.

17 Lipovetsky, *The Empire of Fashion*, pp. 145–90.

18 Lipovetsky, *The Empire of Fashion*, p. 125.

## 8. Tourism

1 Bauman, *Postmodernity and its Discontents*, p. 93.

2 According to the World Tourist Organisation, tourism accounts for over 10 per cent of world GNP. Eight per cent of the global workforce is employed directly or indirectly in tourism. In 2000, 700 million people visited a foreign country. The long-term growth trend for global tourism, registered in 2008, is 4 per cent per annum.

3 In 1999, the proportion of overseas travellers to the United States who used a package-tour was 22 per cent ('travellers' includes a number of other categories apart from tourists, including business visitors).
On the history of the British package-tour, see Roger Bray and Vladimir Raitz, *Flight to the Sun: the story of the holiday revolution*, Continuum, London, 2001.

4 Boorstin, 'The Lost Art of Travel', *The Image*, pp. 77-117.

5 Leed, *The Mind of the Traveler*, p. 1. Leed's book is a knowledgeable and reflective history of travel in its many forms.

6 Leed, *The Mind of the Traveler*, p. 5.

7 Dean MacCannell, 'Staged Authenticity: Arrangements of Social Space in Tourist Settings', *American Journal of Sociology*, vol. 79, no. 3, Nov. 1973, pp. 589–603.

8 In 2006, there were 40 million visitors to Las Vegas, with 13 per cent of them international. Fifty per cent nominated their reason for going to Las Vegas as vacation or pleasure, 10 per cent for gambling, 10 per cent for conventions, and 4 per cent went for a wedding.

## 9. Democracy

1 The American presidential system, radically adapted from the English foundation, has problems of its own. The most serious, the capacity of the Congress to paralyse the president, is not new, and was observed by Walter Bagehot in his classic study on *The English Constitution*, pp. 79–83.

2 Putnam, Leonardi, & Nanetti, *Making Democracy Work*.

3  Putnam, Leonardi, & Nanetti, *Making Democracy Work*, pp. 167–85.
4  Putnam, Leonardi, & Nanetti, *Making Democracy Work*, pp. 115, 175–6, 181.
5  Putnam, *Bowling Alone*, pp. 43, 60, 81, 98, 100, 112.
6  Putnam, *Bowling Alone*, p. 115.
7  Jeff Blunden prepared the *Golf Industry Report* for Ernst & Young (Sydney) in 2005. It is thorough, clear, persuasive — and ominous. The 1970s and 1980s were growth decades, with club membership across the country increasing by 16 per cent and 26 per cent respectively. In the 1990s this slowed, and between 2000 and 2003 membership declined by 4 per cent to about 470,000. All the signs are that this trend will continue.

   Blunden calculates that 8 per cent of Australians play golf. The Australian Bureau of Statistics puts the figure at 6 per cent, but their figure is based on less extensive sampling.
8  The comparative figures in New Zealand are 12 per cent, with Sweden an impressive 20 per cent.
9  Bagehot, *The English Constitution*, p. 67.
10 Tocqueville, *Democracy in America*, part 1, chapter XVI.
11 See, for example, Bork, *The Tempting of America: the political seduction of the law*.
12 This is a theme developed at length, and persuasively, by Jeffery Alexander, in his book *The Civil Sphere*.
13 Weber, 'Politics as a Vocation', *From Max Weber*, pp. 77–128.
14 Between 17 per cent and 25 per cent of Americans regularly attend church in the early years of the twenty-first century. Gallup polled regular American church attendance at 35 per cent in December, 2004. However, this was a poll-based survey — asking people themselves about their behaviour — rather than a count-based one registering numbers entering the church doors. Sociologists have calculated that poll figures for church attendance should be discounted by as much as a half, to take account of the degree to which people exaggerate or lie on this subject — whether out of guilt, self-deception, or in the belief they will help the local church by claiming they attend regularly when they don't.

   For instance, C. Kirk Hadaway and P.L. Morler studied Protestant and Catholic attendance counts and found the rate at about half the poll figure — 'Did You Really Go to Church This Week? Behind the Poll Data', *The Christian Century*, May 6, 1998. Hadaway's 2005 figure is 21 per cent regular attendance (private communication).

In Australia, the 2001 National Church Life Survey put the weekly attendance at Christian churches as 8.8 per cent of the total population (*2001 Church Attendance Estimates*, Occasional Paper No. 3, J. Bellamy and K. Castle, February 2004). The Catholic component was 15 per cent of Catholics attending weekly, which equates to 4 per cent of the total population. This figure seems reliable as it was based on comprehensive surveying of parishes across the country over four weeks (information from Bob Dixon, director of Pastoral Projects Office of the Australian Catholic Bishops Conference). The Protestant figures appear more vulnerable, and need discounting. We may conclude that between 6 per cent and 8 per cent of the Australian population attended a Christian church weekly, in 2001. The figure is declining.

The British figure looks like roughly 5 per cent, with France and Germany lower again.

15 Daniel Jonah Goldhagen, in *Hitler's Willing Executioners* (Knopf, New York, 1996), has proved how pervasive and spontaneous the persecution of Jews was, and that it was not just the work of a fanatical minority.

16 Lipovetsky, *The Empire of Fashion*, pp. 107–11, 125–6.

## 10. The Motor Car

1 Quoted in Graeme Davison, *Car Wars*, p. x. Davison's book is a compelling and perceptive history of the car, in terms of the way it has transformed life in one Western city, Melbourne.

2 Robert S. and Helen M. Lynd, *Middletown*. Harcourt, Brace, New York, 1929.

3 Rothschild, *Paradise Lost*, pp. 74–5.

4 Rothschild, *Paradise Lost*, p. 205.

5 McLuhan, 'Motor Car, The Mechanical Bride', *Understanding Media*, pp. 232–40.

## 11. The Do-It-Yourself Home

1 In 2007, Bunnings Warehouse had 250 stores and revenue of $5,000 million—putting it in the top 50 Australian companies (*Business Review Weekly*, 22 November – 12 December 2007).

2 *The Castle*, a 1997 Australian film, directed by Rob Sitch.

3 Tania Lewis, in *Smart Living*, explores the growth of the DIY lifestyle TV shows, contrasting ordinary experts with celebrities like Martha

Stewart and Nigella (especially ch. 6).

4  Putnam, *Bowling Alone*, pp. 97–100.

5  The 1941 film *Citizen Kane* projects a Coliseum-like warning to DIY culture.

6  Satirised in the sociologically acute film, *Fight Club*.

## 12. The Personal Computer

1  Arendt, *Human Condition*, p. 147.

2  Putnam, *Bowling Alone*, p. 95.

3  Quoted in Putnam, *Bowling Alone*, p. 169.

4  Mark Tremayne (ed.), *Blogging, Citizenship and the Future of Media*, Routledge, London, 2007.

5  Tim Adams, 'The Knowledge', *Good Weekend*, *The Age*, 18 August 2007.

6  Penelope Debelle, 'A Space of her own', *The Age*, 4 August 2007, Insight, p. 10.

7  Danah Boyd, www.danah.org/bio.html.

8  Sal Humphreys, 'In Search of the Next Level', *The Australian Literary Review*, December 2006, pp. 14–15.

9  Putnam, *Bowling Alone*, p. 179.

## 13. Nature

1  Surf Life Saving Australia, the association of the 305 clubs around the Australian coast, claimed a membership of 112,000 in 2007.

2  'Ideal landscape' is Pierre Rosenberg's term, *Nicolas Poussin*, p. 289. The *Matthew* was painted as a pair, with the *Landscape with St John on Patmos*.

3  As most fully argued by Anthony Blunt in his Mellon Lectures, *Nicolas Poussin*.

4  One exception, in which God appears in a painting, is the 1641 *Miracle of St Francis Xavier*, a commissioned work that is so stiff and awkward, as Alain Mérot has remarked (in *Nicolas Poussin*, Thames & Hudson, London, 1990, p. 123) as to be uncharacteristic of Poussin.

5  Peter Berger introduced the term 'the sacred canopy' into modern sociology in a book of that title. What he rather meant, as admitted in the text, is 'sacred cosmos' (p. 25). Berger argues in a following volume, *A Rumor of Angels*, that the revival of Christianity will depend on new ways of discovering 'signals of transcendence' in the everyday world

(p. 52). He also suggests that Christianity must maintain its devotion to a single, distant and other, creator God, to counter the mysticism of the East.

6   Gerard Manley Hopkins, 'God's Grandeur', lines 1–8.

7   Rainer Maria Rilke, 'Nature, Man and Art', in R. Ellmann and C. Feidelson (eds,), *The Modern Tradition*, Oxford University Press, New York, 1965, p. 409.

8   J.B. Leishman and Stephen Spender translation of Rainer Maria Rilke, *The Duino Elegies*, Hogarth, London, 1968, pp. 24–8.

9   The relationship between the eighteenth-century English landscape garden and Poussin is a reciprocal one, in the sense of a special affinity between the two. Poussin paints his ideal landscapes in the middle years of the seventeenth century. Their form is then imitated by several generations of painters, especially in France. The influence is also spread through etching copies. The English gardens start to appear in the early eighteenth century — some key dates, Castle Howard and Stowe in the first half of the eighteenth century, and Blenheim in the 1760s. It is later in the century that the aristocracy purchases its major Poussins. Notable landscapes include *Snake Landscape* (Sir Robert Strange, 1773), *Body of Phocion* (Lord Clive, 1774), and *Ashes of Phocion* (Earl of Derby, 1776).

10  The 2005 participation rates (in millions) in the United States show the leading sports in nature as walking (86), fishing (48), bicycling (43), hiking (30), and golf (25), as against basketball (30), baseball and softball (29), football (24), and tennis (11), *Statistical Abstract of the United States,* US Department of Commerce, Bureau of Census, Washington, 2008.

The Australian figures for 2007 are similar, with walking (25 per cent of the population over the age of 15), swimming (9 per cent), cycling (6 per cent), golf (6 per cent), tennis (5 per cent), cricket (4 per cent), and bushwalking (3 per cent). These are Australian Bureau of Statistics figures — in the case of golf, the Australian Sports Commission found, in 2003, that 8.2 per cent of the population play golf. The Sports Commission figures are based on more extensive sampling than the ABSs'.

11  'Hook, Line & Sinker', *Good Weekend, The Age,* 18 January 1997. One-third of all Australians will fish at least once a year, making fishing by far the most popular participant sport (discounting walking as a 'sport').

12  In fact, golf predates Calvinism in Scotland, suggesting that the cultural

affinity works in part the other way round, that a people with a passion for golf will be attracted to Calvinism. The oldest surviving club is not the Royal and Ancient at St Andrews, 80 kilometres from Edinburgh, but The Honourable Company of Edinburgh Golfers, founded in 1744, who play at Muirfield — their modern course relocated 30 kilometres from Edinburgh.

13 Michael Murphy, *Golf in the Kingdom*, Penguin, New York, 1997.

14 Carroll, *Guilt*, pp. 79–80.

15 For a reading of Poussin's pair of Phocion paintings, see my, 'What Poussin Knew', *Quadrant*, vol. 41, no. 7–8 (July 1997), pp. 16–52.

## 14. The Nightmare — if it all goes wrong

1 By 2003, the average Australian household was spending 2.3 per cent more than it earned each week (*AMP.NATSEM Income–Wealth Report No. 9*, November 2004).

2 In the United States between 1960 and 2000, child obesity rose from 4 per cent to 14 per cent, and adult obesity from 13 per cent to 33 per cent ('Childhood Obesity in the United States', *Institute of Medicine of the National Academies*, September 2004). By 2000, 60 per cent of Americans were overweight.

3 In the United States, the number of hard-core pornography titles released rose from 1300 in 1988 to 13,600 in 2005. Average monthly visits to Adult websites rose from 18 million in 2001 to 75 million in 2005, by which time there were four million pornography websites, 12 per cent of all websites. By 2006, revenue in the United States from pornography reached $13 billion. (Jerry Ropelato, 'Internet Pornography Statistics', *Internet Filter Review*, 2007.)

4 Furedi, *Culture of Fear*.

5 Martin Seligman, 'Boomer Blues', *Psychology Today*, October 1988; Michael Rutter & David J. Smith (eds.), *Psychosocial Disorders in Young People: time trends and their causes*, Wiley & Sons, New York, 1995.

6 Gail Bell, 'The Worried Well', *Quarterly Essay*, no. 18, 2005, pp. 57 & 59.

7 Steyn, *America Alone*.

8 Daisy Sindelar, 'Netherlands: Week of Violence Leaves People Questioning Tradition of Tolerance', *Radio Free Europe*, 10 November 2004.

9 The Archbishop of Canterbury, head of the worldwide Anglican

Church, commented in February 2008 that it was inevitable that aspects of Islamic Sharia law become incorporated into British law. His comment was met by a howl of angry reaction from across the political spectrum, signalling the low likelihood of this eventuating. Melanie Phillips, in her book *Londonistan* (Gibson Square, London, 2006), has documented the degree to which British elites have turned a blind eye to, and sometimes even facilitated, a creeping Islamicisation of institutions and practices.

10 Birth rates also remain relatively healthy in Ireland and in Scandinavia.

## 15. Resilience

1 In the West, there is reason to be more confident about the Anglo sphere than the rest. Since the defeat of Napoleon at Waterloo in 1815, the globe has experienced close on two centuries of Anglo supremacy. Economic power has generated world power. In this period, the Anglo nations have become used to fighting wars and winning the major ones.

The two institutional creations that drive the modern world—the capitalist economy and parliamentary democracy—were both made in England. They form two legs of the tripod that is Western civilisation. In the nineteenth century, nearly all innovation came out of England. This was true at the technological level—blast furnaces for steel, railways, steamships, giant steel bridges, and post and telegraph. It was true at the institutional level—the mass production factory, the insurance company, cabinet government, the museum, and the department store. It was also true at the everyday social level—organised sports including soccer, tennis, golf, and modern horse racing; mass tourism, luxury hotels, whisky, and fishing; and modern journalism, the detective novel, and Romanticism (Claudio Véliz, *The New World of the Gothic Fox*, University of California Press, Berkeley, 1994, ch. VI). There were, at the same time, notable exceptions—such as German philosophy and music, and French art.

In the twentieth century, the United States took over, and remains, by a vast margin, the most creative society on Earth—in science, in technological innovation, in organisational development, in design, in architecture, in high culture, in media and entertainment, and in lifestyle. This ranges from New York to Las Vegas, from Harvard to Hollywood, from Silicon Valley to the Pentagon, from the skyscraper to the motor car, the jumbo jet to the Personal Computer, and from pop music to fast food. It is difficult to name a handful of major inventions or innovations of the last 60 years that have not come out of America. Regular prophecies of the decline of the United States continue to flounder—the speed of its recovery in the 1980s from the demoralising disaster of the Vietnam War was a sign of the nation's phenomenal resilience.

Both industrialisation and democracy are intricate creations germinating out of the culture of the people—its history, traditions, and institution building capacition. We should never underestimate the enduring potency of *genesis*—its legacy. There may be a confidence deriving from a sort of instinctual knowledge, in the Anglo sphere of the West, that we as a people are moving and acting in a world which we know well, for we created it.

# INDEX